STORIES OF LIGHT IN A DARK WORLD

Skipping Winter

THE MOSAIC COLLECTION

CANDACE WEST * SARA DAVISON
ANGELA D. MEYER * DEB ELKINK
ELEANOR BERTIN * STACY MONSON

Published by The Mosaic Collection
Minneapolis, Minnesota
mosaiccollectionbooks.com

Cover design by Indie Publishing Services

From The Mosaic Collection
Our mission is to change hearts with the gospel through fiction.

Welcome To
The Mosaic Collection

We are sisters, a beautiful mosaic united by the love of God
through the blood of Christ.

Several times a year, The Mosaic Collection releases faith-based
novels and anthologies in a variety of genres. Our stories range from
romance and suspense to literary and women's fiction.

Join our Mosaic reader family and discover soul-affirming stories
of truth and hope at www.mosaiccollectionbooks.com

Join our Reader Community, too!

Find us at www.facebook.com/groups/TheMosaicCollection

BOOKS IN
THE MOSAIC COLLECTION

MID-YEAR ANTHOLOGIES

Before Summer's End: Stories to Touch the Soul

Song of Grace: Stories to Amaze the Soul

All Things New: Stories to Refresh the Soul

Dancing in the Rain: Stories to Shelter the Soul

Sounds Like a Plan: Stories of Change and the God Who Doesn't

BirdSong: Stories of Promise and Hope

CHRISTMAS ANTHOLOGIES

Hope is Born

A Star Will Rise

The Heart of Christmas

A Whisper of Peace

A Thrill in the Air

A Weary World Rejoices

Skipping Winter

JOHNNIE ALEXANDER

The Mischief Thief (Rose & Thorne #1)

When Memory Whispers (Echoes of War #2)

Journey of the Heart (An Unseen Valor Novella #1)

Beneath a Rare Blue Moon (An Unseen Valor Novella #2)

BRENDA S. ANDERSON

A Beautiful Mess

Pieces of Granite (Coming Home Prequel)

Broken Together (written with Sarah S. Anderson)

Chain of Mercy (Coming Home #1)

ELEANOR BERTIN

Lifelines (The Ties that Bind #1)

Unbound (The Ties that Bind #2)

Tethered (The Ties that Bind #3)

Flame of Mercy (Burning Bright #1)

Flicker of Trust (Burning Bright #2)

SARA DAVISON

Lost Down Deep (The Rose Tattoo Trilogy #1)

Written in Ink (The Rose Tattoo Trilogy #2)

This Little Nowhere, Nothing Town

Every Star in the Sky (two sparrows for a penny #1)

Every Flower of the Field (two sparrows for a penny #2)

Every Bird That Falls (two sparrows for a penny #3)

The Color of Sky and Stone (In the Shadows #1)

JANICE L. DICK

The Road to Happenstance (Happenstance Chronicles #1)

Crazy About Maisie (Happenstance Chronicles #2)

Calm Before the Storm (The Storm Series #1)

Eye of the Storm (The Storm Series #2)

Out of the Storm (The Storm Series #3)

DEB ELKINK

The Red Journal

The Third Grace

Vagabond Come Home

CHAUTONA HAVIG

Spines & Leaves (Bookstrings introduction)

Hart of Noel (Bookstrings "Noella")

Twice Sold Tales (Bookstrings #1)

Clock Tower Bound (Bookstrings #2)

MILLA HOLT

Into the Flood (Seasons of Faith #1)

Through the Blaze (Seasons of Faith #2)

Within the Storm (Seasons of Faith #3)

Amid the Ashes (Seasons of Faith #4)

After the Frost (Seasons of Faith #5)

Home Town Melody (Rhapsody of Grace #1)

Small Town Harmony (Rhapsody of Grace #2)

Old Town Symphony (Rhapsody of Grace #3)

ANGELA D. MEYER

This Side of Yesterday

Where Hope Starts (Applewood Hill #1)

Where Healing Starts (Applewood Hill #2)

Where Joy Starts (Applewood Hill #3)

STACY MONSON

When Mountains Sing (My Father's House #1)

Open Circle

LORNA SEILSTAD

More Than Enough

Watercolors

CANDACE WEST

Through the Lettered Veil (Windy Hollow #1)

Among the Kindled Embers (Windy Hollow #2)

OTHER

Totally Booked: A Book Lover's Companion

CONTENTS

CANDACE WEST

Valor Passage

VALOR PASSAGE

Candace West

Chelsea Thatcher's idea of skipping a Deep South winter is racing toward a blizzard in the Smoky Mountains of North Carolina. After all, what is better than holing up in a cabin with family, hot chocolate, cinnamon rolls, books, and an unwelcome guest concealing unfinished business in a pillowcase?

Snowballing just got personal.

For the pigeons Cher Ami, William of Orange, Tommy,
Mary of Exeter, the horse Sergeant Reckless,
the English Pointer Judy, the mongrel Chips, and Simon the cat

Brave beyond measure

Are not two sparrows sold for a farthing? And one of them shall not fall on the ground without your Father.
Matthew 10:29 (NIV)

1

Welford, Arkansas

January 2025

I'd never known Pawpaw to sucker punch anyone. Until then. And of all people . . . me.

Shoving myself from the table, I glared across at my twin brother, Charles. "What was he thinking?"

Charlie scrubbed his jaw with his palm while darting his eyes away, no doubt to hide the twinkle of humor rising. "Chelsea, get a grip. He had a good reason."

"Care to enlighten me?" A huff escaped my bottom lip, lifting the bangs from my forehead.

He shrugged. "I haven't the foggiest clue."

"Yeah. So I figured." The kitchen chair squealed against the 1970s orange-and-avocado linoleum floor as I pushed farther from the table and rose. My work boots rumbled through the farmhouse in perfect rhythm with my pounding head as I stormed toward the screen door. The main door already stood aside to allow the mild January breeze to freshen the rooms. Typical for southeast Arkansas.

I stepped onto the porch and gulped, tucked my fingers into the hip pockets of my jeans, and swallowed once more. Closed my eyes.

Pawpaw had been gone six excruciating months. No amount of his preparations had readied us for this vacuum. To soften it, he had instructed us to wait until New Year's to open a gift from him—one for Charlie and one for myself.

We had never made a big deal at Christmas because our dad had died on that day. We reserved the first of January to refresh and thank the Good Lord for His blessings.

From the portals of Heaven, Pawpaw had dropped Mon Petit Chou—his darling little cabbage—right smack dab into my lap.

Not a literal cabbage. An 81-year-old stuffed racing pigeon, his prized possession second to the family Bible. Under a glass case, Chouchou had perched on one leg and unblinkingly studied me from Pawpaw's desk since the day Charlie and I had arrived at the farmhouse eighteen years earlier.

At twenty-six, I still hadn't won our staring matches. I learned to avoid her. Ignore her. Even going so far as to drape her case with an old tablecloth whenever I cleaned the study.

Mon Petit Chou never had the satisfaction of watching me dust Pawpaw's bookshelves. Well, except once when Charlie called me a chicken. He never compared me to any kind of winged creature from that day forward, though.

Charlie's soft sigh reached me as he stepped onto the porch. He fumbled with an envelope before angling it my direction. Pawpaw had scrawled my name on top and sealed it. The familiar, spidery handwriting brought an ache to my throat.

My brother shook the envelope slightly. "He probably explained everything in here."

Everything. The truth of *everything* settled in the pit of my stomach.

I shook my head. "Pawpaw knew I hated her."

"Feared her, you mean."

"Spare me." I scowled, my inner child yelling *Take it back*. I drew in another long, steadying breath. "I don't understand." My voice cracked.

Charlie took my hand and plopped the envelope into my palm. "Give him a chance. Don't you think you need to come to terms with this whole thing? Chouchou is not your enemy."

"I don't have to make peace with a stuffed bird."

Shaking his head, Charlie jammed his hands into his overalls' pockets and stepped to the edge of the porch. He scanned the landscape—the pasture bordering one side of the place, the ancient oaks shading the lawn, and the gravel driveway snaking into the woods before emerging in the world beyond home.

He frowned. "You beat all."

I gritted my teeth against the words scorching the edge of my tongue. A quiet soul, Charlie didn't waste words, unlike me. He mastered filling a sentence with more thought than I could fire off in an entire paragraph.

A very unfair advantage to my excuses.

We were a veritable Marilla and Matthew Cuthbert in the flesh.

A smirk twitched my lips at the silly thought, but it vanished when I glanced down at Pawpaw's handwriting. I slid my finger under one corner of the envelope and tore it open. My heart hammered as I withdrew the letter, then unfolded it.

Instead of writing a long explanation, Pawpaw had expressed his thoughts in the center of the page.

Chouchou saved me out of a jam more than once. She'll do the same for you. If you get to know her, you'll discover you're both a lot alike.

Love you always

My arm dropped to my side, the note dangling between my fingers. Disappointment and grief mingled with my anger.

Charlie cut a glance at me. "Well?"

"Nothing." I held the page up as he leaned closer to read it.

Charlie smiled slightly, his hazel eyes meeting mine and crinkling around the corners. "That's just like him."

"I'm so glad you think it's funny."

"I don't." He straightened to his six-foot-three height. "I'm ready to talk when you are."

"Don't hold your breath." I folded the paper and slid it into the envelope. Turning, I reached for the screen door and yanked it open.

Charlie's alarmed voice trailed my swift steps. "What are you doing?"

"The right thing—what should've been done long ago."

"Chelsea."

The threshold creaked under Charlie's boots as he followed. Snatching a large flour-sack hand towel from the countertop, I shook it out, then draped it over Mon Petit Chou's case before lifting it onto the crook of my arm.

At the back door, I grabbed the truck keys dangling from the peg and slipped outside before my brother stopped me.

As if he really could.

I paused on the step outside of *Vintage Adventures* and straightened my shoulders. Never mind that my ex-sweetheart owned the antique shop. Since it was the only one in town, I had no other choice.

Sweat prickled the nape of my neck as the mild breeze tangled my reddish-brown hair around my face. Mon Petit Chou's case bit farther into my arm as I shifted its weight to one side and tugged the door.

The brass doorbell clanged as I sidled inside the shop. The scent of old books, quilts, galvanized metal, dust, and memories assaulted me, and I resisted the urge to cringe.

At the back of the shop, the double doors swished as I set the case beside the cash register—a huge brass contraption from 1911.

I braced myself against the worn oak countertop and waited to face Wyatt Newton. Instead, his brother Wesley—the youngest of six boys with *W* names—rounded the corner of one of their many booths. I released a pent-up breath.

"Well, look what the cat dragged up." A grin hitched up the corners of his mouth.

"Hi to you too, Wes. And it's *what the cat dragged in.*"

He dismissed my correction with a wave and eyed the case still draped with a hand towel. "Is this what I think it is?"

"See for yourself." I folded my arms as if it would somehow bar the stirring of my conscience.

Wes's smile widened as he tugged off the towel and bent down to peer closer. "Chouchou. You beautiful girl."

"I don't know what you see in her."

"I see history and a chance to make some serious cash." He raised his eyebrows and tipped up his chin. "I bet you're glad Wyatt ain't here."

At sixteen, his business sense—but not his tact—rivaled Wyatt's. I cleared my throat. "Watch it. I can take this elsewhere."

Wes bit his lower lip, regret erasing the grin. "Sorry. You know me, Chelsea. Just a clumsy tease. I haven't forgotten what she meant to your pawpaw." He pointed to a place beside Mon Petit Chou's one leg. "Do you know what this is?"

I focused on a cuckoo clock mounted on a wall behind Wes and shrugged. "It's an old medal."

"Not just any old medal. It's the Dickin medal. It was awarded—"

An ache rose in my throat. "Never mind all that. Just tell me what it's worth."

Wes sighed. "Are you sure you want to sell her?"

"Look. I'm not changing my mind. It's better with someone who will . . . appreciate it."

With his index finger, he tapped the top of the case and eyed me. "Five hundred dollars."

My tight jaw unhinged. "That much?"

He nodded. "Maybe a bit more, but I've gotta make a little profit too." A wayward, sandy curl dropped against his forehead, reminding me of Wyatt. Another pang of regret I'd rather forget. I needed to close the deal before he showed up and scattered my composure to bits.

"I'll take it."

Wes's eyebrows rose. "Are you really sure you want to do this?"

Was I? A twinge of hesitation needled me, a sudden, unexpected feeling. I blinked against the memory of Pawpaw's face. I was selling his treasure, something almost as dear as family.

I angled a glance at Mon Petite Chou. Her stare met mine. For a moment, I held it, but . . .

"I have to." My lips quivered as I focused my gaze elsewhere.

As Wes filled out a receipt, I turned away from the pigeon while ignoring the burning behind my eyelids. The faint melody of Taps and the tri-folded stars and stripes clutched in Charlie's hands edged into my mind.

No. Not here. Not now.

I balled my fists, then stretched my fingers. Pulled in a long, slow breath.

"Here ya go." Wes laid the cash on the counter.

"Thanks." I nearly choked on the word. "Find it a good home." I folded the money and stuffed it deeply into my pocket.

"No worries. Lots of folks will fight over her."

"See you." I shoved open the door and stepped into the sunlight, itching to keep walking and never stop. Leave *everything* behind. Forward momentum equaled freedom.

However, I'd perfected running away in place.

After sliding into the truck seat, I turned the key, and the engine roared to life. No matter how fast I sped toward home, the haunting melody still pursued me.

2

"It ought to be a sin to sit on a porch in January."

Charlie grunted at my remark, stretching his legs where he sat on the steps. He'd said less than five words since I had returned.

The remnants of the sunset faded from a blue patch of sky stretching above the trees. A few stars winked into view. With the tip of my boot, I pushed the porch swing into a gentle motion.

"Still miffed?"

"Not mad." His broad shoulders rose, then fell. "Just . . ."

Never one to vocalize his emotions, he allowed the rest of his unspoken words to trail off. He tunneled his fingers through his chestnut hair and raised his head heavenward. Thinking of Pawpaw and Jesus, no doubt.

I squirmed, the back of the swing biting into my shoulders. The Lord had been quiet since Pawpaw's homegoing, and I couldn't understand it. Wasn't He near the broken? These days, my prayers didn't seem to rise higher than my bedroom ceiling.

Charlie, however, radiated peace despite all of it.

I pretended to brush some dust from my britches. "I know you're not happy about the bird—"

"Chouchou."

"I can't stand the sight of it any longer."

"If you understood, you'd feel different." He threw a narrow glance at me over his shoulder. "But you never gave Pawpaw a chance to explain. Nor me."

My cheeks blazed against the cool breeze. "Maybe y'all didn't understand. Have you ever thought about that?"

"Pawpaw understood. That's why he entrusted you with Chouchou."

I leaned forward. "Wait a second. Did you want it? If so, I can go and get it."

Charlie huffed and crossed his arms. "She was never rightfully mine. She's yours, like it or not."

"You're not making a lick of sense."

"Ditto."

The hairs at the nape of my neck prickled. Charlie and I rarely argued, and his disapproval poured over me like hot molasses, clinging to every inch of my conscience.

My phone buzzed, cutting off my retort. I lifted it from the seat and saw my cousin's name appear at the top of the screen.

Chloe: Looks like we're getting snowed in this weekend. Just the kind of winter you've always wanted. Throw some clothes in a bag and get yourself trapped up here with us. Now. We're stocked up on hot chocolate and cinnamon rolls. Pry Charlie loose and bring him too.

My fingers hovered over the phone for several dizzy seconds. Valor Pass, North Carolina,

was situated deep in the Smoky Mountains with breathtaking vistas overlooking a serene valley nestled like a hidden gem from the rest of the world. The perfect place to ditch a deep-fried Southern winter for a genuine one.

In the heart of the valley, Chloe and her husband had built a cabin to raise their growing brood of kiddos.

"It'll be snowing in Valor Pass this weekend." I scooted to the edge of the seat. "Chloe wants us to come and get stranded with them."

"Too much to do around here, but go ahead if you'd like. I can manage." The sharp edge of Charlie's voice had mellowed. "It'll do you good."

The tightness in my ribcage eased as I glanced down at the phone to type my answer.

Charlie can't. But keep those cinnamon rolls warm for me.

Two seconds later, the screen flashed to life with Chloe's ringtone. I dashed to the steps

and planted a swift kiss on Charlie's forehead before answering.

I swept my finger across the screen and lifted it to my ear. "Chloe-girl, I'm packing now."

"What were you thinking? Trying to sell Chouchou?"

Wyatt's incredulous voice filled the truck's speakers while I sped northeast on the Interstate. I gripped the steering wheel as my mouth ran dry. I could almost see the lines buckling his forehead, his firm jaw tightening while he waited for my answer.

"Woah. What do you mean *trying?* It's a done deal."

"Not by a long shot. Wes doesn't own the store."

"You let him conduct business all the time."

"Not with something this important."

My thumbs drummed the steering wheel in rhythm with my whirling thoughts. "It's my right to decide what to do with Mon Petite Chou."

"You need all the facts before you decide."

Facts. A pesky, inconvenient word. "I know plenty."

"Not enough to make an informed decision." He paused with a low groan. "I can't take Chouchou until you're sure you can part with her."

I rolled my eyes at him, not that it mattered. "I'm positive, Wyatt."

"That's what you think." His voice dropped lower. "I'm coming to Valor Pass."

The muscles down the length of my spine tensed. "You're WHAT?"

"Let's see. I'm about two hours behind you. A fair chance to prepare for battle."

The seatbelt tightened across my chest as I braked behind a slower car merging into

traffic. "You've got a lot of nerve, you know it? I'm not changing my mind. You might as well turn around."

"Not gonna happen. We need to settle things."

My forehead throbbed as my internal alarm bells erupted. "We have. Please, Wyatt, go home."

"I can't." The deep timbre in his admission brought unbidden tears to my eyes. The road blurred only a moment before I blinked. He continued. "Besides, Chloe told me she made extra hot chocolate."

The smile in his tone warmed me to my toes, and I imagined his blue eyes sparkling. I shook myself. "Is that so? I sense a conspiracy."

"Nah. Call it a happy coincidence." Road noise rumbled in the background. Wyatt cleared his throat. "Please don't be mad at me, Chelsea. I wouldn't be coming if it wasn't important."

Well. How to respond to that? I steeled the breathlessness out of my tone. "Be prepared to get stranded."

"With you and Chouchou, I'll manage to keep warm."

As I hurried to end the call, Wyatt's chuckle quickened my traitorous pulse. For good measure, I pressed the gas pedal a few more miles per hour over the speed limit.

After all, it's impossible to shut one's eyes while driving. Well, not impossible, but definitely not recommended.

During the long hours to Valor Pass, I discovered the problem with solitary road trips. The past crawls into the passenger seat and wears out its welcome.

I was eight years old when Dad was killed in Desert Storm in Iraq. The following days remained blurred in my mind, but the details of his memorial service had never faded. As Pawpaw and Granny's only son, he had prearranged to be laid to rest in his hometown, knowing how important it was to them.

The whole world seemed to cry at Dad's funeral. The clouds loomed overhead, emptying cold sheets of rain that soaked us to the skin. At the graveside, the small canopy above our heads did nothing to stop the howling wind.

My teeth chattered at the memory.

After the closing prayer, we hurried to our car, where Mom tugged two suitcases from the trunk and handed them to Pawpaw. She bent to hug Charlie and me.

"The visit with Pawpaw and Granny will be good for you. It'll be just for a few days."

My brother and I scrambled into the backseat of their vehicle as the rain pounded the car roof harder. Pawpaw shut the door and helped Granny inside.

With a small wave, Mom ducked into her car, then drove in the opposite direction.

As we traveled several miles to the farm, the sky brewed, ripping through the trees like an invisible menace, rocking them in its fierce grip. I huddled closer to Charlie and pinched my eyes shut as he wrapped his arm around my shoulders.

We wound through the twists and turns of the shady lane. The mid-afternoon shadows darkened the cab of the car like twilight. Minutes later, the car's wheels sloshed through the gravel in the driveway, and Pawpaw parked.

Charlie and I dashed for the front door, which our grandparents kept unlocked. I twisted the knob and stumbled inside. Behind me, Charlie tripped over the rug but quickly recovered.

He reached for the light switch and flipped it. Nothing. "The power's gotta be out," he mumbled.

The house was dark . . . too dark. Rubbing my eyes, I stepped farther into the living room. We hadn't visited Pawpaw and Granny since I was four. My hazy mind fumbled for familiar details but remembered nothing.

Against the wall, the large outline of a bookcase drew my attention. Peering closer, I shuffled toward it.

Outside, a bolt of lightning blazed through the darkness, illuminating a glass case with a dead bird. Eye level. Mere inches from my face.

I screamed as a blast of thunder rattled the windows.

The next thing I remembered was Granny's soft hands easing me from under the kitchen table, her arms closing around me while I sobbed hysterically into her dress.

Pawpaw moved Mon Petit Chou to his study that very night. He tried to explain, but I couldn't stand to hear it.

"Not yet, honey," Granny had whispered while she rocked me. I buried my face in her shoulder, the faint smell of her rose-scented lotion washing over me.

A few days later, when I tried to tell Mom over the phone, she had only scoffed and called me silly. I suppose I was foolish about a lot of things during the first several weeks at Pawpaw and Granny's.

The weeks stretched into months. Mom's phone calls turned into letters. The winter drifted into spring while the letters evolved into the occasional postcard. Summer's heat mellowed into fall, the gusty breezes scattering gold and red leaves over Dad's resting place.

Charlie and I stopped checking the empty mailbox.

As it turned out, a few days lasted forever.

Stop.

Unclenching my jaw, I turned up the A/C and angled the vent toward my face. The cool air skimmed over my skin and through my hair. Outside, the gently rolling hills gradually surrendered to taller ones. The foothills of the Smoky Mountains stretched around me like a welcoming embrace.

The vistas sported a slight pink flush, a promise of coming snow. I murmured a prayer of gratitude.

Valor Pass lay beyond, and I couldn't get stranded fast enough.

3

"Howdy stranger." Grinning, Chloe skipped down the cabin's front steps. Shrugging into a coat, I bumped the door of the truck shut with my hip.

She tugged me into a bear hug. "Ah, you smell like sunshine and popcorn."

I laughed. "More like road grime and watery soda."

"I have the cure." Chloe surveyed me with discerning brown eyes. "Our brainless chatter will clear up your muddled musings."

On cue, the cabin's front door swung open to squeals splintering the crisp air. Four-year old Ben and five-year old Amelia danced on the porch in their sock feet while their dad, Luke, emerged behind them, smiling. A miniature collie wriggled and barked from a nearby window.

I waved. Chloe looped her arm around mine. "See, I told you."

While we sauntered toward the cabin, I filled my lungs with clean air and gazed at the view. The valley sprawled out in front of us, sheltered by the tree-covered mountains in every direction. The tumbling, rushing sounds of the creek whispered from behind the house. A veritable feast for the senses.

"I'd never tire of this," I said. "Food for the soul."

"Our little corner of heaven on earth. We're so glad you came." She squeezed my arm, and I returned the gesture. She lowered her voice. "I hope you're not too upset about Wyatt coming. I didn't have the heart to say 'no.'"

"I can't say I'm thrilled, but I'll make the best of it. He's a great guy. I just . . ." I shrugged.

"Say no more. We'll make it work."

I pinned her with a mock glare. "As long as you don't run out of hot chocolate."

She smirked, her pert nose wrinkling as she flipped her blond hair over one shoulder. "I wouldn't dare."

The next moment, as we topped the steps, Ben and Amelia swallowed me with sweet, sticky kisses and hugs. My soul soaked it up like dry ground absorbed a long-awaited rainfall.

Sharing a snowstorm with Wyatt might not be too bad with Chloe and her crew always nearby.

"Come in, come in." Luke gestured us inside.

I stepped into the warmth of the vaulted living room. The aroma of the fireplace enveloped me as Daisy, the collie, zipped back and forth across the rug, barking happily. I knelt and called her.

The ball of fluff bounded into my arms, her pink tongue lapping empty air as I arched my head out of reach, laughing. My, but it felt good. Like balm to a wound.

I ached for Charlie. He needed this as well. I should've twisted his stubborn arm and hauled him along anyhow.

When the excitement settled somewhat, I stashed my bags in the upstairs loft bedroom, donned an oversized fleece plaid sweater and lounge pants, then traded my thin crew socks for a fuzzy, lavender pair.

Chloe giggled when I entered the kitchen. "You look the part."

"I'd be sweating if I were home."

An impish twinkle gleamed in her eyes. "Luke checked the forecast again. Oh, girl, you're so getting snowed in. And with you know who."

I rolled my eyes, ignoring the fluttering in my stomach. "Save those sweet, corny ideas for your next recipe."

"Speaking of which . . ." She plopped a stained index card on the countertop. "You can lend a hand with my latest disaster."

Pursing my lips, I scanned the ingredients. "False modesty never looked good on you. You're a master cook, way better than me. Own it."

Chloe chewed a fingernail. "Well, not much better."

"Don't feed her ego, Chelsea." In the living room, Luke crawled on his hands and knees with the kids on his back.

"A wise man would keep out of this conversation, especially if he wants to eat." Chloe arched an eyebrow.

For good measure, Luke roared, and the kids' squeals filled the house. *Could Wyatt and I ever be like this?*

The unbidden thought jolted me. With a tight smile, I cut a glance at Chloe, who shrugged and started pulling pots and pans from the cabinet. Her head wagged.

"The possibilities are endless."

I popped her with a hand towel as punishment for reading my thoughts.

A light snow had started when Wyatt arrived. My insides knotted as I brought up the rear of the welcoming crew. Too bad I couldn't morph into a house cat or something. Like a coward, I hid behind Chloe, which did me no favors since we were almost the same size.

In the twilight, Wyatt moved toward us with an easy, unhurried stride. Nestled in the crook of his arm was, no doubt, Mon Petit Chou's case, shrouded inside a jumbo pillowcase. After the initial greetings, he angled himself around my family and zeroed in on me. As though I were the only one on the place.

An unspoken apology lingered with the uncertainty in his gaze.

A girl could get lost in that blue haze.

Could I melt so easily? Forget the flecks of snow speckling his hair and broad shoulders, the utterly lost expression on his face while he cradled a stuffed pigeon. The faint dimple in his chin. The blatant nerve of my heart. Dipping my head, I forced a smile, then bolted indoors.

The family buzzed happily while I sank onto a nearby recliner. Chloe slipped her hands under Mon Petit Chou's case and lifted it into her arms. She winked at Wyatt. "I know the perfect place for Chouchou. She'll love our book nook."

"I'm sure she will. Thanks." Wyatt nodded.

Resisting the urge to grit my teeth, I chewed my bottom lip and stared at the floor. Why did everybody treat her as though she were alive? She was dead. Like a lot of other things.

A pair of boots appeared at the edge of my vision. Wyatt. "Looks like I made it in time."

In time for what, I wanted to snap. *To ruin my weekend? To disturb my peace?*

He continued. "The snow's coming down harder by the minute."

Slowly, I gathered my wits and ventured a glimpse at him, praying my turmoil didn't show. "You may regret getting stuck with us."

He shook his head. "I'm sorry. I know how much this getaway means to you."

Faint, weary shadows pooled beneath his eyes. Tension stiffened his usually pleasant lips. He'd driven long hours for something I'd been retreating from most of my life. Anger wouldn't do us any good.

Sighing, I straightened and rubbed my knees. "You know I never stay mad at you for long."

And I discovered I meant it.

His eyes warmed as his mouth relaxed into a smile. "Thanks."

The evening progressed through supper and board games. Our tense laughter eased as we rediscovered bits and pieces of our old camaraderie. When the clock reached the kids' bedtime, Chloe and Luke carried them to their rooms for stories and prayers.

I scooped up the remaining two cinnamon rolls onto a plate, took them into the living room, and set them on the coffee table.

Wyatt patted the sofa cushion beside him. "I won't bite."

I hesitated before opting for honesty. "I know, but it's a bit weird since our breakup."

He held up his hands. "We're still friends. Let's keep it there for now."

"For now?" I frowned.

Hurt shadowed his face. "I'm not giving up, but I'm not pushing either."

Crossing my arms, I tilted my head to one side. "Then why did you come?"

His gaze captured mine for several dizzying seconds while he patted the cushion once more. "Let's enjoy the evening for what it is. No talk of the past, present, or future. The fire is nice, the dessert is waiting, and the company is perfect."

A grudging, breathless laugh escaped me. I settled on the sofa a little farther from the spot he'd patted. "What do we discuss?"

"Why talk? Sometimes it's better to listen." Lifting a cinnamon roll to his mouth, he relaxed against the seat and watched the crackling fire.

I followed suit and closed my eyes as the soft texture of the dessert released the flavors of vanilla and cinnamon. Outside, the wind howled around the eaves of the cabin and whistled through the trees. A cozy, safe feeling. Mostly because Wyatt sat only a few feet from my side without needing to press me for answers or drone on about nothing.

One of the things I love about him.

I choked mid-swallow. Hunching, I coughed while smacking my chest. Immediately, Wyatt slid closer. "Are you all right?"

I nodded. Wyatt hurried to the kitchen and returned with a small glass of water. "Take a sip when you can."

After the cough subsided, I set the glass on the coffee table. Wyatt studied me.

I shifted my eyes to the view outside. Beyond the low lamplight, sheets of snow flew sideways past the huge picture windows, a perfect comparison of light unhindered by darkness. Of clarity overcoming uncertainty.

My doubts had failed to obscure the deeply buried truth. I loved Wyatt, but the realization only highlighted the reasons I dreaded commitment.

"What's wrong?" His question splintered my thoughts.

I wagged a finger at him, my smile weak. "No present. Remember?" I stood, then turned toward the stairs, praying inwardly that he didn't sense my emotions. "Been a long day. I'm going to turn in. See you in the morning."

My hasty footfalls climbing the stairs blotted out his answer.

Too bad they couldn't stamp out the truth.

Once in the shelter of the loft, I slumped onto the bed and buried my head in my hands. Wyatt and I had battled a tug-of-war between our hearts since early high school. Whenever we verged into serious territory, I would call a halt. Through the years, our pattern yo-yoed between intense and casual.

I'd never shrugged off that kid huddled under the table. Ditched and too naïve to realize it.

I wasn't worth the trouble, but Wyatt persisted.

Why?

4

In the morning, clouds still shrouded the mountains, and a steady wind swept through the valley. Snow blanketed everything, an undisturbed canvas ready for Ben and Amelia's mark. Flakes still drifted on the air but not as heavily as during the night.

While the kids tugged on their boots, I pulled my wool hat farther down on my ears, then tucked a scarf around my neck. Beside me, Wyatt slid his hands into a pair of gloves.

He plucked another pair from the rack beside the front door and held them out to me. His eyes searched my face. "You okay?"

I brightened my tone as I took them. "Sure."

"Hmm." He clearly didn't buy it.

During breakfast, I'd managed to keep up with the happy chatter while battling against the churn of my stomach and avoiding Wyatt's gaze. Hiding the truth had never been my strong suit. My eyes always betrayed me.

"Are you sure you're staying in?" I asked Chloe over my shoulder.

Nodding, she snuggled closer to Luke on the sofa. "Us old and wise folks will watch from the window and stay warm."

"Enjoy it while you can." Luke lifted a cup of coffee to his lips. "It gets heavier again this afternoon."

I rubbed my gloves together in satisfaction. "Heaven's dust."

Raising their cups in a toast, they laughed while we ushered the kids and Daisy outside. As they bounded across the yard, I tilted up my face to let the snow graze my skin. The blood in my veins hummed, invigorated by the crisp, clean air.

"Now this is what I call skipping winter." I raised my arms.

Wyatt pulled out his phone and tapped a weather app. "Charlie's in short sleeves. It's 65 degrees."

I grimaced. "That means an ice storm will probably hit in February."

"Hush." Wyatt zipped the phone into his pocket. "I'll pretend I didn't hear you."

"C'mon, let's build a snowman!" Amelia tossed a handful of snow above her head while Ben stuck out his tongue to catch flakes.

Their giggles punctuated occasional bickering as Wyatt and I helped them roll the snow and stack the balls almost four feet high.

"Are we having a contest?" I panted as we settled the snowman's head on top.

"I never do anything halfway." Wyatt winked.

The tingling of my face intensified as I turned my attention elsewhere. Amelia jabbed two sticks into the snowman's sides. "He wants a toy."

"What's he saying?" I whispered, leaning closer to his charcoal grin.

Amelia copied my movement and widened her eyes. "I know." Pressing a finger to her lips, she turned and dashed to the porch.

"What's she doing?" Ben yanked my coat, then reached up, wanting to be held.

I scooped him up while Amelia rummaged in a box. "It's a secret. Wait and see."

"This," she yelled, holding up a red jump rope. She jogged to us, waving it in her mittened hand.

"But he don't have legs."

"He don't need 'em." Amelia draped the jump rope in the snowman's *fingers.*

Ben pointed. "How's he jump?"

Amelia put her hands on her hips. "He does when we ain't watchin' him."

"He don't have legs," Ben whined, rubbing his eyes.

Wyatt touched my elbow and dipped his head near my ear. "That's our cue." To Ben, he held out his hands. "Do you smell hot chocolate? Are you ready for a piggyback ride to the house?"

A sunny grin dissolved the scowl. "Yay!"

As Amelia and I trailed them, I struggled not to notice Wyatt's chummy ease with the kids. He had brothers, after all. Why wouldn't he be a natural? I dismissed the thoughts. My heart did stupid things to my brain.

One morning down. Now the afternoon to go.

"Care to talk?"

I lifted my eyes from the novel in my lap. Wyatt's head emerged at the top of the loft stairs. He rested his hand on the rail.

My mouth ran dry. "Do you take rain checks?"

With a wry grin, he stepped into the room and glanced out the window behind me. "Sorry. Not a raindrop in sight."

"Smarty pants." Laying aside the book, I straightened my legs and rose from the chair, my hopes to escape dashed while the rest of the house napped.

He gestured toward the far end of the loft. "How about the nook?"

"Lead the way."

Tucked partly beneath the angled ceiling, the book nook had its own wall separating it from the rest of the loft. Within the miniature world, stories filled colorful shelves from the floor to the ceiling. Its large window sported a wide, cushioned seat piled with plush pillows begging to be cuddled, while a view of the frosty mountains drew the eyes outward. A perfect spot for daydreaming.

Except that Mon Petit Chou perched on the sill as though surveying the snowscape. Chloe's creative idea, no doubt.

I lowered myself onto the chaise lounge in the opposite corner while Wyatt chose the window seat. Folding his arms, he sat on the edge of the cushion as far from the fluffy pillows as possible—a humorous sight if his expression hadn't sobered.

"Where do we start?" he asked.

"I don't know." I grabbed a pillow beside me and hugged it to my stomach.

"Before you let Chouchou go, you need to hear her story."

My fingernails dug into the pillow's fabric. "I can't, Wyatt."

His shoulders sagged. "Then you'll have to find someone else to sell her."

"But I trust you." A sudden idea flashed through my mind. "Why don't you keep the bird?"

"I can't afford her."

My mouth slacked. "It's not like you need to buy feed and water. Really, I'd rather you take it home. Pawpaw would approve."

Wyatt scrubbed the side of his lightly stubbled jaw, his frustration surfacing. "Do you really think he would approve of my paying $500 for a $25,000 bird?"

The pillow I clutched slid onto the floor. For several long moments, we stared at one another. Suddenly, my chest started heaving as though I had been running. I couldn't get enough air. My heart hammered against my ribcage.

"What?" I finally gasped. The amount was incredible.

Wyatt slowly rose and approached me. Kneeling on the shag rug, he captured my trembling hands in both of his warm ones. "You have to know her story before you make a decision."

His gentle insistence nearly undid me. My eyes smarted. He continued, "I'm sorry. I don't want to hurt you. You've endured enough pain, but I care too much to let you avoid the truth. I'm here. Chelsea, you're so much more than that little girl hiding under the kitchen table in a thunderstorm. You're the bravest person I know. And you are worth fighting for."

How did he know my deepest fear? Brave? I ran from anything or anyone who might crush me. I had bolted every moment our feelings had drifted into the delightful unknown.

I'm here.

Two tears streaked down my cheeks as I slammed my eyes shut. The image of Mom driving off contrasted with Wyatt pursuing me almost seven hundred miles to walk my valley. I shuddered.

His hands left mine, and then the pads of his thumbs wiped the moisture from my skin. "Chouchou is worth fighting for too," he whispered, his voice wobbling.

I swallowed hard, leaning into his touch for a split second before withdrawing to collect myself. "You're right."

"Is it all right if I call Charlie? He knows the details better than I do."

I stood. "Give me a minute to wash my face."

Nodding, he shifted to the chaise lounge while I hurried to the restroom.

5

"How do I begin?" Charlie propped his elbows on the kitchen table at home after angling his phone so that we could see him on the screen. Nearby, beads of condensation pebbled around his glass of sweet tea.

"Start where it's easiest for you." Resisting the temptation to scoot closer to Wyatt, I clutched my fingers together in my lap.

Charlie glanced at the ceiling, then blew a hard breath through his lips. "It was 1944 in the Netherlands during World War II. Pawpaw had fought his way across Europe. The Allies were slowly gaining ground against the Germans, but Pawpaw's unit ran into trouble. The Germans surrounded the troops, and the communications, such as radios, failed."

He paused to take a swig of sweet tea.

"What did they do?"

"In those days, the Army still used carrier pigeons to relay messages. Pawpaw handled and trained them. Mon Petit Chou was one of many. She was his favorite.

"When they were ambushed, she was chosen to carry a message for help. He attached it to her leg . . . the missing one now. Then he let her go."

A sharp pain stabbed my fingers as I realized I was squeezing them too tightly. My pulse ticked up a notch.

"German snipers watched for the pigeons. Some birds made it through. Others didn't." Charlie's chest expanded and fell as he cleared his throat. His gaze dropped to the table.

My heart shriveled with dread. "Did she not make it?"

"No sooner than she'd taken off, a sniper opened fire. Shot her through the chest. She fell, then took off again. The sniper shot at her again. Pawpaw lost sight of her."

No.

I wanted to shout and cry. Seeming to sense it, Charlie glanced at me and lifted a hand. "She made it, Chelsea."

"What?"

"She flew over two hundred miles, arriving at her box in England after four-and-a-half hours. She saved around two thousand lives. Chouchou's spirit was stronger than her wounds. Her leg, the one carrying the message, had also been wounded and had to be amputated."

Overcome, I covered my mouth with my hand, the room swirling around me.

Wyatt steadied me with the soft pressure of his hand on my back. "What happened to her afterward?" he asked Charlie.

My brother hesitated a moment before answering. "She lived about eight months, long enough for Pawpaw to be reunited with her in England. He always believed she'd been waiting for him to return before she eventually—"

I sprang out of the seat. "Sorry. I need to breathe."

Blindly, I scrambled down the stairs and snatched open the door without bothering to grab my coat or boots. Standing at the porch's edge, I tried to fill my mind with the view in front of me rather than the scene within my mind.

Heavy clouds lumbered over the tops of the Smokies. Large snowflakes descended like a thick, speckled curtain, obscuring parts of the valley.

The hush of snowfall, absent of wind, filled me with wonder, calmed my racing pulse. The miracle of its silent touch reminded me of God's fingerprints throughout my life.

His presence endured through the bad and good, overlaying the rough and smooth places. Nourishing my soul while I awaited the renewal of spring. All the while, He had beautified every detail, although I had failed to see it. Especially with Chouchou.

A bittersweet realization tweaked me. Pawpaw's endearment for her had also become mine.

Behind me, the door opened. Wyatt approached with his coat draped over one arm. A soft, hesitant smile played around the corners of his mouth as he shifted the coat onto my shoulders.

"That was a bit intense." He searched my face.

"I needed to hear it, though." I eased my arms into the sleeves and filled my nose with the traces of his cologne.

"Are you okay?"

For a long moment, I allowed myself to get lost in his perusal while he gauged the things I rarely allowed to surface.

I nodded. "For the first time in a long while, I am."

Wyatt's arm rounded my shoulders, and he pulled me close against his side.

From the book nook's window, the purple flush of dawn promised clear skies before another wave of snow clouds would reach Valor Pass in the late afternoon.

Sleep had eluded me most of the night while I wavered between my choices for Chouchou's future. My whispered prayers for wisdom brought peace but no definite answer. Twenty-five thousand dollars would stretch a long way with farm expenses or making repairs to the 120-year-old house. I still could hardly believe it.

But Pawpaw had already known and chosen to keep her.

I lowered myself onto the chaise lounge and opened my Bible. If I kept her, would I ever be able to look at her without a shadow of grief and dread? Sighing, I glanced down at the page and read the first verse that met my eyes.

Are not two sparrows sold for a farthing? And one of them shall not fall on the ground without your Father.

The explosion of a sniper's gun arrested my thoughts along with the image of Chouchou falling from the sky. God was there when she hit the ground.

And He was there when she took flight again.

If you get to know her, you'll discover you're both a lot alike.

I raised my eyes as the first rays of sunlight spilled over the horizon and glittered across the snow. From her case, Chouchou quietly observed the sun's slow rise. A mellow glow haloed her, burnishing the soft gray of her head, shimmering across the blend of green, blue, and lavender neck feathers, her chest, then onto her wings.

For an instant, she lived.

The silence between us grew hallowed.

She would live forever afterward to me. The way she lived to Pawpaw.

I had almost missed discovering a faithful friend and hero. The sun climbed, banishing the shadows from the nook and my mind. Its warmth stretched across the floor and washed over me in a wave of love.

Thank You, Lord.

Thank you, Pawpaw.

Near the doorway, the wooden floor creaked. Holding two steaming cups of coffee, Wyatt popped his head around the frame. "Is it too early?"

"Not for coffee." I swallowed, a little nervous. "Or you."

He beamed, a pleasant, ruddy flush spreading from his neck to his forehead. "Same here."

After handing me a cup, he paused, a curious expression raising his brows. "You're keeping Chouchou."

"I've discovered I can't part with her."

"I knew you had it in you." He fished a small pouch from his pocket and sat beside me. "Here. I put her Dickin medal in this because I didn't want to risk losing it while traveling. There's little value without it."

"She's priceless to me." Setting the cup on the coffee table, I took the pouch.

"Listen to you defending her already." He winked and sipped from his mug.

With a cheeky grin, I tipped up the bag and caught the medal in my palm. I'd never held it or bothered to observe it closely. The aged bronze was engraved on both sides with a wreath. One side displayed her name, her army group, the date of her heroic action, and her service number.

Mon Petit Chou

I turned it over.

For Gallantry. We Also Serve.

I bit my lip. "Without her bravery, I wouldn't exist. She saved not only Pawpaw's life, she saved Dad's. Charlie's. Mine. What a coward I've been."

Shushing me, Wyatt wrapped the fingers of his free hand around one of mine. "Courage always comes at the right moment, when we need it. You and Chouchou are the bravest souls I know."

I squeezed his hand, self-conscious and anxious to lighten up things. "I owe you $500, by the way."

"Ah, yes. I'll hold you to it."

I stroked the medal with my thumb, tracing the simple letters of a complex story. Another thought struck me.

"Remind me to kill Wes when we get home."

Wyatt's deep laugh rumbled through the loft, threatening to wake the entire household. I laid the medal beside my coffee.

Capturing his face between my hands, I silenced him in the best possible way.

A NOTE FROM THE AUTHOR

I learned of the Dickin medal while watching the British Antiques Roadshow when one was valued at £30,000. That is roughly $39,000 US. The medal belonged to a racing pigeon named Mary who served during World War II.

Going online, I began researching the Dickin award and its recipients. The rest, as they say, was history.

Another pigeon named Tommy intrigued me. During a race, he was blown off course by a storm and subsequently ended up in the hands of the Dutch Resistance. He successfully carried a coded message to England, which led to the destruction of a German arms factory. Like Chouchou, he also was shot and wounded but successfully completed his mission. He lived until 1952. He was not stuffed, however. The devotion and gallantry of these birds touched me deeply.

Chouchou's story is loosely based on two carrier pigeons, Cher Ami and William of Orange. Cher Ami, whose name means *dear friend,* served with distinction during World War I. He sustained a chest wound and lost one leg when German snipers opened fire. Miraculously, he made it to England with a message that saved around two thousand lives. William of Orange served during World War II and saved a few thousand lives during similar circumstances. He was not wounded, however.

In the UK, members of The People's Dispensary for Sick Animals (PDSA) wanted to recognize these courageous animals for their gallantry and devotion to duty. Maria Dickin, the founder, developed this award in 1943 to be the highest award for valor, equivalent to its human counterpart the Victoria Cross. Since its creation, seventy-five animals have been honored. Among these are thirty-eight dogs, thirty-two pigeons, four horses, and even one cat.

These animals also had trainers or handlers who bonded closely with them. Some of the trainers were fortunate enough to carry *their* animal home after the war, especially if their animal was a dog. These animals were considered fellow soldiers by the troops who depended on them.

Today, Cher Ami resides in the Smithsonian Museum. Yes, he is stuffed. You can also look him up online and find a picture of him standing proudly on his one leg. The Royal Signals Museum in Dorset, England, commemorates William of Orange. The Dock Museum in Barrow-in-Furness, England, acquired Tommy's medal for £30,000 in January 2025, and it is on display. Mary of Exeter is buried in Ilford Animal Cemetery in London along with Simon the cat, another Dickin medal recipient.

I hope you, dear reader, will forgive any liberties I took while fictionalizing and combining their stories.

These extraordinary animals deserve to be remembered.

Candace

ABOUT THE AUTHOR

Candace West was born in the Mississippi delta but grew up in small-town Arkansas. She is a graduate of the University of Arkansas at Monticello. Ever since the age of twelve, she dreamed of writing inspirational fiction. Over the years, she has published short stories as well as poems in various magazines. By weaving entertaining, page-turning stories, she hopes to share the Gospel and encourage her readers. Read more about Candace and her books at candaceweststoryteller.com.

TITLES BY CANDACE WEST

THE MOSAIC COLLECTION: NOVELS

Windy Hollow series

Through the Lettered Veil
Among the Kindled Embers

THE MOSAIC COLLECTION: ANTHOLOGY STORIES

"A Garland of Grace" in *A Star Will Rise*
"Forever Mine" in *Song of Grace*
"The Key" in *All Things New*
"McDonald's Farm" in *Dancing in the Rain*
"The Angel Voices" in *A Thrill in the Air*

Valley Creek Redemption Series

Lane Steen
Valley of Shadows
Dogwood Winter

an in the shadows novella

Only the Ocean Knows

sara davison

ONLY THE OCEAN KNOWS

Sara Davison

Alain Temauri is desperate to leave the cold, dreary weather behind, along with memories of the girlfriend who broke his heart when she walked away. Last year, his younger brother Rav's trip to Tahiti, their parents' birthplace, changed his life. Could it do the same for Alain? Along with the warm breezes and tropical sands he expected, he encounters one shocking revelation after another about his family that he definitely didn't foresee. Taking his therapist's advice, Alain shares his heart and tangled emotions with the Pacific, since the ocean never gives up its secrets.

Unless, of course, it does . . .

Who shut up the sea behind doors
when it burst forth from the womb . . .
when I said, "This far you may come and no farther;
here is where your proud waves halt"?
Job 38:8,11 (NIV)

DECEMBER 26TH

Alain Temauri reached for the well-worn novel he'd brought with him to his mother's place. An inch from the spine, he stopped and pressed his fingers to the slightly dusty side table next to the armchair. As an English professor, he taught at least one Jane Austen novel every semester. *Persuasion* was one of his favorites. Or had been.

He and his girlfriend Carly had read the classics to each other—*Wuthering Heights, Jane Eyre, To Kill a Mockingbird, The Great Gatsby.* Each one compelling, and yet something drew them to *Persuasion* over and over. Hence the worn-thin cover.

But Carly was gone, wasn't she?

Alain didn't blame her. He didn't even blame the friends who had convinced her to walk away when, after three years, he was no closer to proposing to her than he had been the day they had met.

That wasn't true, although he could see how her friends and family might think so. How even Carly might think so, given that he had never broached the subject, as much as he might have wanted to. How could he? How could he possibly ask a woman as full of light and life as she was to commit herself to a man from whom light and life had departed when he was seven years old? Or maybe he'd never had either of those things. If he had, he couldn't remember.

Certainly what happened that fateful night when his alcoholic, abusive father dragged his older brother Tane into his truck and then proceeded to ram that truck into the side of a car, killing a classmate of Tane's, had stolen the last of the light from Alain's life.

He'd been able to pretend, when he was with Carly, basking in the overflow from her sweetness and warmth, that maybe a little of that glow emanated from him. Until he couldn't pretend anymore. Even then he was unable to send her away, only tell her that if she had any sense, any self-preservation at all, she would go.

Maybe it was that—his voice added to the chorus of others—that had finally persuaded her.

In any case, she'd left. And for every moment of the three months, two weeks, and six days since, he had tried to let go of her, of the memory of the look she had given him after telling him it was over, stumbling to the door, and disappearing from his life forever.

It wasn't working.

Summoning all his courage, he grabbed the book and flipped it open. A photograph fluttered to his lap. Picking it up, he stared at it a moment—a picture of him and Carly, laughing together over dinner on the second anniversary of their first date. Man, they'd laughed a lot. As they usually were, her green eyes were warm with a hint of mischief. Even now, in a photo, he could barely tear his gaze from them.

Then a flash of red caught his eye, and Alain lowered the picture. A crumpled ball of Christmas wrapping paper lay on top of a few pieces of wood in the bronze box next to the woodstove. After tucking the photo into the front of the book, he returned it to the side table and pushed to his feet. Snatching the paper, he grasped the silver knob at the end of the black metal stove handle and wrenched it down so he could pull open the door and toss the paper in. The fewer reminders that Christmas had just passed, the better.

He'd spent the day with his mother. Remarkably, Tane had shown up in the afternoon bearing gifts, the first Christmas his older brother had spent with them in three years. Tane had some kind of highly classified undercover police job they knew very little about. He was rarely able to come home, so that had been one bright light in what had otherwise been a dark holiday season for Alain.

Only Rav, their youngest brother, was missing. Rav had spent the previous Christmas in their parents' homeland of Tahiti, searching for roots, meaning, purpose—everything that was missing in Alain's life as well.

Apparently, Rav had found all those things. In the sweet, adorable redhead Annie. In his interactions with the assorted and eclectic group of tourists he'd spent the week before Christmas with after stumbling upon something called the Back Door Christmas Tour Company. And most impactful of all, according to his little brother, in his newfound relationship with God. So this year he and Annie had returned for a reunion with *the family,* as they referred to the friends they had met there.

As happy as Alain was for Rav, he couldn't wrap his mind around any of it. Would it have helped if he'd taken his little brother up on the invitation to go with them to Tahiti this year? If he'd taken the same journey, retraced his brother's footsteps, was there any chance he might have found some of those answers for himself?

He wandered over to the window. Icy rain pinged against the glass. Typical late-December weather in their hometown of Pemberton, British Columbia. Lucky Rav, basking in the sun while the rest of them shivered in the cold and damp. Alain pressed his fingertips to the glass. Was it too late to change his mind? He slitted his eyes, imagining that he was gazing out over the brilliant turquoise ocean, sandy beaches, palm trees waving in a warm, gentle breeze.

The thought of going to Tahiti *was* appealing. Could he afford it? Financially, not really. He'd been a university professor only a couple of years and was nowhere near getting tenure or a decent salary. Mentally, physically, and emotionally, though, he was starting to wonder if he could afford *not* to go.

As long as his mother was okay. After his dad went to prison when they were kids, it had taken *Maman* a long time to recover. She was doing well now and was more than capable of being on her own. Even so, Tane, Alain, and Rav always felt better when at least one of them was in town. With Tane AWOL most of the time and Alain teaching in Vancouver, that responsibility usually fell to Rav, but he wouldn't be back for another week.

Alain headed for the kitchen. Xaviar—the stray Rav had met in Tahiti and brought home with him and that they'd all adopted as another brother in the family—sat at the kitchen table eating a sandwich.

"Hey, kid." For fun, knowing how much Xaviar hated it, Alain ruffled his hair.

"Hey." Clutching the sandwich in one hand, Xaviar swatted Alain's fingers away with the other. "You're lucky you wear glasses."

Alain laughed, their *little brother* one of the few people who'd been able to make him do that in recent months. "Or what?"

Xaviar had been wrongly convicted and done two years of hard time after his biological older brother set him up to take the fall for his drug dealing. His arms were covered in tattoos, and he had developed a pretty convincing façade of toughness and detachment, which he'd likely needed to survive behind bars. What he didn't want anyone to know was that he was a total softie—one of the kindest and most decent people Alain knew.

"You do not want to find out," Xaviar muttered, his faint Spanish accent making even the threat sound lyrical. He shoved the last bite of sandwich into his mouth and used the side of his hand—the grease he was never fully able to wash off from his job working on high-end sports cars visible in the lines on his knuckles—to direct a few wayward crumbs onto his plate.

Alain laughed again. "Yeah, okay."

Tane strolled into the kitchen and headed straight for the counter, where their mother had left out bread, meat, and cheese for them to help themselves to while she was volunteering at the local food bank. She'd done that every Friday since discovering that doing something for others was one of the most helpful ways for her to find healing herself. She'd also returned to the faith she'd raised her young boys with, although so far only Rav had followed her along that path.

Alain took a plate down from the cupboard and handed it to his brother.

"Thanks." Tane nodded as he took it.

Alain leaned back against the counter and said, as nonchalantly as possible, "How long are you planning to be home?"

His brother offered him a wry grin. "Trying to get rid of me?"

"Not at all." Not only had Tane's classmate been killed in that accident, but Tane had been thrown through the windshield. He still bore the scars from the broken glass down the side of his face and across his chest.

Even so, when their mother withdrew into herself, Tane had stepped up and taken care of Alain and Rav, kept their lives from going off the rails. They owed him everything and missed him desperately when he was gone.

"I just . . ." Alain drew a line across the linoleum with the toe of his sneaker. It was a crazy idea, wasn't it?

Tane stopped spreading mustard on the bread. "What?"

"I was sort of toying with the idea of taking a trip."

His brother's eyebrows rose. "Really?"

Alain didn't blame him. He'd never left the province. As far as he knew, Tane hadn't either, although if he traveled the world for work, Alain and Rav wouldn't know it. Rav's trip to Tahiti last Christmas had been the first time any of them had left the country that Alain was aware of. "Yeah. Just feeling the need to, you know, get away for a few days."

Tane considered him a moment before asking, "Where would you go?"

Xaviar pulled the dishwasher door open and slid his plate into a slot on the lower rack. "Tahiti, right?"

Alain blinked. "How do you know that?"

"I've seen your face when Rav and I talk about it—you're drawn there like he was."

Huh. Alain hadn't been aware he had a *face* when the topic came up. The thought of visiting the country of his forefathers *had* always resonated somewhere deep inside, so maybe.

"You should go." Tane speared a tomato slice and set it on top of the three pieces of ham he'd laid across his bread.

"Yeah?"

"Yeah." He unscrewed the top off a jar of dill pickles. "I know things have been tough for you lately. A trip would do you good." He grabbed a fork and fished around in the jar for a pickle. "I can stick around a few more days."

"I'll be here too," Xaviar added as he closed the dishwasher door. "Your *maman* will be fine."

If Alain had hoped either of them might offer him an excuse to give up his ridiculous quest, they clearly weren't going to indulge him.

"You hear anything from Carly?" After setting the top slice of bread on his sandwich, Tane reached for a knife and cut it in half diagonally.

"No. I don't expect to. She was way too good for me, anyway."

Tane and Xaviar exchanged a look.

Alain frowned. "What was that?"

"What was what?" His brother tossed the knife into the sink with a clatter.

"That look you two just gave each other."

Tane paused in the act of twirling the bread bag to close the top. "It's just that you've said that before, and you're the only one who believes it."

"I'm not the only one. Carly broke up with me—she must believe it."

Another look passed between Tane and Xaviar.

Alain gritted his teeth. "Stop doing that." Obviously the two of them had been talking about him. With Tane home so rarely, when had they gotten so chummy? There was something about Xaviar, though. With their brown skin, Alain, Tane, and Rav had looked different than most of the other kids at school, and their fellow students had always been mean to them. After the accident, the cruel taunts and bullying had become unbearable.

The lesson had been drilled into Alain—people hurt you. People let you down and betray you. Books are safe. People leave. Books are always there, waiting patiently for you when you need them. They offer an escape from the harsh realities of life. From childhood, he had preferred the company of books and had only ever let his guard down to allow a very few people into his life—his mother and brothers, a small group of friends, Carly. And every year, despite his determination that it wouldn't happen again, his students. So, when Xaviar landed in their home without warning, it shocked Alain how quickly the kid won him over simply by being himself. Obviously, he'd had the same effect on Tane.

Of course, they did have in common that they had all been deeply hurt and betrayed by the people who should have been their fiercest protectors. So there was that.

His older brother twisted a tie around the end of the bag and set it on the counter. "Carly doesn't believe that either. I know she was the one to officially end things, but only after you pretty much shoved her out the door."

"Because I had nothing to offer her. She deserves better."

Tane clasped Alain's shoulder. The dark eyes that met his were haunted, as they had been since the night of the accident, and his chest clenched. He hated how much pain his brother had been forced to endure with no one to rely on the way Alain and Rav had always relied on him. Well, no one but his two best friends, Johnny and Beck, anyway. Thank goodness he had them even now, as they'd all gone to the police academy and then disappeared together into whatever dark, shadowy world Tane inhabited.

His brother's grip on his shoulder tightened. "Look. No one understands better than I do how hard it is to let go of the lies you've been told about yourself your whole life. But at some point we both need to find a way to do that. Like Rav has."

Alain sighed. "Maybe you're right."

"It does happen. Occasionally." Tane let go of him. "So go to Tahiti. See if you can find the answers you're looking for there. If God and I were on better terms, I'd say I would be praying for you, but you know *Maman* will be."

"Me too," Xaviar piped up. "Rav and Annie as well."

Alain wasn't sure how much stock he'd put in those prayers, even his mother's. Like Tane, he struggled to believe that God, if he did exist, could truly care about any of them. If he did, why hadn't he protected them from all the terrible things that had happened to them as kids?

In any case, he would go to Tahiti, follow in his little brother's footsteps. He would leave the dreary winter weather and his heartache and Carly and all the memories he had of their time together behind him. Maybe, if he could do that, he actually might find the answers he was seeking and be able to move on with his life.

DECEMBER 27TH

The pavement outside the Fa'a'ā International Airport in Tahiti was wet, as though it had rained recently. Now, though, a late-afternoon sun fell across Alain's shoulders as he worked his way through the throngs of people being dropped off or waiting for their rides. It was still warm—close to eighty degrees—and a light breeze carried the salt-tinged scent of the ocean.

In the distance, Alain could make out the dark shape of mountains behind a gauzy veil of mist. Even though he'd been born and raised in British Columbia and his hometown was surrounded by the Rockies, mountains and ocean never failed to move him, and he stopped a moment to take in the sight.

It had been tricky, not to mention wildly expensive, to book an extremely last-minute flight during the busiest time of year for tourists. So far he hadn't been able to find accommodations, but surely there'd be an available hotel room somewhere on the island. First, as he hadn't eaten since five a.m. and it was now five p.m. local time, dinner was his priority. After a good meal, he might have the energy and enthusiasm to start searching for a place to spend the night. Worst case, he knew Rav well enough to know that he and Annie would have separate hotel rooms, so he could let his brother know he was in the country and crash in his room for the night—or a few nights—if needed. He'd save that as a last resort. Rav and Annie were here to catch up with the friends they'd met last year, not to play host to him.

Besides, being the third wheel to a deliriously happy couple while trying to recover from a devastating breakup was not Alain's idea of a good time. He was happy for his little brother, but not happy enough for that.

A taxi approached, and he raised his hand. The driver veered to the curb, and Alain tossed his bag onto the back seat before climbing in after it.

The driver, a young man wearing a Tahiti FTF cap—the national football team—half turned to look back at him. "*Où aller?*"

Alain knew enough French from his public-school upbringing in Canada to understand the question—where to?—but looking like a local might become an issue if everyone assumed he was fluent. He checked his phone for the address of the restaurant he'd chosen after perusing the options during his flight. "*Place Tu-Marama, s'il vous plait.*"

The driver looked at him slightly askance. No doubt Alain's accent had given him away immediately. "The Meherio Tahitian Bistro, yes?"

Alain didn't miss the fact that the man had switched to English, which felt like a small failure on Alain's part. This was the land of his people, after all. He should have tried harder to learn the language and how to speak it like someone who actually belonged here. His *maman* would have taught him. She could have taught him a lot of things about this country, about his past, if he'd asked. Why had it never occurred to him to do so?

An unusual small spark of defiance lit inside him. "*Oui. Merci.*"

The driver's lips twitched but he only nodded and shifted around to face the front.

What did it matter if his language skills weren't great? Alain didn't plan to interact with a lot of people here. This was a solo quest. The thought of meeting a bunch of strangers like Rav had left him cold.

He stared out the side window as the driver wound the cab in and out of the traffic leaving the international airport. Papeete, the capital city of French Polynesia, was only a few kilometers away, and he wanted to soak in as much of his first view of the country as he could before they hit the city limits.

The palm trees he'd dreamed about seeing while standing in his mother's living room were everywhere, along with all kinds of other trees, shrubs, and lush foliage. To his left, the teal water of the Pacific Ocean stretched out as far as he could see, dotted with white sailboats. The waves of this same ocean crashed against the coastline of his own province, yet his home and his homeland felt worlds apart.

Far out on the water, a lone surfer crested a wave, riding it for several seconds before coming out of the tunnel and skimming along the surface. Alain watched him, mesmerized. Maybe he should try surfing while he was here. He almost laughed. Rav and Xaviar drove to the ocean to surf almost every weekend in the summer. Although they always invited him, Alain had yet to accept their offer. Life was dangerous enough without taking unnecessary risks. Jumping on a plane to come here was the most adventurous thing he'd ever done. His heart was pumping from the sheer audacity of the decision, which, he had to admit, was making him feel more alive than he had in a long time. Possibly ever.

He rolled down his window to breathe in the aromas of sea air and tropical flowers. As much as he had second-guessed this spontaneous trip while driving to the airport and waiting to board his flight, he was glad he had come. Even if he didn't find the answers here that his brother had, the warmth and beauty were already driving away a little of the dark cloud that had hovered around him for so long.

Maybe this was all he needed—a little time to himself surrounded by breathtaking scenery. He'd stuck three or four books into his suitcase, including, after a full minute of standing next to his bed considering the possible ramifications, that worn copy of *Persuasion*, the photo of him and Carly still tucked inside.

Traffic grew heavier as they reached the outskirts of Papeete. Less than five minutes later, the driver pulled to the curb in front of the restaurant. Alain paid and thanked him before grabbing his bag and climbing out of the car.

He'd booked a table on a patio overlooking the ocean beneath a wooden overhang. After the host seated him, he tucked his overnight bag beneath the empty chair across from his. The benefits of traveling on his own. Scanning the menu, he tried—really tried—to look only at the French and not cheat by reading the English translation. After getting the gist of the description of *Poisson du lagon à la vapeur*, he gave in and read the details to make sure he wasn't ordering anything crazy. Steamed lagoon fish with ginger and herbs and a side of grilled vegetables. Seemed safe.

The server was a tall man around Alain's age and dressed in black pants and a black golf shirt. Like the cabbie's, his lips twitched as Alain stumbled through ordering in French. When he finished, the man nodded and said, "Very good, sir," as he reached for the menu. His dark eyes were warm and friendly, which tempered Alain's humiliation. With his intense love of words and story, he'd always considered language his thing. Apparently he was limited to one. The server disappeared inside, and Alain leaned back in the surprisingly comfortable white chair with rounded back to take in the view.

Palm tree fronds waved in every direction. Fancy white sailboats were moored at the dock in front of the restaurant, floating gently on the turquoise water. Large white flowers hung upside down on the branches of trees filled with green, glossy leaves. A soft floral scent drifted on the evening breeze, and Alain breathed it in. Definitely an improvement over the bare branches and cold, drizzly weather at home, as beautiful as British Columbia was most of the year.

The server set a bamboo basket of food in front of Alain. The aromas of herbs and spices drifted from the fish and the vegetables, and he took another deep breath. "*Merci.* Thank you." A compromise.

With a small chuckle, the man said, "*De rien, monsieur.* You're welcome."

Alain unwrapped a black cloth napkin from around his cutlery. "Can you tell me what those white flowers are called?" He pointed to the large ones he was pretty sure were emitting the heavenly scent of . . . coconut? Jasmine? Both?

"That is the Tiare flower, sometimes called the Tahitian gardenia."

Oh. Rav and Annie had mentioned that flower in their stories from last Christmas. "Is that the one that women wear on the right side if they are single and the left if they are taken?"

"*Oui.* Exactly." The man cocked his head. "You are not from here, *monsieur?*"

Good question. *Was* he from Tahiti? Although his heritage was rooted here—in the volcanic soil of this beautiful country—not really. Of course, he had never felt completely home in Canada either. A foot in both worlds. "My parents are from here. I was born in Canada."

"Canada." A strange look fluttered across the man's face. "I have a relative there, I believe. If he is still alive."

People from other countries often didn't realize how vast Canada was, so Alain half expected him to mention the relative's name and ask if he knew him. Instead, someone at another table lifted a hand, and the server nodded in his direction. "Enjoy your meal." He dipped his head and was gone before Alain could respond. In any language.

His stomach rumbled in response to the hours it had gone without food and the enticing aromas carried by the steam rising from the fish and vegetables. He took his time eating, enjoying every bite as the sun sank lower in the sky and splashes of fuchsia and orange dropped onto the surface of the ocean.

Carly would have loved this view. She adored sunsets. The ocean too, for that matter. And flowers. And palm trees. Like him, she had never left Canada, although she'd told him numerous times she would love to come here and learn more about his country. Alain had always put her off. Sadness rippled through him like the tiny waves skimming the surface of the ocean. Why hadn't he brought her here when she asked? Would it have changed anything for them?

The splashing of the waves onto the shore reminded him of her favorite quote from *Persuasion,* the one she pulled out whenever she was attempting to talk him into one crazy adventure or another. Planting her hands on her hips—a prerequisite posture for this particular speech, apparently—she would say, "I hate to hear you talk about all women as if they were fine ladies instead of rational creatures. None of us wants to be in calm waters all our lives."

Alain slammed the door on that train of thought. He was here to get his mind off of her and their failed relationship. If this little trip of his could start him on the process of getting over her, that would be really great.

The server—Hiro, according to his name tag—returned to Alain's table and gathered up his plate and cutlery. "Would you like to hear the dessert choices?" he asked, nodding toward a cart set up near the door into the restaurant.

"No, thank you." Alain touched a hand to his stomach. "It was delicious, but I've had enough."

"I'm glad you enjoyed it." He lifted the plate. "I will take this to the kitchen and return with your bill."

"*Merci.*" Alain couldn't resist. If he didn't accomplish anything else this trip, his new goal was to get someone to keep talking to him in French and not switch to English as soon as he opened his mouth.

The man smiled before disappearing into the restaurant. He returned a moment later with the bill in a leather folder in one hand and a portable credit/debit machine in the other.

Lost in his musings and in the breathtaking scene in front of him, Alain hadn't noticed that he was the only patron left on the patio. Twinkling lights on strings around the wooden overhang and twined through bushes and around sailboat masts had come on, bathing the small harbor in soft, yellow light.

Almost dark. Which reminded him . . .

He flipped open the folder and checked the amount on the bottom of the bill, which wasn't helpful as it was listed in French Pacific francs. He didn't ask for a translation into Canadian dollars, just nodded as though he was fine with the amount and then leaned forward to retrieve his wallet from the back pocket of his cargo pants. "Do you happen to know of any good hotels that might have rooms available?" He slid the card into the slot and tapped in his code, leaving the man a generous tip despite his clear amusement at Alain's attempts to speak the language.

Hiro winced. "It could be a little difficult for you to find a place this late. It is a very busy time here in Papeete." The receipt curled around the bottom of the machine, and the server ripped it off. "Let me see. Perhaps you could try . . ." He started to hand the paper to Alain and then stopped, his eyes narrowing as he studied it. When he looked up, that strange look that had fluttered over his features earlier had returned. "Your name is Alain Temauri?"

"That's right."

The man pressed a hand to his chest. "My last name is Temauri as well. Hiro Temauri."

"Huh. Is it a common name here?"

The man lifted his shoulders. "I'm sure they exist, but I have never met another Temauri." He glanced around at the empty tables on the patio before gesturing to the seat across from Alain. "My customers have gone. May I sit?"

"Of course." Alain's head spun a little as he reached beneath the table for his bag and tugged it free of the chair. Was it possible he and this Hiro were related? He'd never met any family outside of his parents and brothers. They were the only Temauris he knew of who had come to Canada, although it was certainly possible there were others scattered across the country.

Hiro sat down and leaned forward, his forearms pressed to the table. "The relative I have in Canada is—or was—my father's brother. His name is Raimana Temauri. Do you . . ."

Alain's shock must have shown on his face as the man's dark eyes fixed on his. "You know him, yes?"

His throat had gone dry, and Alain reached for his water glass and took a sip. When he set it down, he wrapped his fingers around it, the condensation cool against his suddenly heated skin. "Raimana is my father's name." Was it possible there was more than one Raimana Temauri in Canada?

"Is your mother's name Emere?"

Alain let go of the glass with one hand and ran damp fingers across his forehead. "It is, yes." How crazy was this, that he happened to come to this restaurant tonight and be waited on by the cousin he never knew he had?

A huge smile broke across the server's face as he straightened. "Then you will not go to a hotel. You will come home with me. You are family."

Alain's head continued to spin as he climbed into the passenger seat of his cousin's dilapidated purple Jeep. The top was down, and he gripped the frame as they drove along the Circle Road that ran around the perimeter of Tahiti, the largest island in French Polynesia.

"My *papa* and I live in Tiarei, a small community on the water about twenty-five minutes east of Papeete," Hiro informed him.

Alain nodded, trying to wrap his mind around the fact that his cousin was driving him to his house, where he would stay with him and his dad, Alain's uncle. He hadn't seen or talked to his own father since he was seven years old, but he couldn't remember him ever mentioning a brother or any other family in Tahiti. In fact, he'd never wanted to talk about Tahiti at all. What could possibly have happened to make him so unwilling to share about this beautiful place with them?

His mother had never mentioned family either. Had he or Tane or Rav ever asked? Maybe not. From the time they were little kids, they had all been in survival mode. Sitting around reminiscing about the past had not been a big part of their existence.

He shifted a little to look at Hiro. "Will your dad mind me crashing at your place?"

His forehead wrinkled as he took his eyes from the road to glance over at Alain. "Crashing?"

Ha. He wasn't completely fluent in English then. Not the slang words, anyway. "Yeah. It means to sleep somewhere. It can also mean to show up without an invitation, either of which would apply here."

"Ah." His cousin shifted his attention to the front. "Not at all. My *maman* died a few years ago, so it is too quiet in our home. *Papa* loves to have people around." Hiro ran his fingers up and down the steering wheel. "His memory is not good now. He is often confused. I worry one night I will come home and he won't know me."

Given the sorrow weaving through the words, Hiro and his father were close. What would that be like? "I'm sorry."

"Thank you. It's been hard. He is my only family. Or he was. Until tonight." Hiro shot him a grin. "Unfortunately, I don't know how much he will be able to tell you about the past."

"That's okay. It will be good to meet him." Alain's black-framed glasses had slid a little down his nose, and he pushed them into place with one finger. "Has he ever mentioned my brothers and me?"

Hiro's dark eyebrows rose. "You have brothers?"

"Yes. Tane is older and Rav younger."

"Wow. Three cousins. Even more family." Hiro steered the Jeep around a slow curve in the road. "No. He never mentioned you. To be honest, I don't know if he is aware of you. He and your *papa* did not speak after Raimana left Tahiti."

Alain frowned. "Do you know why?"

"No. I asked my father about his family once, and he only said that he had one brother, Raimana, who married a woman named Emere and moved to Canada. He didn't seem to want to talk about it, so I didn't push it. I did write the names down, though, in case I ever went to your country and wanted to look them up."

"I wonder why he wouldn't want to talk about his only brother."

"I don't know." He glanced over at Alain. "Your parents, they are well?"

His throat tightened. How was he supposed to answer that? "*Maman* is good. Now."

"Now?"

"Yes." The wind was whipping the hair he hadn't taken time to get cut in a few months, and Alain shoved a handful behind one ear as he stared out at the water to their left, moonlight sparkling on the surface. Was there any reason not to tell Hiro the truth? He sighed and rested his head against the back of the seat, turning it slightly in his cousin's direction. "Dad used to drink. A lot. When he did, he was . . . violent with *Maman* and us."

Hiro didn't look over this time, although a shadow fell over his features. "I am sorry to hear that."

"It was hard. Then, when I was seven, he got angry at Tane, who was nine, because he was trying to protect *Maman*. Although Dad had been drinking, he dragged Tane into his truck and took off. I have no idea where he planned to take him because he drove through a stop sign and hit a car."

His cousin's knuckles gleamed white in the semi-darkness. "Was everyone okay?"

"My dad was, of course. Tane was thrown through the windshield."

Hiro winced. "Oh no."

"Yeah. He was hurt badly. He still has scars on his face and chest from all the stitches. The worst part, though . . ." Alain stopped and stole another look out at the water, the beauty of the night keeping his emotions from spiraling out of control. "A boy in Tane's class was in the car. He was killed, and his sister has been in a wheelchair ever since."

His gaze still on the road, Hiro reached over and grasped his forearm. "I am sorry, Alain. I cannot imagine what all of you have gone through." He returned his hand to the wheel.

"It was terrible. My dad went to prison and he is still there. *Maman* could barely function for a long time. Once Tane came home from the hospital, he took care of me and Rav. I don't know what would have happened to us if he hadn't."

"I would like to meet both your brothers."

"I hope you can. I know they'd love to meet you. Tane is still at home, but Rav is actually in Tahiti with his girlfriend, Annie, for a few days."

Hiro's face lit up. "You must invite them to come for dinner."

Alain laughed. "They don't even know I'm here yet, let alone that I will be staying with family we didn't know we had."

"God is good to bring us together like this, *non*?"

Alain gazed out over the water again. Surrounded by such incredible beauty, it was hard to argue against some kind of creator. Whether that creator was good or not, he had yet to decide.

His cousin didn't press him on that, only pointed to the right. "Here is our place."

Alain studied the two-story wooden cabin with thatched roof and large, wraparound porch surrounded by flowering shrubs and palm trees and set back maybe fifty feet from the water. Not fancy, but the house and property were neat and well kept. No neighbors that he could see, so it looked as though they had the waterfront area to themselves. Not a bad place to hang out for a few days.

Hiro parked his vehicle in front of a small garage. Alain twisted to grab his bag from the rear seat before climbing out and following his cousin inside. He gestured to an opening to their right. "*Papa* will be watching TV." He started that way, and Alain trailed after him. What would his uncle be like? Anything like their father? That thought tightened up his muscles a little. Hiro had said his *papa* liked to have people around, though. His father had never wanted any of them to bring friends home. Hopefully that was a good sign.

"*Papa?*" Hiro approached the older man sitting in a recliner. Alain lingered near the doorway, waiting for his cousin to break it to his father who he was.

"Hiro!" He clapped his hands together once. "*Eaha ta oe i afa'i mai na'u ?*"

"He asks what I have brought him," Hiro translated for Alain. He held up a black plastic container. "*Korori ravioli, pata uouo e te vanilla no Taha'a, Papa.*"

His father clapped his hands again. "*Te mea mau ta 'u i hinaaro!*"

Alain didn't understand what they were saying, but he did get that they were speaking Tahitian. His parents had used their native language with each other when they wanted to discuss something they didn't want their sons to overhear. Or sometimes when they were fighting and didn't care who overheard them. He repressed a shudder at the memory of nights huddled in his bed, his hands over his ears in a vain attempt to block out the yelling. And the hitting.

Hiro laughed. "He says that is exactly what he wanted. Which he says every night."

Alain thought back on all the times his father had complained about what *Maman* had made for dinner. Occasionally he would throw it in the garbage and demand she make something else. One memorable night he had swept an arm across the table, sending all their plates full of food flying across the kitchen linoleum.

Yes, this man was obviously nothing like his brother.

"I have brought you something else, *Papa*. Or rather, someone else."

Although he had switched to English, his father looked up from the container Hiro had handed him, interest sparking in his dark eyes. How many languages did these people speak, anyway? "Who?"

Hiro half turned to Alain and gestured for him to come closer. As he came up to stand next to his cousin, his uncle's eyes widened. He set the container on a small table next to his chair and clambered to his feet.

"Alain, this is my *papa*, Vateo Temauri. And this is—"

Before he could introduce him, Alain's uncle clapped his hands the way he had when his son brought him dinner. "Raimana, my brother. You have come home at last!"

Of the three of them, Alain did look the most like his father. People often commented on the resemblance, which he'd always hated. They both wore glasses, but beyond that, Alain had inherited his father's curly hair, the shape of his face, his nose. His entire life, every time he had looked in the mirror, he had been reminded of the man he despised, the one who had very nearly destroyed all their lives.

So, he couldn't fault his uncle for thinking that was who he was looking at now. He was likely about the same age his father had been the last time his brother saw him. And Hiro had said his memory was failing. Did he have dementia? Carly's grandmother had been diagnosed with Alzheimer's several years ago. She was a very sweet woman but often mixed up the people who came to see her with those in her past. Typically the family played along, not wanting to upset or confuse her.

Hiro cast a stricken look at Alain. "No, *Papa*. This is Alain. Raimana's son."

Alain touched his cousin's elbow. "It's fine."

His uncle advanced toward him. As though his son hadn't spoken, he clasped Alain's forearms. "I never thought I would see you again." He let go and pulled him into a tight embrace, his gray cardigan soft against Alain's bare arms.

Okay, then. Apparently Alain was going to be his father. For tonight, anyway. It was a small price to pay for free accommodations and time with family. Hopefully his uncle would be thinking more clearly tomorrow, and they could explain to him who he was. Until then, Alain might hold off on inviting Rav and Annie over for that dinner. It would likely be easier for his uncle if they gave him a couple of days to get used to his presence.

"*Papa*, sit. Your dinner will be cold."

His uncle let go of him and stepped back. Hiro rested a hand between his father's shoulder blades and guided him back to the recliner. "You eat. I will show our guest to his room. He will be tired from his travels."

His father nodded as he wiggled to the back of the chair and reached for the container again. "Yes. He has come a long way. We will talk tomorrow, brother."

Alain nodded. "Of course. Good night."

His uncle had already grabbed a fork and speared a mouthful of ravioli, so the two of them left him to it. Hiro led Alain up the stairs to the second floor. They walked along the narrow hallway until Hiro stopped and pushed open a door. "Here is our guest room." He pointed to a small door across the hall. "There are towels in there. Help yourself to anything you need."

Alain wandered over to a chair in the corner and set down his bag. The room was small but neat with a double bed, a dresser, and two large windows. A small wooden desk sat beneath one window, overlooking the ocean.

Hiro switched on the lamp next to the bed, bathing the room in a soft glow. Definitely not a bad place to hang out.

"This is great, Hiro. Thank you."

"You're very welcome. I'm just happy you're here." He ran his palms over the front of his black dress pants. "I'm sorry my father confused you for yours."

Alain shook his head. "It's okay, really. My . . . ex-girlfriend's grandmother had Alzheimer's, so I get it. It's better not to argue with him. And I do look like my dad, so I don't blame him."

Hiro contemplated him a moment, his dark eyes clearly seeing far more of Alain than should be possible after such a short acquaintance. Would he ask about his ex-girlfriend? Calling Carly that out loud for the first time had actually hurt Alain's chest. He really didn't feel like talking about her. Not tonight.

As though he could sense that, his cousin only nodded slightly. "Hopefully he will know you tomorrow. Some days are better than others, although he does seem to be lingering in his own world longer and longer." The sorrow that had threaded through his words earlier had returned. His cousin was lost in grief, like Alain was. Maybe God really had brought them together. He would reserve judgment on that.

"I'm looking forward to getting to know you both better."

Hiro's ready smile returned. "Yes. I am as well. I am off now until after New Year's. Tomorrow I am taking *Papa* to the Papeete Market. Would you like to join us?"

Alain had heard about that market from Rav and Annie, who'd explored the attraction last year with their tour group. "Sure. I'd love to."

"Wonderful. Come down to breakfast whenever you are ready, and then we will go." He nodded and started for the door.

"*Bonne nuit, mon cousin,*" Alain called after him.

Hiro laughed at that. "*Bonne nuit. Dors bien.*" He stepped out into the hallway and closed the door.

Alain sank onto the edge of the bed, the white bedspread soft beneath his palms. What had just happened? So far this spontaneous trip had been full of surprises he could never have foreseen. What, exactly, would the next day bring?

DECEMBER 28TH

"Raimana!" Uncle Vateo rose from the table and strode toward Alain, pulling him into a hug the way he had the night before. Alain couldn't remember his father ever hugging him. *Maman* was also frugal with her physical affection, although she had warmed up a little in recent years. Even knowing his uncle believed he was hugging someone else, Alain briefly relaxed into the embrace before Vateo slapped him on the back a couple of times. "We have much to discuss, *non*?"

At least he was speaking English to him. It might be tricky for Alain to explain why he wasn't fluent in either Tahitian or French like his father most likely was, having grown up here.

A smirk crossed Hiro's face. "Yes, sit, *Raimana*." He waved a hand toward the chair across from Vateo. "I will bring you the *firi firi*."

Alain rolled his eyes, which only broadened the smirk. Apparently his cousin had come to terms with his father thinking of Alain as his long-lost brother. "*Firi firi?*"

"You will see. It is delicious, I promise you."

It smelled delicious. The aromas of fried dough and hot grease permeated the air, along with the nutty scent of coffee. Alain drew in a deep breath as he pulled out his chair and sat down. A platter of fresh fruit sat in the center of the table.

Hiro placed a mug of coffee and a plate of fried dough in front of him. "Enjoy."

He suspected he would. His cousin nudged the platter of fruit closer, and Alain used his fork to spear pieces of pineapple and papaya and transfer them to the plate next to the dough. Hiro hadn't oversold the *firi firi*. Alain detected a hint of coconut in his first bite of the sweet fried dough.

When they'd finished their fruit and *firi firi*—the best breakfast Alain had eaten in a long time—they climbed into the Jeep, and Hiro pulled onto the Circle Road for their return trip to the capital city. Every few minutes, Uncle Vateo would point out a landmark. Then, without fail, he would twist in his seat to peer into the back at Alain and say, "You remember, Raimana."

Each time, Hiro would glance in the rearview mirror, his eyes filled with amusement. Alain's response was considerably more complicated. The situation was bizarre, him being forced to step into the shoes of the father who had wreaked such havoc on their family. The man who had caused the haunted look in Tane's eyes and the jagged scars on his body. It felt almost a betrayal to his older brother—and to Rav and *Maman*—to passively go along with the imposture.

On the other hand, from the little Alain knew of Vateo, his uncle appeared to be as good a man as his father was villainous. If, in his confused state, it made him happy to pretend he had his brother back after all these years, was there truly any harm in it?

Time would tell. For now, Alain was determined to relax and enjoy the market with his newfound family. Palm trees lined the side of the road as they drove along the streets of Papeete. Downtown, Hiro parked the Jeep, and the three of them climbed out and started for the massive gray building that housed the indoor booths of the market. Hiro rested a hand on his father's back to guide him by brightly colored shirts and dresses hanging on display in the booths facing the street and waving in the breeze.

They wandered past blue and white and red umbrellas sheltering the outdoor stands in the paved lot around the market. More booths were set up inside the warehouse-like structure. A group of men in floral shirts and straw hats sat on overturned buckets playing music on an assortment of stringed instruments. The scent of flowers mingled with the aromas of fresh fish and spices. Alain's senses went into overload as he attempted to take in the riot of color, the sounds of singing and vendors calling out and children running and playing.

They passed counters filled with Tahitian pearls and jewelry, straw hats and bags, leis and grass skirts, and more flowers. After an hour or so of browsing, they reached the food court. Hiro pointed to an empty table. "I will go get us some lunch if you will wait with *Papa*, Alain."

Probably a good idea, since Alain didn't recognize most of the offerings listed on chalkboards or on display in glass cabinets. "Here." He tugged the wallet from his back pocket and withdrew a credit card that he held out to Hiro. "I'd like to get lunch for the two of you."

His cousin lifted his hands and shook his head. "No, no. You are our guest."

"It is a thank you for welcoming me into your home."

Hiro hesitated before reaching for the card. "All right. *Merci.* But we will buy the fish for dinner."

"Deal." Alain returned the wallet to his pocket.

"Anything you like or don't like?"

"I like pretty much anything, although I'm not sure how excited I am about the *poisson cru*. I tend to prefer my fish cooked, not raw."

Hiro grinned. "I'll let you get away with that today, since it's your first day. But you *will* be trying it before you leave the country. You cannot come to Tahiti without eating our national dish."

Alain returned the grin. "Got it." As much as he liked seafood, the thought of raw fish in coconut milk, as popular as it was here, had never appealed to him. His *maman* had made it a few times, but he'd always gotten out of eating it. If Hiro insisted, however, he would. Rav had ordered it when he'd been here last year and enjoyed it, although Annie had refused to try it.

Hiro disappeared into the throngs of marketgoers as Alain settled at the table across from his uncle. For a few minutes, the two of them listened to the music and watched the people passing by. Then Vateo leaned forward and grasped his arm. "Raimana. Do you remember when we came here as boys?"

Panic flared. What should he say? He had no idea what it would have been like to grow up in Tahiti, and he didn't have a clue what kind of child his father had been, so he couldn't fake either.

Thankfully, his uncle continued without waiting for a response. "We drove *Maman* and *Papa* crazy, running loose in the old building, hiding among the clothes or behind the flowers."

Alain chuckled as he gazed around the market. Was this the same building his father had run around in? Likely not, since it didn't look that old. Still, it sounded as though the market was similar back then. He narrowed his eyes a little, attempting to picture his dad and uncle as young boys, racing around and laughing as they peered out between racks of floral shirts at their parents frantically looking for them.

He'd never heard his father laugh. When had he lost that sense of fun and adventure? What had turned him so hard and angry?

For most of his life, Alain had refused to give his dad much thought. The family rarely talked about him, and dwelling on the past brought only heartache. Being here, though, in the country where his father had grown up, getting to know Raimana's brother and nephew, it was impossible to put him—or Alain's childhood—out of his mind.

As much as he was enjoying the company of both of them, the old hurts and anger he had buried so deeply that even the therapist he had seen off and on for years hadn't been able to unearth them were breaking free of all the dirt piled on top of them and rising like something out of a zombie apocalypse movie.

Which terrified Alain. What would his therapist advise him to do in the situation? He pursed his lips. Likely he would suggest Alain write down everything he was feeling and then crumple up the paper and throw it away or burn it. Or maybe, since he was in Tahiti, he could toss it into the ocean. They probably didn't take kindly to tourists throwing litter into the Pacific, though.

Still, the idea of putting his thoughts and emotions to paper was worth considering. He'd tried it before but had never been able to bring himself to go deep, to see his pain written across the page in black and white. If this was rock bottom, maybe breaking down and trying the writing technique would start him on the journey to healing. At this point, he was open to pretty much anything that might ease the unbearable pain in his chest.

Before he could formulate a response to his uncle's comments, Hiro returned with three sandwiches made with baguettes. "Chow Mein sandwiches," he announced as he set one in front of his father and then Alain before handing him back his credit card.

Alain eyed the messy-looking offering in front of him. Noodles on a sandwich? "I've never heard of this sandwich."

"It is native to this country." Hiro tugged out the chair next to his *papa*. "A fusion of Chinese and French influence and Tahitian ingenuity. Delicious combination."

It did smell delicious, although Alain had no idea how he would eat it without spilling noodles everywhere.

Hiro had looped a bag over one wrist, and he pulled out three water bottles and a small paper bag that he set in the middle of the table before settling on his seat. "*Haupia*," he said.

Alain raised an eyebrow as he stuck his card into his jacket pocket. His cousin turned the opening of the bag toward him and lifted one side so he could see the small white squares inside. "Like a custard made from coconut milk and chilled."

Alain nodded. Whatever they were, the little squares looked delicious. And the sandwiches, messy as they might be, were much more appealing than raw tuna in coconut milk, although he suspected his cousin would keep his word and force him to try that dish before he left to go home.

Everything was even better than he'd expected. None of them were able to keep from spilling noodles and bits of chicken and cheese onto the table, but Hiro and Vateo laughed freely—at themselves and at Alain—and after a few slippery bites, he joined them. By the time they finished the filling meal, he was definitely ready to walk again. They strolled around the market for a couple more hours. Then Vateo started to lag a bit, and Hiro touched his back. "Why don't we choose the fish for supper, *Papa*, and then we will go home."

His father nodded. The two of them headed for one of the many booths displaying fresh fish on ice. Alain started to follow them, but then something caught his eye at another booth, and he meandered over. A set of four empty, long-necked bottles about five inches high sat on a table. Which, like so many other things, reminded him of Carly.

Ever since they'd watched Nicholas Sparks's *Message in a Bottle* together, she had fallen in love with the concept and sought out every book she could find that included people communicating that way. So it would be fitting if he used that device to help him let go of her. If he wrote out his feelings and tucked the paper into one of those bottles before tossing it into the ocean, that wouldn't be considered littering, would it?

He liked the idea. Very symbolic, letting the currents of the Pacific Ocean carry away the anguish that must have started here, on this island, since Hiro said something had transpired between his father and Vateo before his parents left for Canada. Had whatever happened here caused Raimana's spiral into alcohol and violence?

If his uncle continued to believe that Alain was his father, would the past come to light this week as he spent time with him? Did he even want to know the history of his family?

In any case, writing out his feelings might help him let go of the anger and bitterness he had carried around with him for far too long. He grabbed from his pocket the credit card Hiro had returned to him and, when a woman in a grass skirt and lei headpiece came over, pointed to the bottles.

If there was a God and he did decide to take pity on Alain and order the waves around like Jesus did in that Bible story where he calmed the storm, maybe they would carry all thoughts and memories of Carly far enough away that he could finally let her go.

After the fabulous meal Hiro had cooked them using the fresh fish, vegetables, and fruits they had brought home from the market, he and his *papa* settled in the living room to watch an old *Matlock* episode. Vateo had continued to chat with Alain as though he were his brother, telling stories of a fun-loving, mischievous boy Alain could not reconcile with the Raimana he knew.

With too many thoughts spinning through his head to concentrate on the show, he gathered up a notebook, pen, and one of the bottles he had purchased at the market earlier and wandered down to the ocean.

Someone—Hiro, maybe, or his dad when he was younger—had strung a hammock between two trees on the beach. Alain tossed the book, pen, and bottle onto the hammock before continuing to the edge of the water.

For a long time, he stood in the sand, watching the waves roll onto the shore, listening to the cry of the sea gulls as they swooped and rose above the water, and breathing in the scent of brine and seaweed.

As the sun sank down closer to the horizon, casting the first rosy glow over the water and the long, weathered wooden pier he hadn't noticed last night in the dark, he made his way to the hammock and settled in.

His head propped on a small, waterproof cushion, he flipped open the notebook and pulled the cap off the pen, sticking it on the other end for safekeeping. What should he write? His therapist had often told him that if he was overwhelmed by thoughts or emotions, he should mentally step away and observe the tangled mass with a neutral eye, pick out the one that was most prominent, and deal with it first.

Closing his eyes, he pictured the mass as a jumble of strands of wool of various colors. Which most fully captured his attention? Slowly, one strand—a deep mustard yellow—separated itself from the others. Could he name it?

Was it heartbreak? Maybe. He visualized reaching for the end of the yellow strand of wool and tugging on it, freeing enough length to drape it across one palm.

Alain stuck the end of the pen with the cap on it into his mouth. If it was heartache, was it because of his relationship with Carly ending? He pondered that for twenty or thirty seconds. That heartache was there, absolutely, but it was a tributary flowing into a much larger body of water—the heartache that had started years ago, when Alain was a young boy.

Maybe it was finally time to deal with it. He flipped open the notebook and stared at the blank page. Where should he begin? Just start dumping his feelings onto the paper? He'd heard of writing a letter to yourself as a strategy, but the idea felt a bit silly to him. Someone else then? His father? Tane?

Carly. For the past three years, she was the one he had gone to when something was bothering him, and she had always listened and then offered him a wise, compassionate response that inevitably made him feel better. Although he had never gone deep with her about his past—despite her inviting him countless times to do so—he'd still opened himself up to her more than he had anyone else in his life. Even Tane or Rav.

So, she was the one he needed to write to now.

He pressed the nib of the pen to the paper and paused a moment, gathering his thoughts, before beginning to write.

Dear Carly,

Wow. I miss you. I want you to know I don't blame you for leaving. Of course I don't, since I'm the one who told you to go. Even so, I need to be honest with you about how I am feeling. I know. Shocker. You try to get me to open up to you for years and now, after you have gone, I'm finally ready to do so. Or willing, anyway.

So here goes. My heart hurts. Everything hurts, actually, but it's coming from the heart. So many things happened to Tane and Rav and me when we were kids. Some of them I told you about but a lot I didn't. I pretended that was to protect you from all the ugliness, and that was part of it. The bigger part, though, was that I was afraid.

Alain stopped writing and tapped the end of the pen against his front teeth. Ah. Not heartache, then. Fear. But what had he been afraid of? Being hurt, physically or emotionally, most likely. The very few times he'd gone to his father to share his pain over being bullied at school or feeling like an outsider, his dad had shut that down fast. Told him he was being a baby and he needed to toughen up. Sometimes even hit him to, presumably, hurry that process along.

Being rejected, definitely. The way his classmates treated him had taught Alain that he didn't belong and never would. Was that one of the reasons he had pushed Carly away?

He pictured again that piece of yellow wool. He'd pulled it out enough to fit across his palm—the length of the facts of his upbringing, which was as much as he had ever been willing to share with Carly or his therapist. Not the way those facts made him feel about himself or the world, though. That would take pulling that thread out a lot more. All the way out, maybe.

The thought sent icy chills rippling through him. What better time to do so than now, though, when he had the opportunity to tear open his chest and pour out his heart onto the page? Then he could fold up that paper, stick it in a bottle, and toss it into the water. Only the stingrays and fishes and coral would witness his anguish. Maybe, in sending it out to sea, it would be gone from him so that he could at last draw in a breath unrestricted by all those tangled strands of wool.

Jaw clenched, he pressed the pen to paper again.

I've never shared that with you, how afraid I was of being hurt, of being rejected. Someone told Rav once that there was something in his eyes, as though he wanted to reach out but was afraid of having his hand slapped away. I understand that far more than I want to.

But I'm tired of being afraid. I want to let go of that fear. Maybe this will help, writing it down, sharing it with you even though you will never read it.

He stopped again and gazed out over the water. At the waves cresting and breaking and crashing lightly against the shore. The sheer vastness and power of the Pacific was breathtaking. Could it have formed by chance? It seemed unlikely. Was he ready to acknowledge an intelligent designer? A benevolent God who had not only created the universe but actually cared about him? Loved him, even? Who didn't want him to be afraid? That seemed equally unlikely although, for once, he didn't immediately reject the idea.

Exhaling, he lowered his head again.

I've been thinking about God lately. It's hard not to when I'm sitting here on a shore in Tahiti surrounded by palm trees and bushes of Tiare flowers and a warm evening breeze sweeping in from the ocean to brush across my face like a caress.

His cheeks warming, Alain glanced around. Maybe that was a bit much, but it *was* the truth. While he had no idea if this little exercise was going to work, he did understand that it only would if he told the truth. To her and to himself for once in his life.

So maybe, between sharing my feelings on these pages and opening up my mind and heart to the possibility of a divine being who is nothing like my father, I will discover that there is hope for me yet.
Yours forever,
Alain

He contemplated the closing words. Given his recent commitment to complete transparency, could he say that?

Yes. Absolutely. No one else would ever *supplant her in his affections,* as Jane Austen would say. Carly had been his one true chance at happiness, and he had tossed that away as surely as he was about to toss a bottle into the ocean.

Speaking of which . . . Alain tore the page from his notebook, rolled it up carefully, and then popped off the top of the bottle with his thumb so he could tuck the paper inside.

Then he replaced the stopper and clambered off the hammock. He'd have to go out a ways so the current would carry the bottle out to sea and not back into shore.

He trudged through the ankle-deep volcanic black sand this country was famous for until he reached the pier and meandered along it to the very end. Hopefully that would be far enough.

He gazed at the teal-blue water for a moment and then, before he could change his mind, pulled back his arm and hurled the little bottle as far out into the waves as he could. There. He'd just shared the first of his deep secrets, revealed a part of his heart he never had before. As terrifying as it was, he was comforted by the fact that the bottle was already bobbing away from the shore, transported on an invisible current.

He rubbed a palm over his chest. The perpetual ache there actually had eased a little. So maybe there was something to this exercise after all. Even if someone did come across the bottle one day, they wouldn't know who either Carly or Alain was. Besides, he would be long gone from Tahiti by then.

Only the ocean would know who had scribbled the words on that torn notebook paper. And the ocean would never tell.

DECEMBER 29TH

The rich aroma of coffee greeted Alain when he strolled into the kitchen the next morning. He'd been determined to help cook and not allow Hiro to make all the meals for the three of them, but his cousin was already pulling a dish from the oven.

"I was planning to help with breakfast," Alain said as he took a mug down from the cupboard and filled it from the carafe.

Hiro waved an oven-mittened hand through the air. "It is no trouble. My *maman* taught me to make this when I was a boy, so it is easy for me." He carried the dish to the table and set it on a hot pad next to the ever-present platter of fresh fruit. Then he removed the lid with a flourish, releasing the aromas of cinnamon, coconut, ginger, and nutmeg.

Alain leaned closer, inhaling the steam rising from what looked like a bread pudding. "That smells so good. What is it?"

"*Pain patate.* A pudding made from cornmeal with sweet potatoes, avocado, coconut milk, and spices."

"Yum." His uncle's mug was nearly empty, and he grabbed the carafe again and filled it for him.

Vateo's face lit. "Thank you, brother."

Apparently he was still lost in his own world. How did he know enough to speak English to Alain? Was that the language he and his brother had communicated in when they were kids? "You're welcome."

He returned the pot to the burner before settling on a chair. He was about to dig in when his uncle clasped his hands together. "Dear Lord, thank you for this food and my son who prepared it. And thank you that my brother is home at long last. Amen."

"Amen," Hiro echoed.

Alain nodded before sticking his fork into the pudding. Even if his uncle thought he was someone else, it felt surprisingly good for someone to thank God for his presence. Mulling that over, he took his first bite of *pain patate*. Flavors exploded over his tongue, and he groaned in pleasure.

Hiro had been watching him. A smile broke across his face. "Good, *non*?"

"Amazing. I need to get this recipe from you."

His cousin's face softened. "My *maman* wrote it out on a card for her box. You can take a picture of it. Hers was much better than mine."

"I find that hard to believe." Alain took a swig of coffee to wash down the bite. "What was your *maman* like?"

"She was wonderful. Very sweet. She loved to laugh and to take care of everyone. One of those people who always lit up a room. Right, *Papa*?"

Vateo's features had softened like his son's as he described the woman they both clearly missed dearly. "Yes. Heiana was a wonderful woman. Like your Vairani, Raimana."

Vairani? Alain glanced across the table at his cousin, whose forehead had wrinkled.

"Raimana's wife is Emere, *Papa*."

His father waved his fork through the air, sending bits of pudding spraying across the table. "Not that wife, although she is also wonderful. I'm talking about your first wife. Emere's sister."

Alain's mouth dropped open slightly. His father had another wife before *Maman*? How did he not know that? What had happened to her? He looked at Hiro again, who shook his head and shrugged before shifting a little on his chair to face his father. "I never knew Vairani. What happened to her?"

Vateo's dark eyes misted, his fingers trembling as he shifted the salt-shaker closer to the pepper. "She died. Remember, Raimana? We lost both her and your little girl. It was a terrible, terrible time."

Alain and Hiro left Uncle Vateo in his recliner watching a football match and climbed into the Jeep.

The top was still down, and Alain tipped back his head, letting the ocean breeze whip through his hair and clear some of the cobwebs from his mind as Hiro steered them north along the Circle Road toward Taravao. The idea that they were traveling away from Papeete, where Rav was, left Alain oddly bereft, although according to Hiro they were only going about thirty kilometers. They were heading to Tahiti Iti Diving, the only diving center on the Tahiti peninsula, according to his cousin. When he'd made the suggestion after breakfast that the two of them go diving, Alain hadn't been thinking clearly enough to refuse.

"I've always found that, when you're feeling completely underwater, the best cure is to actually go underwater," Hiro had declared.

Well, if Alain had ever felt as though he was about to go below the surface for the third time, it was now. What had just happened? Not only had his father been married before—to *Maman's* sister, no less—but they'd had a child who died? A half-sister to Alain and his brothers? He was beginning to feel as though, after boarding that plane in Vancouver, he had flown straight into an alternate universe.

"You hadn't been hoping for a quiet, relaxing time away free of shocking revelations about your family, had you?" One wrist resting on the steering wheel, Hiro offered him a rueful smile before returning his gaze to the road.

Alain ran a hand down his face. "No, of course not. My plan was to come here so I could have my life completely turned upside down and sideways."

"Well, we do like to make sure our guests aren't bored."

He snorted a laugh. "I'll give you that. I am not bored."

His cousin shot him another look. "Do you want to talk about what you learned today?"

"I'm not sure there's much to say. I need to let it sink in a bit. Maybe your *papa* will tell us more later about how Raimana's first wife and his daughter died and if that somehow led to him and my father falling out."

"He might. He's staying pretty firmly in the world in his mind, longer than he ever has. Your presence, I believe. Or, to him, the presence of his brother."

"I guess so." Alain gazed out the window, the bright blue sky, endless ocean, and swaying palm trees calming him. As much as it had thrown him in the beginning, stepping into his father's shoes was giving him a glimpse into his own past, which he never would have expected. The fog swirling around much of his childhood was clearing a little. Whether that was a good thing or a bad thing remained to be seen.

Hiro wheeled the Jeep into the parking lot of the Phaeton Bay marina. Rows of sailboats lined one end of the lot, near the ocean. The two of them headed for a low, white building with blue trim, the diving center. Inside the door, a small wooden bar to the left filled the place with the aroma of slightly stale coffee. A table to the right held racks of pamphlets. Hiro had called ahead, and in minutes they had changed into wetsuits, and he was following his cousin out the front door and down to the dock, where a yellow raft-like boat with small overhead canopy sat bobbing alongside a dock.

Alain had never done anything like this, and he was trying hard not to fixate on what might be involved. Which wasn't difficult when his mind was filled with thoughts and questions he had no idea what to do with. He was practically dragging his feet under the load of them, and right before they hit the dock, he shot a look at the crystal-blue sky. *Look. I have no idea if you're there. Maybe I'm starting to think you are, that you must be. If so, can you help me process everything that has happened? And I don't just mean everything that has occurred since I arrived in Tahiti but about Carly and, well, my whole life pretty much. What has all of that been about, anyway?*

"*A ou'a i roto!*" Their guide, a guy about their age with long, dark hair pulled back in a ponytail, a red T-shirt, khaki shorts, a Chicago White Sox ball cap, and tattoos on every bit of exposed skin Alain could see, smacked the edge of the boat with his palm. Alain didn't have to speak Tahitian to understand they were to get into the boat, so he climbed over the side, planting one foot and then the other on the middle of the floor.

"*O Enoha to'u i'oa.*" The guide pressed a hand to his chest.

"He says his name is Enoha," Hiro translated for him before giving their names to the man, who nodded and flashed them a bright, toothy smile.

There weren't many places to sit. Enoha stood at the helm close to the back of the vessel, so Alain and Hiro made their way to the front. The bench set in the prow was small, and Hiro waved for him to take it as he lowered himself to the bottom of the raft and sat with his back against the side.

"*E piti ahuru minuti te maoro o te tere,*" the guide called out right before the roar of the motor filled the air.

Hiro leaned closer to shout, "He says the trip will take twenty minutes."

Alain nodded. He turned on his seat so he could scan the horizon as they flew across the surface of the ocean. Ten minutes into the trip, the guide hollered something, and Hiro smacked Alain's knee and pointed behind him. "Look!"

He spun around in time to see a hunchback whale spinning through the air before landing in the water with a massive splash. Okay, that was pretty amazing.

"Cool, *non*?" His cousin tapped his knee again with the back of his hand. "I never get tired of that. So majestic."

"It really is." Alain stared at the spot where the awe-inspiring beast had disappeared. Once again, the thought that there had to be a designer behind the creation of something that breathtaking struck him.

They reached the diving area, pulled on all their gear, and received instruction on how to dive and how to communicate with each other and with the guide, who would remain in the boat. The tattooed man had switched to heavily accented English after the first bit of information Hiro translated for Alain. As much as Alain was hoping for one local not to switch to English, in this case, when his life might be on the line, he appreciated the gesture.

As soon as they were ready, they both flipped backwards off the side of the raft and began to swim, the fins propelling them downwards. Rav had told them a story about kayaking with the other tour group members last year when the kayak he and another man were in was surrounded by sharks. Given his current situation, Alain wished he hadn't heard that story, although any apprehension dissipated rapidly like the bubbles rising from their oxygen tanks as they entered the enchanting world beneath the surface.

They glided over the speckled coral reef. Everywhere Alain looked through his mask he saw fish of every color, pattern, and size. The brilliant purple ones fascinated him, and he made a mental note to ask Hiro or Enoha what they were called.

A sting ray glided by, inches from his hand, and he stared at it, mesmerized. Whatever kind this was, the back of it was covered in greenish-black spots. Massive turtles drifted past them, and endless schools of fish, flashing as the rays of sun caught their sides, swam by.

Alain barely knew where to look. All he did know was that, when their two hours were up, he had to force himself to climb into the boat and leave the spectacular sights behind. Maybe closing his books once in a while, pushing himself out of his comfort zone, wasn't a bad idea. He might even tag along with Rav and Xaviar next time they went surfing.

He sat on the floor this time, his eyes scanning the surface of the water for another whale as they zipped along. No hunchbacks obliged them, but at one point three dolphins did leap into the air in perfect synchronization, which more than satisfied him.

Hiro had been right. This was exactly what he had needed. The heavy load had lifted, the wind and water washing away his earlier shock and confusion.

Back at the diving center, they thanked Enoha, changed back into their clothes, and crossed the lot to the Jeep.

Hiro smacked him on the back. "Good, right?"

"Amazing. Really. Thanks for suggesting it."

They reached the vehicle, and his cousin stopped and faced him. "I'm glad you enjoyed it, but I'm sure you still have much to work through. Why don't you call Rav and invite him and Annie to join us for dinner tonight. Something tells me that you could really use your brother right now."

Hiro had been right about that too. As soon as his cousin mentioned Rav's name, the desperate need to see his little brother filled Alain. He hadn't brought his phone, so as soon as they arrived at the house, he excused himself to go to his room to text him.

For several moments, he sat on the edge of the bed, staring at the blank screen. Where did he even begin? Finally, he typed *Hey. I made the spontaneous decision to come to Tahiti a couple of days ago.*

In less than thirty seconds, Rav responded. *Really?? Where are you?*

Here we go. Alain shifted a little on the bed. *Actually, I met a cousin of ours, Hiro, at a restaurant the first night I was here. I'm staying with him and his dad.* He took a deep breath before adding *Dad's brother, Vateo.*

It took a little longer for Rav to respond this time. After a minute or two, his message appeared. *Wow. You're full of surprises, aren't you?*

Alain let out a humorless laugh. *It's been a surprising trip. Hiro wants you and Annie to come for dinner. Are you free tonight?*

No hesitation this time. *Of course. When and where?*

Alain texted him the address and the time—six p.m.—that Hiro had suggested.

Got it. Looking forward to meeting our family. Before Alain could respond, another message appeared. *Any more surprises I should know about?*

His brother had no idea. *A few. I'll fill you in when you get here. One thing you should know is that Uncle Vateo is a little confused. He thinks I'm Dad, which has been . . . interesting.*

Nothing happened for a few seconds. Was his brother absorbing the mention of their father like Alain had needed to when he first came up?

At last the words appeared. *Sounds like we need to talk. Are you doing okay?*

Alain had no idea how to answer that. He settled for *I'm hanging in there. I really want to see you.*

I want to see you too. We'll be there at six.

Alain set the phone on the bedside table. Two hours. He should go down to help Hiro make dinner, but he needed a minute. Restless, he pushed to his feet and wandered around the room. When he reached a small door he hadn't yet checked behind, he turned the knob and pulled it open. As suspected, a closet with a few shirts hanging on the metal rod and several boxes piled on the floor against the back wall. Another one—a white shoebox—sat on a high shelf.

Obviously Hiro and Vateo used this closet for storage. Alain really shouldn't be poking his nose in where it didn't—

He froze as the words scrawled across the side of the box on the high shelf registered. *Raimana Temauri.*

Alain slammed a palm against the door frame. His dad had a box of stuff here? What could possibly be in it? He glanced around the room, although he'd closed the door behind him. Then he swung his gaze back to the box and stared at it for a full minute. Should he look inside? Part of him screamed that it was none of his business, while another part asked if his father wasn't *his* business, then whose was he?

Before he could give himself too much time to think about it, Alain stepped into the closet, reached up to grab the box in both hands, and lifted it off the shelf. After backing out of the tiny space, he carried it over to the desk in front of the window and set it down. He gripped the lid on both sides but paused before lifting it. Was he opening a Pandora's box here? Maybe, but all the evil in the world had definitely not been confined to this little white container the way it had been to hers. The evil was already out there, all around them. He'd seen enough of it to know that for sure. Besides, after everything he'd learned this week about his father, what was one or two things more? Maybe whatever was in here would answer a few questions and set his mind at ease. If so, it would be helpful for him to find those answers before Rav came, so he could share them with his brother as well.

Alain lifted the lid and tossed it onto the desk next to the box. Not much inside, only a few photographs. So innocuous looking, but pictures could do a lot of damage. They could also offer clarity, which he desperately needed right now.

With a sigh, he lifted the first one. His father dressed in a navy suit and blue-and-red-striped tie, his arm looped through the elbow of a woman who bore a distinct resemblance to *Maman*. Vairani. Given the simple white dress that fell just below her knees and the flowers she cradled in her other arm, this was their wedding day.

They were gazing at each other and smiling. Wow. Had he ever seen his parents look at each other that way? Definitely not.

He set the picture in the box lid and lifted the second one. Vairani again. Alone this time, standing in a field of flowers to her knees. Actually, not completely alone. A baby bump was obvious beneath her flowing yellow blouse. If what Vateo had told them at breakfast was true, that would be Alain's half-sister.

The idea jarred him as much now, studying the photo, as it had that morning, and he dropped the picture on top of the wedding one and reached for the next. His dad, sitting in a rocking chair cradling a baby and gazing down at the swaddled child with as much adoration as he'd bestowed upon his wife the day they were married.

His father was capable of love, then. Or he had been at one time in his life. Alain had often wondered.

The thought sent a pang through his chest, and he lowered that photo to the box lid and reached for the last one. A little girl, maybe three or four, skipping on the walkway in front of a small, thatched-roof house. Like Vateo and Hiro's, it was nothing spectacular, but it was freshly painted and well maintained.

Alain lifted the photo closer to his eyes to examine the rope the girl was using to skip. It looked unusual—maybe six strands woven together to create a kaleidoscope of color. Not like any skipping rope he'd ever seen.

He touched a finger to the girl's cheek. Was this his half-sister? What was her name and what had happened to her and her mother? Would Vateo be able or willing to share that with him? He set down that photo as well before peering into the box. A small, white piece of paper lay on the bottom of it, and he picked it up. The spidery handwriting—his father's—sent a jolt of shock through him. He scanned the handwritten words. *Who shut up the sea behind doors when it burst forth from the womb... when I said, 'This far you may come and no farther; here is where your proud waves halt'?*

Hmm. Powerful words. Poetic, even. Were they referring to the ocean? Who had the authority to speak to it that way? God, he supposed. Were these words from the Bible? Alain frowned. What was a Bible verse doing in a box of his father's things? Nothing in the man's words or actions suggested he'd ever cracked open that book.

Stil holding the piece of paper, he checked the box again. Empty. No real answers then, only more questions. Not even that hope that Pandora had been left with once the evil had flown away.

Just an unexpected flicker of grief over the loss of this little girl he'd never met, hadn't even realized existed. Which was crazy.

To keep the water from crashing over his head again, he scooped up the pictures, set them and the Bible verse in the box, and replaced the lid. He'd leave it out to show his brother and then return it to the closet shelf and close the door on it forever.

Alain hadn't expected dinner to be as much fun as it was. Hiro kept them all laughing with stories of the worst customers he'd waited on at the restaurant, and Rav and Annie shared their interactions with the tour group members they had met and bonded with so deeply a year ago—Septima and Sojourner, the seventy-something African-American sisters from South Carolina, Gregory from Australia, and Maeva and Nino, their hosts. They had all returned for the reunion this year except for Xaviar. Why hadn't he come? Could he not afford it? Alain winced. Should have thought to ask that. Although he worked sixty hours a week at his dream job, Xaviar was still apprenticing at the garage, so he likely didn't bring home a huge paycheck.

Alain had not been the most unselfish person the last three months, had he? Consumed with his own heartbreak, he'd barely checked with *Maman* to see how she was doing. When he got home from this trip, he was definitely going to do better with both of them. Rav and Annie as well. And Tane, whenever he was home.

They lingered over their meal. Not *poisson cru*, thankfully, but *poulet fafa*—chicken cooked in coconut milk and taro leaves. When Alain had come down from upstairs, Hiro had looked up from running water over vegetables and stilled, contemplating him for a few seconds in that way of his. No doubt Alain wore the effects of seeing those photos on his face or in his eyes. As usual, Hiro didn't push him to share, only turned off the water, dried his hands, and planted a palm between Alain's shoulder blades to guide him out to their backyard. There, he showed off their underground oven, which he claimed was what gave the dish its unique taste. Whatever it was, the chicken was truly delicious.

Alain had insisted on preparing the *firi firi* for dessert, which, given how quickly the bits of fried dough disappeared, hadn't turned out too badly for his first attempt. When he passed the plate to his uncle, offering him the last one, Vateo smiled at him. "Thank you, Raimana."

It was the first time he had called Alain his father's name that evening, and although he'd tried to prepare his brother, Rav still jerked slightly. Annie covered his hand with hers, and he smiled at her, the tension easing from his shoulders. Some kind of silent communication passed between them before she nodded.

Rav cleared his throat. "Um, Annie and I have some news."

Alain set the empty donut platter on the table. "What's that?"

"We're getting married."

He blinked. "What? When?"

His brother looked a little sheepish. "In two days. New Year's Eve. On the beach here in Tahiti."

Alain immediately squelched the tiny spurt of something—sorrow? jealousy?—at his brother finding the love of his life, his soulmate, while

Alain was still wading through a slough of grief and regret over the loss of his. Tonight was not for sadness, though, only joy. He pushed back his chair and rounded the table to wrap his arms around his brother before slapping him on the back and letting him go to give Annie a hug. "I'm happy for you both." A glint caught his eye, and he lifted her hand to examine the ring he hadn't noticed earlier—a Tahitian pearl surrounded by two small diamonds on each side. Perfect.

"Yes. I am happy for you as well." Hiro shook Rav's hand before wrapping an arm around Annie's shoulders and squeezing. "More family." He grinned as he stepped back. "God is good, *non?*"

Rav and Annie's response to that was considerably more enthusiastic than Alain's had been when his cousin said those words to him. The thought that maybe God *was* good, better than Alain had given him credit for, did cross his mind, and he found himself nodding.

Hiro didn't miss the gesture. His eyes met Alain's for a few seconds before he clapped his hands. "All right then. *Papa*, it is time for *Wheel of Fortune*. The rest of you go relax. I am on clean-up duty."

Alain's protest died on his lips when Hiro inclined his head slightly in Rav's direction. All right. He did need to speak to his brother.

Annie linked her arm through their uncle's. "May I join you, Vateo? I love *Wheel of Fortune*."

Vateo's face lit up as he patted her hand. "*Bien sûr, ma chérie.* Of course."

Annie was still chatting away to him when the two of them disappeared through the living room doorway.

Alain nudged his brother—whose gaze had followed his fiancée as she crossed the room. "Can I show you something upstairs?"

"Sure." Rav carried two platters over to the kitchen area and set them on the counter. "Thank you for dinner, Hiro. Everything was amazing."

He dipped his head and flashed his usual smile as he picked up the plates. "It was my pleasure, cousin."

Rav followed Alain up to the guest room. Inside, Alain gestured to the small chair at the desk. "Sit. I want to tell you something first."

"Okay." Rav sounded a little apprehensive as he walked to the chair and pulled it away from the desk to turn it around, facing Alain.

He settled on the edge of the bed. "So, it's been a crazy week."

Rav nodded. "I gather that. Discovering close family members you didn't know you had is pretty huge."

"Yeah, about that." Alain ran a palm over the top of the wooden footboard. "Did you know Dad was married before?"

Rav frowned. "What? No. He was?"

"Apparently. Vateo told me. At least, he reminded Raimana of that fact."

"Who was he married to?"

He studied a few scratch marks etched into the wood. "That's the really crazy part. Her name was Vairani. She was *Maman's* sister."

"Wow." Rav blinked rapidly as though attempting to take that in, which Alain completely understood.

"I know. And there's more."

His brother gripped both arms of the chair as though bracing himself. "What?"

"They had a daughter."

Rav stared at him for several seconds before blowing out a breath. "We have a sister?"

"Had. Something happened to the two of them. I'm not sure what yet. From what I can gather, Vateo and Raimana were close before that. I'm guessing that somehow the deaths of Dad's wife and daughter destroyed the relationship between the brothers and led to Dad marrying *Maman*, leaving Tahiti, and never speaking to—or about—his brother again."

Rav let go of the chair to run the side of his hand over his forehead. "I mean, are you sure? Vateo is wonderful, but his mind . . ."

"I know. But yes, I'm sure." Alain stood and crossed to the desk to grab the shoebox and carry it back to the bed. Perching on the edge of the mattress again, he set the box next to him, lifted the lid, and took out the photographs, leaving the piece of paper on the bottom. "Here." He held them out to Rav.

His brother took them and studied each one carefully before sliding it to the back of the pile. When he'd gone through them all, he lifted his head. "Wow."

Alain managed a weak grin. "You said that already."

"I don't know what else to say."

"I get it. It's a lot to take in."

His brother held out the photos. "You're handling this pretty well. I mean, you've had more to take in than me, since you were able to at least prepare me for some of this. Plus, you were already going through a hard time. How are you not losing it completely?"

"I've had my moments, believe me." Alain set the pictures in the box. "But I've been doing some of the stuff my therapist told me to, like writing down what I'm feeling. And I've been . . ."

Rav tilted his head. "What?"

"Thinking about God a little."

"Really."

"Yeah. I mean, it's so beautiful here that it's hard not to think about whatever or whoever created it all. And you and Annie and *Maman* and Xaviar and Hiro and Vateo all believe he's real and cares about us, and it seems like you share this . . . peace or joy or something. That makes me want to know more."

Rav nodded. "That's amazing, Alain. If you ever want to talk about that or anything else, I'm here."

"I know. I just have a few more things to work out in my head before I'm ready."

"I understand."

"Besides, you're going to have other things on your mind for the next little while."

Rav grinned. "Can you believe it?"

"Actually, I can. I knew the first time I saw you and Annie together that the two of you were meant for each other."

"I knew the first time I saw her too. I just had to convince her."

"I doubt it took much persuading."

"Are you really okay with it? I know it's not the best timing for you, after what happened with . . ."

"Hey." Alain set the lid on the box. "As far as I'm concerned, there's never a bad time for one of my brothers to be happy. You don't have to worry about that."

Rav exhaled. "Okay, good. I feel the same way."

"I know." Alain carried the box to the closet and slid it onto the shelf. "Will you tell Tane and *Maman* and Xaviar, see if they can fly here?"

Shadows flickered over his brother's face. "I want to, believe me. But with Annie's mom gone and her father's new wife refusing to have anything to do with her, she won't have family there. It doesn't feel right for me to have everyone. Besides, it would cost them a fortune to get flights now, if they even could with such short notice. You'll come though, right?"

"Of course. I wouldn't miss it."

"Good. We'll invite Hiro and Vateo, and our friends from the tour group will be there. That will be enough." He didn't sound convinced, but it wouldn't help for Alain to argue with him. He closed the closet door. Firmly.

When he returned, Rav pulled him into a hug. "I'm really glad you're here, big brother."

"I'm glad I'm here too."

They made their way downstairs. The *Wheel of Fortune* episode was just ending, and Rav and Annie said their goodbyes before leaving.

Hiro grabbed the cloth to wipe off the counter. "You doing okay?"

"Yeah." He was. Kind of remarkable, as Rav had pointed out. Even so, he wouldn't be able to sleep tonight until he did one more thing.

Dear Carly,

It's been a wild day. In the past, whenever anything happened to me, you were the first person I wanted to call so I could tell you all about it. I wish I could call you now. To be perfectly honest—which is the whole idea of these letters—I wish you were here. Every time I try something I've never done before like flying to a different country or going scuba diving, or when I see something breathtaking like a humpback whale rising from the ocean or fish a shade of purple you would love since that's your favorite color, or learn a new bit of information about my family like how my dad was married before and had a daughter, I start to reach for my phone to let you know. And then I remember.

Each time, it hurts as much as standing in the doorway watching you walk away. So I need to try and get past you being the first person I think of. And I need to let go of wishing you were here next to me. Maybe most of all I have to stop asking myself how I could have ever let you walk away. I only did because I felt . . .

The pen stilled on the paper. Alain gazed out the window. He'd raised the pane before sitting down at the desk in his room, and the soothing sound of waves curling onto the sand eased a little of the tension from his body. He felt what? Closing his eyes, he called that jumbled mass of wool to his mind. What strand leapt out at him tonight? After a few seconds, one did emerge—a blue as soft as the moonlight sparkling and dancing on the rippling waves.

Unworthiness. He blew out a breath. Couldn't argue with that one. He'd wrestled with it his whole life. He'd never been good enough for his father. He'd never believed that anyone at school would want to be his friend, which had turned out to be a self-fulfilling prophecy.

Although Carly had told him over and over that she loved him and that he was everything she had ever wanted in a life partner, Alain had never been able to fully believe that. The sense that he wasn't good enough for her and didn't deserve to be that happy, along with his fear of rejection and failure, had been a lethal combination. The one-two punch that had knocked him out of contention, that had led to him pushing her away. He saw that now, clearly.

Alain tugged on that thread until the full length of it fell coiled into his palm. Then he touched the tip of the pen to the paper again.

I felt unworthy. Unworthy of anyone's love, especially yours. And God's. So I pushed you away just like I have pushed him away all my life.

It's too late for me to stop doing that with you, but maybe it's not too late to stop pushing God away.

I'm going to try, anyway. What is helping a little is starting to see that maybe God has something to do with everything I am seeing around me, everything that's happening to me. Do you believe that? I wasn't sure I did until I came here, but whenever I consider the possibility or try talking to him, I do feel something inside—a faint, shimmery sensation like the wisps of fog drifting in front of the mountains here. Whatever it is, I want more of it.

Because like I told Rav tonight, the people I care about who have opened up their minds and hearts to the possibility of a loving God are filled with this mysterious peace and joy that I want. That I need.

Wherever you end up, whoever you end up with, I hope (and, for what it's worth since I really have no idea how to do it, I pray) that you find that peace and joy too.

Yours forever,

Alain

He paused a moment, letting the words he had written seep into every part of him before tearing out the page, rolling it up, and sticking it into another bottle.

The house was quiet, so he crept down the stairs, unlocked and slipped out the front door, and padded in his bare feet across the sand and along the pier, the odd sliver of wood from a weatherworn board pricking his toe or heel.

When he reached the end, he stood a moment, letting the soft rays of moonlight fall over him and breathing in the cool, salt-tinged air before flinging the bottle as far as he could out into the dark waves.

Then he tipped back his head, taking in the myriad of golden stars shimmering over the country, the land of his people. They shimmered over his home country too. Was *Maman* looking at them, or Tane? Was Carly?

Most importantly, was the one who had scattered the golden stars across the night sky looking down at him?

That mysterious warmth drifted through his chest. Maybe he was. Alain pressed a palm to the spot, his eyes still fixed on the glittering sky. *Okay, look. I promised to pray for Carly, so here it is. Could you help us both to find that peace and joy I've been longing for? Thanks.*

Likely that wasn't close to the way he was supposed to do it, but it was the best he could do tonight. Hopefully the prayer, rough and unpolished as the wooden boards of the pier, would carry him through tomorrow and whatever *shocking revelations* the day might bring.

DECEMBER 30TH

"Did you have a good talk with Rav last night?" Hiro swiped a towel over the last plate from the breakfast Alain had made them—scrambled eggs and bacon—before setting it in the cupboard.

"I did. Thanks for inviting them. It helped."

"Good." Hiro draped the towel over the handle of the stove. "If there is ever anything you want to talk to me about, I've been told I'm a good listener."

"Actually"—Alain rinsed out the dish cloth and squeezed the water from it before hanging it over the faucet—"I did want to show you something if you have a minute."

"I have all the time in the world."

Which was one of the many things he loved about Tahiti—the island way of slowing down and enjoying every moment of life. Very different than his North American mindset, and likely much healthier. He started for his room, his cousin trailing behind him. The sounds of *The Price is Right* followed them from the living room, where Vateo had settled in his recliner after they'd eaten.

Hiro followed Alain into his room and stopped as he opened the closet door and took down the box. "I found this in here. Since it had my dad's name on it, I opened it up. I hope that's okay."

"Of course." Hiro lifted a hand. "You have more right to it than *Papa* or me, I think." He walked over to stop next to Alain. "Did you find anything interesting inside?"

"Only a few photos of my dad's first wife and their daughter, which confirmed Uncle Vateo's story that he had been married before." He offered his cousin a chagrined look. "Not that I doubted . . ."

Hiro waved a hand through the air. "It's okay. I understand. It's funny, though. While *Papa* often gets details wrong about recent events, like what we just ate for breakfast, everything he has told me about the past so far seems to be correct. Those days are much clearer to him now. The present is slipping from his grasp."

The sorrow was back in his cousin's voice, and Alain touched his arm. "I'm sorry. That must be very difficult to watch."

"It is, although you coming here has made it easier, as though no matter what happens now I am not alone in the world. I have God and I have family."

"Yes, you do."

"God's timing is perfect, *non*? Bringing you and Rav and Annie and hopefully one day soon Tane and your *maman* into my life just as I was starting to think I would soon have no one."

Alain couldn't deny his cousin's assertion. "It is, yes. It's been perfect timing for me as well. I needed to be reminded that God is real and that he actually might love me. *Maman* took Tane and Rav and me to Sunday school when we were kids, but I'd kind of forgotten everything I learned there. It's been coming back to me this week."

"Good." Hiro slapped him on the back. "I will pray it continues to do so."

That meant more to Alain than he would have believed a few short days ago. "Thank you." His throat had thickened a little, and he cleared it and lifted the box. "Anyway, I thought you might want to see the pictures. Vairani would have been your aunt and their daughter your cousin."

"I would. Very much."

Alain carried the box to the desk and set it down. After removing the lid, he held out the photos to his cousin. The white piece of paper lay on the bottom, and he slid a finger beneath it to lift it up. "Do you recognize this?" He read the words to his cousin, ending with *"This far you may come and no farther; here is where your proud waves halt."*

Hiro nodded. "Yes. It is from the Bible. The book of Job. Job has been questioning God, and God demands that Job tell him who commands the ocean and all created things. Basically, he is telling Job to remember who he is speaking to."

What was a verse like that doing in the box? Was it one that meant something to his father? "Hmm. Good lesson for all of us, I guess."

"It is." Hiro leaned back against the desk and flipped through the photos the way Rav had the night before, studying each one carefully before sliding it to the back of the pile. He stilled on one, his eyes narrowing as he lifted it closer to his face.

"What is it?" Alain came around to stand next to him so he could see the photo.

"This skipping rope." Hiro touched the tip of his finger to the rope the little girl—Alain's sister—was jumping with. "It looks familiar."

"Really?" He narrowed his eyes to bring the rope into sharper focus. "It's unusual, isn't it. Did you see it in a store?"

Hiro shook his head. "No. I'm sure it is handmade, not from a store. Not even from the market. But I have seen a little girl using one like it in front of a house between here and Papeete. I drive back and forth from the city almost every day, so I have seen it often, and I noticed it because, like you said, it is so unusual."

His heart rate had ratcheted up. As unlikely as it was that the rope his cousin had seen was the same one, it might be worth checking out. "How do you feel about taking a drive?"

A smile crossed Hiro's face as he handed him the photo. "Let's go."

"This is crazy, right?" Alain's gaze followed the path of a flock of sea gulls, dipping and rising over the water. "There's no way this skipping rope or the girl could have anything to do with our family."

Hiro lifted his shoulders. "You never know. It is a small country." As usual, he'd rested one wrist on the top of the wheel, as relaxed and casual in his driving as he was in every other aspect of his life, from what Alain had observed. "It's good it is the holidays, so she won't be at school." He shot Alain a grin. "More perfect timing."

Alain huffed a laugh. "Seems like it." A red sign with the number 32 on it flashed by. He'd noticed those signs before. What did they mean? "What are those red and white signs with numbers on them for?"

"Ah. That is because of the Notre Dame Cathedral in Papeete. It is considered Point Zero."

"Point Zero?" The wind whipping by them was scented with tropical flowers, and he drew in a slow breath.

"Yes. It is the point from which all distances are measured on the island. The numbers mark the kilometers from the cathedral."

Huh. Was that an acknowledgement that the church was the center of the island? Of Tahiti? If Alain's roots were buried deep in the volcanic soil of this country, was that what was driving his own growing acknowledgement that he was not doing well with himself as the center of his life, that he needed God? Maybe. He certainly felt as though he needed God now to guide him through the potentially choppy waters that lay ahead.

None of us wants to be in calm waters all our lives.

Carly's favorite quote from *Persuasion*. Alain got it, although he'd clung to a life preserver while being buffeted by stormy waters often in his life. Right now, calm waters, like the quiet ocean he gazed out over as they drove, sounded pretty good.

Hiro stepped on the brakes to slow the Jeep. Were they here? Questions crowded into Alain's mind. What would they say to this girl if she was home? They'd have to make sure one of her parents was around, not talk to her alone. Maybe they should have thought this out a bit better.

Hiro pulled to the curb and turned off the engine. "Ready?"

"Not really." Alain smiled weakly.

"Even so, we are here. And there is the girl." His cousin inclined his head toward the front yard of a neat wooden house, painted a blue that matched the waves of the ocean across the street. Two young girls, maybe seven or eight, stood in the driveway, bouncing a small red, blue, and white ball off the garage door to each other. No skipping rope around that Alain could see. Maybe they shouldn't bother . . .

Hiro pushed open his door and dropped lightly onto the asphalt. All right. They were actually doing this. Alain climbed out of the vehicle and followed his cousin across the road. He walked up the small path leading to the front door. Good call, not going straight to the kids.

Both girls stopped playing and turned to face them. One of them planted a hand on her hip and called out, "*Qui êtes-vous?*"

Alain remembered enough French from school to know that she was asking who they were.

Thankfully, Hiro answered. "*Nous sommes ici pour parler à votre mère ou votre père. Sont-ils à la maison?*"

Alain caught mother, father, and home, which gave him the gist of his cousin's question. Was either of her parents home?

"*Maman,*" the girl called out, trotting ahead of them to the door and flinging it open. "*Deux hommes sont ici.*"

Hiro shot Alain a grim smile. "She says two men are here. That should bring her mother quickly."

The words were barely out of his mouth before a woman maybe a few years older than Alain appeared in the open doorway, a large bowl tucked under one arm, her towel-covered hand resting inside it. She set the bowl and towel down on a table inside the door and wrapped an arm around the little girl's shoulders to pull her closer. "*Oui?*"

"Do you speak English?" Hiro asked her.

"*Oui.* Yes. A little."

"Okay then. We're sorry to bother you, but we found this picture at home and thought this skipping rope looked like the one your daughter uses."

Alain tugged the photo from the pocket of his shirt and held it toward the woman.

She took it and gazed at it a moment before looking up. Alain tried to gauge the emotion on her face. Surprise? Suspicion? "Where did you get this picture?"

"It was in a box of family photos," Alain said. He rested a hand on the wooden stair railing. What was happening? The woman definitely appeared to know something about the picture. The question was what? And why did she look so shaken?

She glanced at the picture again before meeting his gaze. "What family? What is your last name?"

"Temauri. I am Alain and this is my cousin Hiro."

The photo shook in the woman's hand as she held it out to Alain. "I think you both better come inside."

"Sit." The woman gestured to a couch in the small, tidy living room. "I will get us something to drink."

"Please don't go to any trouble," Hiro protested.

The woman shook her head, the long, dark hair she had pulled into a ponytail swishing across her back. "It is no trouble." The young girls had followed them into the house, but she shooed them back outside to play before grabbing the bowl and towel and disappearing into the kitchen.

Hiro wandered over to the couch, and Alain took the spot next to him. "What do you think is happening?"

"I have no idea, cousin." Hiro tugged the cushion behind him up a bit higher before settling back against it. "But something is happening for sure." He nodded toward the kitchen. "She knows the girl in the photo."

Alain had gathered that much. Did the name Temauri mean something to her? Was she a relative? Vateo had been right about everything so far—he couldn't have been mistaken about Raimana and Vairani's daughter dying, could he? Alain straightened as the woman walked back into the room, carrying a tray with a jug of lemonade and three glasses on it. Alain pushed to his feet and took the tray from her, setting it gingerly down on the table in front of the couch.

"Thank you." The woman tucked behind her ear a strand of hair that had come loose from the ponytail. She poured lemonade into all three glasses, ice clinking against the sides, before handing them each one. Then she took the last glass and sat on an armchair facing the couch.

For a moment, she didn't speak, only gazed down at her glass. Hiro took a sip of his drink. Alain studied the slices of lemon floating in the glass, giving her a moment to gather her thoughts.

Finally, she looked up. "My name is Raina Temauri. The little girl in the photograph is me."

Alain blinked. So Vateo *had* been confused. Or was Alain wrong about the little girl being his sister who died? If she wasn't, then who was the girl in the picture, another cousin? When he couldn't even think how to respond to that, Hiro leaned forward.

"We thought the girl was the daughter of Raimana and Vairani Temauri."

"Yes." Sadness flickered in the woman's dark eyes. "They were my parents. They died when I was four, and my uncle took me to . . ." Her forehead wrinkled and she looked at Hiro. "*Une SOS village d'enfants.*"

He nodded. "An orphanage."

"Yes. Orphanage." Her voice rasped, and she took a drink of lemonade and then wiped her fingers across her bottom lip.

"But, Raina . . ." Alain shot a helpless look at Hiro. His cousin nodded. Alain drew in a deep breath as he shifted his attention back to her. "I believe your mother died, yes, but your father did not. Raimana married Vairani's sister, Emere, and they moved to Canada. They are my mother and father."

She fisted a hand and pressed it to her mouth. They waited thirty seconds before she lowered her fist and whispered, "My father is alive?"

"Yes."

"Then why would he send me to an orphanage?"

"I don't know. I'm sorry." Alain ran a thumb through the condensation on the glass. "I came to Tahiti a few days ago for the first time. I didn't know I had family here until I ran into Hiro and we realized we were cousins. His *papa* is Vateo, Raimana's brother."

Raina pressed her fingers to her lips. "That is my uncle. Uncle Vateo. I haven't seen him since he took me to the orphanage." She contemplated them both for a few seconds before letting out a small laugh and lowering her hand. "So, you are my half-brother and cousin."

"That's true, yes."

"Any other family I don't know about?"

Alain rested the glass on one knee. "I have two brothers, Tane and Rav. And Rav is getting married on a beach here tomorrow." A crazy idea—although no crazier than anything else that had happened the last few minutes—popped into his head. "Would you like to come to the wedding? You could meet Rav and Annie. I know they would love to see you."

Raina ran a hand down the side of her face. "I don't know. Maybe. This is a lot."

"Of course it is." He understood the feeling completely. "I'll tell you what. They are getting married on Tautira Beach at six tomorrow evening. Very relaxed."

The woman shot another look at Hiro.

"*Décontracté*," he told her.

"Ah." She nodded.

"Come if you want to," Alain added, "but no pressure."

When her forehead wrinkled slightly, Hiro smiled. "*Pas de pression.*"

Her lips quivered when she tried to smile. "Okay. *Merci.* I will think about it."

Alain leaned forward to set his glass on the tray. They had over-whelmed this woman—his sister, which was going to take a while to sink in—enough for now. "We should go."

Hiro set his glass down as well and stood. "It was good to meet you, Raina."

"You too." She rose and, when Alain pushed to his feet, grasped his forearms. "A brother." She let out a shaky laugh. "Three brothers. And a cousin. I cannot believe it. I truly thought we were all that was left of our family."

"I can't believe it either."

"My . . . our father, he is okay?"

Telling her the truth would be even harder than telling Hiro. "He has had a difficult life. I don't think he ever got over your mother dying."

She nodded and let go of his arms. "I can understand that. Losing the love of your life, there is no pain like it."

Her words sent an arrow of pain driving deep into his chest. For her and for himself. "Your husband?"

She shook her head. "He was a policeman. Killed . . ." She turned toward Hiro. "*En service?*"

"On duty. I'm sorry."

"*Merci.* Thank you. It was four years ago, but it is still hard."

Great. Alain hid a wince. "I'm sorry too." The sound of girlish laugh-ter drifted inside, and he smiled despite the ache. "What is your daugh-ter's name?"

The sadness faded from her eyes. "Vairani. After my mother. I wanted her name to live on."

"It's beautiful." Alain tugged the wallet from his back pocket, flipped it open, and withdrew a business card. "Here." He held it out to her.

"I hope you'll come tomorrow, but if you don't, please call or email me anytime."

She accepted the card and stuck it in the front pocket of her beige capris. "I will."

Hiro and Alain went outside and down the porch steps. The girls were skipping. Vairani was using the jump rope from the picture, while her friend's was a pink rubber one, the kind available in any store.

Raina came out after them, stopping on the porch and planting her hands on the wooden railing to gaze at the girls. "That rope was the only thing I had with me when I went to the orphanage. My father made it for me when I was very young."

So, Hiro had been right about that. "It's beautiful."

"I always thought so. I loved it. When my uncle told me my parents were gone and he was taking me somewhere else to live, I refused to let go of it."

"I'm glad you did, since it helped us to find you."

Her smile was stronger this time. "*Moi aussi.* Me too."

She followed them down the stairs, and her daughter stopped skipping, dropped the rope into a coiled heap, and ran over to her.

Once Alain had settled on the passenger seat of the Jeep, he looked at them—his sister and his niece. Raina had wrapped her arms around Vairani and pulled her back against her. Both of them watched as Hiro turned the Jeep around and drove by their home.

Alain lifted a hand, and both Raina and her daughter did the same. He watched them in the rearview mirror until Hiro drove around a curve and the two of them faded from sight.

Clutching his copy of *Persuasion*, Alain settled in the cushioned wicker chair in the corner of the porch. Hiro and Vateo sat on wooden chairs in front of the window, a checkers game on the table between them. The two of them were easy with each other, bantering back and forth and mocking each other for their moves.

Alain smiled to hear them, although the fact that he and his father had never had even a moment like that did sting. Maybe a little less now that he had come here and met more family who cared about him and what he was going through.

Hiro had kept his promise and made *poisson cru* for dinner. Alain had mustered up all his courage to try a bite—and been pleasantly surprised. The coconut milk made the dish nice and creamy, and the lime juice gave it a fresh, zesty flavor. Honestly? It might be the best meal he'd had in Tahiti, and he'd eaten a lot of amazing food since arriving in the country. Even so, he had hoped to avoid giving his cousin the satisfaction of knowing how much he enjoyed it. Given Hiro's smug smile after Alain had taken a few bites, he had not been successful.

He flipped open the book and tugged free the photo of him and Carly. The sight of her still stung. Not less than before, although maybe not as sharply. He doubted he would get over her for a long time, if ever. Still, for the first time since she had left, seeing the two of them together didn't stir up only pain. It also carried with it faint echoes of their time together. Echoes tinged with joy and love and laughter swirling like a frame around the edges of the photo.

With a sigh, he tucked the picture inside the cover and slid a finger between the pages where a bookmark held his place.

"Raimana."

Alain looked up. His uncle had turned in his seat to look back at him. He closed the book and set it on the small glass-topped table next to him. "Yes?"

"Before you leave, brother, there is something I must say to you."

That sounded serious enough that Alain stood and pulled out the third chair at the table, the one between his uncle and cousin, and lowered himself onto it, giving Vateo his full attention. "What would you like to say?"

"I need to ask you to forgive me."

Alain exchanged a look with Hiro. What could Vateo possibly have to ask Alain's father forgiveness for? "Forgiveness for what?"

"I know you were furious with me when I told you not to marry Emere. Although she was a good woman, you did not love her. You were drawn to each other in your shared grief, I know, but you loved Vairani still. I worried that you would grow angry with Emere for not being her sister. I could tell already that you were, even if neither of you could see it." His uncle waved a hand feebly in the air, fingers trembling. "Even so, I said harsh words that day, words I regret and have always wished I could take back. Words that drove you to another country and that kept us apart for many years. And for that, I am truly sorry."

Alain reached for his uncle's hand and held it between both of his. "I forgive you, Vateo."

His uncle released a deep breath, his entire body slumping as though he'd been holding something inside for a very long time. "Thank you."

"Can you forgive *me* for the things I said?"

A smile crossed Vateo's lips. "I can. I forgave you a long time ago. And I want you to know that your daughter is safe. I took her to the home like you asked and made sure it was a good place. Although I did not agree with you giving her up, maybe it was for the best. Maybe you would have only been angry with her, too, for reminding you of her mother."

Alain's chest tightened. Although he would never have wished for his half-sister to grow up without a family, life at home with an angry, violent father would have been far worse.

He glanced at Hiro again. His cousin inclined his head, so he patted his uncle's hand. "It was for the best. She was well taken care of, and she grew up to be a wonderful woman with a beautiful girl of her own. She named her daughter Vairani, so her mother will never be forgotten."

His uncle nodded. "That's good." He sighed. "I know you have always blamed yourself for what happened. But it was not your fault, Raimana. That storm came up so fast, and you in your little boat . . ." Vateo rubbed trembling fingers across his forehead. "You could only save one of them. If you had kept trying to rescue Vairani, all three of you would have died. Your wife would have wanted you to save your child, as you did."

Currents of electricity traveled through Alain's body. No wonder his dad had left Tahiti. And given up Raina. Which must be what Vateo had meant when he said they had lost them both—Vairani to the sea and Raina to the orphanage. For his father, the memories of that day, of his desperate attempts to save his wife and daughter, would have been unbearable. And in this tiny country, surrounded by ocean, he would have lived the experience over and over. *Maman* as well, after the loss of a beloved sister. "Maybe you are right."

Vateo squeezed Alain's fingers. "I'm glad we talked before it was too late. I'm going away, you know."

He frowned. "You're leaving? Where are you going?" Tingling prickles crawled across his skin. What if his uncle tried to go to Canada to see his brother? This ruse only worked if Vateo never saw the real Raimana, never bore witness to the kind of man his brother had become.

Vateo chuckled. "I'm not taking a trip, brother. I'm going away here." He tapped the side of his head. "My boy, Hiro, is doing his best to keep me with him, but I can feel it. I'm trying to stay, for his sake, but I slip away from him a little more each day."

Alain's throat tightened. He risked another look at his cousin, whose dark eyes were shimmering.

Hiro reached across the table to rest a hand on his father's arm. "It's okay, *Papa*. You can go if you need to. I will be okay."

Any last tension seeped from Vateo's body. "I know you will be. God will be with us both." He turned back to Alain. "I need to go to bed now. I love you, brother."

"I love you too." He let go of his uncle's hand. "Sleep well."

Vateo rose and wandered behind Alain's chair. When he reached Hiro, he clasped his son's shoulder. Hiro covered his father's hand with his own, and they stayed that way for a few seconds, until Vateo let him go and continued into the house.

Alain gave his cousin a minute before saying, "Are you okay?"

"I think so." Hiro's voice rasped a little, and he cleared his throat. "I had no idea he understood what was happening to him."

"That must be incredibly difficult, although he seems more at peace with it now."

"More at peace about what happened between him and Raimana as well. So, thank you for that." Hiro pressed a hand to the tabletop between them. "I don't know if you believe in God, Alain, but I know in my heart that he brought you here to us at this moment in time to set my *papa's* mind at rest over everything that happened in the past and whatever might happen in the future."

Alain drew in a breath of cool evening air. "I'm not sure I would have agreed with you before I came here, but now I think I do."

Hiro leaned back in his chair. "You've changed."

Alain let out a short laugh. "It's only been a few days."

"Even so. I can see you are on a journey, as we all are, but already you have drawn closer to what you are seeking. And you know what the Bible says: 'You seek me and find me when you seek me with all your heart.' So keep going on that journey, cousin. If you ever want to talk about it, I am here."

Alain nodded. "And I will be here for you, whatever happens. You will not be alone in the world."

The sorrow lingering in his cousin's eyes cleared when he smiled. "For the first time in a long time, I believe that what you say is true."

Alain stood at the edge of the ocean, the wind swirling around him whipping up roaring waves that pummeled the shore and licked at his bare toes. This was the wildest he had seen the sea, and the sight and sound of all that power called to something deep and primal inside him, sending adrenaline coursing through his veins. The words on that slip of white paper took on new meaning. Was that why the words meant something to Dad? Because he was well acquainted with the power of the sea and what it could give—and what it could take away?

A wave crashed against the pier, sending a plume of water cascading into the air. What kind of being could order these waves to halt on the shore and go no farther? The kind of being—the kind of God—he would continue to seek when he left here, as his cousin had encouraged him to do.

His time in Tahiti was drawing to a close. Tomorrow would be a busy day with the wedding and then he would fly home on New Year's Day.

The past week had been nothing like he'd expected. He'd been forced to step into his father's shoes. With all Vateo's revelations, Alain now had a faint glimmer of understanding as to what had happened to his dad to turn him into such a deplorable father and human being. It didn't excuse the way he had treated *Maman* or any of them, but it helped a little, knowing how desperately lost in heartbreak and grief he had been when he left his country. And that the one good thing he had done was protect his young daughter from himself.

Alain knew now that he was part of a bigger family than he'd dreamed. And maybe—he gazed up at the sky, the stars partially obscured tonight by a thin, gauzy haze but still vast in number—he was part of something else, something bigger than himself. Bigger than all the universe. He needed to have some serious talks with Rav about all of this.

Sinking down onto the sand just out of reach of the curling waves, he removed the notebook and pen from his shirt pocket. He took a few seconds to breathe deeply, the aroma of the Tiare flower drifting on the breeze, before pressing pen to the paper.

My dear Carly,

What a day it has been. I met a half-sister and a niece I didn't know I had. And I had a moving conversation with my uncle that has gotten me thinking. Believing I was my father, he expressed regret over harsh words spoken between them and asked forgiveness. When I offered it, a burden appeared to be lifted from him.

That conversation showed me the power of letting go of the past, of forgiving ourselves, of being forgiven. So, I want to ask you to forgive me. I was so afraid to give you my heart when we were together. And you deserved that. You deserved all of me because you so freely offered all of yourself to me. I wanted to accept it, and I wanted to tell you how much I loved you in return, but I was too foolish and afraid.

Because of that, what I feel now, beyond even fear or unworthiness, is regret.

Alain paused. He hadn't needed to think about that or visualize the tangled strands of wool. His uncle's admission that he had always regretted his final words to his brother had on its own tugged that piece free in Alain's mind. Regret. Another terrible burden to bear. As Vateo had been able to do, Alain needed to let it go as well. Carrying around anger and sorrow and bitterness and resentment had destroyed his father, eaten him from the inside out.

And Alain didn't want that. He wouldn't wait thirty years to ask forgiveness, as his uncle had done. Or refuse to ask for it at all, like his father. He needed to do it now.

I have to let it go, all of it. Therefore, what I most want to say to you is that I'm sorry. I'm so sorry I let you down, that I pushed you away, that I hurt you. Even though you will never read these words, I hope and pray that you somehow know that.

Yours forever,

Alain

P.S. I did want to marry you. More than anything. Every thought and dream and plan I had of the future included you. In the words of Captain Wentworth in Persuasion, "A man does not recover from such a devotion of the heart to such a woman! He ought not; he does not." And I promise you I never will. So, I have to ask you this: If I'd had the courage to tell you how much I loved you, how desperately I wanted us to have a life together, how badly I wanted you to be my wife, what would you have said?

Although he would never get an answer to that question, it helped to ask it, if belatedly. Clutching the top of the notebook in one hand, he ripped out the page with the other. Then he returned the pad to his pocket and scooped up the bottle sitting on the sand next to him. After rolling up the paper, he tucked it inside, replaced the topper, and pushed to his feet to carry the bottle to the end of the pier.

He hurled it as far out into the raging water as he could. More secrets for the ocean to keep. Clasping his fingers behind his head, he gazed at the mountains nearly lost in the mist glowing in the light of the full moon.

One last time, he visualized that ball of wool. He'd drawn out fear, unworthiness, and regret. There were other, paler threads, but the biggest ones were gone. He had sent them out to sea. The remaining pieces were less tangled, so maybe, with time and prayer, they could be smoothed out. Maybe even used to make something beautiful like those strands his father had braided together to create the unusual skipping rope that, decades later, had drawn a family together.

In this moment, surrounded by beauty, he knew with certainty that a designer—much more powerful and creative than his father—was already working inside him, weaving the peace and joy he had seen in Rav and Annie and Xaviar into Alain's heart and life in ways he was just beginning to perceive.

He'd been wrong, then. As with Pandora's box, when all the evil had flown away, hope had been left behind after all.

DECEMBER 31ST

The wind from the night before had died down, and the mist cleared as the sun rose. A beautiful Tahitian day—perfect for a wedding. Alain had texted Rav first thing to see if he needed anything or wanted him to come early. His brother had assured him that everything was in place and the wedding would be so simple that he didn't need anything except for Alain and Hiro and Vateo to be there.

Since he doubted they would come, Alain didn't mention that he had extended an invitation to Raina and Vairani, especially since Rav didn't yet know they existed. His little brother had enough to think about today.

Hiro had made *farina*—a porridge made from breadfruit flour that *Maman* often made and that Alain had always really liked. A platter of fresh fruit occupied the place of honor in the middle of the table, along with an assortment of pastries and croissants Hiro had gone out to get from a nearby bakery.

Alain made a pot of coffee and was lifting three mugs down from the cupboard when Vateo wandered into the room.

His face lit up when he saw Alain. "*Qui est-ce?* Who is this? Hiro, you didn't tell me we had a guest."

A look passed between Alain and Hiro. Clearly his uncle had returned to their world.

"*Papa*, this is Alain. Raimana's son."

Vateo clapped his hands. "Raimana's son! My nephew." He strolled over and pulled Alain into a hug. When he stepped back, he kept a hold on Alain's upper arms. "It is so good to meet you. Your father and I have been visiting. We had a wonderful conversation last night and made peace between us at last."

He remembered that much, then. Alain nodded. "I heard that. I was very happy for you."

His uncle smacked him lightly on both arms before letting him go. "I am happy as well. So come, let us celebrate with a good meal!"

They laughed and chatted over the food. Vateo peppered Alain with questions about *Maman* and Tane and Rav. Thankfully—maybe because he believed he'd just spent the last few days with the man—Vateo barely mentioned Alain's father, so he was able to focus on how well his mother was doing and Rav's and his careers and what little he could share about Tane. When he mentioned that his little brother was getting married today and they were invited to the wedding, his uncle was overjoyed. "To love and peace and family," he declared, lifting his mug of coffee into the air.

Hiro and Alain clinked their mugs to his. After the events of the past few days, the toast held much more meaning for Alain, and he sipped the coffee as though it were celebratory champagne.

Love and peace and family. *Thank you, God, that you have brought all three into my life this week.*

The prayer caught him by surprise. That it had come without thought most of all, but also that, for the first time in his life, talking to a deity he couldn't see or hear didn't feel awkward or forced. Maybe because it had come straight from the heart that, as Hiro had pointed out, was already beginning to change.

And although neither he nor his brothers drank, Alain would happily raise a mug of coffee to that.

Both hands stuck in the pockets of his shorts, Alain contemplated the view—the waves that had gentled to soft whitecaps today, the mountains ringing the shore, the palm fronds swaying in the breeze. What an unexpected experience this trip had turned out to be. How different would it have been if he hadn't gone to the bistro that first night and run into . . .

Something bobbing in the water along the shore, clinking lightly against the black sand, snagged his attention. A bottle. Oh no. One of the messages he had sent out had been dragged back in, likely because of the tumultuous waves the night before.

Splashing through the shallow water, he made his way to it and crouched to scoop it up. He'd carry it to the end of the pier and try again. He took one step in that direction before stopping. Wait. The paper inside this bottle was pink, not white like the ones he had written on. Obviously someone else had had the same thought as him.

Likely he shouldn't read it, only toss it back into the sea. He took another step toward the pier and stopped again, something stilling his trek. The back of his neck prickled, and he glanced around. Seeing no one, he lifted the bottle to eye level and scrutinized it. Maybe he'd read it before returning it to the Pacific. He wouldn't know the person who had written it, and whoever it was had left it out here for anyone to find, so it wouldn't be a violation of privacy, right?

Without giving himself any more time to think about it, Alain used his thumb to pop the stopper out. The bottle was the same as the ones he'd used, which wasn't surprising, since he'd gotten his at the very popular Papeete Market that most locals and tourists regularly visited. Turning the bottle upside down, he tapped it against his palm. The paper caught in the neck, and he used his finger to pin it against the glass and draw it out.

Dropping the bottle onto the sand, he slowly unfurled the pink paper. Five words had been written across it in a beautiful handwriting he knew as well as his own.

I would have said yes.

He froze. Carly. But how?

Alain spun around. The woman who had broken his heart three months earlier stood ankle deep in sand ten feet from him. She wore a floral sundress that swirled around her legs, one hand holding back the long, blonde hair the wind was blowing around her face.

"Carly." He breathed the word as though, like Uncle Vateo the day before, he'd been holding it in for a long time.

"Hi, Alain."

"What are you doing here? How did you know where I was?"

"Annie called me. She invited me to her and Rav's wedding today."

"Ah." She hadn't come for him, then. Of course she hadn't. They were over. Although, the words she had written in her note . . . Did they mean anything or were they only hypothetical, like his question had been?

"She also mentioned that you seemed sad the other night and she was worried about you. Since I've been worried about you as well, I asked her where you were staying, and she gave me your uncle's address."

His heart was pounding in his ears as loudly as the surf the night before. "Then you know I discovered family here."

"I do. Partly from Annie and partly from reading your letters."

"My letters?" Plural?

"Yes." She wore a cotton bag with palm trees printed on it across her chest, and she slid one strap off her shoulder to dig around in it before fishing out three pieces of paper. "I couldn't sleep, so I went for a drive this morning and ended up here. As the sun was just coming up and it was too early to knock on your door, I wandered down to the water and saw three bottles floating around the edge. When I realized they each had a message inside, I couldn't resist opening them."

So, the ocean had given up its secrets after all.

Alain managed a shaky grin. "Of course you couldn't." He lifted the note. "Did you mean this?"

"Absolutely." She held up her fist, his three letters clutched in her fingers. "Did you mean these?"

"Every word."

"Then here's another one." She reached into the bag again and pulled out a second bottle, a piece of pink paper already rolled up inside. The mischievous glint in her eyes when she looked at him squeezed his chest. Man, he'd missed that look.

"Should I throw it in the water?" Her lips twitched.

"How about we skip that step?" This felt like a dream, as though she were nothing more than an illusion his overactive imagination had conjured up. Part of that alternate universe he'd wondered a few days ago if he had somehow been transported to. If she was, he had no desire to return to reality.

Alain started toward her, his bare feet sinking into sand. When he reached her, he stopped and held out his hand.

Carly set the bottle on his waiting palm, her fingers brushing over his skin. The tingles of electricity dancing across his hand and up his arm were real. Very real.

He swallowed, his gaze fixed on hers as he pulled out the stopper and worked the paper free. When he unrolled it and read the words, his heart, already thundering, ratcheted up another notch.

I would still say yes.

He looked up. "You would?"

She lifted a hand, her eyes warm and laughing. "Ask me and see."

"I don't have a ring."

"It doesn't matter."

Well, all right then. Alain started to go down on a knee, but she grasped his hand. "Don't. I want to see your eyes."

He straightened, his gaze locking on hers. "Carly Travers." How could he even begin to say everything that was on his heart? Maybe Jane Austen could help. "I offer myself to you with a heart even more your own than when you left." A beautiful smile broke across her face, and he lifted the back of her hand to his mouth and kissed it.

Abandoning Jane, he pressed Carly's hand to his chest, over the pounding of his heart. "From the moment I met you, I knew you were the one I was meant to spend my life with. Can you forgive me for being foolish enough to let you go and agree to marry me, so we never have to be apart again?"

Her eyes glittered in the sunlight as she gazed up at him. "I do forgive you. And to quote Jane, as you have done so eloquently, my affection will be yours forever. So yes, Alain Temauri, I will marry you."

Still holding her hand to his heart, he cupped her cheek with his other, her skin soft and sun-warmed beneath his. Lowering his head, Alain touched his lips to hers. The feel of her, the soft hair blowing across his hand, felt like coming home. A home he had believed was closed and locked to him forever. When he lifted his head, she rested hers against his chest, and he wrapped his arms around her and pulled her close.

A salt-laden breeze brushed over them, carrying with it the heady aromas of the sea and sand and Tiare flower—the scents that would always draw him back to this country and to this moment with the woman he loved.

The one he had tried to leave behind but who had, at the perfect time, come anyway.

EPILOGUE

Alain and Carly strolled side by side along the black sand, following Hiro and Vateo as the four of them made their way to the rows of white chairs and a small archway covered in flowers. Tautira Beach offered a spectacular view of lush green mountains, fluffy white clouds drifting across the peaks like a flowing train.

Hiro half turned to look back at them. "The mountains and valleys of Tahiti Nui," he announced.

Alain nodded. "Beautiful."

Rav and Annie were waiting for them when they arrived at the site where the ceremony would be held. His brother wore a white shirt and khaki pants, while Annie's dress was white and billowy, swirling around her calves—perfect for an island wedding.

Although Alain and Carly had agreed to keep their engagement news to themselves for today, not wanting to take anything away from Annie and Rav, Annie still glanced from him to her before reaching for Carly's hand and tugging her farther along the beach, their heads close together.

Alain watched them the way Rav's gaze had followed Annie as she left the kitchen with Vateo the other night. Then Rav cleared his throat, and Alain shifted his attention to his brother, his neck warming.

Rav embraced Hiro and Vateo before directing them to their seats. When he returned, he raised both hands, palms up. "Carly? How did that happen?"

"She said Annie called and invited her to the wedding."

"Ah. Little schemer."

"I'm glad she did. We talked earlier and have worked things out."

Rav punched him lightly in the shoulder. "I am happy for you. Both of you."

"Thanks. I am happy for you too." Alain gestured to the ceremony site. "Are you ready for this?"

"To marry Annie and begin our lives together? I've never been more ready for anything." A slight shadow crossed Rav's face. "Only it doesn't feel right, doing this without *Maman* and Tane and Xaviar here."

"Good thing you won't have to then."

Tane? Alain spun around. The three of them—Tane, *Maman*, and Xaviar—were making their way carefully across the dark sand. As they drew closer, Rav closed the distance between them and threw his arms around his mother. "I can't believe you're here." He let her go and hugged Tane and Xaviar before stepping back. "That any of you are here. How did you know we were getting married today?"

"I called them." Annie came up to slip her hand into his, a smug look on her face.

Rav's eyes glowed as he looked down at her. "You've been a busy little beaver, haven't you? I heard you called Carly as well."

"I did." She inclined her head toward the chairs. "I also called him."

Rav turned to look. Alain peered past him at a man sitting a few chairs away from Hiro and Vateo. When his brother turned back around, his forehead had creased. "Your father?"

"Yes."

"What about your stepmother?"

She shook her head, her smile dimming slightly. "She refused to come. But I wanted him here, Rav. Him and everyone you and I love the most. That's why I called your family. We couldn't get married without them."

"I agree." He pressed a kiss to the top of her head, his eyes misting. "Thank you."

Alain contemplated them. The two of them were so happy together, fit so perfectly. Just like he and . . .

Carly returned, brushing the back of her hand against Alain's as she stopped next to him. *Maman* was distracted admiring Annie's gown, but Tane and Xaviar immediately zeroed in on the gesture before sharing a look. This time Alain didn't mind so much. They'd be happy for him and Carly, he knew that. And so would *Maman*, who loved Carly and Annie like daughters and had cried off and on for days after Carly left.

Before his brothers could comment, Annie said, "And here comes the rest of the family."

They all turned as a group of people approached. Alain didn't need Rav's introductions. From the stories he'd heard, he immediately recognized the sisters from South Carolina, Septima and Sojourner, who hugged them all as though they were long-lost relatives. Gregory from Australia had a woman on his arm, Netta, and the two of them were gazing at each other adoringly. Alain hadn't expected that, given that, according to Rav, the year before Gregory had still been grieving the loss of his wife. Although he had never met the man who'd gone through that near-death experience with Rav when sharks circled their kayak last year, Alain was thrilled for him that he had found love again.

Maeva and Nino, the tour guides who prayed for and then opened their home and hearts to a select group of tourists each year, had come as well. Alain understood what Rav meant now when he said that he couldn't explain it, but that in a few short days this group of people had become family to him and Annie. Each of them greeted Xaviar like a brother or son, swarming around and hugging him. Septima even pinched him on the cheek before the lot of them went to find their seats.

Annie linked her arm with Carly's. "Come help me with the flowers. You'll stand up with me, won't you?"

Carly readily agreed, and they left to make their way to the end of the makeshift aisle. Alain's gaze followed them, his heart full. The two of them were as close as sisters, and Annie had been nearly as torn apart as he had been when he and Carly broke up.

Hiro bending close to say something to his father caught his eye, and he turned to his mother. "*Maman*, there's something you should know. I met Uncle Vateo and his son Hiro this week."

At her sharp intake of breath, Rav and Xaviar each moved to her side. She stared at Alain. "Heiana?"

He shook his head. "She died a few years ago. I'm sorry."

Sadness drifted across her face. "I'm sorry too. She was a wonderful woman."

"Uncle Vateo said the same about you."

"He did?"

"Yes. I'm sure he will be happy to see you again."

Her dark eyes widened. "He is here?"

"Yes, with Hiro."

For a moment, she gazed out to sea. Was she praying? Maybe, because calm settled over her features, and she drew in a deep breath. "I would like to see them as well."

"Come on, *Mamá* Emere." Xaviar held out his bent arm. "I will take you to them."

She beamed at him as she slid her hand through the crook of his elbow, as she always did when he called her that. Everyone needed someone to call *Maman*—or, in the case of Xaviar and his Latino heritage, *Mamá*—she'd informed Alain and Rav. Sometimes it seemed as though she forgot Xaviar hadn't actually been born into the family. Fair, since most of the time they all forgot that. He watched as they strolled over to the chairs. Vateo stood and met them a few feet from his seat, drawing *Maman* into his arms. Smiling, Alain faced his brothers. No doubt they had questions, especially Tane.

Tane raised an eyebrow. "Not sure what to ask first. You and Carly?"

The warmth of her brief touch against his hand still radiated up his arm. Alain would be more than happy to fill his brothers in, but they had more urgent matters to discuss at the moment. "Look, I'll give you all the details, I promise, but for now, I need to tell you . . ." Two figures appeared in the distance, and his breath caught. Raina and Vairani.

Rav followed his gaze. "Who is that?"

Alain turned back to his brothers. "That's what I need to tell you. It's a long story. But the short version is that, like I told Rav earlier this week, Dad's brother Vateo told me that Dad was married before, to *Maman's* sister Vairani. And they had a daughter."

Tane shifted, but he didn't otherwise react. Years of training, no doubt. Alain shot another look at the girls, who had nearly reached the beach. "What I didn't know at the time was that Dad and Vairani and their little girl were caught in a storm one day. Vairani died, but Dad was able to save his daughter."

"She's alive?" Rav stared at the woman and little girl coming toward them.

"Yes."

Tane's brow furrowed. "So, these people are . . ."

"Raina, our half-sister who grew up in an orphanage after Dad and *Maman* left for Canada, and her daughter Vairani, our niece. Raina's husband was a police officer killed in the line of duty, so it's just the two of them. They thought they were alone in the world until Hiro and I tracked them down this week."

"Wow." Tane shook his head. "A sister and a niece. That's pretty wild."

"You couldn't just stick to the registry like a normal guest, could you?" Rav nudged Alain in the ribs.

He let out a short laugh. "They are a gift. A gift from God."

Both brothers shifted their attention back to him. Rav's eyes lit as he clasped Alain's forearm. "I'm sure you're right about that."

Tane's gaze lingered on Alain for several seconds. Then he said, "You've found a way to let go of the lies, haven't you?"

Alain nodded. "I'm on the right path, anyway. Toward that end and toward understanding Dad and the way he is a bit better."

Tane clasped his shoulder. "I'm happy for you, little brother. Truly."

His throat tight, Alain nodded. "Thank you."

The girls were only a few feet from them now, and he extricated himself from his brothers to go meet them.

"*Bonjour, Oncle Alain*," Vairani greeted him, as full of spunk as she'd been the day they had come to her house, which he loved. He needed to come back here as often as his professor's salary would allow—get to know his family better. He and Carly. Joy flowed through him at the thought.

Alain grinned. "*Bonjour,* Vairani." He grinned at his half-sister. "Raina." He hugged her, and, when he let her go, she smiled at him and slid an arm around her daughter's shoulders. "I hope it is okay that we are here."

"Of course. I'm thrilled you came." He gestured to Tane and Rav. "Come meet your other brothers." Tugging gently on one of Vairani's dark braids, he added, "*Ton Oncle Tane et ton Oncle Rav.*"

His niece skipped ahead of them, heading for his brothers. As he and Raina followed her, Alain scanned all the people seated on the white chairs waiting to witness the ceremony that would unite Rav and Annie forever.

As his about-to-be sister-in-law had said, all the people he loved in the world and all the ones who loved him were here on this beach, surrounded by the breathtaking handiwork of the one who had scattered the stars across the sky and whose voice even the wind and the waves obeyed.

A Note From the Author

Dear Reader,

Have you ever tried running away and leaving all your problems behind? How did that work out for you? The problem with running away, of course, is that we bring ourselves with us. Every thought, every memory, every heartache, every mistake we have ever made hides away in our hearts and minds like the sneakiest of stowaways.

The good news is that, wherever we go, God is there as well. As King David said in Psalms 139:7-10, "Where can I go from your Spirit? Where can I flee from your presence? If I go up to the heavens, you are there; if I make my bed in the depths, you are there. If I rise on the wings of the dawn, if I settle on the far side of the sea, even there your hand will guide me, your right hand will hold me fast."

As Alain discovers, God is not only there when he finally reaches out for him, but he has always been there. He has been waiting to take Alain's fear and unworthiness and regret from him and replace them with more peace and joy and love and family and hope than he could have ever imagined.

My hope and prayer for each of you, dear friends, is that you will never run *from* God, but that you will, every day of your life, run *to* him. I promise you that, when you do, you will experience the ocean-deep love and grace that only the one who commands the wind and the waves can offer.

Blessings,

Sara

ABOUT THE AUTHOR

Sara Davison is the author of numerous romantic suspense series, as well as the standalone, *The Watcher*. A finalist for more than a dozen national writing awards, including the Christy Award, Davison is a HOLT Medallion, Cascade, and two-time Carol Award winner for romantic suspense. She lives in Ontario with her husband, Michael. Like every good Canadian, she loves coffee, hockey, poutine, and apologizing for no particular reason.

Get to know Sara better at www.ontheedgesuspense.com, or find her on Amazon, Instagram, BookBub, Goodreads, and Facebook.

TITLES BY
SARA DAVISON

THE MOSAIC COLLECTION: NOVELS

The Rose Tattoo Trilogy
Lost Down Deep
Written in Ink
Sharp Like Glass (2026)
This Little Nowhere, Nothing Town (story collection)

two sparrows for a penny series
Every Star in the Sky
Every Flower of the Field
Every Bird That Falls

In the Shadows Series
The Color of Sky and Stone

THE MOSAIC COLLECTION: ANTHOLOGY STORIES

"Taste of Heaven" in *Hope is Born*
"Ten Bottles of Sand" in *Before Summer's End*
"Sixty Feet to Home" in *A Star Will Rise*
"I'd Like to Thank the Academy" in *Song of Grace*
"Star Light" in *The Heart of Christmas*
"Scarlet" in *All Things New*
"A Single Spark of Light" in *A Whisper of Peace*
"The Poppy" in *Dancing in the Rain*
"The Other Way" in *A Thrill in the Air*
"Five Things You Know About Me" in *Sounds Like a Plan*
"The Back Door Christmas Tour Company" in *A Weary World Rejoices*
"The Weekend" in *BirdSong*

The Night Guardians Series
Vigilant
Guarded
Driven
Forged

The Day Draws Near Series
The End Begins
The Darkness Deepens
The Morning Star Rises

Standalone
The Watcher

PAUSE that THOUGHT

ANGELA D. MEYER

Pause That Thought

Angela D. Meyer

Betsy is facing the change of life, struggling to navigate wayward emotions and regulate her personal summers in the middle of winter. Then one particularly bad ice storm sets her on her derriere, and she decides she's had enough. With her boyfriend taking a break from their relationship, Betsy teams up with a friend to escape the hostile terrain of winter. Perhaps life will be better in paradise.

To all the women swimming up current through the changes of life.

The righteous will flourish like a palm tree, they will grow like a cedar of Lebanon; planted in the house of the LORD, they will flourish in the courts of our God. They will still bear fruit in old age, they will stay fresh and green, proclaiming, "The LORD is upright; he is my Rock, and there is no wickedness in him."

Psalm 92:12-15 (NIV)

CHAPTER ONE

Betsy stepped out the door of the Jukebox Café onto Main Street and stared at the wintry wonderland. Last week, celebrating Thanksgiving, they experienced summer temperatures. That was the Midwest for you. She pulled her red, knee-length, skirted coat around her curvy hips and tucked the ends of her snowflake-covered scarf inside the collar. The silence of December's cold echoed in the still air. The pavement looked like a sheet of glass. An ice-skating rink if she ever saw one. An hour ago, the roads had been clear. She should have left with everyone else, but apparently, they had more smarts than she did.

Driving home was not an option in these conditions. She reached into her pocket for the keys to the café. "Drats." She'd left them on the office desk, where she had been working. Darn this change of life. It stole her brain cells. Now, staying at the café wasn't an option either.

Ginger and Mike's new house would be the closest haven. Three-and-a-half blocks across a sheet of ice and she would be welcomed out of the cold. She could do this. Betsy inched out from under the overhang and tested the pavement with one foot, then pulled back close to the building where the ice hadn't collected. Even with the tread on her boots, it was slippery. She was bound to fall if she tried to walk anywhere, but she couldn't stay here. She blew out a frustrated breath, filling the air with a plume of fog, then sent a quick text to Ginger to let her know she was on the way.

Betsy pulled on her gloves. Under the protection of the overhang, she walked past two storefronts to the end of the block. She stared at the two feet of ice to the curb and the step down from the curb to the ice-laden street. Did she really want to land on her backside? She brightened as an idea formed. "Well, if I'm to end up on the ground, I might as well choose how." She tucked her wool coat under her behind and eased onto the sidewalk. "Sure hope no one is watching, or I might be the star on someone's social media for everyone to laugh at. That would be my luck. Disclaimer—nobody was harmed in the filming of this video." She chuckled at her monologue.

Betsy scooted the distance to the curb, then lowered herself to the street and turned backward for leverage. She pushed off the curb with her feet and sent herself flying across the icy road. On the other side, she placed her palms on the curb behind her and raised herself onto the sidewalk. No overhang on this block, so the sidewalks were thick with ice, too. She repeated her process of traversing the icy path until she reached the next block. Pausing to catch her breath, she laughed, surprised she was having fun. "Look, Mom, I'm butt-sledding."

Hanging a right, she stayed on the sidewalk and coasted down the slight hill to the first house, then eased onto the lawn and walked across the grass, where there was traction. At each driveway she was back on the ground, maneuvering across the ice. Shaking her head, she made it to the end of the second block, then faced left. One street, two drives, and three yards to Ginger's place.

Betsy was preparing to cross the last drive when Mike exited his house and waved. Betsy hollered, "Wait there. I've got this." Sitting down at the edge of the pavement, she demonstrated her ice crossing ability with ease. Mike laughed. After one more lawn and with a belly aching from laughter, she arrived at her destination.

Mike helped her off the ground. "You never cease to amaze me, Betsy."

She brushed off the back of her coat. "That was unexpectedly fun. Regardless, I'm done with winter. I'll be heading south using some of that money my hubby left me to finally take a vacation."

A door slammed, and Ginger stepped out onto their porch. "Hot chocolate, anyone?"

"You're talking my language, girlfriend." Taking Mike's arm, Betsy allowed him to help her up the steps that he had already treated with ice melt. "Let's get this party started, folks."

Betsy muttered as she slushed her way through melting ice to Lillian's house. "Fine mess I've buried myself in this time." Two days ago, back at her house after the ice storm had blown over, Samuel, the man she was dating, had called to check on her. In a moment of perimenopausal angst, she had let her frustrations regarding an argument they'd had earlier in the week spill out all over him like sticky molasses. An argument about the best way to organize her kitchen. For goodness' sake. He was simply offering some suggestions about making things flow better. From sink to cupboard, he said. She shouldn't have cared, but it burrowed under her skin. What had she been expecting when she ranted at him? An apology? A commiseration over her internal struggles? It sure wasn't silence. The man was infuriating. A little understanding would be nice, but in his unmitigatedly gentle way, he had suggested that if they couldn't have a friendly difference of opinion, then they needed to step back from their blossoming relationship for a bit and think things over. Couldn't she have kept her trap shut for once?

Untwining her scarf, she breathed a sigh of relief as the cool air lowered her internal temperature. "God, help me to stop being so prickly about everything. Samuel is a good man. Besides, I don't care to be alone for the rest of my life."

Betsy climbed the steps to Lillian's front door and rang the bell. She was probably in her studio. After several minutes, the door opened, and Betsy's willowy friend beckoned her inside. Auburn tendrils had escaped from a loose bun and framed her face. The apron she wore over one of her twirly skirts was covered with splashes of paint, confirming Betsy's suspicions. "What are you working on this time?"

Lillian hung Betsy's coat and scarf on a rack. "Randy's Christmas present. Come on, I'll show you."

Betsy followed Lillian to her studio. Typically one to work with industrial art, her friend was a creative genius with any medium as far as Betsy was concerned. Betsy didn't have a creative bone in her body. If she took paintbrush in hand, any artwork she produced would resemble a mishmash of a child's attempt at Picasso.

Lillian paused at the door to her workspace. "It's different than my usual. Something Randy has been asking me to do." She stepped aside to allow Betsy entrance.

Betsy stared at the painting in front of her. At once awed at her friend's talent and discouraged at her own lack of special abilities, she swallowed back disappointment in herself. This was not about her. She took a deep breath and approached the piece in progress. "This is amazing."

"Thank you."

The painting depicted the view of the river from Table Rock at sunset, a popular place for picnics, meditative afternoons, and marriage proposals. Betsy had yet to enjoy its romantic potential, though her friends knew it well. Someday maybe. Or perhaps she would find her own spot.

"In my humble opinion, you need to do more paintings."

"It was more satisfying than I thought it would be." Lillian pulled off her apron and hung it on a hook. "What brings you here today? You look like a woman on a mission."

"How long did you say Randy would be gone?"

"He'll get back a few days before Christmas."

Betsy clapped her hands. "Perfect. Plenty of time."

Lillian crossed her arms. "What crazy idea do you have this time?"

"I'm done with winter. I'm done with men. I'm done with this intolerable change of life." Betsy plopped a fist on her hip. "Don't give me that look. I know how much your doctor is helping you, and I promise to think about making an appointment." Betsy relaxed her shoulders. "For now, I intend to forget about all of it and escape. I've made reservations at a resort in Maui. Come with. You won't have to pay for anything. I finally broke into some of the money my husband left for me when he died. I'm taking a vacation, and I don't want to travel alone."

Betsy scrunched her shoulders. "We would leave day after tomorrow."

"Wow. That's not much time to get ready." Lillian tapped her chin with a finger. "This is important to you, isn't it?"

Betsy nodded.

Lillian laughed. "Why not?"

CHAPTER TWO

Bags checked, Lillian and Betsy joined the line of passengers waiting to pass through security. Betsy unbuttoned her jacket and fanned herself. Newly painted red fingernails flashed back and forth. She leaned toward Lillian. "I suppose I didn't really need to escape to some tropical resort. I have my own personal summer with me wherever I roam."

"I haven't had to deal with that one much. Yet." Lillian stepped forward as the line moved. "We can always live in our swimsuits while we're at the resort."

"You can get away with that, but with this body? No way. I'll be in the pool and submerged to my neck when I'm wearing mine."

"Don't be so hard on yourself, Betsy. You look great."

Betsy fought the tears. Her now-dead husband—God rest his soul—from early on in their marriage had complained about the shape of her body. He'd often referred to her as fat or too big for her own good, even though she was only size sixteen. It seemed that at least once daily he had told her she needed to lose ten pounds. Not that she hadn't tried. He would even throw out her fudge when she wasn't around. As though he was a picture of health. She crossed her arms. It was hard to see herself as any different than what he had called her all those years ago. And now, with the change? Gaining weight was her nemesis. At least one of them.

Lillian elbowed her gently. "Hey, didn't mean to bring you down. Change topic?"

Betsy nodded.

"Did you bring a book?"

"Yep. I brought my e-reader with plenty of suspense choices. You?"

A TSA agent waved them forward. "Put your things in a bin and walk this way." He pointed to the metal detector.

While Lillian filled her bin, Betsy put her carry-on and purse on the belt. It had pained her to trim down from what her friends called her bottomless purse to one no bigger than a fanny pack. Her shoes went into a bin.

"Ma'am?" One of the agents walked over to her. "You need to place your jewelry in there, as well, or you might set off the alarm."

Betsy took off her dangling earrings, bracelets, and rings and tossed them in with her shoes. She hated this process of being looked into and through in ways that felt intrusive.

The two ladies made it through security without any issues. After Betsy reassembled herself, they paused at a monitor to check the status of their flight. Betsy had a hard time finding it in the long list of numbers until Lillian pointed it out. So far, so good. If the flight continued on track, they wouldn't miss their connecting flight and could make it to their destination tonight. They stepped away from the monitor and Betsy landed on someone's foot.

"Watch what you're doing." The man raised his voice. His irritation bled through his well-tailored expression.

Betsy cringed. "I'm so sorry."

The man scowled and continued his walk down the terminal.

Betsy switched her carry-on from one shoulder to the other. "I'd be bummed if he was on our flight."

"I've heard some awful stories about how people can be on flights these days."

A running child zigzagged past them. A woman ran after him. Betsy sidestepped and bumped into a chair. The woman hollered a quick "Sorry" and kept chasing the youngster as Betsy lost her balance, fell, and dropped her carry-on. The contents spilled out of her unzipped bag. Betsy's makeup, container of snacks, and her collection of pens scattered across the floor. Lillian grabbed the bag and stopped the leakage as an apple rolled toward the middle of the wide hallway, where people dodged to miss stepping on it.

Berating herself for not securing her belongings, Betsy snatched the bruised piece of fruit off the floor and tossed it in the trash before returning to her flight mate to stuff everything back in the carry-on. She glanced at her phone. "Drats! I've made us late. We need to skedaddle."

Running the rest of the way, they arrived at the gate and checked in moments before the flight attendant announced that boarding was about to begin.

"That was close." Laughing, Lillian glanced at Betsy.

Betsy leaned over, resting her hands on her knees and trying to catch her breath. She hated to admit her friends were right. She was out of shape. They had been after her for ages to join their walking club. "I see that look, Lillian. And yes, when we get back to Preston Hill, I'll get serious about exercise." According to her doctor, exercise would also help with some of the lovely symptoms she was experiencing in this new season of life. "For now, I'm planning to enjoy this trip." She pulled a small plastic baggie out of her carry-on. "Fudge?" She popped a small piece into her mouth.

Lillian accepted the offer, then they moved forward as the flight attendant called for their grouping of passengers to board.

Lillian and Betsy added their carry-ons to the overhead bin, then sat in their assigned seats. Lillian in the middle and Betsy, who tended to be a bit claustrophobic, on the aisle. They introduced themselves to an older woman sitting in the window seat as a loud commotion broke out a couple rows back. The young child who had caused the demise of Betsy's dignity in the terminal cried and clung to his mother.

The man who had rudely inserted himself to view the monitors sat in the aisle seat and glared at the pair waiting to crawl over him to their seats. "Will I have to put up with that crying the whole trip?"

The mother nudged her child close to her. "He'll be fine once we get seated. He's tired and wants his dad."

"I'm not switching seats."

"His dad isn't on the flight. We just need to sit in our own seats. Could you let us into the row, please?"

The older woman next to Lillian spoke up. "Poor child. That man is making him more upset." The woman tsked and shook her head.

Betsy squeezed her eyes shut and said a quick prayer. This was supposed to be a pleasant flight. *I don't want to change seats, but I see what you're doing, God.* She checked with Lillian and the woman sitting in the window seat about switching seats, then waved over the flight attendant. Betsy explained her and Lillian's willingness to exchange seats with the woman and child. The lines around the attendant's mouth melted away. "Bless you. I'll make the arrangements."

Twenty minutes later, Lillian and Betsy were situated in their new seats, and the child was quiet. The plane taxied onto the runway. Other than an eye roll when he had to allow them past, the man had ignored them. Thankful for his silence, Betsy took the opportunity to examine him. There was not one sandy brown hair out of place on his head. Thick and slightly wavy, it stayed put well. No wrinkles marred his collared knit top, and his dark blue jeans had a crease ironed into each leg. His speech sounded cultured. In her mind, there was every indication he was well off. However, despite any advantage of knowing the man, her encounters with him led her to think he wouldn't be easy to get along with. She should give the man the benefit of the doubt. God knew *she* hated to be misjudged.

As the plane gained speed to take off, the claustrophobic portion of Betsy's brain sprang to action. She quietly recited the twenty-third Psalm and her anxiety eased.

CHAPTER THREE

Betsy stood on the balcony and watched the ocean move back and forth from the shore in the early morning hours. Her wildflower-print sundress blew gently against her legs. After an uneventful arrival and check-in last night, she and Lillian had soaked in the hot tub before succumbing to the allure of sleep. Today, she wanted nothing more than to read her book and eat delicious food.

Lillian joined her. "I wasn't expecting the luxury suite. Thank you for bringing me."

"My pleasure." Betsy slid her feet into her pink sequined flip-flops. "I'm ready for breakfast."

As if on cue, Lillian's stomach growled. "Let me throw on some clothes, and I'll be ready to head down."

From the balcony, Betsy spotted poolside cabanas. She grabbed her beach bag. Reading beneath the shade of the large tent with the tropical breeze flitting over her sounded divine.

Lillian joined her, dressed in jeans and flowy tunic. They took the elevator to the restaurant on the main level. Hawaiian-themed Christmas decorations hung around the perimeter of the room. The buffet was open, but few people populated the indoor sitting area yet.

"Let's sit outside." Lillian grabbed a plate for herself and gave one to Betsy. They each chose a Belgium waffle smothered in syrup, an omelet, and a side of fruit.

The dining patio had filled with early risers. The gentle hum of conversation surrounded them. They claimed a table situated in the shade and far enough away from the door to avoid foot traffic. As they sat down, the waitress arrived at their table and took their order for drinks. Betsy leaned back in her chair and sighed.

Lillian unrolled her napkin and set her silverware on the table. "I didn't realize how many activities are available here. Did you see the brochures in the room? What should we do first?"

Betsy swallowed a bite of waffle. "I'll be reading or swimming today. What piques your interest?"

Lillian rested her elbows on the table, a huge grin spreading across her face. "Horseback riding."

"You'll enjoy that."

The waitress arrived with their drinks, interrupting their conversation.

Lillian took a sip of her orange-mango-pineapple drink and voiced her approval to the waitress, then turned to Betsy and described the adventure promised in the brochure.

Betsy listened as she watched a couple of women about their age looking for seats. They seemed as opposite as friends could be. The taller one, dressed in a floral romper, wore her red hair in a long braid hanging down her back. The woman flowed through the crowded dining hall the way Betsy imagined a mermaid would glide through the sea. The other woman wore straight-legged jeans and a dark blue, fitted T-shirt. She had styled her dark hair in a medium-length bob. Her steps were sure, yet her gaze darted around the dining space like a deer about ready to run.

When the taller of the two spotted them, Betsy waved and pointed to the empty seats at their table. "I hope you don't mind, Lillian."

"New friends are always welcome."

The ladies weaved their way through the crowd and joined Betsy and Lillian.

"You guys are life savers. I'm Aspen, and this is Megan." The mermaid friend set her food on the table. "We thought we might have to eat standing up. You sure you don't mind us sitting here?"

"Not at all." Lillian moved her plate to make room for Megan as well. "What brings you to paradise?"

Aspen grinned. "Relaxation and fun. You?"

Lillian and Betsy spoke in unison. "We're skipping winter." They burst out laughing.

"There must be a story there." Megan poured maple syrup on her pancakes.

Betsy chuckled. "A recent ice storm convinced me it was time to get out of town. For the whole story, news at eight."

Lillian elbowed her friend. "And . . ."

Betsy pointed a fork in Lillian's direction. "You are *not* telling everyone about my personal summers."

"I feel the pain." Aspen added salt and pepper to her eggs.

"Me too. Sounds as though we're all in a similar boat." Megan dragged a bite of pancake through the syrup on her plate. "Since we're not talking about summer"—she paused and everyone concurred—"what do you do when you're not skipping winter, and where are you from? I stage houses for selling and have recently moved to Omaha, where Aspen lives."

"Oooh." Betsy clapped. "That sounds fun. What do you do, Aspen?"

"I'm a house sitter. I'm working in Omaha right now, but I'll house sit anywhere. What about you, Lillian?"

"I'm an artist, mostly industrial art for businesses." Lillian pointed at Betsy, then herself. "We're both from Preston Hill, Nebraska."

Megan positioned her elbows on the table. "That's wonderful. My art talent reached its height in elementary school. Betsy, you?"

"I guess you could say that I'm spending my time figuring out what to do with my life. I'm thinking about possibly, someday, maybe opening a business." Betsy reminded herself to slow down on the plausible deniability in case starting a business never happened. Time to be positive. "I've been slushing around ideas since my husband passed several years ago, but nothing stands out as the best idea. Nowadays"—Betsy leaned forward and whispered—"with the change and my scrambled brain cells, it's even harder to narrow it down to one thing."

"Well, hello, ladies. We meet again." A deep voice from behind Betsy and Lillian addressed their new friends.

Betsy cringed. It was the unmistakable sound of rude-dude's voice from the airplane. What were the odds of them landing at the same resort? She was curious what the man's reaction would be when he recognized her and Lillian.

The man set his plate on the table closest to Megan. Keeping his gaze on her, he completely ignored everyone else. "I didn't introduce myself. I'm Greg. Do you mind if I join you?"

Megan directed his attention to the others.

Greg looked around the table. "Ladies? Do you mind more company?" He offered a blinding smile as though trying to win over a company bigwig. When his field of vision included Betsy and Lillian, he narrowed his eyes and pursed his lips. Then the ice melted as quickly as it formed. "I need to apologize to you both for my behavior in the terminal and on the plane. I am sorry for my rudeness. It's been a difficult couple of weeks. Family drama. I had just come from—" He let out a heavy sigh. His eyes watered and he shook his head. "I'm sorry, it's too hard to talk about. Still, that's no excuse. Please, accept my apologies."

"We all have rough days. You don't need to explain about your family. I'm Lillian and this is Betsy."

"Thank you for understanding. Does that mean I may join you beautiful ladies?"

Betsy waved toward the chair. "Make yourself at home." She understood all about family drama throwing people off their game.

"Thank you." Greg sat, then looked from Aspen to Megan and back to Aspen. "Have we met before?" I'm from Omaha, Nebraska. I've lived there for about a year, and I work at Scott and Mitchum construction company. Ring any bells?"

Aspen tilted her head. "I don't remember ever meeting you."

"It's said that we all have a doppelgänger. Maybe I've seen yours somewhere."

"That could explain it." Aspen took a sip of her drink. "What brings you to Hawaii, Greg?"

"Vacation. Saved up my vacation days, and here I am." He focused on Megan and began chatting with her.

Betsy listened to the conversation that she and Lillian were mostly left out of. There had to be more to this story.

She and Lillian finished their breakfast and lingered for another half hour, then made their excuses and departed for the day.

CHAPTER FOUR

Betsy headed for the pool and found an empty cabana. She settled into one of the loungers and started her e-reader. Lillian was off to horseback riding. More power to her. Betsy had no desire to be at the mercy of one of those powerful and beautiful creatures. She would watch from a distance, thank you very much.

She found her bookmarked place in the story and lost herself in its drama. Invested in the rising action of the story, Betsy was startled when water sloshed on her feet. Three young boys were jumping into the pool a few feet away from her, creating a swathe of water in the wake of their cannonballs. Where was their mother? She opened her mouth to instruct them about poolside etiquette, then shut her mouth as she remembered rude-dude's response to the crying child on the airplane. She snickered. If only she knew them. It would be more fun to splash them in return.

"Boys." A woman's voice commanded the young lads' attention. "You're too close to the other guests. Come over here so you don't splash everyone." Her instructions precipitated the boys' disappearance out of Betsy's line of sight.

Betsy opened her e-reader and attempted to find reentrance into the story world but found her mind wandering. Giving up, she pulled her hat down over her face. A nap in the middle of the day sounded heavenly. Taking deep breaths, she relaxed and started to doze off when a deep voice jerked her to full awareness. The distinctive timbre of his voice left no doubt in her mind that it was Greg.

"I told you . . . no, you listen to me. I'm doing my job. I'll get you the information."

Thankful that the curtained cabana concealed her presence, Betsy eavesdropped on the one-sided conversation. Not her finest moment, but he wasn't making it easy *not* to hear. She furrowed her brow at the intensity of Greg's voice.

"I know what I'm here for. I've already located the person in question." His voice faded as he walked away.

Betsy peeked around the curtain. Who had he found? Why was he looking for said person? Was this a missing person situation? She tapped her fingers against her e-book reader as the ideas twirled in her head. Maybe there was an inheritance involved. Could someone be in danger? Or was he an assassin? Should she call the police?

She halted her mind's trajectory. This wasn't a novel and, besides, the police wouldn't give any attention to a one-sided conversation that could mean a myriad of things heard by a fortysomething woman dealing with perimenopause. She blew out her breath. More information was needed.

Stuffing her e-reader into her beach bag, she headed back to the room to change. Time to put on her sleuthing hat. Tonight she would convince Lillian to be her co-conspirator.

Lillian stared at Betsy. "Do you remember what happened the last time you tried to play private detective? You promised you would stick to reading mysteries, not create them.

"What if someone *is* in danger? Can't we just keep our eyes open? We don't have to follow him or anything." Betsy scrunched her shoulders.

"Fine. That's it. No chasing anyone or sneaking around. Deal?"

"Deal." Betsy pulled out the brochure listing various activities in the area. "Now for the real reason we're here." She handed the paper to Lillian.

"You want to do an escape room?"

"You know me better than that. Third choice down."

"A mystery dinner? I have nothing to wear." Lillian held the back of her hand to her forehead in a dramatic pose.

Betsy snickered. "It says here to dress in something that people would have worn in the nineties. We can wear our Hawaiian shirts."

"That simplifies things. Okay, girlfriend. This is your vacation. I'm simply along for the ride."

Two hours later, Betsy and Lillian exited the elevator walking arm in arm. Guests milled about the lobby dressed in beachwear.

Betsy stared at the sign outside of the events room announcing an evening of Beach Bingo. "Great. It's obvious I missed the mark. Again." Ever since the change had started in earnest, she had been discovering—at the most embarrassing times—all sorts of loopholes in her thinking. It made her tired. It was like navigating through eel-infested waters.

"No, you don't. Your hormones will not ruin our night of fun. A year ago, it wouldn't have mattered if we confused events. You would have marched right in there dressed the way you are and stolen the show. Besides, Hawaiian shirts work for a beach party, too."

Betsy perked up. "Fair point."

"Hold your head up, and let's have some fun." Lillian led Betsy into the room. "Evidently it's an equal opportunity mixer." She pointed to Greg on the other side of the room.

Betsy followed the direction of Lillian's finger. All thoughts of disappearing fled. "And there's Megan and Aspen, too, over at that far table. I wonder if he's here with them."

"Shh. I may regret pointing Greg out to you if you insist on shouting our business to the whole room."

Betsy saluted her friend. "Aye aye, captain." She pulled Lillian to a spot with a better vantage point for observation. They watched Megan and Aspen meander to the buffet laid out for the event. Greg pulled out his phone and took a picture. From that angle, the image could include the two girls.

Betsy tugged on Lillian's sleeve. "Did you see that? Do you think he could be a stalker?"

"Betsy! He's probably taking a picture of the whole room. Everyone else is capturing the event, too."

Betsy's avid curiosity deflated. "You're right. I'm sure I'm making more of this than I should. Let's get some food." As they approached the buffet, Greg joined Megan and Aspen. He smiled and chatted with them a bit, then glanced over at Betsy and Lillian before hurrying out of the hall.

"What do you make of that, Lillian?"

"He would rather hang out with women his own age than someone our age?"

Betsy elbowed her friend. "Funny. Real funny. We're not *that* much older."

"Forget about him. Let's have fun tonight."

Betsy followed Lillian to the buffet, where they joined Aspen and Megan.

Aspen passed on Greg's apologies for not staying. He had a meeting to verify the authenticity of some artwork his boss sent him to purchase. He had been attempting to contact the seller all day, and he was finally available.

Betsy focused on her plate. That was probably what the phone conversation she'd heard earlier was about. She gave herself a lecture regarding her insatiable curiosity and love for an interesting story that often landed her in deep water. Greg's business wasn't any of her business, after all. She focused on the cuisine offerings. Especially the desserts. There was enough chocolate to keep her hormones content for a few hours.

CHAPTER FIVE

Betsy pulled her Monet-inspired tunic and bright turquoise tights from her suitcase and dressed quickly. Lately, any inclination to dress in her usual vivacious style had withered to a shadow of what it used to be, but she had packed a few of her favorite clothes anyway. In case being on vacation inspired her. Squaring her shoulders, she grabbed her beach bag and headed for the elevator.

Although Betsy had encouraged Lillian to enjoy separate activities, she was a bit disappointed to be alone. She shushed the voice in her head that called herself unwanted. "Thank you, Jesus, for loving me when I'm unlovable."

When the elevator doors opened to the lobby, Betsy stepped out and almost ran into Lillian.

Lillian took a step back. "Hey! Are you sure you won't join me snorkeling?"

"Can you really see me snorkeling? You have fun. I'll enjoy the winery a whole lot more."

"If you're sure." Lillian hugged Betsy, then caught the elevator to return to their room.

Before Betsy could delve into her emotional state of mind, her stomach growled. Distracted from her downward-tracking emotions, she hurried to the buffet and piled her plate with bacon-and-egg casserole and a waffle loaded with chocolate hazelnut spread. She nabbed a spot near the large picture windows and watched a middle-aged couple holding hands and looking at each other lovingly as they walked toward the exit.

She swiped a tear from her cheek. Why had she ranted at Samuel before she left on this trip? She deserved his hitting the pause button on their dating. It was becoming more obvious that it was time to follow Ginger's advice to make an appointment with the menopause specialist and get these hormones under control. In the meantime, she owed Samuel an apology. She reached for her phone, then hesitated. Food first to fortify herself. Then a private place to call him.

Betsy climbed into the van heading out to a nearby winery for a wine-and-cheese-tasting tour. She felt much lighter after having made her apologies to Samuel. They weren't necessarily back together, but at least they were talking to each other.

Betsy sat next to an older woman dressed in jeans and a purple tunic. Her brown, mid-length hair was pulled back into a ponytail.

She smiled when Betsy joined her. "I'm so glad I won't be sitting alone. Ever since our first visit, my husband, Freddy, prefers to hang out at the resort when I do the wine-tasting tour. I'm Anne."

"I'm Betsy. You've been to this resort before?"

"Every year since Freddy retired from the police department. We live in Wisconsin but need a bit of summer to get through our winters these days. We were thinking about moving to a state farther south, but with our kids and their families still in Wisconsin . . ." Anne shrugged. "What are grandparents supposed to do?" Her smile was infectious.

"I definitely needed a bit of summer this year." Betsy fanned herself. "External summer, that is. I'm cold one minute, hot the next."

"Ahh. I remember those days well. So does my husband."

"Any advice for surviving?"

Anne spent the remainder of the drive sharing stories from her journey through the change. Each one with a bit of a lesson attached but always spoken from a place of hope.

When they approached their destination, she placed her hand on Betsy's arm. "You'll get through this, and so will your man. Remember to take a step back when you feel overtaken by the darker emotions. It will keep you from a world of regret in your relationships. And take your friend's advice about that doctor. You'll be glad you did."

"Thank you for your encouragement." When she was older, Betsy wanted to be at least a little bit like Anne.

The van stopped, and everyone piled out. A second van pulled up, and another group disembarked. Betsy spied Megan and Aspen deep in conversation. She started to call out to them, but their groups headed in different directions. She would catch them later. For now, she was enjoying the company of her new friend.

As they walked toward the first building, a forest-green Lexus parked in a space across the lot from the vans. Greg exited the vehicle and walked in the direction of the other group. Was he looking for the girls? They better be careful.

Betsy and Lillian's friend group sat on the beach enjoying the sunset and dessert. Anne entertained the girls with stories about her husband, Freddy. He joined in from time to time, patted her arm, and kissed her on the cheek. He, the introvert, and she, the perpetual friend to everyone she met. They obviously loved each other and enjoyed one another's differences.

Betsy sighed. The belonging soothed her anxiousness that had been gathering in her heart for the past . . . well, for a while. After Ginger had married Mike, Betsy hadn't been able to hang out with her bestie as much as would have been nice. Lillian was her next bestie, but she also was busy with her spouse. Not that Betsy expected anything different, but she had been lonely.

She had Samuel, but he was as different as night and day from Betsy, and at times she felt as though she were the lesser of the two. Betsy contemplated how different from each other Freddy and Anne were, and yet they obviously loved each other deeply. Betsy needed to change the way she thought about her relationship with Samuel. Yes. That was what she would do. She closed her eyes, allowing the voices to dance through her head. A smidgen of who she really was beyond any change of life began to bloom again. God's peace enveloped her. She would be okay.

Greg appeared at the perimeter of the group, a drink in hand. "Hey, Megan, mind if I join you guys?"

Betsy watched the exchange. The man was persistent. She would give him that. *Lord, protect Aspen and Megan if there is anything untoward in his intentions.* It would be dangerous to trust a stranger too quickly.

"There's a chair right here. You're welcome to join us." Freddy pointed to an empty chair nearby.

Greg seemed to notice the older gentleman for the first time. He nodded and retrieved the chair, then placed it next to Megan.

Betsy put on her sleuthing hat. "Did you enjoy the vineyard today, Greg?"

Greg hesitated and glanced down at the drink in his hand before answering. "I went snorkeling today. Have you been yet?"

"I'm not sure I would enjoy snorkeling. I tend to get a bit claustrophobic." Betsy jotted down a mental note about his sidestep.

"They don't take you down deep. You're right at the surface and can pop up if you're uncomfortable. You might get a kick out of it." Greg took a sip of his drink.

Lillian pulled her feet underneath her. "You really should try it, Betsy."

Betsy covered her ears. "I can't hear you." She laughed. "Someday. Very far away. Tomorrow, I'm learning how to do the hula." Betsy put her arms in the air and pretended to dance while still sitting.

Anne patted her arm. "I'm not too fond of snorkeling, either. I watch the videos of other people doing it."

"That's my kind of undersea adventure." Betsy relaxed in her chair.

"Ziplining, though, is an adventure you need to try." Anne grinned. "Right, Freddy?"

"Absolutely." Freddy looked at the women around him. "I know when I should agree." He winked.

Betsy's eyes widened. Anne ziplining? That was completely unexpected.

Anne laughed. "So, which will it be? Snorkeling or ziplining?"

"I don't think . . . well . . ." Betsy sputtered her way to declining the invitation to snorkeling but considering ziplining. After all, it might be fun to fly. Once the attention reverted to the others, her mind continued to puzzle over Greg. If he lied about being at the winery, then he must have something to hide. Right? She remembered her promise to Lillian to only observe, and began backpedaling her thoughts about Greg. Maybe she had him all wrong.

Anne whispered to Betsy, "I noticed him there, too. That Lexus stood out in the parking lot."

"I was starting to think I had mistaken someone else for him."

"No mistake." Anne shook her head. "Those girls need to be careful."

"I couldn't agree more." If only Betsy could convince the girls of it.

Two hours later, Anne and Freddy made their excuses and returned to their room, with a promise to find them at breakfast. Lillian and Betsy were quick to follow their example.

"Wait up." Megan and Aspen called out to Betsy and Lillian.

Megan slid to a stop in the sand and reached out to Betsy to balance herself. Aspen, coming in at a more leisurely pace, patted her friend on the back. "Congratulations. You did indeed run faster than me."

Megan stood. "You weren't even running."

"My point exactly." Aspen linked arms with Megan on one side and Betsy on the other. "Hot chocolate, anyone?"

"Always." Betsy patted her ever-present beach bag. "And I have fudge."

Lillian excused herself and went to their room. The others ambled into the almost empty lounge area and prepared mugs of cocoa, then settled into cushiony chairs placed in the far corner. Aspen took a bite of Betsy's decadent, creamy chocolate. "Amazing. Do you make this yourself?"

Betsy nodded.

Megan licked her fingers. "You could sell this."

"Hear, hear. I agree." Aspen popped her last bit into her mouth. "Betsy, I need your help convincing Megan to attend an event on the other side of the island with Greg. She's not interested."

Betsy took a sip of her hot chocolate. "I don't mean to be a party pooper, but Greg lied about not being at the vineyard. Anne and I both saw him."

Aspen waved her hand as though she were swatting at a mosquito. "We know. We ran into him there."

Megan leaned forward and spoke softly. "He said he was picking up the artwork that he told us about last night. He asked us not to mention anything for security reasons. When you asked if he was at the winery, I'm sure he didn't want to talk about it in such a public setting."

Aspen nodded. "And by the way, I work at the same company where Greg said he works, and I finally contacted my boss in Omaha. He confirmed that Greg does work for him. He sent me a picture to verify. He also said that, if he had a daughter, he would let her date him. Does that ease your mind?"

Betsy knew how hard it was these days to find an honest man. If he checked out with Aspen's boss, then as long as Megan liked him, who was she to stand in the way of romance? Betsy nodded. "That does make me feel better. Just be careful, Megan."

Megan folded her paper napkin into a small square. "It's only been two days since we met him. And I don't know if I even *like* him enough to spend more time with him. Besides, it takes more than a few days to decide if someone is trustworthy. Betsy's right about being careful."

"Don't let fear keep you from something fabulous. What if it was a double date?" Aspen raised her eyebrows.

"If he loses interest before we get back to Omaha, then all his attentions are for show."

"True. But are you okay if he hangs out with us on vacation?" Aspen bumped her elbow against Megan's arm.

"Sure." Megan picked out another bite of fudge.

Betsy pondered the exchange. Something was off about the whole Greg situation, but she did breathe easier knowing that Megan wasn't walking into a potentially compromising situation with the man. She slapped one hand down on her knee and stood. "Ladies, I'm leaving you to your conundrum. Let me know how things progress with this Greg fellow." She waved goodbye and went to her room.

At this point, all she could do was keep her eyes open and pray.

CHAPTER SIX

Betsy twirled, allowing her long dress to swirl around her legs. She imagined a grass skirt swishing back and forth. What would Samuel think of this? "You said this is a *basic* hula class, right?"

Lillian swayed her hips from side to side. "Focus on having fun. You'll do fine."

"Easy for you to say. You've done this before."

"For five minutes at a birthday party when I was seven." Lillian giggled. "You should have seen me. I had no coordination as a child."

The attendees quieted their chatter as the hula teacher began her instruction. She explained that the hula was a storytelling dance conveying Hawaii's history, culture, and narratives. She shared the history of hula, the time it was outlawed, and how, years later, another king brought the hula back. Once the attendees understood the importance of the dance, she demonstrated each move they would learn today, explaining its meaning and how it fit into the story the dance was telling.

Samuel would enjoy this. He was always asking her to take ballroom dancing classes with him. It was time she accepted the challenge. She smiled at the idea.

The teacher turned on the music and went through the dance a portion at a time, allowing the attendees to practice the moves together. Betsy relaxed, allowing herself to fully enjoy the process. Even the mistakes.

By the end of the lesson, Betsy could do the entire dance. After the music ended, the teacher thanked them for coming and invited them to return and learn another dance.

Betsy danced her way over to Lillian. "Can we come back tomorrow?"

"I was hoping you would go ziplining with me."

Betty grimaced. "Can I think about it?"

"Sure. We'll figure it out later." Lillian gave Betsy a hug. "I want to visit with that couple over there for a bit. I met them when I went horseback riding."

Betsy waved her off. "You know me. Never met a stranger." She watched Lillian interact with her new friends until her attention was drawn down the beach to her right. Wearing sundresses, Megan and Aspen were traipsing through the sand with Greg. From behind a cabana, a guy dressed in shorts and a flowered shirt—similar to half the men on the beach—popped out and rushed toward the trio. Betsy watched as he grabbed Megan's purse, pushing her down in the process, then dashed down the beach toward Betsy. Greg bent next to Megan.

As the man drew closer, Betsy made out a giant octopus tattoo traveling up his leg. She looked around for help, but no one else seemed aware of what had happened, and Greg was still focused on Megan. Betsy kicked off her sandals, lifted her dress high enough that she wouldn't trip on it, and ran to intercept the thief. Plowing him down as though she were a linebacker wouldn't be wise. She spied a nearby group of kids jumping rope. Running over, she grabbed a spare rope, which was lying to the side, and waited in a spot with a clear view of the thief's trajectory. It would take a miracle for this to work, but she might as well try. As the man passed, she whipped it out in front of him, tripping him as it wrapped around his sea-creature-covered leg. The purse flew out of his hands, and he scrambled to get untangled.

Surprised that her efforts had worked, Betsy let out a whoop. Not bad for an out-of-shape perimenopausal woman. The thief ran off, leaving the stolen purse in the sand. Betsy made a beeline to retrieve it, but Greg beat her there, grabbed the purse, and headed back toward Megan.

Lillian ran to Betsy. "That was great. Are you okay?"

Betsy pointed her chin down the beach. "More worried about her." With Lillian trailing along, Betsy marched toward their new friend. They arrived as Greg handed Megan her purse.

"Thank you, Greg. So glad you were able to stop him." Megan let him help her stand.

"Anything for a lady in distress." Greg glanced at Betsy as though waiting for her to contradict him.

Betsy met Greg's gaze and considered his attempt to impress his love interest. It wasn't worth pointing out that she was the one who had saved the day. At least Megan wouldn't have to worry about someone stealing her credit card or anything else of value. Dealing with fraud was the worst.

Betsy focused on Megan. "I saw that guy knock you over. Did he hurt you?"

"I'm a bit sandy is all. And embarrassed."

Betsy patted her purse. "Nothing a bit of chocolate won't cure. Want a bite of some fudge?" Betsy included Aspen and Greg in the invitation.

Megan laughed. "Sure."

After the three friends had picked out their chocolate, Betsy walked with Lillian back the way they had come. She had to text Samuel about her latest escapade, taking down a thief.

Betsy stared at the sign outside the door of the events room. "How are they planning on doing a scavenger hunt here? This sounds too complicated. And all for a ten-dollar prize? After running down that thief today, I could have used a nice, relaxing night in."

"From the woman who plays detective?" Lillian looped her arm through Betsy's.

"Fair point."

"And the jackpot isn't ten dollars."

"Spit it out."

"Try a day at the spa for two."

"That's what I'm talking about." Betsy marched through the door, pulling her friend with her into the gathering crowd. "Let's get our food and nab a seat at the front while they're still to be had."

"Slow down, girlfriend. They opened early for the buffet. We have plenty of time."

Betsy came to a sudden stop, just inside the room. Lillian bumped into her from behind. Betsy pulled her friend close and pointed toward a far corner of the spacious hall. "Isn't that Greg over there?"

"Leave the guy alone. He's not some vicious crook. You heard what Aspen's boss said." Lillian started to walk away.

"That guy with him. I think he's the thief."

Lillian looped her arm through Betsy's. "How can you tell that from here? Most of the men are dressed in flowered shirts."

"Fine. Let's preview the buffet. I can see better from there anyway." Betsy kept an eye on the two men as she and Lillian weaved through the maze of tables and lined up on the far side of the buffet. "This spread is incredible." In addition to a wide array of fruit, there was a variety of meat choices. Despite the placards attached to the serving pans, she was unfamiliar with the dishes, but it looked to her like the options included some sort of pork, fish, and chicken. Quite a few other dishes that were new to her graced the lineup.

Lillian leaned closer. "I think that's Spam Musubi."

"Spam? I've heard stories about spam." Betsy shrugged. Forgetting her mission for coming tonight, Betsy loaded her plate. Including the Musubi. Why not take a chance?

Lillian nudged Betsy with her elbow. "They're coming this way. Take a close look. You'll keep wondering if you don't see for yourself."

The two men were deep in conversation. Greg stopped and got right in the man's face. The mystery guy shook his head. He reminded her of the thief, but nothing definitive stood out. It was possible she was wrong. The unknown man glared at Greg, who finally handed him an envelope.

"Did you see that?" Betsy strained to see if the man had a tattoo on his leg.

"Can you tell if it's the same guy?"

"No."

"Unless you know he's the thief, it's not our monkey, not our circus. It probably has something to do with that art deal."

"Traitor." Lillian's suggestion made too much sense. Once again, Betsy's crazy ideas were running rampant. Trying to soften her response, she bumped shoulders with Lillian. "I know you're watching after me."

"Let's try and win that spa day."

"Deal." Betsy followed Lillian to a table at the front of the room, glancing back over her shoulder one last time. Her gaze collided with

Greg's. He smiled and waved at her before he left the room. Was there money in the envelope? Was the guy grabbing Megan's purse a set up?

Reining in her thoughts, she told herself to forget it.

CHAPTER SEVEN

Betsy tapped her bright red fingernails on the counter as she waited. The hotel clerk lowered her horn-rimmed glasses on her nose and glared at Betsy, who scrunched her shoulders and mouthed an apology. Turning, Betsy admired how the sun glinted off the Christmas decorations draped on the fake palm trees in the lobby.

"You must be Betsy."

Betsy pivoted and faced a man a head taller than she and obviously well versed in working out. A smart choice for security detail—if anyone had cared to ask her. "That would be me."

"I'm Vince, head of security. You had some questions?"

"My friend's purse was grabbed yesterday. Her name is Megan Davis. We retrieved it, but she filed a report so that maybe it wouldn't happen to any of your other guests. I was wondering if you had caught the guy yet."

The man leaned against the counter. "You're the woman who stopped him."

Heat rose through Betsy's body and onto her face. "No one else was doing anything." She crossed her arms.

"If I could find a dozen as determined as you, we might not ever have any trouble around here." Vince pushed away from the counter. "That being said, you could have been hurt, so please leave the rescues and recoveries to our security team."

She plopped her hands onto her hips. "I think not. If I had, Megan would be without her passport, her ID, and her money. I won't stand idly by and let someone be hurt or taken advantage of."

"I respect you for that. However, as head of security, I have to ask you to stand down if any other situations come to your attention." He interrupted Betsy's protest. "I'm not listening to any other plans you may have about saving the day. Otherwise, I would have to do something about it. Capiche?"

Betsy narrowed her eyes. It wasn't actually permission, but she didn't want to get kicked out of the resort. She nodded. "Got it. Now, about my friend's incident report. Have you found out anything?"

"We filed a report with the police as well. Fortunately, the security footage from that area gave us a clean picture of his tattoo, which was enough for the police to link him to other such incidents. However, the footage didn't show a clear shot of the man's face. They're still working on identifying him. This happened yesterday. You'll have to be patient."

"Hopefully they'll find him soon. Thank you." Betsy started to walk away, determined to keep her eye out for errant octopuses climbing up a man's lower limb.

"There's a video that's gone viral you ought to see."

Betsy turned. "Viral?" Suspicion and dread tap danced on her insides as she took his offered phone. There she was in action mode roping the thief like he was a calf in a rodeo. She gasped and covered her mouth as she considered the reaction of her friends in Preston Hill, who were probably viewing this as they spoke. How would Samuel react?

"You always get your man?" The humor in the security officer's tone of voice as he took back his phone registered in her brain. His smirk told her he was enjoying her antics.

Several other guests gave her a thumbs-up as they walked past. A slow chuckle built inside her chest until she couldn't contain it.

"You're famous now." The guard winked and walked off, leaving Betsy sweating in her own personal sauna and wishing for a dunk in an ice bath. How could a few simple words and one wink bring on a menopausal response? She stamped her foot. She was so done with this. She grabbed a brochure from the front counter and fanned herself all the way out to the shuttle, where Lillian waited. Why had she allowed Lillian to talk her into ziplining?

Betsy buckled her hard hat in place, then attempted to step into her harness. Her feet tangled between the straps, and she landed on her rear end. Someone laughed, and a flush spread up Betsy's neck. Standing, she waited for help in order to avoid any further embarrassment.

After she was properly harnessed, she listened intently to the instructor's safety reminders and how-tos of ziplining.

Half an hour later, they were in line to ascend to the platform, where they would begin their flight through the air with the greatest of ease. A day ago, Betsy had thought it inconceivable that she would attempt this. She shifted under the unfamiliar weight of the pulley in her right hand and tightened her grip on the harness that would carry her through the forest for the next couple of hours.

Lillian tapped her on her shoulder. "Relax, friend. Someone's watching you."

Betsy refocused on the moment and noticed the youngster ahead of them. She guessed he was older elementary age. She relaxed her grip on the harness as he tugged on his mother's arm and pointed back at Betsy. The woman's countenance brightened. "Aren't you the woman who used a jump rope to stop that thief on the beach?"

Betsy raised her hand. "That would be me."

"My son thinks you rock. And so do I."

The tour guide called for the next in line. The pair in front of them moved forward.

"Thank you." Betsy smiled.

Lillian adjusted the gear she carried. "And *you'll* rock this ziplining, too."

Another call went out for the next in line. The young boy balked at getting on the platform. His mother looked at Lillian and Betsy. "He's not quite ready for stepping off the platform. Mind trading places?"

"No problem." Betsy understood how he felt. Was it too late for her to back out of this crazy stunt of an idea? She took one look at Lillian, knew she would never get away with it, and resigned herself to a terrifying adventure.

As the two friends passed the mother-and-son duo, Betsy turned to the kid. "You'll do great. I don't like heights, and I'm not particularly brave, but I'm doing this. And if I can do it, you can, too."

He offered a tentative smile and nodded. His mom mouthed a thank you. The tour guide called for the next in line to ascend the platform. As Betsy took the final steps, she berated herself for speaking up. She had effectively taken away any possibility of backing out of this lunacy. She moved into position on the right side of the platform. Lillian waited on the left side. The tour guide placed Betsy's pulley on the line and hooked on her halter and safety lines. Once he ensured she was safe to sail through the air, he prepared Lillian for flight.

The tour guide instructed them to stand at the edge of the deck and wait for him to give the all-clear. After a brief conversation with someone on the other end of his walkie-talkie, he told them it was time to step off the platform.

Lillian and Betsy looked at each other and stepped off the platform together. In the moment between standing firm on the platform and the cable taking on her weight, Betsy's stomach caught in her throat. The pulley began sliding along the cable, and Betsy clung tightly to the bar of her pulley above her head and squeezed her eyes shut.

"Open your eyes, Betsy. It's beautiful." Lillian's voice reached her from across the empty space between them.

Maybe if she didn't look directly below her, she would be okay. Betsy opened her eyes and took in the scenery around her. She was surprised that she rather enjoyed it.

Too soon, they arrived at the next platform and were unhooked to make room for more adventurers. She turned in time to see the young kid flying toward them with his arms and legs spread and a grin on his face wider than the Missouri river.

After his harness was unhooked, he ran over to Betsy. "I did it. I did it." He flung his arms around her for the briefest of moments, then ran a few feet away before he stopped abruptly and came back for his mother.

They traveled by ATV to the next line, which was quite a bit longer than the first one. It was only five to six feet off the ground for part of the trip and Betsy had the sensation of zooming at the speed of light.

"Betsy, hold my hand." Lillian reached across the space between them.

"Do I have to let go?" She gripped the bar tighter with one hand, then grabbed Lillian's extended hand. "This is great!" Laughing into the wind, she released her grip on the bar with her other hand, trusting the harness she sat in. "Look, Ma, no hands." She starfished, spreading her arms and legs the same way she had seen the young kid do. She couldn't wait to tell Samuel all about their adventures.

The air rushed past her, and all too soon, she came in for a landing on the next platform and was directed to the bridge they needed to cross to reach the final line. Betsy gaped at the foot bridge—a suspension bridge to be precise—they needed to cross. Their tour guide explained that it was the longest suspension bridge in Hawaii at 360 feet. He assured them it was completely safe, though they might feel it moving with the wind. Betsy froze. She was afraid of heights.

Unaware of Betsy's conundrum, Lillian headed across, chatting to someone else from the tour.

The young kid and his mother from the first line walked past Betsy. She took a deep breath and stepped onto the bridge. She paused and looked over the side.

She squeezed her eyes shut. "The Lord is my shepherd." This was worse than the ziplines. "He leads me beside still waters." She dared to open her eyes and found the kid staring at her.

He tilted his head. "You know, I don't like heights, either. And I'm not particularly brave, but *I'm* doing this. And if *I* can do it, you can, too."

Betsy squinted at the kid. "Using my own words against me?"

"Is it working?"

"I think it might be." She eased her way forward. The occasional glance over the side revealed more of the beautiful handiwork of God. The one who held her in his hands. No matter if it was while she crossed this bridge or navigated her way through the change. Tension oozed out of her body. Standing tall, she finished crossing the bridge with confidence and high-fived the kid. "Thank you." Only one more line left.

By the time they finished the final line, Betsy was exhausted but happy. They returned their equipment to the starting point of their adventure and headed out to their shuttle. A group of teenage boys waiting near the door hollered at her and waved. They were on a church youth group outing and recognized her from the video of her roping the thief. They insisted on taking a picture with her. The group crowded next to her, and their leader snapped the image, then texted her a copy.

She laughed all the way back to the resort. What a trip this was turning out to be.

CHAPTER EIGHT

Betsy climbed out of the car and stared at the helicopter sitting on the helipad. Lillian had finally convinced Betsy to take a helicopter ride on their last full day at the resort. After surviving ziplining, Betsy figured that an open-door helicopter ride would be a breeze. Literally. She laughed. Yesterday, that thinking had sounded reasonable. Now? Not so much. She glanced over at Aspen and Megan visiting with Greg. Lillian and Anne chatted a few feet away. The only one missing from their resort friend group was Anne's husband, Freddy. He had chosen to hang out at the beach because he hated heights. If only that excuse had worked for her. She followed her friends to the office.

An hour later, after being duly educated about helicopter riding safety, Betsy followed the others outside. They were loaded onto the helicopter and buckled in with more reminders about safety. Lillian and Anne sat in the front seat next to the pilot. The rest of them were buckled in behind the pilot. Greg sat next to the right hole where the door should be, and Betsy sat on the left side with the Omaha girls between them. Why couldn't she have been in the middle? Better make the best of it. Goggles on. Headphones on and sound checked. Phones secured on lanyards. They were ready to take off.

The helicopter rose off the ground, the roar of the machine bleeding through Betsy's earphones. The pilot flew them out over the water, then banked left to travel back inland. Looking at the water below with nothing but her seatbelt keeping her from falling out, the full effect of the doors-off tour took her breath away. The helicopter leveled out, and she had to admit that the beauty of the West Maui Mountains was spectacular. The pilot described various points of interest along the way. Betsy took photos of the Kohau Falls, seen in *Jurassic Park*, and the Wall of Tears with seventeen waterfalls, several of which were hundreds of feet high, before the pilot headed across the channel toward Molokai.

The water rushed past underneath them as they neared Kanaha Rock, an island bird sanctuary that looked like a swimming turtle. Along the coast of Molokai, the tallest cliffs in the world greeted their flight, and the Papalaua Falls cascaded over 250 feet. Too soon, the pilot headed back across open water to Maui.

As Betsy watched the surf breaking on the reefs below, she realized how relaxed she felt. Samuel would have enjoyed this, too. Maybe they could come back together someday. A flush crawled up Betsy's neck. She was getting a bit ahead of herself. Would he be interested in continuing their relationship when she returned? She prayed this pause on her overwhelm had given her the perspective she needed to wade through the change with more grace than she had exhibited so far.

A few more minutes and they were back at the airport. Once everyone was standing on solid ground, they gathered in front of the helicopter for a picture of them all together. *Lord, I know you're with me through this season. Help me hang on to this peace I'm feeling right now.*

An hour later, Betsy dropped onto the couch in their suite at the resort. What a day. She pulled out her phone and watched the video clips from her ride in the sky. She posted three of them to her social media before following Lillian's example and taking a short nap before dinner with their new friends.

Betsy slipped on her red flats and examined her final appearance in the mirror. Her bright floral tunic over white leggings was a statement of sorts and the red flats the exclamation mark. Not bad for a hormonally challenged woman figuring out how to hold on to her mojo in the sometimes treacherous season of the change. She added a touch of bright red lipstick and a dab of perfume before she and Lillian joined their new friends for dinner. Freddy and Anne had suggested a luau.

Lillian, Aspen, and Megan walked a few car lengths ahead of them, leading the way to their shuttle. Arm in arm, Anne and Betsy trailed behind the other women. Freddy and Greg followed at the rear. They made quite the mishmashed entourage. Six days ago, they had been strangers, and now, if Betsy was any judge of character, they would be exchanging Christmas cards for years to come. Except for Greg. He didn't seem like the greeting card type of guy.

Anne patted Betsy's arm. "You're much more relaxed than when we met. Adventuring suits you."

"It's what the good doctor ordered." Betsy pointed upward.

"He is indeed good."

A car sped past, then squealed to a stop slightly beyond the girls at the front of their group. Betsy gaped as a man wearing a face mask and baseball cap exited the car and grabbed Megan. She screamed and fought against him. Lillian and Aspen hit the man with their fists and purses.

A second man, wearing a mask and graphic T-shirt, jumped out of the car and pushed Lillian and Aspen away, knocking them to the ground before he helped baseball-cap-guy tug Megan toward the car. Betsy told

Anne to stay back, then ran to help Megan. Greg zipped past and pulled baseball-cap-guy off Megan before punching him in the face. Both assailants joined forces against Greg.

The driver rounded the car, wrapped his arms around Megan, and dragged her, kicking and scratching, toward the vehicle. Betsy had to help her get away. She rushed forward and hit the driver over the head with her bag. He pushed Megan to the ground and turned to face Betsy. Aspen leapt on his back, and Lillian flailed him with her purse.

Anne squatted next to Megan while Freddy helped Greg fight off the crazed duo from the car. When a security guard rushed out of the resort and shouted at the attackers, the would-be abductors ran back to their vehicle and took off.

Greg hurried to Megan, who was lying on the concrete. "Are you okay?"

"What happened?" Megan sat up with Greg's assistance.

The security officer shook his head. "There've been a couple of attempted tourist abductions on the island recently. They've become more aggressive each time. You were lucky. Do you mind coming in and filing a report? It will help the police find these guys."

Freddy rested his arm around Anne's shoulders. Lillian, Aspen, and Betsy huddled together out of the way and watched.

Greg helped Megan to her feet, and they followed the security officer inside. Greg had thrown himself into protecting Megan without any hesitation. The evidence pointed to Betsy being wrong about the guy.

Unless . . . it had all been staged.

Betsy shook her head, refusing to visit that rabbit hole again. He and Megan would make a great couple.

Betsy left the rest of their group waiting outside and followed Greg and Megan. Vince, the head security guard, nodded at her. "You have

quite a team there. If you guys ever want a job in paradise, give us a call."
He winked and walked out of the building.

CHAPTER NINE

Finally packed, Betsy moved her suitcase and carry-on into the living room portion of their suite. After the debacle with the attempted abduction last night, the group of new friends went to the luau and enjoyed a fun evening together. It had been as much to help Megan past the trauma as it was having a last evening together. Megan had basked in the attention of Greg all night.

Greg apologized to everyone for any misunderstandings he caused and answered all their questions. Including what he knew about the abduction attempt. Evidently, someone in the art world threatened his boss, and Megan became their target. On behalf of his boss, as a way of apologizing, Greg paid for the group's luau.

Why had Betsy allowed so many minor things about him to invade her head space? Was she trying to prove she was still useful? Whatever the reason and despite loving mysteries, she was moving on from her wayward suspicions.

Lillian joined Betsy. "I'm definitely ready for breakfast now."

"Me too. I'm glad we didn't take an early bird flight with Greg and the Omaha ladies."

Betsy made a beeline for the door. "I hope they stay in touch."

The two friends hurried downstairs for the breakfast buffet. Freddy and Anne were waiting for them outside of the restaurant. They were leaving for another part of the island for the rest of their holiday and wanted to say bye. Anne hugged each of the other women and promised to keep in touch. She tucked her hand through her husband's arm. "Keep being you, Betsy. Don't let this changing season change who you are at heart."

"Great advice." Lillian rested an arm on her friend's shoulder.

Betsy swiped at the moisture gathering in the corner of her eye as Anne and her husband left. Samuel had said something similar about the importance of being true to who she was even when her world felt as though it was falling apart. And to remember she wasn't alone on the journey. She was too stubborn, and it was time that changed. She looped her hand through Lillian's arm. "I hear those omelets and pancakes calling."

They joined the short line and chose their food. With plenty of open spaces, they found seating near a window. Lillian sat opposite Betsy with her back to the door.

"I need a chef to fix me breakfast every morning." Betsy closed her eyes and savored a bite of pancake drenched in maple syrup.

"Didn't you say that Samuel is a great cook?"

Betsy's eyes flew open, and she felt her face grow hot for reasons other than hormones. "I better take that into account…" She did a double take when a tallish man in a Hawaiian shirt breezed through the restaurant doors. His gaze landed on their table. "Were you expecting—"

"Lillian, my love." The man snuck up behind his wife as she started to turn.

"Randy!" She practically leapt from her seat and threw her arms around him. "What are you doing here?" She turned to Betsy. "Did you know about this?"

Betsy shook her head.

Randy put a finger under Lillian's chin and drew her attention back to him. "Would you enjoy spending Christmas in paradise? I've already booked a room through the new year, assuming—"

"Yes."

Betsy clapped her hands as they kissed. They had an amazing Christmas ahead of them.

After a full day of travel, the plane taxied to the terminal at Omaha International Airport. It had been a pleasant flight. Every one of the passengers had been in a festive spirit. Before Betsy skipped town, creating a Christmassy atmosphere in her home—which was normally a delight—had been reduced to one more thing on her list to get done. But in her heart, Betsy felt things shifting back to normal. Her new normal. She was growing excited about decorating her house for Christmas.

After the pilot turned off the "fasten your seatbelt" sign, Betsy grabbed her carry-on from the overhead bin as well as the one belonging to an older woman sitting next to her. Betsy was ready to get home. Ginger and Mike should already be here to pick her up. The resort had the best sleeping accommodations that she had ever had at a hotel, but tonight it would be wonderful to sleep in her own bed.

After waving down an airport golf cart for her elderly seatmate, Betsy headed to the baggage carousel. She double-checked her messages for pick-up information from Ginger and Mike. Nothing. They were still nowhere in sight as she approached the crowd waiting for their luggage.

One man stood out from the rest. Samuel. Standing five foot seven to his six feet, she had always enjoyed walking beside him. And handsome? He was a looker with green eyes that captivated her heart each time their gazes met.

Her steps faltered, then she hurried her pace until she stood in front of him. "You came for me."

"Of course." Samuel took both her hands in his. "Betsy, you brighten my world."

"But you wanted a break in our relationship."

"More of a pause. Betsy, you are one of the most alive people I know. I hope someday you can see yourself the way I do."

"I think I've made a start on this trip."

"I saw the videos online—as did everyone in Preston Hill." He laughed. "I can't wait to hear the rest of the story."

"It's a lot easier on vacation. Back home?" She glanced at her feet. "I'll probably need a lot of help."

"I'll be right here." He cupped her face with both his hands. "Merry Christmas, my love."

Betsy's eyes widened. His *love?*

He drew her close and kissed her. He was definitely a keeper. Vacation in paradise had been nice, but Betsy preferred to do her living in Preston Hill with those she loved. She leaned into Samuel's embrace and returned his kiss. Confidence surged through her as though someone had pulled back the curtains in a dark room to let in the sun.

God was bringing her through life's changes—whatever they were—a stronger, better person.

A Note from the Author

I hope you had as much fun reading about Betsy as I had writing "Pause That Thought." One thing I know is the best place to find inspiration for stories is smack dab in the middle of reality. That butt-sledding part in "Pause That Thought"? Yep! I did that on a particularly icy day in the winter of 2024. LOL. Perimenopause—been there, done that, too! Not a single health provider asked how I was handling the change nor offered options to help me get through in one piece. By the grace of God, I live to tell the tale. Although now that I'm (clear throat) a few years past that phase of life, I really wish someone had informed me of better ways to deal with symptoms.

But I digress . . . it's getting through today's changes that has our attention right now. Whether it's peri- or postmenopausal or other health issues, family drama, an overly stuffed life with not enough time to breathe, financial burdens, or some other challenge, God lights the way for us to get through it with encouragement from his Word, the strength of a friend to lean on, hope that fills our heart during prayer, or simply resting in our time with him. He is our Shepherd.

Like Betsy, with God guiding us through life's changes—whatever they are—we can be stronger, better people.

Angela

ACKNOWLEDGMENTS

A huge thank you goes to my family for their patience when my time is consumed with writing and always being there cheering me on! And my appreciation is broad and wide for my Mosaic sisters! They are always there with a wealth of knowledge to share and a willingness to help when needed. Without a doubt, I wouldn't be publishing my books today without them.

ABOUT THE AUTHOR

Angela D. Meyer writes fiction that showcases God's ability to redeem and restore the brokenness in our lives. Now that her two children she homeschooled are grown, she works as a Chiropractor's Assistant. When she's not at work, she stays busy writing and learning how to grow things. She enjoys sunrises and sunsets, hanging out with friends, a good laugh, and reading. Someday, she would love to vacation by the sea. Learn more about Angela's books and subscribe to her newsletter at www.angeladmeyer.com

TITLES BY
ANGELA D. MEYER

THE MOSAIC COLLECTION: NOVELS

This Side of Yesterday

The Applewood Hill Series
Where Hope Starts
Where Healing Starts
Where Joy Starts

THE MOSAIC COLLECTION: ANTHOLOGY STORIES

"The Jukebox Café" in *Hope is Born*
"Returning to Christmas" in *A Star Will Rise*
"Jillian's Refuge" in *Song of Grace*
"Reinventing Josie" in *All Things New*
"Reclaiming Tomorrow" in *A Whisper of Peace*
"Rekindling Her Dream" in *Dancing in the Rain*
"Gifting Christmas" in *A Weary World Rejoices*

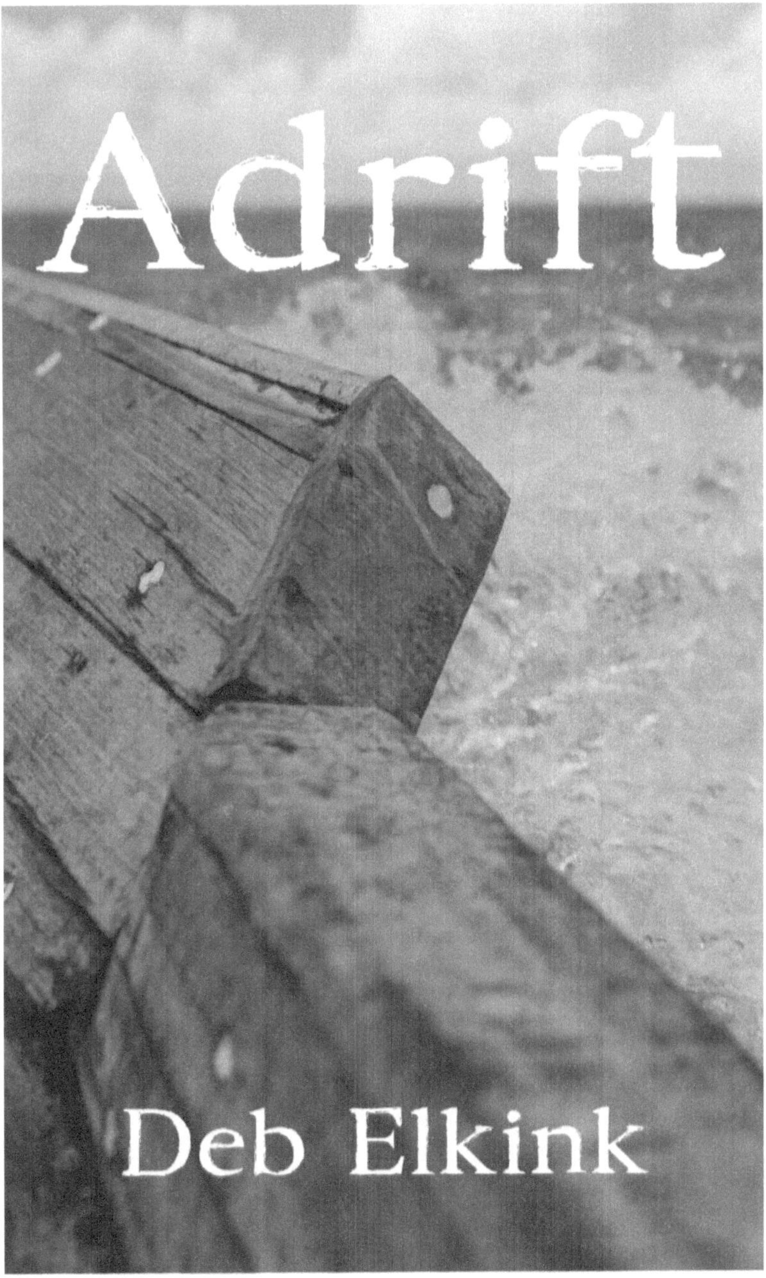
Adrift
Deb Elkink

ADRIFT

Deb Elkink

Kallum MacVicar, wetting his feet in academics, volunteers for a month-long teaching stint at a mission school on a tropical island, avoiding a harsh Canadian winter while earning college credit. He meets local Bahamian beauty Samara Hanson, who is eager to swim on her own but is flirting with personal disaster.

Are Kallum and Samara in over their heads?

There is one spectacle grander than the sea, that is the sky;
there is one spectacle grander than the sky, that is the interior of the soul.
(Victor Hugo)

"I am the light of the world.
Whoever follows me will never walk in darkness,
but will have the light of life."
John 8:12 (NIV)

ADRIFT

Kallum MacVicar tossed his backpack into the rear of the floatplane alongside the boxes and tarped containers stacked from the floor to the top of the cabin. He swung into the right-hand front seat.

"Welcome to your missions adventure, my friend." The pilot, Chad, wore aviator sunglasses and a headset. He stuck out his hand. "Good to see you again outside the classroom."

"Way outside." Florida was a whole world apart from northern Alberta and its frigid winter realities. Kallum shook the older guy's hand but would rather have given him a hearty man hug, having recently sat under Chad's enlightening talks as visiting lecturer on Johannine literature. Kallum also had Chad to thank for this winter reprieve—the perfect suggestion for his undergrad project.

"Wait until you taste island life." Chad grinned as though he knew something Kallum didn't, then clicked his hand mike and spoke into it. "Miami Center, Cessna 206, November one seven niner four, departing marina. Request taxi and departure instructions."

They were soon airborne and soaring between crystalline waters and billowing cumulus cells, buffeted by turbulence but able to chat if they raised their voices above the noisy cabin hum and whir. The deep blue ocean covered the curve of the earth as far as Kallum could see. He caught an occasional flicker of the plane's shadow on the water, and blinding sunlight glinted fiercely back at him from the briny expanse.

"How high up are we?" Kallum hadn't flown often enough to even estimate the distance from plane to ocean's surface.

Chad waved his hand towards the cockpit dials. "Altimeter shows us at 7,500 feet."

Right. Kallum had forgotten to look at the Cessna's instrument panel, not that he understood many of the light aircraft's readings anyway. He'd taken his one-hour freebie session a whole year ago, at his first thought of getting his private pilot's license. If he could ever afford lessons.

"And we're going, um"—Kallum checked for the right gauge—"178 knots an hour?"

Chad nodded. "Yep. Should take us under two hours to hit the shoreline of Eleuthera."

And a well-earned respite from his studies. Kallum had done his research before applying for the dean's approval on his winter interim proposal. That is, he'd contacted Chad for a written reference and to request a ride on his island-hopper cargo delivery route. He'd asked his parents for a loan to cover medical insurance and unanticipated expenses. And he'd read all he could regarding the so-called "out islands"—thirty or so inhabited spits of land amongst thousands of cays and islets and atolls in the chain making up the archipelagic Commonwealth of The Bahamas.

Of course, only a few of the islands qualified for Kallum's month-long vacation-assignment, which was to put into practice what he'd been learning in college—his steppingstone to ultimate enrolment in seminary for a theological Master of Arts degree, still some years off. Kallum's top grades and his connection to missionary pilot Chad had assured he'd get the placement at Morningstar Secondary Academy—an outreach supported by international churches and serving families scattered throughout the maritime nation.

Chad leaned towards Kallum. "Looking forward to your first teaching post?"

"Sure am. I'm calling my series 'The Theme of Light According to Saint John.'" He'd be instructing about a hundred students during five one-hour periods weekly through January, concentrating on the necessity of gaining knowledge, or *episteme*, of Scripture and then applying that through wisdom, or *sophia*. Kallum's beginning Greek study was holding him in good stead, and his choice of subject matter should please the New Testament scholar-pilot, who'd turned him onto John's themes in the first place.

"Ah, good stuff." Chad gave a validating thumbs-up. "That leaves you enough time for getting to know the community, touring the island, and catching the waves."

"I'm counting on it." Kallum couldn't wait to expound in the classroom—he'd been given such a great education himself and was itching to share it with willing younger minds—and the intercultural immersion would add depth to his vocation. As for water sports, that wasn't really his thing. Except maybe lake fishing.

"Morningstar's principal has a reputation for turning out high-scoring pupils."

"Good to know." Kallum's foreign volunteer participation under Edward Hanson would look good on his résumé. He'd been pumped to receive the board's acceptance letter along with a personal invitation to billet with the Hanson family. "I guess he's used to interns."

"Yep, good guy." Chad's eyes slid sideways towards Kallum. "First time traveling?"

"Not really." He was twenty, after all, even though he still lived at home for the time being. "I mean, my parents took me and my older brother as kids on trips to Montana for cattle sales. And one summer we drove south along the coast through the Redwoods." Saying it aloud really did make him sound inexperienced and hinted at his introversion.

But Chad didn't flinch. "The way the girls flocked around you during my class at the college was a trip of its own." He smirked and punched Kallum in the shoulder. "You've got a gift with the ladies, man."

"I hadn't really noticed." Kallum's cheeks burned.

Chad chortled. "Nothing to be ashamed of. Just keep up those top marks of yours."

Kallum rubbed the stubble on his chin. He hadn't considered feeling ashamed. Besides, not having a girlfriend at his age wasn't a defect, was it? As Chad intimated, it wasn't as though he didn't get offers. Mom and Dad had taught him caution, that's all. No wonder his confidence lay more in his intellect than in his communication skills, raised as he was on an isolated farm with an audience limited to the household—though he sometimes preached to the chickens for practice. But he sure did know his scholastic material, having been homeschooled by his resourceful mother.

Chad busied himself on the radio, checking weather or something, so Kallum focused on the view. The pillowy clouds and cradle-like swaying of the plane, along with his sleep deprivation due to the economy seventeen-hour flight schedule zig-zagging down to Miami, almost lulled him into slumber. He resisted, and eventually small islands came into view—gashes of lush green torn into the brilliant turquoise waters, outlined by pale sand beaches.

Even so, Kallum must have dozed off momentarily. He jolted awake with popping ears, and he plugged his nose to swallow. They'd descended almost to sea level and were banking steeply to the right.

"Get an eyeful of that," Chad said, pointing.

Kallum sucked in a quick breath. A long, narrow island sharply divided the cobalt of the Atlantic Ocean depths from the teal-green tropical shallows on the other side. "Is that the Glass Window Bridge I read about?"

"Top tourist site on the island, supposedly the narrowest place on earth at a mere hundred feet across. It was originally an intact limestone arch, according to early seafarers." Chad leveled the plane's wings, then radioed the tower for landing guidance. Returning the mic to its hook, he smiled over at Kallum. "Welcome to one of the prettiest places on earth."

"You sound as though you'd like to live here."

Chad raised one eyebrow. "It's got its dark underbelly."

"Oh?"

"I'm an aviation missionary. I wouldn't be coming to Bahamas if it were actually heaven. Neither would you."

"True, that." Kallum chewed his lower lip. "I hear they get horrific hurricanes at times."

"Yep. Another Category 5 blew its way through here a few years ago. My organization is still catching up with the disaster relief for that one." Chad jerked his thumb towards the crates in the back of the plane. Then he frowned. "But I wasn't talking only about physical storms. The people here need spiritual truth."

Chad squinted at him, and Kallum wondered what that older, more mature sight might be sensing about his soul. No one was perfect, after all, but wasn't Kallum here for the same purpose as Chad? And wasn't he doing his best to get all the knowledge of the Word into his head so he could help others through spiritual storms?

The pilot shut him out for a while then, following instructions from the island's tower and answering in cryptic pilot lingo—"Say again" and "Roger." Flying southerly, Chad lined up the Cessna's nose with the island's shore as they further descended, then touched down on the water, skipping twice as Chad worked the rudder. They taxied on the surface of the gentle waves to the docking facilities, and then Chad shut the plane down.

"Wow, that was amazing."

The corners of Chad's eyes crinkled. "Your first seaplane landing?"

"Poetry in motion, bro."

Chad twisted around to grip Kallum's backpack as well as a carton labeled "Eleuthera for Hanson" and hefted them over the seatback onto Kallum's lap. "Give my best to Eddy."

Kallum tipped his head sideways. "You're not coming with me to the school?" He glanced around at the palm trees fanning the eternal blue of sky and sea, at the row of picturesque, candy-colored colonial houses along the beach road.

"Nope. I've got to bounce on over to Exuma with parts and supplies before sunset. I'm often in the vicinity of these islands, so I might see you again before your return trip."

"How do I get to the academy?" Kallum opened his door to the warm breeze.

Chad pointed towards a golf cart. "My buddy Bembe is expecting to transport you in his fine chariot." He bopped Kallum on his head—"Take her easy"—and then, as Kallum unfolded his tall frame onto the wooden dock, Chad's tone changed. "And don't get into any trouble."

Kallum gave him a mock salute. What trouble could he possibly encounter on this paradisiacal island? He was ready for anything.

Samara Hanson had a secret.

She stared into the mirror as she sat before her bedroom desk, dusting copper blush onto her cheeks and expertly applying smoky liner to her lids. She was more polished in her daily life than any of her friends all dressed up—especially as she remembered them at last spring's high school graduation, with their pudgy bodies squeezed into tacky polyester gowns.

Yes, Samara had a secret she held close to her heart. A girl needed her own inner life, after all, particularly when held captive by parents who both insisted she stay home this year, without pay, to help with the school's administration. Or so they said. Samara suspected it was a ploy to keep her naïve for a while longer. Well, no one was going to rob her of her classified information until she exposed it when and to whom she wished.

Beneath the sluggish ceiling fan spreading around another layer of mugginess—no air-conditioning for the school's staff family—she heard her three teen brothers boiling into the house after last period. They tumbled past her open door, tearing off their hand-me-down uniforms before reaching their room, two of them in hot pursuit of the third.

"We's goin' to break ya harm!"

"Yinnah tink so, eh?"

Samara gritted her teeth and barked above their chaos. "Speak proper English, you bounders." Her words were authoritative, convincing to her own ears, even rather British.

They settled down, then, certainly knowing that, if their mother heard, she'd get after them for using the dialect. Mama ensured all four of her offspring were good examples to the resident kids and to the parents who sent them to Morningstar Academy.

Good examples. Samara was sick and tired of being a good example. What she would give to cut loose now and then.

She studied her reflection more closely—a perfect Bahamian cocktail of rich mocha complexion nearly dark as Mama's, untamed curls almost blonde as Daddy's, pouty-full lips, and Nordic-blue eyes that held ice. She snapped up her phone and took a quick selfie. She was photogenic, no denying it. The island boys thought so, too, and posted their random pics all over the 'Net. Come to think of it, that exposure might be a factor contributing to her current hush-hush plans. There's nothing like a little social media publicity to shoot a girl to fame.

"Samara," her mother called from the kitchen of their three-bed-room-plus-den home—a low cement bungalow with one single, pathetic bathroom. "Samara, I need you."

"Coming." She was always needed by someone. Her father couldn't do without her computer skills, her mother required help in the kitchen, and her siblings' homework was too difficult for them—or all three scoundrels were on the spectrum. She turned off the light of her makeup mirror and padded barefoot down the hallway.

Mama met her with an armload of linens fresh off the line. "Please make the guest bed. And, for heaven's sake, tie back your unruly hair."

Samara fixed a smile on her recently glossed lips. "Yes, Mama." She bunched her hair into a messy self-knot that would surely soon break free. "Another intern coming from the US?"

"Canada this time."

Samara bundled up the bedding and burrowed her nose into their wind-borne scent while her mother scuttled off on another of the never-ending chores demanding her attention. The family's last visiting volunteer who'd used these sheets—an old-maid Floridian librarian with a perm, of all things—had brought her own pillow. That sort of said it all. Nothing was quite good enough for her—not Mama's peas and rice or Daddy's Swedish pancakes or even Samara's hotdogs roasted on a stick over a beachside fire. Not the academy's collection of books or its lending check-out system or its abysmal return rate. And the woman was squeamish about cockroaches, offering the Hanson boys no end of delight as they caught the insects in the schoolyard and seeded them into her daily life with increasing frequency and creativity, invariably sending Mama into a cleaning frenzy.

Just then a ninth-grade dormitory student happened by the open kitchen door. "Miz Samara, can I lend a hand wit' ya bed?"

"I can do it myself." She flared her nostrils.

"You wex?"

"No, Taja, I'm not angry." These kids should keep their islandish noses out of Samara's business. But, then, she'd been one of them not so long ago. She half shrugged. "Just busy. Run along, now." Dorm kids like Taja, sent here from another of the out islands by Christian parents skeptical of the public system, at least got the chance to *go* somewhere. They weren't stuck like Samara.

Kallum loved what he was seeing. Perched on the edge of his faux-leather seat, he reveled in the colors and smells and sounds of the island as the golf cart Bembe was driving on the left-hand side of the road trundled by open-fronted food stalls, and a straw market where women were weaving bags, and a group of chanting girls with cornrow braids taking turns at skipping rhythmically in and out of a double jump rope.

Bembe had a booming voice and a substantial belly that moved with his laughter. In a heavy accent challenging for Kallum to decipher, Bembe introduced himself as janitor, driver, and general fix-it guy for Morningstar Secondary Academy. He was married, he asserted, to the best cook in all of Bahamas, and according to him the missus kept the bellies of the four dozen residential teens filled with johnnycake and pig feet souse and the best guava duff the world had to offer.

"You ain't never eat guava duff?" Bembe's shaggy, graying eyebrows popped high.

"I don't even know what duff is." Kallum had tasted guava, of course, peculiar foods being part of Mom's curriculum.

Bembe's eyes bulged, and he howled in jollity. "You po' skinny white bey left to starve wit' no guava duff."

Kallum, at nearly six feet four and able to bench-press 250 pounds thanks to years of pitching bales at home, chuckled out loud. And Bembe had no idea of Kallum's own Canadian mixed bloodline—Scots enrichened by Cree, giving him an appetite for both shortbread and bannock.

"So tell me about duff." He listened to Bembe's description of a dough-wrapped fruity dessert laden with cinnamon and allspice, steamed, and topped with butter-rum sauce.

This next month might see Kallum gaining weight.

They pulled onto the school compound, comprised of several flat-roofed, aqua-painted, concrete buildings forming an open-ended square. At Bembe's boisterous "Hiya, Mr. Hanson! You in de office?" a raw-boned man in his early fifties, with ruddy cheeks and wearing a suit jacket, emerged from one of several doors facing the interior courtyard.

Hanson immediately called back through his office door, "Ladies, please present yourselves for introduction." He stepped towards the golf cart, his expression pleasant, welcoming. Kallum slid out of the cart and onto the yard's rough pavement.

"Special delivery, sir." Bembe lumbered out of the vehicle, placing Chad's package and Kallum's knapsack on the ground. "Got ya box and"—he pointed his chin at Kallum—"ya bey, so I'll park dis old gal now."

Mr. Hanson dipped his head towards the driver. "Thank you, Bembe." He turned to Kallum. "And you must be the new teaching aide. Pleased to meet you, Mr. MacVicar."

"Just Kallum, please."

"I'm Edward Hanson, at your service." They shook hands, but Kallum noted the man didn't suggest associating on the basis of his first name. So "Mr. Hanson" it was to be. For all the propriety, he seemed a humble man, his sloping shoulders suggesting not so much disappointment as, perhaps, heavy personal burden.

Kallum's dad had the same posture.

The three full-time female teachers made an appearance to greet him, and then two other women stepped onto the porch of an adjacent building.

A glance at the younger one took Kallum's breath away.

Mr. Hanson cleared his throat. "My wife, Nacheline Hanson."

Kallum dragged his gaze from the beauty towards the stern, slim lady who was untying and removing her floral pinafore apron. She said, "I hope your journey wasn't too tiring."

Her enunciation was much more succinct than Bembe's *patois*. Kallum kept his eyes fixed on Mrs. Hanson by sheer willpower until, after a few more pleasantries, the woman said, "This is our daughter, Samara."

Finally. Kallum's eyes latched onto Samara. He let the left side of his mouth tug upwards in what his best buddy called his "babe grin."

"Nice to meet you." He stretched his hand to shake hers. Samara's skin was incredibly smooth, her plump lips only hinting at the shadow of a smile. And those outta-this-world eyes!

"My pleasure." She said it like a caress. And it only got better with every detail Kallum took in about her.

Samara was stunning. Her hair was the wildest bouquet of astonishing blonde curls. Almond-shaped, striking blue eyes were set above sculpted cheekbones. She stood about five feet nine or so, wore jeans with a simple white T-shirt, and had the silhouette of a movie star.

Kallum gathered his wits and closed his gaping mouth, hoping he hadn't salivated. The Hanson parents didn't appear to notice, but he caught humor glimmering from beneath Samara's lashes.

Mrs. Hanson said, "You must be hungry. I've set out a light supper." She indicated the way, and Kallum grabbed his backpack, fumbling as well with the box until Bembe stepped out of the shade.

"I'll get dat for you, bey." He stooped to scoop up the package, nabbed the bag out of Kallum's grasp, then turned towards the office. Kallum's laptop had better be in one piece when he saw it again.

"Mind if I wash up first?" Kallum smelled frowsy—a word he'd learned from Bembe along the way. Stray dogs on the beach smelled frowsy.

Over salad, cornbread, and cold chicken, all six Hansons quizzed Kallum about his life. The three boys were full of jostling fun and would likely be in his classes.

Trying not to allow Samara's allure to distract him, Kallum applied himself to informing the host family of the essentials: Mom and Dad farming in Alberta, an older brother with wife and kids, Kallum's biblical education at a local college, and his interest—if not proficiency—in both Latin and Greek.

But it took only one smothered yawn by him for Mrs. Hanson to declare, "You're tired."

Principal Hanson rose from his chair. "Kallum, sleep in tomorrow morning. We usually cancel Friday afternoon anyway, as boarding students must take time to commute to their homes. We don't expect you in the classroom until Monday. And I suppose you'll want to brush up on your lesson material, anyway."

"That sounds great." But Kallum's notes required only a cursory going over, prepared as he was for his lectures. He yawned openly now. "Maybe I can get the lay of the land here over the weekend?"

"Good idea," Mr. Hanson agreed, "although we do attend services on Sunday." He paused as if expecting Kallum to acknowledge his own agreement to go to church, which of course he wouldn't want to miss.

"I'm the alternate-week pianist." Mrs. Hanson sat a little taller. "Our boys are in the choir for special performances—you should have seen them in the Christmas pageant—and Samara here teaches Sunday school. In addition to her regular hours in Morningstar's office, of course."

The girl's lips curved demurely, but her manicured nails tap-tap-tapped on the tabletop as though she was stifling impatience.

Mr. Hanson shooed his sons off to do their homework. "At any rate, I can spare Samara from her office duties for the next while to act as your guide."

Mrs. Hanson, packing up dishes, paused with her hands full. "Are you sure, Edward?"

"How else is the girl going to learn responsibility, Nacheline?" Mr. Hanson turned back to his daughter and continued. "Samara, you can show our visitor around Eleuthera."

Kallum almost choked on his mouthful of water. To be chauffeured around a tropical island by an enticing beauty would be any guy's aspiration.

Samara leaned in. "I can drive the golf cart?"

Mr. Hanson nodded gravely. "Just be home by sundown, before six." He dug into his pocket—"Here's money for gas"—and dangled the keys in front of her. "Bembe will help me with some construction tomorrow anyway, and he'll be using the van—rather than the cart—for hauling lumber. But I expect you to be careful."

"You can trust me, Daddy."

Samara blinked over at Kallum, her eyes sparking, and he wondered how much trust his preceptor should put in *him*.

Samara sauntered to her room after supper, jingling the keys and not believing her luck. At last, a break from the abysmal boredom of the office! How long might she draw out the privilege? She plopped belly down onto her bed with her notebook opened to a clean page. Samara had some planning to do.

Tourist season in Bahamas was not her favorite, despite the fascinating visitors. For one thing, the roads were clogged. On such a narrow island, it wasn't easy to make good time—especially in an underpowered golf cart. It would easily take all day to hit the major sights, even without stopping much.

She nibbled the end of her pen, then scribbled a list of possibilities beginning first thing tomorrow. Never mind that Kallum might want to sleep in—someone that good looking had no right snoozing the day away when he might be sharing her company. They'd check out the bridge and some of the island's other geographical anomalies, maybe take in the botanical plant preserve, keeping an eye out for iguanas and parrots along the way.

And they couldn't miss the beaches, of course, crowded as they were right now with off-island snorkelers and divers—Bahamians themselves generally not being swimmers. She was one of the exceptions and had earned the nickname "Angelfish" for her love of the water and, of course, for her obsession with showing off her latest swimsuit. She ran her left hand over her waistline and hip. Yes, Kallum must definitely experience the beaches, but maybe on this first day of overview she'd just point them out. She jotted down some of her favorites—Ten Bay for collecting shells, Rainbow Bay for snorkeling, Lighthouse Beach with the most romantic sunsets.

Samara clipped the pen onto her list and rested her chin on fisted hands. Should she suggest they ferry across to Nassau one day during his stay? It took three hours and was pretty expensive, not something she could afford to do very often on her own. She couldn't ask Daddy for that. He was already paying for gas around the island.

The Hanson family had more money than many islanders, but Mama and Daddy were not rich by any means, and all expenses had to be okayed by the mission board. Her parents maintained total transparency.

So when she'd slipped off alone to Nassau a couple of months ago using all her babysitting cash, a friend had to cover for her. No one could know yet about her clandestine activities. Samara quivered and sat up, back against the wall, flipping to the end of the journal to read again her vague annotation to self: *André / Potters Cay / r. on Shirley / Over the Hill / Queen's Staircase / pink door / flames.* No street number.

Her delicious secret.

Exhausted, Kallum climbed between crisp sheets made up on a cot in a room the size of a closet, which suited him just fine—reminded him of camping. He dropped into immediate sleep only to awake in the middle of the night to the rumbling croak of a frog near his open window, the murmur of waves far in the distance, and thoughts of that luscious girl sleeping under the same roof a wall away.

There was no returning to dreamland for Kallum. He pushed off his covers and sat on the edge of his bed, raking his fingers through his thick hair to push it off his forehead. He reached for his laptop and dashed off a quick e-mail to let his parents know he'd arrived safely, but it wouldn't send—likely too far from the school office Wi-Fi.

Oh well. He couldn't get online, so he might as well go over his classroom notes in the cool of the night and occupy his mind with constructive images. Two birds, one stone.

Clicking his file open, Kallum scanned the synopsis of his initial lesson, priding himself on the succinctness of his notes. He loved a good outline.

He would introduce the apostle John as the author of the gospel, the letters, and the apocalyptic Revelation—prolific writer, that guy. Kallum would then explain the setting, the background and history and author details, and his proposed main themes before bringing up the lesson title: "The Light of Knowledge." He'd close the class with an assignment to find and circle all occurrences of the words "light" and "knowledge" in their own Bibles.

A neat and tidy session to kick off his overall subject thesis.

Kallum shut down his computer and checked his watch. Five o'clock already and still inky dark outside. He'd lie down again for another stab at sleep, but first he'd fetch a glass of water.

Kallum inched opened the door to avoid squeaks. The last thing he wanted was to waken his hosts. In the glow from his phone, he took several soft steps in the direction of the kitchen but happened to let his eyes wander through the gaping doorway of Samara's room.

A ribbon of moonlight draped across her prone form, highlighting the curve of her waist and hip, the floss of her hair an angel's nest crowning her head. He gripped the doorframe, mesmerized by the sultry loveliness of the girl, before he turned his eyes away.

He couldn't get back to sleep.

Three hours later, with a hearty breakfast of sardines and grits filling his belly, Kallum climbed into the open golf cart with Samara at the wheel. He suffered a spasm of fear as, exiting the compound, Samara swung into the far lane, narrowly avoiding another vehicle barreling down the wrong side of the road. Correction—the *left* side of the road.

Samara smirked. "Hang on tight, Kallum. I'm going to show you how we do it in Bahamas. We have to make good time if we want to catch everything between here and the top tip of Eleuthera."

Good time? The cart wouldn't likely hit twenty miles per hour.

But the girl brimmed with enthusiasm as, dodging broken asphalt with one hand on the wheel, she pointed out the features along their route. The skies were clear, sunlight flashed off the water, and Kallum slowly relaxed into her guided tour—if anyone could actually relax with those potholes.

Here was a place for cliff jumping, there was a spot known for its howling winds and rugged breakers. She drew his attention to a cruise ship moored in a bay, they dashed into a convenience store for soft ice cream, and she forced him into a dive shop to buy flippers for some future snorkeling event. At Governor's Harbour, they admired quaint, pastel houses with verandas and shutters and steep-pitched roofs. At Gregory Town, they devoured a huge platter of tender lobster with a side of deep-fried conch fritters. They crossed over the Glass Window Bridge Kallum had viewed from the air, even more scenic from this perspective—especially as it now included the vision of spectacular Samara.

"And here is where it all began." Finally Samara parked the cart at their northernmost destination on Friday's list and tossed her hand towards a path in the weedy sand leading off to a rocky bluff. "Ready to walk a bit?"

They approached a large cavern marked with an identifying placard, and Samara said, "This is known as Preacher's Cave."

"Right, I read about this." Maybe Kallum could finally contribute his research knowledge to her anecdotes. "A band of seventeenth-century English Puritans in search of religious sanctuary got shipwrecked on a reef near here."

"Yes, on Devil's Backbone."

"Fitting name." A factoid he'd missed in his Wiki reading. "Well, anyway, the stranded group held the island's very first worship service right here. In fact . . ."

Kallum's voice trailed off as he realized these were the same mariners the pilot Chad had referenced as the discoverers of the Glass Window, who'd established the first permanent settlement on the island. Hmm, that might come in handy as an illustration when he was teaching. Hadn't an ancient theologian likened sunlight through a glass window to the grace of God illuminating the human heart?

"They're known as the 'Eleutherian Adventurers.'"

"What?" Kallum shook his head to clear his mind of data. "What did you say?"

"The Puritans called themselves the 'Eleutherian Adventurers.'"

"That's it!" The penny finally dropped for Kallum. He'd known *how* the island got its name, of course, but hadn't put together the *why* of it. "That's what's been niggling at my brain—the meaning of the island's name. *Eleutheria* or *eleutheros* is Greek for 'freedom.'"

"Freedom." Samara breathed out the word with such melancholy, such wistfulness, that Kallum almost melted in empathy.

He wished for something like freedom himself.

And the carefreeness of his first full day had made a deep impression. If this was what missions was all about, he was on board with it.

Even as he thought it, Kallum chuckled at his magical thinking. No, missions work could not be about his own soul's pleasure—he waggled his bowed head as he turned to walk back to the car behind the shapely Samara Hanson—but about what he knew in his rational mind.

Kallum had just opened his laptop to his lecture notes Saturday morning on his bed when Samara broke in without knocking.

"Good, you're wearing bathing trunks. Let's go!" She thrust a couple of towels and a bottle of sunscreen at him, hauling him to his feet. "The golf cart's loaded and the beach awaits."

He'd have resisted; however, in light of her charm, his review could wait until tomorrow. He grabbed his cap with one hand and let her pull him outside with the other.

Mrs. Hanson insisted on first serving up a breakfast hash of corned beef and veggies. Packing a basketful for a picnic lunch—leftover boiled fish, slices of mango—she said to Samara, "Take one of your brothers along."

"I'd love to, Mama, but the golf cart has only two legal seats, and we'll be fully loaded with our snorkeling equipment." Did Kallum detect smugness? Not that he was keen to drag one of the kids along with them. "Anyway, they're still sleeping."

Kallum wiped his mouth and set the napkin onto the plasticized floral tablecloth. "Samara, I'm not really comfortable swimming in deep water. And I've never snorkeled."

Both Mrs. Hanson and her daughter gawked at him. Of course, tourist brochures were all about exploring Eleuthera's marine life—its many creatures and colorful reefs. Landlubber that he was, he'd be satisfied with staying on the shore.

Samara tittered. "There's always a first time."

So Kallum wasn't getting away scot free. Well, it wasn't as though he'd actually *failed* his childhood swimming course at the Y. But his substantial athletic energies had been concentrated on field and court sports such as baseball and racquetball.

"A first time. Absolutely."

And they were off.

It was a perfect day for strolling the soft pink sands and gathering shells—Mom would love the sand dollars he beachcombed, and he could make a cool pendant from a piece of sea-washed green glass. Most of all, he enjoyed the company of Samara—the twist of her wrist, the exquisite tilt of her head. And then she yanked off her sundress to reveal a very becoming—and tiny—fuchsia bikini. Her mama, she said, had fortunately not seen this one yet.

Kallum gave in to her pressure and tried out snorkeling in the shallows. He had to admit getting the hang of mouthpiece and mask wasn't so bad, though he choked on the saline sea a couple of times. He glided along beside Samara in the sun-streaked water teeming with darting schools of bright yellow and vibrant blue fish, staring down at fantastical coral gardens as starfish small and large inched along the sandy bottom and waves undulated. The delightful sense of saltwater buoyancy was brand new to him.

Samara was half fish herself, a lovely mermaid with her floating cloud of bright hair a luminous halo—*aureola* in Latin. She grasped his hand to focus his attention on a giant turtle flying through the waters in the distance, and she didn't let go.

Neither did he.

Kallum stood up in waist-deep water and began flapping towards the shoreline. He removed his snorkel and mask.

"Wow."

"You liked it, right?" Samara stepped backwards out of the surf, not tripping over her fins like Kallum. So he turned backwards, too, and followed her lead, removing his flippers only once they stretched out on the sun-warmed towels she'd thoughtfully spread beforehand.

"That was fantastic." Kallum couldn't put into words the sensations of the past few hours—the rainbow shades of flora and fauna, the thrum of wave and current, the intimacy of Samara's hand in his. Especially the last.

Holding hands was no big thing. Good grief, he wasn't a monk, although he'd kept to his standard of purity in body and soul. He wasn't ignorant intellectually, either; he had complete command of the biological facts of life and love.

But this incredible chemistry he felt with Samara—the draw to her sensuous femininity—was almost overwhelming, especially within the exotic surroundings where no one he knew was watching. He should really keep his mind on his studies, on the classroom he would soon enter as instructor, exemplar, testifier.

At that moment, Samara quickly planted a moist and salty kiss fully on his lips. She reclined onto her elbows again.

Kallum had no time to react. What was he supposed to do with this turn of events? Was the girl even of age yet? Oh, yes, she'd graduated. But wasn't this, at the least, unprofessional fraternization? Mr. and Mrs. Hanson would be correctly appalled.

Then Samara said, "I've never really had a boyfriend before." She sat straighter and crossed her arms, chafing briskly.

"You're shivering." And like a brother—no, not like a brother—he encircled her shoulders and nestled her close to his warm side, rubbing the gooseflesh on her outer arm. But he kept his lips out of range. For now.

After Samara—dry and fully dressed again—returned with Kallum to Morningstar, she ignored Mama's greeting and dashed into her room for her hinged wooden box to retrieve the manila envelope from the Nassau studio. Boyfriends get to know a girl's secrets. She pushed open Kallum's door to expose his broad, brawny back to her sight. He jumped, then dragged his T-shirt down over his torso before turning around.

"Can we talk?" Samara kept her trembling voice low because her mother was only a hallway away. She closed the door behind her, knowing she'd get blasted by her parents if they happened by, and then she sat on the edge of the cot. It took Kallum to the count of three before he lowered himself down beside her.

"What is it?" He sounded more concerned than curious.

Samara wet her lips, her stomach fluttering. "I want to show you something." She didn't open the envelope yet.

"Okay . . ." He drew out the word. No doubt he was skeptical; they didn't know each other that well yet. But they would.

"It all started a couple of months ago," she began. She wouldn't give him everything at once, only a bit at a time. "I went to Nassau for a photo shoot. I received the proofs last week." Via her friend's postal box, out of Mama's range. She slid her hand into the envelope and extracted the top glossy print.

Kallum used his fingertips to clasp its edges, likely so he wouldn't smudge it. How thoughtful. He didn't seem too shocked at the head-shot, so she added another—the one where she'd slid down her straps to bare her shoulders.

"They're gorgeous pictures." Kallum lifted his lids slowly to take in her real-life, 3-D headshot, his eyes tracking her features as though checking for discrepancies. His amber scrutiny flitted from the top of her still-damp curls, down her forehead, back and forth across both eyes and onto her nose, to rest on her lips, then traced her neck to her *décolletage*. She'd learned that word from the oh-so-attentive photographer.

"I want to be a model." Samara let that part out all at once in a rush of wishing. "I've wanted to be a model since I won the junior beauty pageant when I was twelve—to go to the big city, maybe Paris one day. Can you imagine my parents' horror when I confided this dream?" She laughed but heard her own bitterness. She extracted the third photo, the one with fire in her eyes and bottom lip caught between her teeth.

Kallum drew in a long, slow breath before handing it to her again. "So, what's your next move?" he asked.

She elbowed aside his pillow and propped herself against the wall at the head of the bed. He was asking her about her career objectives, something her parents hadn't ever done. Kallum MacVicar was one very cool dude.

"I'll put together my portfolio and submit it to an agency, I suppose." She didn't suppose. She knew exactly what next steps to take, as the photographer, André—he actually used the little accent on his business name online, *André's Loft Gallery*—had already explained the steps to her. He himself would be her agent, he'd told her. She should just come on back to Nassau after she'd received the envelope of proofs, choose the poses she liked best, and he would pull it all together.

Kallum pushed his hair off his forehead. "Sounds like you've got a plan."

"Really? You like the idea?"

He turned tender eyes on her. "We should all have ambitions of the heart and follow them, Samara. God gave us good gifts and desires, and it's our job to shepherd them."

Warmth flushed through Samara. She was about to cuddle closer for another—a real—kiss when a footstep sounded outside the door. She bounced up off the bed just in time, hiding the manila envelope behind her back.

"Kallum, are you ready for—"

"Hi, Mama. Is supper made?" She slid around her scowling parent, tossing a wink at Kallum, who had leapt to his feet and was blushing fiercely. Let him deal with her mother.

Kallum's first Bahamian Sunday service proved to be unlike any in his Canadian circles. He and the Hanson family walked to the neighborhood church with its peeling-paint, cinder-block walls, and they were welcomed by several eager parishioners, some of whom set down cakes on a table labeled *After Service Coffee Time*. People milled and chattered amongst themselves, but Kallum stood close to Samara, who bumped hands with him when no one was looking.

The family was eventually seated near a rustic cross that loomed over the baptismal tank. Mr. Hanson and his three boys wore wild neckties and white button shirts tucked in at the waist. Mrs. Hanson sported an ornate bonnet replete with plumage and pearls, similar to that of many women in the congregation. In a modest frock, Samara appeared properly chaste under the apprehensive squinting of her parents, who made sure she was seated snugly between them on the splintered pew. Kallum, woefully underdressed in his T-shirt emblazoned with the logo of Calgary's hockey team, was crammed into the family pew nearest the aisle.

Most of the singing was unfamiliar to Kallum—vigorous, to say the least, and full of clapping and jiving, lots of swaying, and even some outright dancing. Ushers passed handwoven tithing baskets that, to be truthful, felt much more human than sending e-transfers through a bank app. And finally, an hour into the service, the worship leader invited the pastor up to deliver his sermon.

To Kallum's considerable surprise, Bembe, the Morningstar handyman, stepped to the podium. He smacked his huge Bible on top of the pulpit, its tattered edges visible to Kallum from where he sat, and in booming tones the pastor addressed his congregants.

"Good mornin' and welcome, sisters and brothers—exspecially our visitors." Bembe beamed directly at Kallum, who prayed the man wouldn't ask him to stand.

Right from the beginning of the sermon—the very long sermon—Kallum struggled with the style and the content of Bembe's preaching. Everyone else appeared comfortable with his pace and pidgin-laced English, judging by the frequent and fervent shouts of "Amen!" There was no overhead screen to give hints of what passage he was expounding, and in fact Bembe flipped around in his Bible so deftly that Kallum wouldn't have been able to follow even if his phone's app could connect. No signal through those thick walls.

Kallum figured out Bembe's theme quickly enough, though he couldn't ascertain any outline or logic to the sermon. The preacher began in the book of Genesis—Kallum caught that reference—where the Holy Ghost hovered over the face of dark waters, over the surface of the deep. Bembe said something about Noah's floodwaters overtaking the wicked, who had left the straight paths to walk in dark ways, who were darkened in their understanding and separated from the life of God, who knew God but didn't glorify Him because their thinking had become futile, their foolish hearts darkened.

When Bembe mentioned Moses—who by the power of God brought down blinding darkness over the land of Egypt, whereas God called blind eyes to open and captives to be freed—one of the congregants shouted, "Let my people go!"

When Bembe declared that humans love darkness instead of light because their deeds are evil, and made reference to unhealthy eyes plunging the whole body into darkness, and warned about the sinner's destination as the place of no return, the land of gloom and outer darkness, a woman exclaimed, "Dey all mix up like conch salad—tingsy and trapsy folk."

At this, Mrs. Hanson, whispering in Kallum's ear, kindly translated for him. "She means sinful people are confused, materialistic, and untrustworthy."

Kallum mulled this over as Bembe carried on, his words and pronunciations only so much glossolalia—an incomprehensible jumble not aligning with Kallum's vocabulary, not in sync with his own precise English. And yet, although the cultural presentation was so unfamiliar, Kallum could follow the thread of real truth.

The unending sermon finally ended with Bembe's admonition: "Put aside ya deeds of darkness, friends. Awake an' cast off dem deeds of darkness, fo' you do not belong to darkness. The people walkin' in darkness have seen a great light. Dat light shines in darkness, an' darkness has not overcame it."

So, yeah, the theme was clear in the end and actually the twin of his own lectures about light, beginning tomorrow.

As the congregation mingled later, eating homemade desserts—such as Coconut Jimmy and Cassava Pone—Kallum listened in to the after-sermon chatter to see if he could identify any linguistic rules organizing their vernacular. Instead he overheard two withered women with shock-white hair prattling in whispers about the island's dark arts, incantations, rituals. About Pastor Bembe's references to bottomless waters, to the creatures of the deep, to Leviathan—the gliding serpent, the coiling serpent, the monster serpent of the sea. And to Jonah, hurled to the roots of the mountains, the realm of the dead, banished to the currents and breakers, seaweed wrapped about his head.

Kallum, too, had been feeling underwater ever since arriving in Eleuthera. Maybe it was jet lag—no, there was a difference of only two hours between Eleuthera and home. Maybe it was the strangeness of the culture, or the change in food, or maybe it had something to do with the utterly, breathtakingly, extraordinarily attractive Samara Hanson.

He should call home and talk to Dad, but the cell charges were so high. He gnawed at his thumb nail. On second thought, maybe he'd wait until after he'd had a day or two in the classroom and then write another e-mail.

Bembe approached him with a round woman about half his height holding a plate of something that looked very sweet and slightly mushy.

"Here you go, bey!" Bembe snagged the plate from his missus and thrust it towards Kallum. "Dis is de guava duff I axed have you ever ate. World's best. Taste it an' tell me I'm wrong."

In late afternoon, Mrs. Hanson called Kallum from the kitchen, holding out the home phone receiver. "It's for you." Maybe over his hesitancy, she continued, "Your parents."

"Kallum." Mom sounded relieved. "You got there without trouble?" In a muffled aside, she said, "Honey, our boy is safe."

"Sorry, Mom." He should have made sure his e-mail actually sent. "Internet connection's not great here."

"Dad and I wanted to check on you, that's all."

"I think I can't get online unless I'm close to the office."

Mrs. Hanson, drying dishes, raised her head and nodded affirmation.

"Don't be burdened to keep in touch, unless you get homesick." Mom chuckled, which made Kallum smile. "Or call back collect if you have any sort of emergency."

So like Mom and Dad—they wouldn't want to saddle the Hansons' ministry with long-distance charges or place expectations on their grown son. He replied, "I don't foresee any emergencies, but okay." Not that phoning from the kitchen would be very private. Then again, he shouldn't need privacy in talking to his folks, right?

Kallum was keen about his first Bahamian schoolroom experience on Monday morning, having planned it out in great detail and looked forward to it throughout his preceding college semester.

He followed Samara down a hallway to the as-yet-empty classroom number 3, his laptop loaded and ready to go with lecture notes and shareable files for session one of "The Theme of Light According to Saint John." But while he was plugging in, just as the school-wide end-of-period buzzer sounded, Samara informed Kallum that most of the students didn't own tablets or even mobile phones and that, anyway, Internet connection for his teaching app wasn't available in classrooms.

"You're joking." Morningstar's technology obviously fell short of basic North American standards.

"We don't have the kind of money the public schools get from our government." She folded her arms across her chest. She was quite adorable when defensive. "And we're not one of those snooty private secular institutions."

"No problem." In spite of her sudden loyalty, Kallum had gotten the idea she wanted to blow this popsicle stand—get away from Eleuthera and the oversight of her parents. He poked her upper arm. "I'll have to ask Morningstar's cute admin to print hard copies of my notes."

Before she replied, teens of all sizes, shapes, and hues began trickling into the room, greeting one another in local jargon—"Whatchusayin'?"—and answering in kind. Several he recognized from church. They straggled to their desks past Kallum and Samara, who stood side by side in front of an antiquated chalkboard.

"Silence!" Samara commanded, as though she herself were the head honcho. "This is Mr. MacVicar, our visiting volunteer teacher for January. He comes from Canada and will lead your daily devotional Bible class this month."

Kallum's heart skipped a beat. He wouldn't exactly have called his research series "devotional."

"Good morning, students." His articulation was firm yet open, engaging. "We're going to be studying—"

"Mr. MacVicar, sir, is it super cold in Canada? Do you have igloos up there?" The girl might have been thirteen—in lower secondary, he was sure, although others were about to graduate.

"Sure, in some places winter can get down to sixty, sixty-five degrees below zero." They hooted at that, disbelieving, protesting that humans couldn't survive in such temperatures. He went on, "And, no, I haven't been in an igloo myself. However, it's said my granddad drank tea with an Inuit friend in an igloo once—on a hunting trip way farther north than our farm."

Several of the kids pumped arms in the air or shouted out their questions: Did Kallum speak French? Had he ever had snow blindness? Was he a hockey player? Did he keep bears and beavers as pets? Was maple syrup as sweet as sugarcane? Had he ridden to school by dogsled?

It took the whole hour before lunch break to fill them in: Yes, a little French and a smattering of other languages. No, but he played baseball. His dog was too lazy to pull a sled. And so on.

When they asked if he had a girlfriend, he glanced involuntarily at Samara—sweeter than either maple syrup or sugarcane—and swiftly diverted his gaze. No, he told them. No girlfriend. But he heard her beside him huff like an irritated cat.

No girlfriend, he'd said? Samara, in the restroom before heading home with Kallum for Mama's fish stew, frowned at herself in the mirror. She'd have to do something about that.

Later in the evening, when her parents had gone to bed, Samara crept into Kallum's room. She whispered to his sheet-draped back, "Can I ask your advice—like, as a man?"

Of course, he wouldn't be able to resist.

As she expected, Kallum turned to face her, then swung his legs over the edge of the cot, chest bare, clutching the bedding at his waist as he sat.

She handed the complete manila envelope over to him, then clasped her moist hands to her chest.

"What's going on?" He angled his head up at her. She sat down beside him so his neck wouldn't get strained.

"I didn't have the chance to tell you the whole story the other day—about my photo shoot." She shivered but with anticipation this time. "There are more proofs than the three I showed you. I wonder what you think about them?"

Kallum withdrew a thin stack of about two dozen poses. The first few included the headshots she'd already shown him and several more of the same. For the next frames, she'd changed into an outfit brought from home—sleeveless dress, wide-brimmed hat. And then André had ordered her to try on the costume he'd designed for her alone, he'd said.

She examined Kallum's face as he shuffled through the glossy eight-by-tens, stopping longer on her favorites—the ones with her rocking a pair of bone earrings and a shark tooth bracelet. She didn't point out the way André had wrapped his fake animal skin tightly around her to show off maximum cleavage—a leopard skin, as if there were any such cats on Eleuthera. André had coached her all the way through, encouraging her to lick her lips or laugh with her mouth wide open or shrug her naked shoulders coyly.

"What is this, Samara?" Kallum lowered the batch of pictures onto his lap, locking her in with those dreamy amber eyes of his.

"Do you like them?" She thought the glam shots were really something. "It's a spiritual theme—same as what Bembe does for his second job, really, except his interpretation is religious."

"Quite a bit different than what Bembe does, I can assure you."

Now Kallum's half-closed lids oozed judgmentalism. Samara's right eye twitched. He'd met only Bembe and no one else yet except those from her family—other than that hour with the batch of students. Sure, he might study the Bible, but what would he really know about Bahamas at this point? About its native mythology?

"These pictures are a cultural expression of our past." She clenched her jaw, ready for his protest. That's the way André had put it—"cultural expression"—and he was a professional, after all.

"Your cultural past? When this country was settled by Puritans? I don't get it."

Samara stared at Kallum. He didn't know about Obeah?

"Long ago, our island ancestors called on the spirits for healing—see the bunch of herbs I'm holding in this picture and the potion I'm drinking from the coconut shell?" It was actually mango juice laced with rum meant to loosen her up, according to André. It had worked.

"Like, jungle magic or something? Voodoo?" Kallum shifted away from her.

"Not really. Slaves were brought here to the Caribbean on the trade route between West Africa and Britain." Did he know nothing of Caribbean history? "They practiced various rituals that blended beliefs together, to help locate missing property, protect against illness, punish slave owners—stuff like that."

"Syncretism." Kallum lifted his left eyebrow. "A mishmash of super-stitions, right?"

Samara bristled. "It's our birthright." Not that Mama or Daddy would agree with her.

"Hmm." Kallum flipped through the portraits again. "I see the artistic direction of the photo shoot, Samara. But what has this got to do with modeling in Paris?"

"Branding." And he was supposed to be educated? "André says he's building a brand for me." American and European women want the sort of look she projected, André had said—the look he coaxed out of her. She was a star already, in his opinion. She would be on the front cover of

Vogue within the year. "And anyway, Kallum, you were the one saying I should follow my heart's ambitions."

Kallum nodded, dubious or maybe disapproving. However, she noticed he didn't actually stop checking out the photos.

Tuesday brought Kallum to the first day of real classroom instruction, and it seemed to be going along fine.

"Yes"—Kallum skimmed the list of student names to identify the girl madly waving her hand with the answer—"Taja. You have a word beginning 'p-h-o-s'?" He'd written it on the chalkboard: *phōs*.

She stood, swiveling her head around at her classmates. "Mr. MacVicar, sir, what about 'phosphoric acid'?"

"Excellent." He wrote her word on the board. "You've been studying your science, I see. Anyone else?"

There were no takers, and so Kallum dove into his first actual lesson. "In Latin, *phos* is the root for such English words as 'phosphorous,' meaning a substance that shines of itself, and 'photo.'" He almost stumbled over the last word as images rushed to his brain. "It originally comes from the Greek *phōs*"—here he pointed to the chalkboard—"meaning 'light.'" He added that word to the rest.

Kallum scanned the blank faces of his pupils. He'd better speed up the lecture.

"The New Testament, written in Greek, uses this root word over eight hundred times. It signifies an interruption of the darkness physically and metaphorically. Can anyone give me a biblical example of physical light?"

Taja squirmed with the answer, but Kallum pointed to another student instead. "Yes, umm . . . Kofi?"

The tall boy slowly unwound himself—like a gecko—and stretched into a standing position. "Mr. MacVicar, sir." His brilliant teeth gleamed white. "Maybe where God said, 'Let there be light'?"

As Kallum nodded his encouragement, the boy sat. "And an example of spiritual light?"

Taja could not be put off. She fairly leapt to her feet this time. "Jesus is the light of the world!" Her face shone in personal witness of the word's meaning, her delight obvious.

Kallum thanked her and addressed the whole class once again. "Over the next weeks, we will be looking at the concept of light through the viewpoint of the apostle John. Don't get him confused with John the Baptist, cousin of Jesus. Our subject is sometimes known as John the Evangelist. Notice that the root of this Greek word 'evangelist'"—he wrote out *euangelistes* and underlined the segment *angel*—"means, simply, 'messenger.' John brought the gospel—the good news of spiritual light."

From this point on, Kallum struggled with the lesson. He kept to the order according to his laptop outline although more slowly than he'd anticipated. He simply had too much information. On each student's desk lay a paper copy of his main study points with room to jot notes, but not many followed along. When he spotted some very droopy teenage eyelids—as well as Kofi in the back row passing notes with a redhead, maybe Gavin—Kallum checked the time on the wall clock and gave them an abbreviated assignment for next class.

"Bring your Bibles tomorrow."

As he cleaned the board and powered down his laptop, Kallum reflected that, over his first two days of teaching, he'd gotten through only a fraction of his planned material.

That evening he spent hours re-evaluating his study plan, condensing, and even memorizing. Samara hung around his door, so he bolted it against her. He needed to focus, and she was much too distracting.

He sprawled on his bed and pulled his laptop close, bringing up his e-mail. He might as well compose a message to his parents, even if he couldn't send it until tomorrow from the office.

Thought I'd drop you a line. This place is awesome, but, Dad, you wouldn't eat half the stuff I've encountered here already. Haha—not like your cooking, Mom. The Hansons are a great family—four kids. The youngest three—thirteen to seventeen—are rambunctious boys. The oldest is a girl, Samara. Very beautiful. The locals all attend the community church—the services are lively, if you know what I mean. I'll have stories for you when I get home.

The rest of week one rolled on in the same vein until Samara claimed Kallum's full attention again on Saturday. She was sporting the earrings and bracelet she'd had on for some of her photos—the really sensuous poses. He recalled every detail.

"Let's go spelunking today, Kallum."

Spelunking, derived from the Latin *spēlunka* for "cave," "cavern," or "den." Kallum asked, "You mean we're going all the way north to the Puritans' landing site?" They'd already seen it.

"Oh, no, we have lots of other caves on the island, like Sapphire Blue Hole and the Hatchet Bay system. But we can stay away from the touristy sites." She touched his elbow, then let her index finger trace a vein down the inside of his arm to his wrist. "I know of a real private one close by that doesn't even have a name."

Kallum swallowed the lump forming in his throat. "Won't we need ropes to get down?"

"No, just a good flashlight, and I have that." She raised it for him to see—a sturdy black one she clicked on to show its piercing beam.

"Isn't it dangerous to explore caves?" He wasn't talking only about physical safety.

"No wild animals—except bats, of course." She tugged on his hand to make him follow, and he gave in.

But as they passed through the kitchen on their way to the outside door, Mrs. Hanson piped up, "Samara, please fetch some grouper for supper."

Samara hid the flashlight behind her back. "Mama, can't one of the boys do it? I was about to take Kallum out to show him more of the island, like Daddy said I should." She snuck a peek at Kallum from beneath her thick lashes. "He's been studying so hard all week . . ."

Nacheline Hanson surveyed her daughter silently, eyes narrowed. "That will have to wait. Please bring enough fish for the seven of us." She opened a spice tin on the counter and withdrew some Bahamian bills. "And after supper, you'll wash the floors, please. Idle hands are the devil's workshop."

Kallum hadn't heard that axiom since his grandmother was alive. He and Samara plodded through the late morning heat towards the beach a few blocks away, the girl uncharacteristically silent with a sour expression. They waded out knee deep to reach two men fileting fish in a wooden boat that had seen better days. Faded white lettering on the battered hull spelled out "Catch of the Day"—whether its name or an ad or both, Kallum couldn't tell.

"Why, Miz Samara, how you doin' dis fine day?" The older man with grizzled white beard must have been in his seventies, and he spoke with the same thick accent used by Bembe—echoed by the classroom kids, too. "An' who you have dere wit' you?"

Introductions ensued—both men named Elijah Curry, junior and senior. Kallum explained his presence on the island and then listened, deeply interested, as the father-and-son team explained the process of spearfishing out on the reef. They pointed eastward over the rhythmic swells to a line of thrashing water maybe a quarter of a mile out.

"Bey, you like to ride along one morning to see how it's done? Not dat you can use our spearguns." Curry Sr. explained some governmental fishing rules, and Kallum assured them he would watch from the dry inner edge of the boat, thank you very much. He might as well give it a go. He'd survived snorkeling already, and, after all, he'd come to Bahamas for a full-orbed experience—the whole enchilada, to mix languages even more.

"How about next weekend?" he asked. He should have a better grasp on the classroom at the close of his second week. "I used to fish with my granddad for lake trout and perch, out near our old family cabin." With a rod, of course, and wearing a lifejacket. The other men nodded, although Kallum suspected they'd never seen either trout or perch. Or maybe even a lifejacket. "In fact, Grandpa had the same outboard motor as yours."

"Is that so? A Johnson two-stroke?" Curry Jr. was easier to understand. "In that case, you come around anytime and take her out for a spin. If you need a break from your classroom."

That Saturday, his second on Eleuthera, marked a turning point for Kallum.

Leaving his new friends, the Currys, on the beach, Kallum and Samara dropped off the fish for Mrs. Hanson and headed out for the cave. Soon they stood at the edge of an almost invisible hole in the ground—an opening about three feet in diameter surrounded by seagrass and wild shrubs. The three Hanson boys, sent along behind by their mother and carrying a second flashlight, slithered down into the cave one at a time.

"Go ahead," Samara said to Kallum. "They know their way around down there. I'll follow you."

She pointed the ray of light onto a rocky ledge inside the cave, and Kallum stepped onto it, then onto the next one. He found his footing on the slippery floor, choking from the stench of—he assumed—bat guano.

"Your turn." His words echoed behind him.

"Give me a hand?"

Kallum reached up to help Samara, her velvety skin captivating him in the deep shadows. Below them and farther on, the brothers whooped, their voices trailing in the distance and then silent. Ahead, a natural skylight had broken through the ceiling of dirt, streamers of tree roots forming a mystical copse below. A cloud of bats, like flying mice, rushed past Kallum's ear and billowed out into the late evening sky. He turned his face away from the daylight and into the pitchy darkness.

Samara shone the flashlight over the graffiti sprayed on the walls—apparently not so private a cave after all—and then along the limestone ceiling dripping with fantastical shapes, candles shedding wax some-times joining the earth in cathedralesque columns. The otherworldly wall formations—like a cross-section of porous bone in a biology text illustration—created chambers exposed by the flickering torchlight as Samara pulled Kallum along behind her, deeper and deeper into the cave. She murmured that they might well have discovered the hiding place of a pirate's hoard, or a graveyard of murder victims, or a secret sacred spot for the witchery of Obeah practitioners.

Every word she uttered bounced in echo. Every step she took, cling-ing to Kallum, propelled them farther in and farther down and father away from the source of light. The quieter the cave got, the louder were Kallum's unbidden thoughts. Dad's terse e-mail answer, received by Kallum earlier today, resonated in the chambers of his mind:

Thanks for the message, Kallum. All reassuring except for your com-ment about the Hanson girl being beautiful. Don't go biting off more than you can chew.

Dad didn't get it. Kallum had popped outside and stepped closer to the office with his computer, then answered his father, briefly and to the point:

Don't worry about Samara, Dad. You just don't know her.

His father must have been sitting in front of his home office desktop because the return message popped right up on Kallum's screen:

I don't know her? Neither do you, son. Keep that in view.

The path ahead of Samara split into two hallways, and she veered to the left into a rocky, rubble-strewn room, where she plopped down onto a boulder cut almost square by the claws of some giant troll.

"Snuggle closer to me. I'm cold." She smoothed gravel from the sur-face as though making a bed. How could Kallum resist?

He draped an arm around her shoulders—those shoulders bared in the photographic images haunting him. Samara reached a hand behind his head, and he let her draw his face close, his lips down onto hers. He gave in and enfolded her in a delectable embrace. Her lips enchanted, her skin beguiled, her curves bewitched. Kallum was spellbound, and Samara shut off the flashlight. But that didn't matter to Kallum; he'd seen the pictures.

Eventually the Hanson brothers' echoing yelps broke into their seclusion, and they clambered to straighten disheveled clothing, tidy hair, move apart. Kallum couldn't look at Samara, so he didn't know if she was looking at him.

But alone later, he saw again in his mind's eye, in his memory, those scintillating snapshots of Samara.

The next two weeks fell into a rhythm for Kallum, a cycle of lesson prep and teaching and marking assignments, of eating regional dishes made by the church ladies, and of playing softball on the neighborhood team. He'd been helping Mr. Hanson and Bembe, too, frame up new doorsills for the compound's buildings. He'd gone out for several rides with the Currys on their boat to the reef, sitting on the middle bench with his feet atop the beat-up icebox, and once took Catch of the Day out on his own with their blessing. And he e-mailed home now and then with general news about the idyllic weather and the strange island vocabulary—and nothing more at all about Samara.

That was the public rhythm, anyway—what others saw, what he showed outwardly.

Lecturing in the classroom followed a pattern now, too. Kallum found himself encouraging less and less in-class, one-on-one engagement, which was so time consuming when he had such a pile of academic data to present. Hadn't he spent the past three years collecting all that knowledge?

Kallum gave the historical background first—what the Old Testament known by the Jewish John had said about the theme of light. He told them about God's glorious dwelling among His people and His mountaintop appearance leaving Moses with a bright, glorified countenance. He explicated the pillar of fire guiding the escaping Israelites and elucidated the seven flames of the golden lampstand in the Temple's holy place. Further, Kallum instructed the students to memorize the Nicene Creed:

We believe in one God, the Father Almighty, Maker of all things visible and invisible. And in one Lord Jesus Christ, the Son of God, begotten of the Father, Light of Light, very God of very God . . .

He taught them how to open their Bibles and follow up a word—such as "light"—by investigating lexicons and dictionaries for its etymology and definitions and by identifying roots in Latin, Hebrew, and especially Greek. He explained interlinear tools and concordances and Strong's numbers and what "context" meant, he pointed them to several commentaries, and he explained how to cross-reference scriptural texts to get the fullest meaning. The principal sat in on the odd class to ensure Kallum's doctrinal correctness and always left the room, Kallum discerned, with the bemused expression of having possibly learned something himself.

As the teens applied all resources at their fingertips and passed his quizzes, Kallum wove in the teaching about the apostle John's view of light. That God, in whom there is no darkness, is light. That in Christ is life, the light of mankind, shining in darkness that cannot overcome it, recreating His followers as bright children of God. That one day in the New Jerusalem, with its radiance like a most rare jewel, the sun and stars would cease to exist in the eternal illumination of the Lord and the Lamb.

Thus, day by day Kallum succeeded in following his lesson outline perfectly.

But in the darkness—oh! the darkness—he met Samara, now indisputably his girlfriend. They'd pass in dimmed hallways to stroke each other's arms. They'd kiss when out for surreptitious midnight walks on the beach. They'd grope behind locked doors without undoing buttons or zippers in a mockery of innocence, Kallum locking out the fullness of the truth he taught in the daytime—sticking to the letter of the law while he shuttered his conscience, failing his own high standards of purity. And all the more when, Samara absent, he would visualize those still photos of her.

On Kallum's third full Friday in Eleuthera, he was passing the open office door on the way to room number 3.

"Kallum, please see me here before lunch today." Principal Hanson—his boss, the man at whose table he ate every day, the father of the girl he craved—must have found out.

Kallum excused his pupils at the noon buzzer and dragged himself, soaked in dread, to the office.

"Sir?"

"Come in and sit down, please." Mr. Hanson dismissed Samara from the corner of the office in which she dealt with admin work for Morningstar, instructing her, "Tell your mother we'll be a bit late for the meal. And close the door behind you, please."

Mr. Hanson turned to Kallum, sat down, and motioned to him to do the same. The principal fiddled with a pen as he spoke, his face flushed. "Something has come to my attention that we must deal with."

He knew. Kallum's own face beaded with sweat. He had only a week left here; would he be kicked out?

"I've been hearing some rumors from the students . . ."

Kallum's guts seized. Had one of them identified him and Samara when they thought they were alone? Had Samara's brothers seen signs and started talking? Maybe Nacheline Hanson in her suspicion had figured it out; they say mothers have a sixth sense about that sort of thing.

Mr. Hanson cleared his throat. "You being my charge, I believe I have a responsibility to do a proper assessment for your Bible school . . ."

Oh no, he was about to be dismissed over his impropriety with Samara. His record would be ruined. His own parents would be embarrassed.

Mr. Hanson coughed into his hand, then finally came out with it. "Your classroom manner is very stilted, Kallum. You're teaching way above these children's heads, and I'm not sure they are actually absorbing your points."

Kallum slumped in his chair, catching himself before actually sighing aloud.

Samara's father seemed relieved, as well, to have spat out his concern, and he loosened up. "The children need application. For example," he suggested, "how is it they are to walk in the light? What did John mean by 'fellowship'? Have they personally chosen light or darkness?"

Kallum kept his eyes averted. Mr. Hanson might have had years of classroom experience, but what did he really know about current teaching methods? Did *he* know Latin? Had *he* studied any Greek at all? Kallum carefully arranged his expression.

"I see. Thank you for the feedback, Mr. Hanson. I can certainly apply that aspect with the students over the remaining lessons."

"That's the attitude." Mr. Hanson nodded, then stood. "I knew you'd catch on to my meaning. I certainly want to send you home with a wonderful reference."

Kallum's back teeth ached from clenching as he left the office. Of course, as this placement in Bahamas was at a very junior level, he'd expected critique from his preceptor. But he detested outright criticism.

Instantly a couple of proverbs zinged through his mind: *Only fools despise wisdom and instruction . . . The path of the righteous is like the light of dawn.*

Kallum shrugged them off. Yes, yes, he knew all that. He didn't have to constantly quote Scripture to be wise, did he?

Then an inner voice reminded him he'd been skipping his morning devotional readings for quite a while now. He rubbed his brow. Wasn't his immersion into the culture, his dedication to giving knowledge to the students, his excellence in communicating biblical propositions enough to satisfy his niggling conscience?

That evening in her room, Samara pored over her envelope of photos once again. Kallum certainly was taken with them. He'd asked to see the collection another couple of times, and the way he'd smiled over it—well, almost slobbered—was proof enough of her beauty, wasn't it? As a model, she could sell her looks, for sure. That's what André had promised.

Samara, suddenly squeamish, hadn't been totally open with Kallum. That is, she hadn't mentioned that, during her photography session, a girl about her age had left André's loft by a side door, when Samara caught a glimpse of another room with a video camera set up in front of a rumpled bed. Maybe it was just André's room—he lived in the rear of his working studio, he'd told her. Maybe it was just André's girlfriend. But he and the girl didn't even say goodbye when she left.

Samara brushed away her faint concerns—it wasn't any of her business. All she needed to know was André was waiting for her decision. She thrilled within. Imagine, her on the cover of *Elle* or *Cosmopolitan!*

Kallum knocked at her door and entered, leaving it ajar—probably so no one would start asking questions. Her brothers and parents were not yet asleep, noisy over a board game at the kitchen table. She snuck in a quick kiss anyway, but Kallum hung back. He stroked his chin, and she could hear the stubble rasping under his hand.

"Something you said that night in the cave got me thinking." Kallum frowned.

That didn't sound good. Samara licked her lips. What if he was, like, going to break it off with her? Not that she'd expected him to stay on in Bahamas indefinitely, and he'd warned her that he planned to extend his studies in Canada. Yet with her about to spring into a big-city career, she'd already been plotting ways to meet him in her travels somewhere, sometime.

She took the plunge. "Thinking what?"

"You mentioned this shutterbug—this André—was the one who contacted you, not the other way around, right?"

"Yes . . ." She drew out the word, unsure of where he was going.

"How did he find you?" Kallum chewed on his thumbnail.

"Online." How else did people meet? "Instagram, TikTok—I forget. The local boys post all sorts of stuff—like, pics they take of me." And she'd posted a fair number of selfies, as well.

"Isn't that sort of risky?"

"What do you mean?" She dug her hands into her jean pockets, suspecting what he might say next. To be truthful, she'd had her own doubts.

"Well, a guy contacts you online out of the blue, says he's got a legit studio—"

"He *does*. I was there." She lifted the sheaf of photos and shook them under his nose.

"Let me see the envelope." Kallum reached towards her bed for it, plucked it up, and read the front of it. "Hmm. Only your address."

"Well, duh. It was mailed to only me."

"No return address."

"What?" Samara craned her neck, and Kallum turned the envelope towards her. He was right—no return address.

"Legit businesses would have a logo or something to indicate the source. Did he give you a business card?"

"I didn't need one—he's got a nice website." She typed *André's Loft Gallery Nassau* into her phone's search bar—she had a decent connection tonight—and passed the screen over to Kallum, who fiddled with it briefly.

"No address there, either. No e-mail. No phone number." He handed the cell back to Samara. "It's basically a splash page with nothing beyond that."

Samara wrenched her phone from him. Kallum didn't know what he was talking about. She'd been there—mounted all four flights of stairs. She'd had these gorgeous proofs taken.

"Samara . . ." He stepped closer and cupped her cheek. "I'd hate to see you get hurt."

"You would, would you?" She bent her face away.

"There are so many scams around. Maybe you should talk this over with your parents?"

Samara froze. What if he threatened her with exposure? "I'm an adult, Kallum. I will do what I want with my life."

"Whoa, girl." He grabbed her elbow, turned her to himself. "No offense intended. Of course you're in charge of yourself."

She sure was. She softened—apparently too soon.

"I just think," Kallum continued, "maybe they could guide you to keep you safe—"

Samara shot to her feet. "I thought you were on my side." Her words were icy cold, as she intended them to be. "Get out."

Just then Mama popped her head into the room and asked if they'd like a bedtime snack of fried plantain. She got no response.

Kallum fled the house and would have slammed the door if the screen door had been slammable. He took off sprinting into the night, heading for the beach and blessed solitude.

What was wrong with the girl? She had a brain like everyone else; why wasn't she using it? Maybe he was wrong. Maybe Samara had found her way into the life she yearned for. But Kallum had a really bad feeling about this André.

He put down his head and got into a tempo, his trainers slapping the ground. If only he were home on the farm right now, he'd go for a run in the bracing cold, maybe, or at least climb up into the barn's sweet-smelling hayloft and nibble on a stalk of rye straw while he—what?—talked to God?

That was the last thing he could do right now.

The spearfishing boat was moored close to shore, barely bobbing on the rising tide. Kallum dragged the anchor into the hull, then pushed Catch of the Day into the shallows, hopping in and hardly getting wet. The Currys would be fine with his borrowing it. He used an oar to launch into the waves and tipped the outboard motor down. He squeezed the primer pump, tinkered with the choke, and pulled, pulled, pulled the starter cord until the engine sputtered to life.

He needed some space.

Samara, seething with indignation, shrieked at Mama, "How dare you snoop through my private things?"

Mama's arms were folded, and Daddy, with all three siblings, came running. Samara scooped the photos off the bed and stuffed them into the manila envelope just before the guys had a chance to see them. That would be too much to bear.

"What have you done, dear?" Mama's voice was full of disappointment.

"Nothing I'm ashamed of." Yet. "I have a right to do what I want with my own body."

"You have a responsibility to care for your body, yes." Mama turned to Daddy and murmured something under her breath about indecency.

Samara didn't care what her mother said or that her father visibly paled. She was done with this scene. She threw herself on the bed in a pout, facing away from them.

As soon as they left, Samara extracted a duffel bag from the bottom of the closet and jammed in her phone, her lip gloss, the packet of proofs, and whatever clothes lay strewn about the room. She tiptoed into the kitchen, snatched the money tin in hopes there was enough cash for a ticket, and took off for the last ferry of the day.

Kallum perched high in the stern and steered the wooden boat towards the reef. The wind in his hair had him feeling better already. The moon cast a broken pathway of its reflection on the cresting waves. He couldn't see any other boats out tonight, which was perfect for his purposes. He cranked the throttle and let Catch of the Day take him farther than he'd yet been. Past the reef, actually, where the Currys didn't venture, though he could still see the lights along the waterfront. Out past the last promontory and into the dark, until the stars sprinkled down on the water. That was where he cut the engine and lay back to examine the heavens.

He bobbed in the quiet waters for a while, emptying his mind of his troubles until, of course, Samara's image came floating along. Samara's *images*, plural. And with them a memory of Dad the day long ago he'd came upon the magazine stashed in Kallum's bedroom footlocker by his seventh-grade buddy. Kallum didn't replay that whole conversation alone under the stars, but he remembered Dad's sage advice.

"You can't stop a bird from landing on your head, Kallum, but you can prevent it from building a nest." Dad had paused, maybe giving his pubescent son time to digest visually. "Inflaming our eyes is one of the enemy's most creative works because a man's eyes are so sensually connected to his brain. And as a man thinks, so he does. So he is."

Kallum had often recalled this reasoning of Dad's and applied it in a dozen ways. However, that was before he'd ever met someone like Samara.

So what would he do about Samara? He could hardly fend her off, although she might not be talking to—or kissing—him ever again, anyway. He was too young to get serious about a woman, and how could they maintain any relationship living half a world apart? He could try to convince her this predator, André, was dangerous. At least that might make up for some of the damage he himself had inflicted on her by not following his own intuition earlier regarding that slimeball, by going along with her flirting and forwardness in the first place.

Who was he kidding? He'd been in his glory these past weeks.

Kallum bit on the dry skin of his knuckle. He could fix this—it was fixable. He'd avoid Samara and thoughts of her luscious body with displacing excuses, he'd promise to keep in touch with her when he was home again, and he'd buckle down to his last days of teaching.

Kallum stretched, the wooden boards tough on his back. He cast around to find the light and couldn't quite make out the shoreline . . . Oh yes, there it was. But when he attempted to start the engine, that old Johnson just sputtered and hiccupped. He tried again and again, then thought to check the fuel level.

The gauge needle sat on empty.

Just then a cool breeze—no, a wind—smacked his spine and jabbed its fingers into his hair. The stars weren't twinkling above anymore, now clouded over, and the ripples suddenly buffeted the boat's rickety hull.

Kallum might be in trouble.

He clutched the emergency oars and started to row, but the sea heaved, and he made no headway. Soon a whitecap or two breached the edge of the boat, and torrential rain pounded down on him—something he'd never encountered during any Alberta summer. All he could do was huddle, sodden, in the squall and hold on for dear life, hoping he wouldn't be swamped.

"One way to Nassau."

Samara pushed the bills under the Plexiglas barrier at the man sitting behind it wearing a stupid little hat. The bus had barely made it to the ferry terminal in time. Though she hadn't seen anyone from home chase after her, she suspected Daddy would soon be on the hunt for her—probably first going to her friend's house, not suspecting Samara's real destination.

The ferry ride was rough, and she could see lightning in the distance to the east. One of the other two passengers reported that an unexpected squall had hit the island moments after they got underway. Thank goodness the transit authorities hadn't caught up with the weatherman and shut the ferry down. She'd arrive in Nassau shortly after midnight, make her way to André's gallery—the shabbiness of the area didn't scare her a bit—stand on his doorstep, and wail aloud in the dark until he came down the many stairs to get her.

And that was when the first tremor of doubt rippled over the surface of Samara's conscience. She brushed it away.

He owed her that much, right?

In the storm, crouching in the boat not knowing his end, Kallum underwent his "dark night of the soul." He'd learned that phrase in a church history class when he'd come upon the sixteenth-century poetry of a Spanish monk; he thought that random thought now. Is this how a person died, with random thoughts chaotic in the head and wreaking havoc in the heart?

Shivering, his arms stiff with his death grip on the edge of the hull, Kallum reviewed not the mere facts of the past weeks but the motivations, the desires, the shady intentions of his soul. What had he expected when he allowed the temptation of his eyes to seduce him? Sure, God loved beauty, created beauty in His own image—no question about it.

Appreciating beauty wasn't the problem, Kallum told himself; worshiping it was. He knew the Bible; he held to the creeds. And he hadn't worshiped Samara—he'd simply *appreciated* her for her God-given looks.

What had God expected, flooding his senses with all that beauty?

Hard shards of self-defense and justification kept gouging at his brain. Even in Eden, perfect mankind couldn't resist beauty. God had made Lucifer the most beautiful of all angels, and Lucifer—that liar—used the beauty of creation to convince Eve, and Eve the beauty of forbidden fruit to convince Adam. Adam had blamed Eve and Eve had blamed Satan.

And now here Kallum was, blaming God.

Had he, after all, fallen into heretical worship of beauty, of creation rather than Creator?

He couldn't in all honesty hold Samara responsible for his faults, either. She had her own issues to sort out, sure, but loving her correctly—as Kallum was meant to fellowship according to the Word—would not look like it had been looking during his stay in Eleuthera. Living by truth meant coming out of the night to live under the scrutiny of God, who exposes all deeds to the light of day. The apostle John had said it well, the very John whom Kallum had been piously spouting for almost a month now, when he wrote that anyone claiming to be in the light—in the *phōs*, in true righteousness that would not cause stumbling—would love his sister.

Kallum was learning a personal lesson in the flesh as he was bounced and flung about in that lone, lost boat.

The worst of the storm lasted, perhaps, two hours, but the boat kept on rocking. At one point, he vomited from motion sickness or from rank fear, and he must have dozed off a couple of times. But out there on the great expanse of the ocean, all alone in a speck of a vessel, just a bit of flotsam beneath the black blanket of eternity, Kallum's heart broke, and he made his confession.

"I was wrong." He said it aloud to the occluded heavens, to the Lord beyond his vision. "I can't fix this. You were right, I was wrong. Help me."

Saturday's sunrise brought Kallum further physical misery, its heat drying his outer garments as well as his poor, parched mouth. After rowing three hours—so, maybe ten o'clock by his estimation, no working watch on hand—he thought he spotted a cruise ship on the horizon. If so, it was nowhere near enough to see him. Waves continued to jostle him. And where were the thousands of little islands said to make up this country? Water, water everywhere . . .

When the sun blazed overtop Kallum, scorching his nose and cheeks, he heard a plane—or maybe he was hallucinating. He slumbered for a while, or passed out, and awoke to the screaming roar overhead of a light aircraft with pontoons diving directly at him, swooping and waggling its wings, passing low enough once again for Kallum to read "N1794" on its fuselage. Wouldn't that be Chad? However, the plane didn't touch down, only flew off again—hopefully to let someone know Kallum's location coordinates.

Indeed, not an hour passed before a speedboat snarled towards him in the distance. The boat operators transferred Kallum to the rescue craft, sat him down in the shade of the canopy, and let him sip water a bit at a time. The second boatman, laden with a tank of gasoline, got

Catch of the Day going and headed out. Kallum learned, on the rescue boat's return trip to Eleuthera, that the Currys had alerted the Bahamian version of the coast guard about their missing boat, likely borrowed by that missionary kid without checking the fuel tank. At daylight, a general alarm had been issued for any private planes and watercraft in the area to be on the lookout. And he learned from the guard that Chad had left a message—couldn't land for the waves, glad he'd spotted Kallum, would see him soon enough.

Kallum couldn't keep his own eyes open. He slept until arriving again at the beach, where the Currys greeted him, and expressed their gratitude over his being safe, and accepted apologies for his foolishness.

No one else was on the beach to welcome the refugee home—no Hanson hosts or sons, no Bembe. And no Samara.

Kallum dragged his sunburnt and now rehydrated body back the few blocks to Morningstar. The compound was in an uproar. Students, not in classes over the weekend, were milling about, some of the girls weeping. Neighbors in housedresses with platters of food, and the other teachers, and Mr. Hanson himself were earnestly talking, not seeing Kallum right away. He caught snippets of comments, and they weren't about him having been saved at sea but rather about Samara and that rascal who'd spirited her off the island.

Kallum jolted as someone gripped his upper arm from behind.

Bembe hissed, "Whatchudoin' here, bey?"

"I . . . the boat almost capsized . . . storm at sea . . ." He was floundering.
"What's going on?"

"Samara run off. Wit' *you*, dey believe." Bembe stepped in front of Kallum and lowered his voice. "Better git behind dese shrubs."

Kallum ducked into the shadow Bembe pointed out. The old fellow explained that Mr. Hanson was right furious, and that Mrs. Hanson hadn't appeared all day though he'd heard her crying through her open window. He recommended Kallum not show his face just yet until the police turned up in one of their scarce squad cars, any time now. And maybe not show his face then, either.

Kallum saw prudence in the suggestion. Samara must have left home about the time he himself had headed for the beach last night—certainly very incriminating at first glance. And apparently the coast guard hadn't transmitted the message to the Hansons yet that Kallum had been found alone in a "stolen" boat. Kallum tugged at his salt-matted hair. News of his rescue would only make the story worse for him, as it might be assumed she had drowned, or something worse, by his hand.

Kallum knew Samara was in deep water, if not the liquid kind. He spoke urgently to Bembe. "I know where she is." Not for an instant did he doubt his own assessment. "Can you get me into the house without anyone seeing me?"

Bembe mumbled a prayer, seeming to implicitly understand the bizarre circumstances. He snuck Kallum around to the other side of the residence and hoisted him into Samara's window. She must have left some clue as to how he would find this André in Nassau. The manila envelope—with no return address anyway—was nowhere to be seen. He attacked her desktop and drawer, finding no clue of phone or paper address book.

He stilled. Hadn't she'd used some sort of journal for her original list of sightseeing destinations as they'd careened about in the golf cart? Yes—he spotted the notebook—there it was. He paged past its lists and scribbles and crossed-off items, cringing in shame at the cupid's heart bearing the initials *KM* and *SH.* He hit the final page bearing André's name scribbled by Samara with the pretentious *l'accent aigu* in place—as though she thought him some famous French artist or something—followed by a cryptic line of what Kallum hoped were directions. He'd have to decode them when he got to Nassau.

Bembe, acting as sentinel outside the window, hissed a warning that someone had entered the front door. No time for Kallum to get his wallet or his phone from his own room.

He leapt from the window onto the crushed-shell surface. "Can you lend me some money, Bembe? And get me to the ferry?"

Nassau at midnight was a creepy place. The area must be crime ridden, Kallum guessed, by the way the loiterers—both guys and scantily clad girls, not very pretty—were skulking around Potter's Cay, the ferry terminal.

Potter's Cay. Hadn't he seen the name on Samara's notation? Kallum pulled the folded journal from his back pocket and turned again to the end. *Potters Cay / r. on Shirley/ Over the Hill / Queen's Staircase / pink door / flames.* If only he had his phone—not that he was sure he'd get a signal. He wasn't about to ask any of the locals for directions. However, there was One he could ask—and he bowed his head right there on the street for a brief moment of humility and supplication.

Kallum paced. At least he'd figured out the first clue, which had been a gimme but proved to him that, yes, he was on the right track here. Shirley must be a road, so he headed south until he found its street sign and turned right. He had no idea what *Over the Hill* meant, yet, as he walked, he found a tourist signpost pointing to *Queen's Staircase* and finally spied an artistic work of graffiti splayed across a concrete wall, featuring the flames of hell. He stood on the spot, pivoting in a circle and surveying the ramshackle houses, until—bingo!—the pink door leapt into his view. He breathed thanks.

Light shone from a filthy upper window.

Kallum found the lock to be easily broken. He charged up the flights of stairs—one, two, three, four—praying, "Lord, protect her. Let her be okay."

On the top floor, a glow leaked from the edges of a door, and he flattened his ear against the cool wood. Voices muttered inside—not shouting or anything—one belonging to a male and then, maybe, Samara.

He banged a staccato on the door, waited to the count of three, and then hammered on it until a man cracked it open.

"Is Samara here?" Kallum thrust his chest out.

The other guy was about five feet seven, with a smarmy moustache and a sneer to go with it. "No Samara here. Maybe looking for *Coco*?" He guffawed at his private joke.

Kallum muscled his way in just as Samara stepped out of a back room, eyes down as she tucked a fake leopard skin around her like a bath towel. He recognized that costume.

Samara was in the middle of a sentence—"It's pretty tight, André"—as she lifted her head and caught Kallum square in the face with her azure gaze. She gasped and almost dropped the fabric.

Kallum held his hands up, both palms out towards her. "It's okay, Samara."

Her expression grew stony, a mask coming down over her visage. She almost spat her words out between clamped teeth. "What do you want?"

André interjected. "Hey, Coco, want me to boot this guy out?" He caught up and brandished what appeared to be a leather whip from the corner, then slapped it repeatedly into his other palm. As if the pipsqueak was any match for Kallum.

Kallum turned to Samara. "What's with 'Coco'?"

"My new identity, and keep it to yourself." She yanked her arm away from his reach. "It's too late to change my mind. You should leave."

Did she mean it?

But Samara appealed to André by tipping her head and gazing at him through half-lowered eyelashes in a vulnerable expression Kallum recognized. Come to think of it, she had no makeup on and looked about fifteen.

"It's short for 'Coconut Jungle Babe.'" André laughed. "The name will sell the vid title. Or maybe you want a piece of the action?" The slimeball jerked a thumb towards the back room. "She's gonna cost you."

At that, Samara moaned, blanching, her shoulders crumpling forward. Finally she was getting it, the situation obviously not what she'd believed.

Kallum gritted his teeth. He cast a glance around the room lined with shelving holding hundreds of CDs. A backdrop screen, a black-and-silver umbrella, and a couple of cameras were set up but no logo, no sign announcing a legit photography business.

He focused again on Samara. "I'm only leaving if you come with me. This is no place for you."

"I don't fit in at home, either." Samara's eyes filled to the watery brim, tears trembling along the bottom lid but not spilling over. She cast a glance at André and bent over at the waist in a dry heave.

Kallum gentled his voice. "The whole community is sick with worry. They miss you, Samara. Better get your clothes on."

The girl straightened, let out one long sigh, and nodded.

The photographer came at him then, and Kallum landed a punch on his nose, knocking him to the floor in a spurting of blood.

"I'll call the cops," the weasel threatened as he slid his butt backwards across the floor to the farthest corner.

Kallum stared at him. "Unlikely." He fastened his grip around Samara's arm and led her into the back room—*lair*, more like—to her clothing, all on a heap on the bed. The filthy pictures plastered on the walls and the video camera and track lighting all in place left no doubt about the purpose of this room.

"Did he . . . *hurt* you, Samara?"

She didn't lift her eyes to him, even when he tilted her chin up with his hand. She shook her head. "He told me to get some sleep because I needed to look good. I locked the door from the inside." Samara still held a fistful of faux leopard fabric, vainly attempting to cover herself. "He fed me mac 'n' cheese and left me alone to watch some of his videos"—she shuddered—"and then ordered me to get ready."

"For a . . . *model's portfolio shoot*?" It wasn't really a question. Kallum let all his disgust settle on that phrase. Had the girl really bought into the lie?

Samara nodded, silent.

In that silence, Kallum kicked himself. His disgust at her gullibility, at André's wickedness, smacked of pretentious superiority. He might as well ask himself if he'd really bought in to his own blindness, his own fantasy. Kallum exhaled a disappointed breath. He had a way to go before achieving maturity himself.

"Get dressed quickly," he said kindly now, but with insistence. "I'm taking you home."

He'd saved her.

Samara could think of nothing else as Kallum dragged her from the fourth-floor studio—more a pit of depravity, she saw now, than the "loft gallery" André had made it out to be. Kallum had had no obligation to rush to Nassau and collect her from her downfall, the troubles she'd brought upon herself. Yet he'd come anyway—he'd saved her from a life she was in no way ready to take on. She gagged at the thought of what she'd been about to do.

"This way." Kallum nudged her towards a street on the right. "The ferry won't leave until daybreak, but we might as well walk in the right direction."

"Right direction," Samara repeated, eyes welling again. The mental fog was lifting after the trauma of finding herself in the predicament she'd brought about. "I need the right direction."

Kallum turned his head sharply at her words as he trod the road alongside her. "Me too." It sounded to her like a confession.

Would Mama and Daddy forgive her idiocy? Would God?

Kallum steered Samara to an all-night coffee shop, where they'd hang out until the day's first ferry sailing. They had a few things to talk about anyway—first, Kallum apologizing for allowing his own passions free rein to take inappropriate advantage of her, and then his suggesting how they might make things right with her parents. Samara wasn't resisting any longer and openly wept, hair hanging like a curtain before her face.

Kallum would have wept, too, but he'd used up all his tears of repentance on Catch of the Day as he'd bobbed alone on the seas . . .

There in the café, Kallum didn't sucker in to vindicating himself. He simply and quietly sat there over his coffee and accepted his part. Samara offered her apology back, with no hugging, as the light of understanding and forgiveness began to dawn in her eyes.

She pulled her phone out and called home to say she was all right, that Kallum was escorting her back safely, that she would explain everything to them later. She gasped as she learned from Mama about the near drowning Bembe told about, shooting regretful looks towards Kallum. Before disconnecting, Samara added that they'd be home in time for church that morning.

Kallum, too, was anticipating his final days in Eleuthera, and he had a sneaking suspicion his approach to his classes would be more application than pontification, more walk than talk. Knowledge of God is not love of God, as that old, dead guy Blaise Pascal taught, the heart having its reasons that reason does not know.

Pastor Bembe was strutting his stuff, impressing Kallum with the last Bahamian sermon he'd be hearing.

"You look out dere!" With a flourish Bembe pointed through the window at the boundless expanse of water—that ever-present reminder to the Eleutherans of their source of life. "You come from de African side of dat great and mighty ocean dat turns around and feeds you. Look in ya books and what you read about de sea? It frets and it foams, the Latin says."

Kallum blinked. Bembe was right—*fretum* was one of the Latin words meaning 'sea.'

"It be a bottomless deep, a *profundum*," Bembe continued. Where had he learned this? Bembe was only warming up; sweat beaded his face as he stomped and thumped, lifting his Bible high. "In ancient Hebrew, de Lord ruled over *mayim* and *tehom*—de abyss of the floodwaters, home of Leviathan, dat drowned de Egyptians chasing Moses and his people. De Greek tells us *thalassa*"—although Bembe pronounced it *dalassa*—"be what Jesus walked upon, what Jesus calmed."

By this point, Kallum had slunk down into the pew and would have crawled beneath it if he could. Here he'd been bragging on his language acquisition as though no one else knew anything about Hebrew, Latin, Greek—heck, even English. What a snob he'd become.

"Now I ax y'all"—Bembe finished, pointing his index finger across the heads of his congregants but seeming to settle on Kallum—"have *you* let de Lord walk upon de turbulence of ya own heart? Have *you* invited de Lord to tame de abyss of ya own prideful soul?"

Had he? Had Kallum allowed his head knowledge to change his heart, his heart to inform his brain and apply complete truth to his spirit? He'd certainly learned more from his academic island project than the books had taught him. He cut his eyes sideways past Mrs. Hanson to a subdued Samara. Yes, he'd made his peace with her, with God, whatever the consequences he might face in the future as he walked in the light.

After church, Kallum phoned home on the Hansons' landline.

"Hi Mom. Is Dad there?"

"Is this an emergency, it being a collect call and all?" Her voice was full of laughter. Likely she was happy to hear from her absent son, evidently not yet knowing about his near drowning. When he didn't answer her question, her tone sobered. "Hang on. He's out in the corral doing chores. I'll call him in."

When Dad got to the phone, panting slightly, Kallum wasted no time. He plunged into his account of the storm—not only the outward tempest but the inward as well.

"So you can see I've been through a bit of a time here, Dad."

"I was picking up on that, son."

"I sort of lost my bearings for a while—in case you hear anything from the college." His parents went to church with one of the profs, who might receive some negative feedback about Kallum's tenure at Morningstar, including his moral failure—the root issue for Kallum.

"Find your way back again?" Dad's voice was gruff, real.

"Yep."

"Got your land legs under you, eh?" Dad chortled. Kallum could always trust him to see life in its true light.

"I remembered what you said to me once, Dad—that God's lamp throws only a big enough pool of illumination to show one step at a time."

A NOTE FROM THE AUTHOR

Dear Reader,

Perhaps you read my story "Aloft" in the summer 2025 Mosaic anthology, *BirdSong*.

My current piece, "Adrift," is a precursor to the last (with possibly a sequel to follow). This story takes place when Kallum MacVicar, only twenty, becomes temporarily unmoored from correct practice while teaching Christian truth. Now, I visited the island of Eleuthera, Bahamas, with my family one winter long ago, escaping Canadian snow, so I'm familiar with many of the spots I mention in this story. And I, too, suffered the beginning of my "dark night of the soul" while there. But God's Word shone a light for me so that, step by step, I found my way through.

Then again, when I was at seminary studying for my Master's degree in historical theology back in 2000, I hit a point in the learning process where my head's knowledge threatened to exceed my heart's application. I was so immersed in the lovely acquisition of *knowing* that, briefly, I minimized *doing*. Even in seminary it's possible for focus to blur. I was soon reminded that Christian belief involves both *understanding* scriptural truths and *trusting* the Lord by walking in the light of His Word. That is, *orthodoxy* (correct doctrine) leads to *orthopraxy* (correct practice).

That said, I would like to again thank in particular my friend Dr. Grant C. Richison for his ongoing exposition of Scripture (www.verse byversecommentary.com) that applies the unchanging truth of the Word of God to personal experience, showing me the light wherein I am to walk. Thanks go as well to my loving and supportive Mosaic sisters (especially, this time, Sara and Elizabeth); to The Word Guild for prayer support; to my family; and to you, my readers, for caring about my characters and their fictional lives.

Deb

ABOUT THE AUTHOR

Deb Elkink writes from a cottage beside a babbling creek in southern Alberta, Canada, a stone's throw from the Montana border and home base
for exotic travels with her husband of half a century. She published her
first bits of writing after graduating university (BA Communications),
then married and spent twenty years as a homeschooling mom and ranch
wife—rounding up cattle, earning her private pilot's license, and cooking for huge branding crews. A second degree (MA Theology, *summa
cum laude*) led to publication of a literary study on the fiction of G.K.
Chesterton (*Roots and Branches*), prepared her as an academic editor,
and jettisoned her into her long-held dream of writing literary fiction
with a theological twist. Her publications so far—incorporating travel
and taste buds and tumults of the heart—include two award-winning
novels (*The Third Grace* and *The Red Journal*) and a collection of short
stories (*Vagabond Come Home*).

Get to know Deb better at www.debelkink.com, or find her on Amazon, BookBub, Goodreads, and Facebook.

TITLES BY
DEB ELKINK

THE MOSAIC COLLECTION: NOVELS

The Third Grace
The Red Journal
Vagabond Come Home: Collected Stories of the Wayfarer's Return

THE MOSAIC COLLECTION: ANTHOLOGY STORIES

"Ever Greening" in *Hope is Born*
"Blue Genes" in *Before Summer's End*
"Reconstituted" in *Song of Grace*
"Taste Budding" in *All Things New*
"Clanging Symbols" in *Dancing in the Rain*
"Scrabbling" in *A Thrill in the Air*
"Aloft" (BirdSong)

Li'l Trip to Paradise

Eleanor Bertin

Li'l Trip to Paradise

Eleanor Bertin

Sun, surf, and sumptuous buffets. For two years, family drama and responsibilities have kept Holly and Shawn from returning to their favourite tropical paradise. Now nothing sounds better than leaving it all behind to celebrate their twenty-fifth wedding anniversary in Costa Rica. When a freak medical emergency overturns their vacation, Holly is blindsided by an even freakier change in her husband, threatening everything they've built together.

"Today, if you will hear His voice,
Do not harden your heart . . ."
Hebrews 3:15 (NIV)

To J

Li'l Trip to Paradise

With a flourish of satisfaction, Holly stroked out ~~Water Plants~~, ~~Empty Fridge~~, and ~~Call Mom~~ from her long and detailed pre-travel list. Boots stamping snow off in the back hall signaled her husband coming in from his last errand. Just for the fun of hearing Shawn's comeback, she held up the page in triumph. "I've checked everything off my To Do list."

Shawn nodded his approval, handing her a soft package. "Ta Da! Now I've checked everything off my Ta Da list." He poked a finger at the trademark Amazon smirk with a matching smirk of his own. "Ho, ho, ho! Another Ama-claus delivery."

Holly grabbed the parcel, trying to keep a straight face. This had been Shawn's running gag throughout the Christmas season. Ama-claus had been extra generous this year. Holly had lucked out with the gifts she'd chosen for everyone—daughters Jasmine and Chloe, her own parents, Shawn's dad, and even the other primary teachers at work had been thrilled. But this package, this one was for her.

"Finally! I'd given up hoping it would get here in time." Holly grabbed a pair of scissors from the kitchen drawer to slit the box flaps apart, tore open the plastic bag inside, and grinned. The burgundy swimsuit's soft, sleek fabric was even better in person. With the weight she'd lost since they planned their anniversary trip six months ago, the suit would look especially good. She could hardly wait to see Shawn's reaction. "You got McFuzz settled in at the kennel?"

Shawn slung an arm around Holly's waist and twirled her to face him. "Done. He's safe and sound, but a more disgusted cattitude you've never seen. So, everything's done. Except for this . . ." He held her face with one hand, kissing her deeply and tenderly as he moved with her again in the slow, adoring dance they had been swaying to now for twenty-five years. He was her everything.

"I can't believe we leave tomorrow," Holly murmured into Shawn's chest, matching her steps to his.

He pulled back to look at her. "By the way, I met your sister at the pet place. She was bringing in that yappy mutt of hers for pruning."

Holly giggled. "Grooming."

"Yeah. That." The smile faded from Shawn's mouth. "She seemed a bit miffed that we hadn't asked her to take care of the cat."

Holly sighed, burrowing back into Shawn's arms as if to escape the turmoil. With Natalie, it was always something, although Holly wasn't usually the cause of her sister's misery. That was Drew's area of expertise, Natalie's grinning buffoon of a husband.

Drew had won Holly's parents over before Natalie ever brought him home to meet them simply because he was studying to be a pastor. He'd looked like a stellar guy. Eventually, Drew and Natalie and the boys made the perfect family. Yet Mom and Dad either didn't notice or ignored the inconsistencies that Shawn and Holly saw—the poor money decisions, the neglected home and yard, the messed-up schedule leading to kids being sick. Holly's sister and her husband were late for everything. Then, two years ago, the shiny, happy mirage dissolved. Drew's "inappropriate relationship with a woman" was exposed, and he was booted out of the ministry. And who did Mom and Dad call to patch Natalie up? The whole mess had drawn Holly and her sister back together after a long cooling between them. In a way, being seen as the stable one, the responsible one, had been gratifying, but it was also exhausting.

Holly bit her lip. Part of the reason she was so looking forward to this trip was the reprieve from her role as Natalie's chief sounding board and problem solver.

"You're sure you're gonna be able to leave all the drama behind for two weeks, right?" Shawn's voice was a delicious rumble from deep inside his chest. As usual, his intuition about what she was thinking was right on the mark.

"Absolutely. Not taking it along. Not gonna think about it. Not even gonna mention it."

"Good girl. You need a break." He tightened his arm around her. "Just think! Nine days in paradise."

"Costa Rica, here we come!" Holly hugged back, then bounced out of his arms to grab his hands. "So, let's go eat."

"Okay, but we'd better make it an early night. Gotta get to the airport by five a.m."

A glow above the city as they approached it woke Holly from her drowsing. The green numerals on the dash clock read 4:45 a.m. She reached over to squeeze Shawn's hand.

"Sorry I fell asleep." She liked to keep her sleep and eating schedules in sync with Shawn's—to feel fatigue when he did and hunger when he did—so they experienced life in exactly the same way. They were a lighthouse, the two of them a fortress against the world.

He stroked her cheek with his thumb. "You've worked so hard to get us ready, I figured you deserved some extra rest."

Holly caught his hand against her face, kissing his fingers. "Have I told you recently that you're the best?"

He smirked. "Nope, never heard that before."

She huffed, delivering a light smack on his arm with the back of her hand, then switched on the dash light to check their passports in her carry-on bag for the umpteenth time. Exactly as she had placed them.

All the familiar routines of the car park and boarding the shuttle to the terminal were awash with the anticipation of the beach. She clutched Shawn's arm as they crunched across the snow-packed parking lot. "I can't wait to leave winter behind."

After checking baggage at the ticket counter and getting through customs, they found their departure area. Shawn rubbed his belly.

"Hungry?" Holly knew his cues. "I could go for some Timmie's about now."

"Sounds good to me." They lined up at Tim Horton's for their coffee and breakfast sandwiches, finding a seat near the boarding gate to munch the sausage-and-egg biscuits.

Shawn buried the last third of his sandwich inside its paper wrapper. "My eyes must have been bigger than my stomach. Are you done?" He held out his hand for her trash, then took the lot to the waste bin.

When he returned to sit beside her, Holly pointed to a sign on one of the duty-free shops down the corridor.

"Li'l Country Store," Shawn read. "Ha! We should check it out."

Holly smiled at him, remembering. They had met on a high school volleyball tournament trip. On the way home, the bus had broken down in Middle-of-Nowheresville, and Li'l LuLu's Diner was the only place that would open up at 11:30 p.m. to feed thirty teenagers with the late-night munchies. Ever since, Shawn had been finding li'l gifts for her. A package of Li'l Smokies sausages, or Li'l Nitro, the world's hottest gummy bears. Holly kept the freezer stocked with Shawn's favourite ice cream treats, Li'l Sammiches, and they collected Li'l Tikes toys for the girls when they were preschoolers. As recently as Christmas, Holly had found a Li'l Chiseler kitchen scraper in her stocking. "C'mon, let's go see what they've got."

At that moment, the gate attendant called for pre-boarding. "Oh-oh! That's us." Holly hooked her arm in Shawn's, and they stepped into the queue with others eager to escape a Canadian January.

Trotting down the long jetway to the plane, Shawn nudged Holly's arm. "Check out Li'l Cowpoke," he whispered. Ahead of them, a slight man, not much more than five feet tall, swaggered along under the largest white cowboy hat known to man. Holly covered her mouth to stifle a snicker, nudging Shawn in return.

They found their seats on the plane and settled in, hand in hand, for the six-hour flight to San Jose.

After take-off, Holly felt Shawn's eyes on her and met his gaze.

"Twenty-five years. How about that, eh?" His fingers trailed up her arm. "Remember that old lady in your church who tried to get you to break up with me?"

Like it was yesterday, Elsie Philpott's earnest, round face floated across from Holly at the tea room where they'd met. A steady stream of Bible verses had flowed from the older woman's thin lips. The most annoying one had been about the dangers of being "unequally yoked." Holly had already been hit with II Corinthians 6:14 enough times that she was sick to death of it. Her mom had used it to plead with Holly. Her youth group leader had brandished it to warn her. Even Dad had quoted it, adding, "You're making a mistake." With brimming eyes, Elsie had predicted lifelong sorrow if Holly married and raised children without a spiritual leader.

Holly's mouth tightened, remembering. Shawn had been a wonderful husband, a perfect father. She huffed. "Elsie Philpott. Someone I'd rather forget. Even my parents said we would never last." She pressed her forehead against his. "Sorry you had to put up with all that. Mom's silent treatment and Dad's heavy talks. All because you weren't a Bible thumper. I'm glad I didn't listen. We were meant for each other. Haven't we proved they were totally wrong?"

"Aw, they weren't so bad. Now that we've got daughters the same age, I totally get it." That was the thing about Shawn. He was a lot better at letting things go than Holly was when it came to her family. She still had a hard time forgiving them for the way they dragged themselves around at the wedding looking gloomy as heck. Good thing her folks eventually saw the light and accepted Shawn. How could they resist? He was such a nice guy.

She gripped his hand. "Drew's heavy-handed ambushes were a different matter though, huh?" Once he found out his brother-in-law wasn't a Christian, Drew made Shawn his special project. Family gatherings grew more awkward as Drew took every opportunity to "witness." What a dork.

Unoffended, Shawn had only made mild, private jokes about Drew's enthusiasm. "He's just immature," Shawn would say. Holly's admiration for how wise and tolerant her husband was had only grown. For her part, she'd stopped speaking to her sister.

Shawn rolled his eyes. "Ah, the two-hour Bible study disguised as 'let's go for coffee.' How 'bout we leave him behind with the snow?" He shifted his seat back as far as the business class seat would allow. Searching her face, his features softened. "Seriously though, haven't we been lucky? We've got our health, great kids—"

"One of whom was born before we could even get to the hospital. Good catch, *Dr.* Gardiner."

Shawn chuckled. "Ha. Nothing to it. But maybe I better stick with diesel engines since no one else ever asked me to deliver their baby. Remember li'l baby Chloe? Twenty years old now and she's still always in a hurry. So yeah, great kids. We've both got good jobs, a beautiful home—"

"That nearly killed us making it livable. Literally, blood, sweat, and tears."

"Ha! The dream home that started as a nightmare. Remember what the realty listing said? 'Great potential. Just needs some TLC.'"

"Little did we know that stood for The Loathsome Cathouse. I'd prefer to forget all those months of disgusting cleanout." Holly shuddered, recalling the vile odor and the three kitten skeletons they had found under mountains of unidentifiable junk.

"But look what we did with it. Would you have wanted it any other way?" He stroked her hand with his thumb. "'Things hard to endure are sweet in memory.' Like I said, we've been lucky."

"More than just luck, don't you think? We've made some good choices over the years."

"You mean like paying our mortgage off early?"

"I'm talking about even before that. For one thing, we didn't get married before finishing our education. Doing the opposite set Drew and Natalie back a lot. Then we waited to have kids instead of having one like they did before graduating college. I mean, did they ever plan ahead?"

Shawn frowned. "I thought we weren't bringing them with us on this trip."

Holly laughed, making shooing motions with her hands. "Whoops! You're right." Leaning her head on his shoulder and closing her eyes, she murmured, "Yeah, we've made a great life for ourselves. We've got everything." She tipped up toward Shawn's ear, humming their song, "Look how far we've come . . . mm, mm . . . You're still the one."

He found her lips, deepening the kiss and stirring welcome and familiar sensations inside her. It was going to be a fantastic vacation. They pulled apart when Holly sensed someone in the aisle next to them.

A young woman not much older than their daughter, Jasmine, flipped her long, dark hair behind her back to bend toward them. Her eyes sparkled as her gaze flicked from Holly to Shawn and back again. "Are you two on your honeymoon?"

Holly and Shawn exchanged surprised glances. "If you call twenty-five years married a honeymoon," Shawn told the girl.

"Seriously? That's amazing! I don't know anyone who's stayed married for that long." The girl's expression dulled for a second, then she brightened, flashing the diamond on her left hand. "My fiancé and I just got engaged. We're thinking about a September wedding. Well, enjoy your trip. It's so nice to see an older couple still in love." She carried on toward the rear of the aircraft.

"Older?" Holly stared at Shawn. They both collapsed in helpless laughter. Holly pushed up the arm rest from between them and snuggled against him. "I guess love and commitment is another thing we have going for us." No need to make the comparison to her sister's marriage. She knew it was on both their minds.

Between offers of drinks and snacks from flight attendants, Holly asked, "What's the thing you're most looking forward to once we get there?"

"Hands down, the sloths. I think they're my spirit animal." Shawn rolled his shoulders and covered a yawn.

"I was expecting you to say the all-you-can-eat buffet, but it's good to see you starting to relax." Holly stretched her legs under the seat in front of her. "Me, I'm looking forward to the beach the most. And maybe some paragliding. Last time, I was too chicken to try the front flips you were doing. This time, nothing will stop me."

Their landing was smooth, the warm, moist Costa Rica air embracing them in welcome. A chatty shuttle bus driver who drove them through the winding mountain roads out to the resort was a comic delight, and their room had a fabulous view of the cove and the sparkling, turquoise Caribbean beyond. Best of all, she'd forgotten how dreamy and relaxing it all was.

Holly came back in from the balcony to find Shawn sprawled across the king-sized bed. He frowned as he rubbed his belly. She tugged at his arm. "C'mon. Let's see what's for lunch. It's been a long time since breakfast, and I'm craving shrimp and calamari."

Shawn wrinkled his nose. "I'm not really that hungry."

"How is that possible?" She patted his flat stomach. "We've had nothing but ginger ale and pretzels since that early breakfast sandwich, and you didn't even finish yours. Come on. The sight of that buffet is bound to give you an appetite."

Shawn rose slowly to his feet, and together they meandered down to the dining room.

While Holly loaded up her plate from the colourful trays of fruit, Shawn's plate looked like hers on the first day of a low-carb diet. "It's okay, we're on vacation. Indulge!" she whispered, helping herself to the eggs benedict.

His feeble attempt at a smile both concerned and reassured her. She kept an eye on him while they ate, happy to see him enjoy the variety of fruit and cheeses.

"I know you wanted to find the sloths first, but why don't we spend the afternoon just lazing around at the beach? I'm dying to work on my tan so I don't look like something that just crawled out from under a rock. Besides, it's already been a long day."

Back in their en suite bathroom, Holly changed into the new swimsuit. The mirror gave its approval, and Shawn would, too. She stuck one leg out the bathroom door, humming a sultry tune as she sashayed toward him.

He let out a low whistle but made no move to pull her onto the bed where he had flopped down again. Disappointed, and feeling a little foolish, Holly put on the new cover-up, pleased with the lacy look of it. Then she spooned next to him on the bed. "Pretty tired, eh?" she asked, running a finger along his jawline. "A nap in the shade will do you good. Let's hit the water."

She tugged Shawn upright, and they gathered sunglasses, hats, and sunscreen, then wandered down the long stone staircase and out to the poolside, where they picked up towels and found a pair of lounge chairs. "Do you feel like taking a dip before we stretch out and get toasted?"

Shawn squinted against the brilliant sunlight. "You go ahead. I just want to—" He groped for the arm of the deck chair suddenly, thumping down hard on the foot end and making the chair upend. Clamping an arm against his middle, he grimaced.

"Babe! What's wrong?"

Shawn didn't answer, only lifted himself off the end of the chair and slid up to seat himself properly. He hugged his torso tight with both arms, his knees slightly raised.

When Holly laid her arm around Shawn, his body felt rigid. And hot. "You're burning up! And you've gone so pale. Do you need a bucket?"

He shook his head, then nodded. A low moan escaped his tightly pressed lips.

Holly searched the pool area for anything resembling a bowl or basin. "I'll be right back." She raced toward the lifeguard, a fit-looking guy who seemed impossibly young. In answer to her, he jabbed a thumb back toward the hotel. Before Holly started jogging up the long staircase, the lifeguard called after her, "Ask for the nurse."

Holly hated leaving Shawn even for a minute, and it seemed forever before she found the nurse on staff. But at least the woman appeared competent. Together they rushed down to where Shawn tossed and turned on his lounge chair. Kids that had been horsing around in the pool now stopped and stared.

Nurse Martina stroked Shawn's forehead with a thermometer and listened to his heart, then pumped up the blood pressure cuff around his arm. Her eyes widened when she checked the temperature reading.

"Too bright," Shawn ground out, turning away from the sun with his eyes screwed shut. "Help me get to the shade." He tried to lift himself onto one elbow, but slumped down, too weak to manage it.

Holly searched Martina's face. "What's wrong with him?"

Martina frowned. "Can you touch your chin to your chest?" she asked Shawn.

He bent his head weakly, but not far enough to satisfy the nurse.

The crease between Martina's thick eyebrows deepened. "We need to get him to the hospital right away." She pulled a two-way radio from her pocket, calling for a stretcher and ambulance. Then she lowered her voice. "We had two cases of bacterial meningitis last year . . ."

Holly's stomach dropped. She glanced at Shawn, hoping he hadn't heard the dreaded words.

Please, God, not that. Don't let it be life threatening! "What about the stomach pain?" Holly gripped the plastic slats of the deck chair. "Couldn't it be food poisoning?"

"What has he eaten today?" Martina asked, as two hotel porters arrived with a gurney. They transferred Shawn to it and lugged him back to the hotel at a remarkable speed. Jogging to keep up with them, Holly filled the nurse in on what Shawn had consumed that day. "No shellfish, either."

An ambulance waited at the resort portico when they reached it. Holly scrunched in next to Shawn. No way was she leaving his side. While the paramedic started an IV, they careened along winding, mountainous roads back to the city.

At the hospital, Holly kept a firm grip on Shawn's hand. A hospital orderly whisked him into the *sala de urgencias.* She whispered reassurances to him during the paramedic's rapid-fire Spanish report on his condition to hospital staff. At the same time, she tried to decipher a clue from the medical jargon about what they might be facing but gleaned nothing. Hopefully, once they saw a doctor, he could explain in English what was wrong. When the curtain was drawn and they were left alone, Shawn's moans became audible. The eerie sound frightened her.

"Get me the chaplain," Shawn rasped.

Stroking his forehead with a damp wipe, Holly wasn't sure she'd heard him right. "What, Babe?"

"Call the hospital chaplain."

"Yeah, right." Holly emitted a sound that was half chuckle, half sob. What a guy. Even in this intense pain he was still kidding around.

"No, really. I wanna talk to someone." Shawn gasped out, a frown of deep concentration wrinkling his forehead.

"I'm here for you, Babe. You can talk to me about anything."

Shawn clawed at the rumpled sheet on the gurney before fixing her with an anguished look. "Please, Holly. I want the chaplain."

"Now? I mean, the doctor might get here any time."

"Now. I mean it, Holls."

That tone and that nickname? He meant business.

"Oo-kayy." She sprang from her chair at his side, skirted his bed with a final worried glance his way, and dashed out of the cubicle. This was so out of character. Was it pain making him delirious? She darted a glance down the corridor in both directions. Did they even have chaplains here? Where should she look for one?

She aimed for the nursing station, where precious minutes ticked by before she could make herself understood. A short, cheerful nurse pointed her in the direction of the chapel. She raced down the hall and turned left as she'd been told.

The wooden door opened on a large, dim room that looked pretty Catholic to her—a bank of candles flickering at the altar, pictures of Mary, stained glass. All so foreign to her Baptist upbringing. She hesitated, puzzling over the contrasts. But what difference did it make? Religion was all the same ridiculous nonsense. *Religulous*, as that funny documentary a few years back had been called. Shawn had said chaplain, not priest, but she'd do anything for him. Besides, she had no clue where else to try.

Antsy about leaving Shawn unattended, Holly paced the width of the vaulted room. She was about to head back to the nursing station to plead for more information when the heavy wooden door creaked open.

"Can I help you?" A sixtysomething man with a thin, gray ponytail, wearing a green polo shirt and khaki shorts, came slowly toward her. His hospital ID tag swung from the lanyard around his neck as he walked.

"My husband asked me to find a chaplain."

"That would be me." He stuck out his hand. "Luis Flores. And you are?"

She shook his hand distractedly. "Holly Gardiner. Would you mind coming with me? I really don't like to leave him. He's in a lot of pain." She hurried through the door that Luis held for her, explaining their situation as they returned down the hall to Shawn's room.

"We just got here from Canada today, and everything was fine. Then all of a sudden after lunch, Shawn doubled over in pain. The ambulance got us here as quickly as they could, but he's in very bad shape." She eyed Luis's open collar, shorts, and sandals. "You're not a priest."

Luis gave a short laugh. "No. Not even Roman Catholic. Born and raised a Tico, but I'm with an American mission agency, filling in this year for the Protestant chaplain, who is furthering his education up in North Carolina."

"Tico?"

"Costa Rican," Luis explained. "Can I ask, what is your husband's faith affiliation?"

Holly's neck stiffened considering this. "None" had been the easy answer on the medical forms she'd filled out for him twelve years ago after a car accident. Nothing had changed since then, either. They still spent their Sunday mornings on long bike rides or cross-country skiing, antiquing, or simply getting chores done around the house before going for a leisurely brunch.

Holly managed to avoid answering Luis's question because they'd reached the emergency cubicle where Shawn lay, still clutching his middle.

He opened his scrunched eyes long enough to hear her introducing Luis. "Can I . . . talk to him alone?" He was looking at Holly.

Holly frowned, confused. "Yeah, okay, sure." She stepped out, walking stiffly to the waiting area near the nurses' station.

Finding a seat in a dim corner, she pondered Shawn's strange request. It spot-lit scenes from the past that she had been only too happy to leave behind.

Holly had been steeped in religion all her life. It was as natural as breathing for her to talk to Shawn about God while they were dating. He had never been antagonistic—simply uninterested. When she invited him to church, sometimes he would even come. Toward her parents, he was always pleasant and respectful. But their dates often ended in arguments, with Shawn retreating into silence.

Sometime during college, after an especially forceful discussion about the truth of the Bible, Holly had asked Shawn what his objection to Christianity was.

"I guess I just don't see the need for any of that."

Afterward, she'd come to a decision. No more pressure. No more invitations to church, or concerts, or other Christian events. No sneaky tuning his car radio to a Christian station. No books or magazine articles left lying around where Shawn might read them. Didn't the Bible say a wife should let her behaviour be the silent influence? Holly had applied the same reasoning to girlfriends.

She snorted, crossing her legs in the waiting room's armless chair. Basing her decisions on the Bible was a thing of the quaint past.

Shawn had made no objection to being married in a church or to her attending services on Sundays. At first, she had thought he might change his mind. But Shawn was a contented atheist. "We're happy without all that," he'd say. Happy to let others believe as they wished. Happy to enjoy the great life they had built for themselves. Live and let live, he'd say.

Yet it was lonely going to church by herself. Once the girls arrived, Holly became more devoted to raising them in the faith. She took them to Sunday school as often as they weren't suffering the sniffles. But she felt the hurt every time she had to witness, alone, some family dedicate their baby to God. The pain of not being able to do that with Shawn was like a sharp pebble in her shoe. To make matters worse, she was annoyed when a zealous man said, "What are we going to do to get your husband into church?" Like Shawn was some stray dog needing to be trained to leash. The comment plucked Holly's every protective, defensive nerve.

As the girls grew older and started getting involved in gymnastics and ringette, it became even harder making it to church. At the same time, a rare sermon on hell made her uneasy with the implications about Shawn's destiny. How could a loving God send such a wonderful, well-meaning man to eternal punishment? For a few months, Holly read and thought, and argued against what she read and thought, and finally she came to a realization.

"I have no belief in a god," she told Shawn one night after the girls were in bed. She had practiced that statement several times in the mirror that week, first whispered, then aloud. Nothing had happened. No lightning bolt struck her, no case of leprosy sprang up on her skin. Only her own smile of relief had met her gaze.

He'd looked up from the Mustang monthly magazine he was reading. "Bravo! Welcome to the real world," he'd said, smiling warmly.

Finally, Holly had had peace. She withdrew her church membership. Once she learned to resist the guilt manipulation of her family and the church members who came at her, life was so much easier. In fact, she had gone into some depth researching the atheist position and found it intellectually satisfying. Shawn left her to it. Although he listened patiently to her conclusions, he was never much invested in the issue. She still enjoyed a good belief-busting podcast every so often.

Now this. This bizarre demand to talk to a chaplain. Holly twisted the dried-out wipe she still held in her hands into a hard rope.

Smiling, Luis emerged from the ward to let Holly know she could return to Shawn's bedside. At the same time, the doctor arrived. From then on, a flurry of tests and consultations led quickly to a decision for surgery.

"No, no. Not meningitis, thank God," the doctor assured Holly and Shawn. "But we fear the appendix may have ruptured." He hurried away, calling out to the staff in rapid Spanish.

Relief at the news it was not meningitis quickly switched to worry again. The word "rupture" struck fear in Holly's heart. Other words like "infection," "abscess," and "risk of death" jumped off the screen when she googled the possibilities amid the hive of medical activity.

An orderly swept the curtain aside and Shawn, his eyes clamped shut again, was rolled away to the operating room without a proper goodbye.

"Señora Gardiner?" A slender nurse touched Holly's shoulder gently. "He is awake now." She bent her finger for Holly to follow her.

Holly rubbed drowsiness from her eyes and hurried toward a room. Shawn lay in the bed, surrounded by a curtain, unmoving. She tiptoed toward him and perched on the edge.

"Hey, Babe," she whispered into the white noise of beeping monitors and hallway clatter.

Groggily he opened his eyes. Though pale, at least his face was free of that grimace. "Hey."

"Feeling better?"

"Fine as frog's hair." His soft croak matched the description.

Holly smiled, stroking smooth the hair on his arm. "Doc said it was ruptured, but he promised they got you all cleaned out."

"Better than Ex-Lax."

She mussed his hair. "You." Bending down, she kissed his face all over. "You had me scared."

"Me too."

"Any pain yet?"

"Not yet. Just a bit loopy from whatever they gave me."

"Can I see?"

"Trust a kindergarten teacher to expect show and tell."

She lowered the sheet and lifted the hospital gown to uncover his surgical site.

"Wound care compliments of the Wizard of Gauze." Shawn's eyebrows tented wryly. At least his wit was still intact.

"It does look pretty bulky. How does it feel?"

Shawn shut his eyes and groped the op site lightly with one hand. "Dry, soft, with some sort of plasticky tape across it."

Holly could barely break a smile. Shawn's face was still pale as death despite his attempt at humour. The thing was, though, he glowed. She had never seen him like this. Like a light from within was seeping out. It must be the drugs. The pain would hit soon enough.

A nurse bustled in to take vitals.

When she left, Shawn reached for Holly's hand. He snaked his head around until she met his gaze. "You have questions, right? Like why I wanted a chaplain?"

Holly did not want to have this conversation. She squirmed, her eyes scanning the uneven paint where the pale green wall met the white ceiling. "You would never have been satisfied with a paint job like that." She jutted her chin upward.

Shawn didn't look, only held her hand, forcing her gaze to him. "Holly, we should have a li'l talk about this."

She gritted her teeth. Now was not the time to be cute. "What if I don't really want to?"

"I know what you're probably thinking, but I *need* to talk about what's happened."

Heat rushed up the back of Holly's neck. She snatched her hand away, putting distance between them by dropping into the plastic chair next to his bed. "So then, talk."

Without looking at him, she could feel his disappointment. She could picture the hurt look on his face caused by her anger. She steeled herself not to give in and soften. The air conditioning system suddenly thrummed loud in the room between them. Down the hall, nurses' laughter punctuated the stiff silence.

"I've never been in that much pain before."

Holly said nothing.

Shawn heaved a sigh. "What kept banging around in my head was a question you once asked. You said, 'If God asks you why He should let you into His heaven, what would you say?' At the time, it meant nothing to me because I was young and healthy. But with the agony I've been in, that came back to me. The worst part was I knew I would be facing my Maker alone. You wouldn't be at my side. No one would. And I knew my good wouldn't outweigh my bad."

Aghast, she stared at him. "But you're a good man, Shawn. The very best. Of course what's good about you outweighs any bad."

"No, Holly, it doesn't. And the thought of being judged . . ."

This didn't sound at all like her upbeat, witty Shawn. Where had all this black talk come from? Holly fidgeted in the hard chair. "That's just superstition. We've left all that behind with the dark ages, remember?"

His voice dropped to a whisper. "Then what happens when we die, hmm?"

Holly went still, her eyes fixed on a small tear in the fabric curtain through which the lowering sun beamed. Shawn was serious. Dead serious, and that scared her. He'd never talked this way before, not even when they used to have those crazy, rambling, and sometimes heated discussions when they were dating. Back when she used to try to convert him. What was it he used to say when she'd bring up the idea of an afterlife? She murmured it now. "I guess we'll have to wait and see what happens." There might have been a bitter edge to her words.

He roused himself to snort softly. "I guess I deserved that. For all the times I answered you that way back in the day."

He remembered those talks? She hadn't meant to say it out loud. His admission melted her. She never could stay mad at Shawn for long. Finally, she turned toward him. "No worries, Babe. I'm just so glad you're out of the woods. Doc says you'll only need to be here a couple more days as long as the antibiotics do their job. You'll get stronger every day, back to your old self in no time. We're gonna beat this, maybe even still enjoy a bit of a vacation while we're down here."

Shawn shifted his gaze upward to the ceiling. "I tell you, the thought of me just ending, of going into the earth, never to live again . . . It tore me up." He shuddered so that the IV line quivered all the way up to the bag. "I was convinced I'd be meeting God soon, and the thought utterly terrified me."

He turned his head on the pillow and shone a beatific smile up at her. Not his wry, teasing smile nor his eyebrow-raised suggestive smile. This was different, an aura that could only be described as glory. "The great thing is, I knew what to do about it. And for that I have you to thank. You and Drew." He reached for her, but she folded her arms against him.

"What's Drew got to do with anything?" She spat his name, dreading what was coming.

"Just like he used to tell me all the time. I needed to get right with God. When you brought Luis here, I got down to business. It's all true. The Bible, everything. It's what I've wanted all my life, even if I didn't know it." He shrugged, his smile never wavering. "I guess I belong to Jesus now." He pulled his other, IV-wired hand over to hold out both hands, pleading. "I wish I'd done this years ago. But like Luis said, it's never too late."

The pulse in Holly's throat throbbed. She searched his face, tried to understand what was happening. If Shawn belonged to Jesus, he no longer belonged to her. Indignation darkened her heart. It spread through to her extremities like a hot dye. How could he? She clenched her ribs, her fingernails digging into the skin.

His self-sufficiency and confidence had attracted her right from the start. Hadn't he often said he was the captain of his life? So now he was giving that up to be a stupid sheep who believed whatever some dusty old book said? Life wasn't supposed to turn out like this.

Betrayal hung an unfamiliar curtain between them that thickened, darkened, as the seconds ticked on.

"Hey," he breathed softly, "you gonna say anything? I thought you'd want to know what's going on in my head."

Holly's whole body tensed. "We had each other. You've always said I was enough for you." She forced out that much but couldn't go on. Instead, the chair clattered backward as she bolted from the room.

Tears blurred her vision as she stormed down the hallway and out into the twilight of the street in front of the hospital. Wasn't she the one who had left behind her Christian upbringing for him? She shuddered to think of her family's cloyingly sweet reaction if she were to return to all that.

Even the cacophony of the traffic-packed street couldn't drown out the clamour in Holly's head. Blindly she fled down the busy sidewalk, not caring where she went. The inland humidity mingled smells of food kiosks with the acrid odors of diesel and sweat on the crowded street.

A thousand logical protests against his belief in a god shouted within her. But from deep down, the most painful question shot to the surface. Did he love her less than she loved him? She sobbed at the thought, tears spurting from her eyes. Flicking them away with an angry swipe, she charged ahead, setting one foot off the curb to cross the street. A horn blasted close to her. She jerked back from the pavement just as a truck careened around the corner. The wind of its rush whipped her hair across her mouth. She would have been hit.

Trembling and panting, she tried to gather her wits. What was she doing? Out here on a street in a strange city, far from the one person she needed more than anyone on earth. Wiping her damp cheeks, she reversed course and slowly trudged back the few blocks to the hospital. But it took more than an hour for her to compose herself enough to return to Shawn's room.

He was sipping apple juice when she came through the door. "Ah, there you are." He set the glass on the over-bed table, shoving it aside to stretch his arms out for her. "C'mere, Babe. I was worried about you."

Holly let herself be enfolded but kept her weight off him. She buried her face in the shoulder of his gown that smelled of bleach.

"Doc says I might be able to leave here the day after tomorrow."

"That's good," Holly mumbled into his neck.

He pressed back gently on her shoulders to where he could see her. "I'm so glad you're okay. But now I'm really tired. Must be the meds. You take a cab back to the hotel, alright?" He pursed his lips for an air kiss. "I'll see you tomorrow."

Holly gave a half-hearted wave and left to make her way back to the hospital entrance. No matter what Shawn said, she knew nothing would ever be the same.

It ended up being a full three days and nights before Shawn was released. He was weak and often sleepy in the six days of vacation they had left.

A jungle excursion to see the sloths was more than he could manage, and paragliding was out of the question. Instead, the two of them lay out at the pool most mornings, then returned to their room for his nap. Holly was becoming nicely browned, but the look was completely lost on Shawn, who had no energy for bed frolics. Which only widened the distance between them.

She could tell Shawn had found something religious on his phone; she would catch him reading it whenever she came back after leaving the room or having a shower. It annoyed her that he shut it the minute she returned to pay attention to her. Like he was feeling for the door to the fortress she had become. A fortress they had always inhabited together. He kept apologizing for ruining their vacation.

"It's not your fault," Holly insisted. "At least you're not in the hospital anymore." What she didn't bring up was the new barrier between them.

On their last evening, Shawn was finally able to enjoy a decent-sized portion of the prime rib dinner. She'd still tried to match her appetite to his, but it seemed a shame to lose out on the fabulous spread at each meal. They played a game of billiards before wandering through the manicured grounds of the resort.

Shawn pointed to an upholstered sofa in the shade of a gazebo. "Let's sit here for a bit."

"You're tuckered out?"

"No, no. Just wanted to sit with you out here."

Holly had an uncomfortable feeling there was more to it. When Shawn put his arm around her and took her hand with his other hand, she knew she was right. She stiffened, bracing herself.

"You know, we've gotta have that li'l chat sometime."

Holly sighed.

"I can feel the divide," Shawn began. "And I don't want my new faith to come between us. If you'd just talk about it. We've always told each other everything, and I really need to share what I've been learning. I mean, it's like this whole new world has opened up to me. Everything's so fresh and amazing. It makes sense of—"

Holly slid out from under his arm abruptly. "Look, Shawn. We're atheists. We think rationally about life." She evaded the hand that reached to take hers again. "I guess I can accept that you've decided to look into religion. But what gets me is, where does that leave me? I don't know what it means for us, for our life. All our years together, all those happy, contented years, are they just wasted? Don't they mean anything to you now?"

"Of course they do, Babe. Nothing can take that from us." He tilted his head, trying to pull her gaze. "This doesn't change a thing between us."

"Yes it does." It came out sharper than she intended. She softened her tone. "You've always been first in my life." Holly leaned into him now. "You're all the god I need. And I thought I was first in yours, too. I thought we liked it that way. It's like we were—I don't know—joined at the hip or something. Like when they tied us together with a skipping rope for those three-legged races we used to run at the neighbourhood block parties. But now everything's lopsided. You're leaving me behind." Her voice cracked. In a bitter whisper she added, "For religion."

He smiled a sad smile at her for a long minute. "If you could just open yourself up to join me—"

Holly frowned. He had no idea what it would cost her to re-enter that world. "That's never gonna happen. End of story."

She was all business as they packed up to leave the resort, navigated check-in at the airport, and boarded their flight. At least she had less regret at having to return to winter. Holly focused on thinking ahead to school starting. She looked forward to being back with her kindergarteners again.

All the while, she avoided Shawn's arms and hands and kisses, knowing her aloofness hurt him but unable to be or do or think what he wanted her to. Still, the longer the cold war lasted, the worse she felt. Like she had lost a body part the way Shawn had. How long would she be able to hold out?

Back in Calgary, winter's early dusk had fallen. Streetlights shone blue on the sparkling new snow.

Shawn merged onto the Queen Elizabeth 2, heading north to Red Deer. He broke the chilled silence. "How long do you figure McFuzz will give us the cold shoulder for leaving him at that place?"

Holly froze guiltily. She stole a glance at him, but his mild expression betrayed no resentment at the cold shoulder she'd been serving up. She stared at his hand, his dear, familiar hand on the shift lever, missing the feel of it. In the last couple of days, he had stopped trying, yet it beckoned her. Could she bridge the gap? It meant opening herself to something she'd thought she was well rid of. And yet, at the critical moment when the threat of meningitis had loomed, hadn't her reflex been to cry out to God? Of course, that had been mere conditioning, brought on by the desperation of the moment. Still, it *hadn't* been meningitis. Shawn was recovering.

Holly clamped her knees together and pressed her arms to her sides to stop her shivering.

They passed the last glimmer of the city's lights, plunged into a darkness that might have been a snug cocoon if not for the wall between them. She foresaw their lives flowing bleakly forward along an acute angle, their paths widening over time until the gap would be too great to straddle. Already she missed him desperately. Only six inches from her hand to his, but the leap seemed impossible. Despite her chill, Holly broke into a sweat, resisting.

Miles passed and she had not answered his quip about the cat. All she could think about was his hand, lit by the green glow of the dash light, what it would mean for her to reach for it. What it would mean if she didn't. She hated the unfamiliar coldness, the separateness, the bitterness in her own soul.

The glow of Red Deer became its lights. Its lights guided them toward home. In some strange way, it seemed a deadline. Fail to reach out and the disharmony would continue to a terrible end. Touch him and everything would change.

Just hold his hand. Let him know you'll try.

Only one more turn before their street corner. Their future hinged on whether she would reach out to him. Shawn made the turn. Only two blocks left. Soon the moment would pass. Maybe forever. Now just one block to go.

Swallowing the hard lump in her throat, the lump made of doubt and fear and pride, Holly moved her hand toward Shawn's. Reaching out at last, she took his warm hand in hers and gave it a li'l squeeze.

A Note From the Author

The idea for this story came to me a year ago when someone dear to me announced she had "deconstructed." Raised in a Christian home, professing Christ at an early age, my friend publicly declared a lack of "god belief." I'm sure this individual never guessed the depth of the hurt this would cause family, church, and friends.

When you build into someone's life, believing her professions of faith, feel like you're both on the same side of the struggle—to have that all swept aside can be devastating. On top of the empty feeling of loss, you feel tricked.

Perhaps you, too, have been left behind by a loved one forging past faith in God to the brave new world of unbelief. We know from Scripture that those who genuinely receive Christ's gift of eternal life can never lose it (John 10:28). We know, too, that not all those who profess belief in Jesus are genuinely saved. ("They went out from us, but they were not of us; for if they had been of us, they would have continued with us; but they went out that they might be made manifest, that none of them were of us." I John 2:19)

Yet no one is beyond the gracious work of the Holy Spirit. Shawn, the happy atheist, is transformed from the inside. This is our great hope, our "secret weapon"—that those we continue to pray for will be drawn to Jesus by His powerful Spirit. May we never give up hope.

Your friend,
Eleanor

ACKNOWLEDGMENTS

Thank You, Sovereign Lord, for Your saving power to reach even the most stubborn of hearts, my own most of all.

Thank you also to Angela D. Meyer for some excellent feedback to help this story make sense and to Deb Elkink for her diligent editing.

Thank you, Reader, for coming along on this writing journey with me and for your welcome and encouraging feedback.

ABOUT THE AUTHOR

From her home in central Alberta, Canada, Eleanor Bertin writes fiction that ponders the depths of God's love and mercy to humanity. Before raising and home-educating a family of seven children for thirty years, Eleanor received a college diploma in Communications and worked in agriculture journalism. She returned to writing in 2016 and has since published five novels, as well as the memoir, *Pall of Silence*, about her late son, Paul.

She and her husband of more than 40 years are the grandparents of ten amazing grandchildren. Along with their youngest son, Timothy who has Down syndrome, they live in the Before of a beautiful century home. www.eleanorbertinauthor.com

TITLES BY ELEANOR BERTIN

THE MOSAIC COLLECTION: NOVELS

The Ties That Bind Series
Lifelines
Unbound
Tethered

Burning Bright Series
Flame of Mercy
Flicker of Trust

THE MOSAIC COLLECTION: ANTHOLOGY STORIES

"Like Wool" in *Hope is Born*
"Love & Unexpected Stress Responses" in *A Star Will Rise*
"How Life Begins" in *All Things New*
"Christmas at the Crossroads" in *A Whisper of Peace*
"Grounded" in *Before Summer's End*
"A Portion of Grace" in *Song of Grace*
"Who Sends the Rain?" in *Dancing in the Rain*

"No Night There" in *The Heart of Christmas*
"Meg and the E-Monster" in *A Thrill in the Air*
"Not by Chance" in *Sounds Like a Plan*
"Unremarkable Sue" in *A Weary World Rejoices*
"Call Me Birdie" in BirdSong

Standalone (Non-Fiction)
Pall of Silence: My Journey from Tragedy to Trust

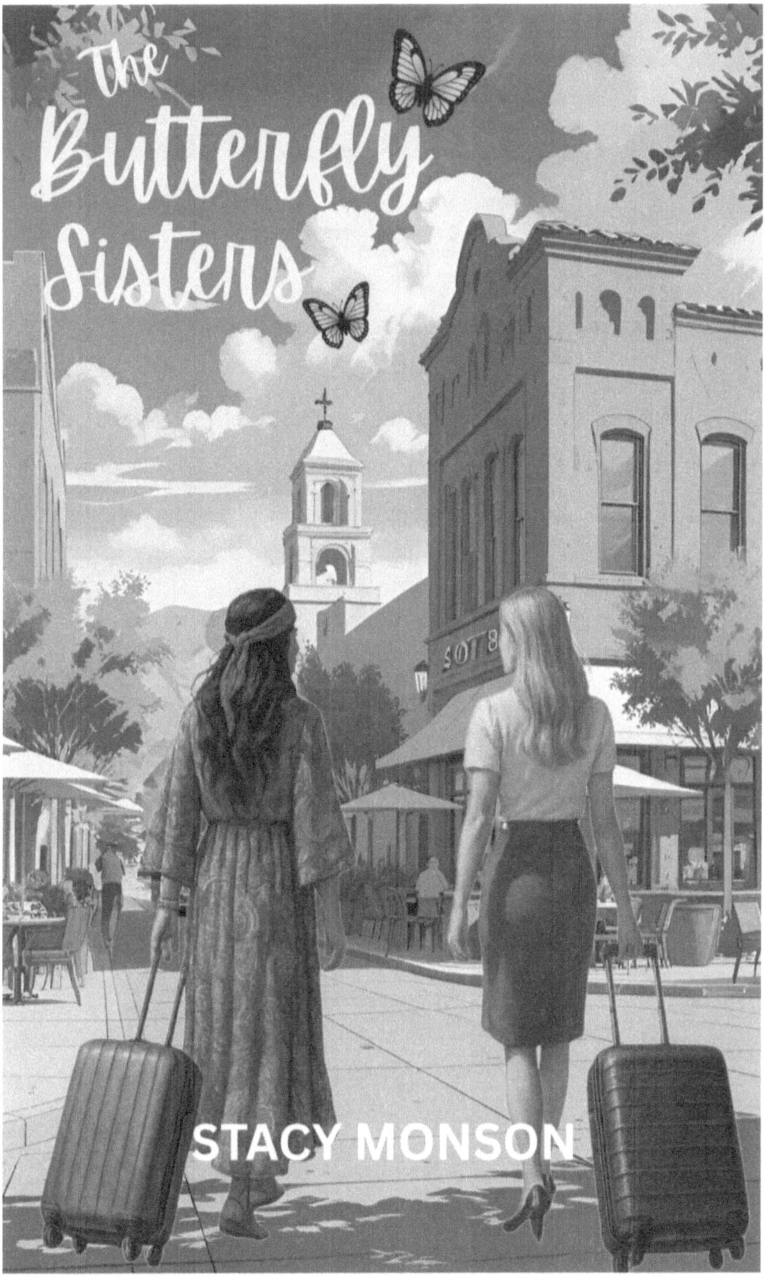
The Butterfly Sisters
STACY MONSON

THE BUTTERFLY SISTERS

Stacy Monson

A heartwarming story of unlikely friendship and finding joy after loss.

Dorothea loves yoga, flowing ensembles of wild colors, and marching to her own drummer. Trixie has spent her life happily in the shadow of the husband she adored; she prefers order and staying in the background. Aside from having the widow title, what could they possibly have in common?

"The Butterfly Sisters" is a lighthearted tale of healing, hope, and the incredible power of being open to the unexpected. Grief isn't a life sentence, but sometimes we find that the person we least expect is the one who helps us find our wings. A story about second chances and laughter through tears, "The Butterfly Sisters" is an uplifting journey from the cocoon of sorrow into the bright light of new beginnings.

CHAPTER 1

"Bobby, why did you leave such a mess?" Dorothea Jackson frowned at the collection notices strewn across the kitchen table. For over three decades, she'd let her husband "run the show," as he'd called their life. Now she'd caught on to how much was show and how little was substance. He hadn't been kidding, as she'd assumed.

Since his death almost two years ago, she'd been waiting to hit bottom, but she remained in free fall. He'd assured her he had everything under control. As a highly paid contractor to human resources departments around the country, he'd advised top companies on how best to care for their valued employees. Why would she think he wouldn't take care of her if something happened to him? She'd believed him.

With a deep sigh that echoed in the hollowness in her heart, she plopped onto the chair, the wood creaking under her. As reality had sunk in, the illusion of their idyllic life shattered like a piece of her pottery. While she'd been free to make and teach ceramics, practice yoga and Pilates, and raise their two children to be life-loving, free-thinking adults, she'd been oblivious to their finances. Apparently, he had been as well.

When the cancer diagnosis came, she'd been thankful insurance had covered most of the treatments, but she'd been forced to wise up to what had actually gone on behind the scenes of their "idyllic life." It had been a rude awakening. Then he'd had the nerve to die and leave her with the mess.

Chin propped on her hand, she turned her gaze to the winter wonderland outside. The third major storm of this winter had dropped another ten inches of sparkling ice particles on top of piles of snow. Yet again she'd be bundling up to shovel herself out of the newest dumping—while the shiny, and enormous, snowblower Bobby had insisted on buying sat idly watching. He'd bought it but never showed her how to run it. She shook her head with a snort. Not that she'd ever try. That monstrous machine would probably drag her down the street and dump her in a ditch. She'd rather snowshoe her way out of the house and find a neighbor to do the snow blowing.

She was tempted to ignore it all, skip winter completely, and hide out somewhere warm and sunny where she could live incognito. Maybe she should move to Florida, where she wouldn't have to deal with winter and she'd be close to the grandkids. She shuddered. But they had hurricanes there, which seemed a lot worse than a snowfall in Wisconsin. A lot worse.

The ding of a text pulled her attention from the window. Speak of the devil. She chuckled. Not that Willow was a devil... anymore. "Hi, Mom! Here's something a friend sent me that I thought sounded fun. What do you think?" She'd included a link.

"Christian Widows Restorative Retreat"—four days of relaxation, spiritual healing, prayer and share times, goal setting, and self-discovery.

"A *widow's* retreat?" She hooted. What could be worse than a bunch of old women sitting around crying into their lace handkerchiefs and sharing memories of their long-dead husbands? Even the word "widow" conjured morbid images of black clothing, a shuffling gait, and thin white hands that trembled. While she'd adored her grandmother, she still couldn't shake that image from Grandpa's funeral. She wasn't about to turn into Granny if she could help it. And not going to a widow's retreat was a solid step away from becoming that.

She gave a thumbs-up to her daughter's text, set the phone aside, and went to the refrigerator to find something else to eat. She'd become an Olympic-level snacker, with too-snug pants to prove it. A widow's retreat. Hardly.

Trixie Tungsfeldt gently closed the photo album she'd looked through for the millionth time, its spine weakened from hours of page turning. Trygg hadn't ever been a fan of being photographed. She'd be forever grateful that their youngest son, the budding professional photographer, had consistently taken real-life photos. They were much better than posed pictures, anyway.

She set her hands on the cover and offered a prayer of thanks for the thirty-five years she and Trygg had shared before the diagnosis. Most of those years had been good until the miniscule changes started—forgetting a long-time parishioner's name, missing an occasional appointment, snapping at her when she asked a simple question. So not like her sweet pastor husband who was large and in charge, as their eldest son often said. Trygg wasn't large, but he'd been the center of their ever-growing congregation. Even when he'd gone into the corporate world to help his friend get his company up and running, he'd been the one everyone went to for answers.

Setting the album on the weathered coffee table, she went into the kitchen for another cup of tea. He'd been adored by the staff and congregants alike. He was funny and inquisitive, with the biggest heart and strongest faith she'd ever encountered. There were so many reasons she'd fallen for the handsome seminary student, but his heart for God and for others, especially for her and the kids, was the main one.

He'd been gone eighteen months now, and she still had no clue what to do with herself. She'd lived in his shadow her whole adult life, content to stay in the background while he preached, taught, counseled, and married and buried people in their churches. Even with the diagnosis, she hadn't given any thought to what her life would look like without him. It had been unfathomable. Still was.

Taking the steaming cup of green tea to the kitchen table, she settled with a sigh. If she didn't get a grip on her life, she'd become one of those old ladies who never left the house and eventually shriveled up like funeral flowers. Never leaving the house didn't sound so bad, but the kids wouldn't allow it. Trygg certainly wouldn't have.

A melody flowed from her phone, and she smiled at the photo of her youngest daughter and the baby that appeared. How she adored that beautiful one-year-old. She answered the call, still smiling.

"You sound chipper today," Tansy said.

"Just smiling at the photo of you and Liam that always pops up when you call. How is our sweet boy?"

"Napping, thank goodness." Tansy was an amazing momma to her two young children, but between mothering and working part-time, she always sounded a bit breathless. "I only have a second before I have to switch out the laundry and start making cookies, but I wanted to know if you've signed up for that women's retreat yet."

Trixie squeezed her eyes shut briefly. She'd forgotten about the widow's retreat the kids had gifted her for her birthday. Maybe "forgotten" wasn't the right word. They so wanted her to move on with life. She so longed for her old one. "Sorry. I keep meaning to check it out."

"Mom." Tansy's voice became firm. "We're not letting you off the hook with this. You need to get out of the house, away from all this snow and cold, and meet some women who know what you're going through."

"Sharing my private life with a bunch of strangers doesn't sound fun, Tan."

"I doubt you'll have to spill your guts to everyone, but it will do you good to go somewhere warm. Spend time in the sunshine, breathe in fresh air that won't freeze your nose shut. And maybe learn something."

Trixie held in a sigh. The kids meant well, but they didn't understand just how much she'd depended on their father to deal with people. With life. Why the gregarious pastor had married such an introverted mouse remained her greatest unanswered question.

"I know it sounds scary, Mom, but I'll bet it's scary for every woman who's signed up. And maybe hearing from other women in your situation will help. Now, I know it's coming up soon, so you get yourself registered, and I'll get your flights set up, okay? Remember, that's all part of the gift."

She wanted to argue, put it off and say a flat-out "no," but something deep inside niggled at her, urging agreement. Wouldn't that surprise everyone if silent, wallflower Trixie marched onto the plane and went to a retreat in Arizona all by herself?

The thought made her nauseous even as she heard herself agree. The joy in Tansy's voice pulled a trembling smile from her. For Tansy and for all of them, she'd put on her big girl pants and do it. It might even make Trygg smile somewhere in heaven.

CHAPTER 2

Dorothea sat back, watching the last passenger file off the airplane. When she had no other excuse, she trudged toward the front, dragging her carry-on behind her.

"Thanks for flying with us," the redheaded flight attendant said as she passed. "Enjoy your time in Arizona."

She nodded and went down the outer stairs. "Enjoy" would be a stretch. Not run screaming out of the retreat center when all the embroidered hankies came out would be success, but it was doubtful she'd enjoy any part of this four-day "retreat." If both kids hadn't ganged up on her, she could have held her ground, but once River joined Willow in expressing concern, she gave up the fight. If it made them happy, fine. She'd give up four days of her life listening to elderly widows bemoan their lot in life just to say she'd done it.

She paused outside the terminal to send a selfie to the kids, proof that she'd actually gotten on, and off, the plane. Her smile looked more like a grimace but, hey, it was honest. She said she'd go, not that she'd enjoy it.

Bobby would have already made friends with the pilot, the gate attendant in the Green Bay airport, and the Uber driver. But that was Bobby—everyone's friend. *Her* best friend. Then the revelation happened right when his cancer was diagnosed. Struggling to keep their marriage intact during his decline, they'd been trapped at home together for two years. The cheerful, handsome blond had morphed into an angry, weakened person who hadn't appreciated anything she did for him. They'd lived as strangers until the last few weeks of his life.

Now her generally easy-going temperament had become a lot more guarded and cynical, a lot less freewheeling. After dealing with debt collectors since Bobby's death, she checked the camera before answering a knock. And she never answered a call from an unknown number. *Fool me once . . .*

The cool air inside the terminal was a welcome change from the blazing sun that had toasted her as she crossed the tarmac. Having left another forecasted snowstorm behind, however, she would not complain about sunshine and warmth. She slid her sunglasses to the top of her head, letting her eyes adjust to the fluorescent lighting. Someone was supposed to meet her at the baggage claim to drive her to the retreat center, so she followed the other passengers who followed the signage pointing the way.

Near her carousel, a young brunette stood holding several signs. *Trixie Tungsfeldt!* Dorothea muffled a snort. That was someone's real name? The other sign said *Dixie Jackson!* and her laughter faded. She should talk, since she'd impulsively registered as Dixie instead of Dorothea, or even Dottie, as Bobby had called her since their first meeting. The memory made her heart ache.

"No one," he'd said with an adorable sixteen-year-old boyish grin, "should have to carry a name as heavy as 'Dorothea.' You're way too pretty. You look more like a Dottie, so that's what I'll call you."

That might have been the moment she fell in love with him.

Spying her large, red paisley suitcase making the corner on the carousel, she veered away from the young woman to wrestle it over the edge to the worn carpet. Bobby had rolled his eyes every time she pulled it out, but he'd carried it without complaining. As he had done most things.

Fraying edges revealed the suitcase's aging state; she just wasn't ready to replace it. It had seen her through many trips with him for work and for fun. She set her carry-on on top, drew a deep breath, and turned toward the perky brunette, muttering "Let's get this party started so I can go home."

Trixie emerged from the ladies' room, luggage in tow, and scanned the emptying baggage claim area. She'd been surprised when her suitcase came down the chute first, relieved that it gave her a few minutes to calm her nerves and use the restroom. Now she had no more excuses to avoid the young lady holding a sign with her name on it.

Squaring her shoulders, she scolded herself for being such a scaredy-cat and started toward the girl. Another woman seemed to be heading that way as well, and they arrived at the same time.

The brunette's face brightened as they joined her. "Welcome, ladies! How fun that you arrived together."

Trixie glanced at the other woman dressed in a brightly colored, flowing outfit that only an aging hippie would wear. "Well, not exactly together."

The woman chortled, there was no other word for it, and her flowered headband bounced as she nodded. "Together but not."

"Well, either way it's perfect timing," the young woman said. "I'm here to get you safely to the retreat center. So, you don't know each other? Let's get introduced then. I'm Hannah. Which one of you is Trixie?"

Trixie waved her fingers.

"It's nice to meet you, Trixie. And that means you're Dixie." She giggled. "How fun is that?"

Trixie and Dixie? It sounded like a bad comedy act. A couple of widows as different as Mother Theresa and Cher. Trixie glanced at the hippie. "Very fun."

"All right. Have you got all your luggage? Good. Since we have a forty-minute drive ahead of us, now would be a good time to use the facilities."

Trixie bit back a smile. Tansy sounded like that with her young children, although it was more like, "Who needs to go potty?"

"We're good? Great. You two are among the last to arrive, so once we get to the retreat center, we can get the party started."

A party of widows. Why had she let the kids talk her into this? Because they'd all had a husband die didn't mean they had anything else in common. Would they have to share what their husband's death had been like? She pursed her lips as she followed Hannah out into the hot, dry air. That wasn't something she shared outside the family. Too personal, too . . . sad. She did enough crying at home; she didn't need to do more here.

In the brown Serenity Retreat van, Hannah kept up a cheerful chatter with Dixie, who had hopped into the front seat. Trixie nodded occasionally. Making small talk had been easy at church, in her element with her husband nearby, but talking with strangers had never been in her "wheelhouse," as the kids called it. Between the bright mishmash of colors, her black hair, and layers of makeup, Dixie was a walking party in her own right.

She glanced at her own pale-yellow monochrome outfit, far more widow-like than Dixie's. Trygg had always complimented her on her hair styles, outfits, even her makeup. Perhaps Dixie's husband had done the same? He'd probably been overwhelmed by her. Trixie had been content to be outshone by Trygg. Everybody couldn't be in the spotlight.

"What do you think, Trixie?"

She started, meeting Hannah's eyes in the rearview mirror. "I'm sorry. I guess I was too busy looking at the scenery."

Dixie snorted. "Which looks pretty much the same—dry, brown, and flat."

Hannah laughed. "It does probably seem like that, but I can assure you Arizona has mountains, pine trees, beautiful flowers unique to the southwest, and even snow in some places."

"No snow, please," Dixie said. "I left plenty of that back home."

"Where are you from?" Trixie was surprised at her own question.

"Outside Green Bay, Wisconsin. You?"

"Holland, Michigan. Lake-effect snow keeps us buried all winter."

Dixie's hoot of laughter startled Trixie. "You're a Gander! Love it."

Gander was a common nickname, but it sounded like an insult from the hippie. "What are you called in Wisconsin?"

"We prefer 'Wisconsinites.'"

Trixie rolled her eyes and turned her attention back to the scenery, heat radiating from the window. Blue sky, blazing sunshine, and more brown terrain than she'd ever seen. It looked as dry as her heart.

Hannah steered the van along the winding driveway and stopped at the front door of the one-level building. She turned toward them. "Welcome to the Serenity Retreat Center, ladies. We're happy you're here."

The one-level, brick-and-stucco building was neat and modest, settled at the foot of what Hannah had called Camelback Mountain. Bright flowers—in vivid blues, yellows, and pinks—gathered in bunches along the walkway. Surprisingly tiny cacti dotted the rock area between the flowers.

It's only for a week. Trixie repeated the words as she pulled her luggage past a natural rock water fountain and into the building. Probably the longest week of her life.

CHAPTER 3

As the door closed behind her, Dorothea—no, she was Dixie now—dropped onto the edge of the king-size bed with a sigh as heavy as her suitcase. "Why did I let them talk me into this?" she said aloud. "I'm already exhausted, and it hasn't even started."

At least she hadn't seen any hankies, although Trixie seemed like a hanky kind of widow. Such a mouse of a woman. How could anyone be that quiet? She'd had an intelligent look in her blue eyes, so there had to be thoughts in her head, but she'd spoken about two sentences the whole ride and hadn't smiled even once.

Lifting her head, she encountered her mirrored reflection. She hadn't been a barrel of laughs either, but at least she'd tried to keep up with the driver's conversation. Heidi? Honey? She blew out a breath that sent her bangs fluttering. She'd never been good with names; Bobby's recall for people always put her to shame. But then, it had been a huge part of his job as a consultant. Spending hours in her pottery studio kept her from having to even meet a lot of people; thus, she'd had no need to develop that skill.

She looked around the room that was nicer than she'd expected, decorated in peaceful, natural tones. The patio doors made the room bright and cheerful. There was a coffee bar and a private bath. The bedside lamps matched the curtains of warm turquoise and browns. Not a bad place to hide if the wailing widows were too much.

Propped against the pillows sat a sheet of paper and a white organza fabric bag of candies. She enjoyed a chocolate heart while perusing the weekend itinerary. The next few days were packed with activities, seemingly every waking moment.

Was she supposed to attend everything? Was there even time to eat? Oh, there were the meals, sandwiched tightly between other things. She did love her meals. Good thing this was an all-inclusive. She'd had to learn to follow a budget the past few months, a new concept since she'd been as free as, and perhaps more than, Bobby in her spending habits.

Her shoulders drooped. If she were honest, the financial predicament couldn't be blamed entirely on him. Her pottery studio was testament to that. She'd probably have to sell it.

"That's for later," she stated sharply, pulling her focus back. "So, when does the party start?" Skimming the sheet again, her breath caught, her gaze flying to the bedside clock. "Right now? Oh, for Pete's sake!"

She grabbed her oversize purse and dashed from the room. Well, at least this was true to who she was. A "grieving widow" but also perpetually late.

Settled safely in the back row of the retreat center's meeting room, Trixie clutched the folder she'd received at the door. Soothing background music floated through the room along with a pleasant aroma of sage and lavender. Five rows of ten seats each were set up theater style facing a one-step stage with a podium.

Floor to ceiling windows along the wall to her right flooded the room with warm sunlight, revealing an outdoor courtyard teeming with desert shrubs, gangly trees, and bright flowers. That would be a lovely place to sit when she needed a break from . . . whatever was about to happen.

Women of all ages, sizes, and colors were scattered through the rows, some looking as nervous as she felt, others visiting quietly with each other. A few were surprisingly young, but most were probably middle age like her. All of these women had lost their husbands. No, the men weren't lost; they were healed and whole in heaven. It was the women who were lost. Especially her.

Tears stung her eyes and her heart, sharp as rose thorns. Lost and stumbling through her own life. She flipped open the flowered folder. A lot of paper for only a few days. A condensed schedule, then detailed daily schedules. A notebook and gel pen in her favorite turquoise. Lists of speakers, entertainment, and resources.

A willowy woman with short salt-and-pepper hair, dressed in a pink blouse and black pants, stepped to the podium and adjusted the microphone as the music quieted. Her warm smile touched on each of them. Trixie automatically smiled in response.

"Welcome, ladies, to the Serenity Retreat Center. Isn't the sunshine glorious?" Women nodded in response. "I know some of you are from Arizona, but most of you have traveled here from across the country and may not know that the weather is *always* perfect here. Well, almost always," she added with a laugh. "I'm Laura Clark, and I'll be your host throughout this Hope and Healing retreat. I'm glad you took the step to sign up and come. It probably felt a bit scary to do so, right? I know I get nervous at the start of every retreat. Put that nervousness aside. We don't bite, and we won't ask you to reveal your darkest secrets."

Laughter rippled through the room as the side door flung open and a woman appeared, colorful clothes fluttering behind as she dashed in.

"Ah, *now* we're all here," Laura said, smiling at the latecomer. "Welcome. Janice will get you a folder, and you can sit wherever you'd like."

"So sorry," Trixie's van-mate said as she slid into the front row.

Laura continued. "As I said, we won't bite. We want you to enjoy your time here. Anything you decide to share will be held in the strictest confidence."

"Sort of a 'what happens in Vegas stays in Vegas' deal?" Dixie said.

Trixie had seen photos of Las Vegas but never visited. Camping had been their idea of fun. Dixie the hippie seemed more suited to Vegas.

"Along that line," Laura agreed with a grin. "You're not required to share anything at all. We are all here because we've experienced the death of our spouse, including me and the retreat staff. But every single experience is unique and will be treated as such. So, with that said, let's look at the materials in your folder. We'll start with the one-page agenda that looks like this." She held it up.

Trixie pulled the sheet out, her stomach churning at everything squished onto the page.

"I see panic on a few faces out there," Laura said, "but you are not required to attend everything you see listed."

Hoping her face wasn't one of the panicked ones, Trixie glanced at the woman a few chairs away, who smiled back and made an exaggerated swipe of her forehead. They shared a smile before turning back to Laura.

"We encourage you to participate as much as possible, and we've included a wide variety of breakout sessions and keynotes that we hope you'll find interesting and informative. But if you need quiet time or a short nap, you are encouraged to do that as well. This retreat is about rest, healing, and caring for yourself."

Grief counselors would be available every day, appointments encouraged but not required. Breakout sessions would include topics such as finances, career planning, AA/Al-Anon, and discovering who they were in this new stage of life.

Trixie bit her lip. She needed to hear the keynote address on that last topic. The roles she'd played the last three decades had evaporated with Trygg—she was no longer a wife at home or the pastor's wife at church, no longer part of a twosome after thirty-five years. No longer even a member of the choir she'd loved, because the music made her cry. At least she still enjoyed volunteering in the nursery.

"We'll also have a lot of fun," Laura was saying. "We'll be holding the Ladies' Olympics Friday evening but have no fear. No special skills are necessary. The focus will be on silliness, revisiting some childhood activities, and cheering each other on. I'm sure the idea of silly fun feels very foreign to many of you. Laughter can seem almost sacrilegious while you're grieving, but I promise you it's in no way disrespectful of your husband, it's acceptable at any stage of grief, and it is truly necessary for your emotional, physical, and psychological well-being."

Laughter. It's what drew her and Trygg together in the first place so many years ago—their love of funny movies, trading one-liners, and enjoying private jokes that made no sense to anyone else. She might miss that the most about him. She'd found little to laugh about since his diagnosis.

"The last thing I want to draw your attention to before we head into dinner is your small group assignment. You'll find a number on your nametag in the upper right corner. All of you are assigned to a small support group of four women. Our prayer is that, as you get to know each other, you'll discover nuggets of shared experiences, perhaps similar viewpoints on some topics, and even someone to share a laugh with at some point.

"Talk about your hobbies, your children or grandchildren, pets, favorite foods or music or vacation spots. We'll provide ice breaker questions you can use each time you meet with your small group to get conversation started. Tomorrow morning will be your first opportunity to meet with your group. Remember"—mischief filled her smile—"we're women and we need to use our 40,000 words each day!"

Laughter and scattered applause answered her. Trixie nodded. She certainly missed talking to Trygg. Molly, her darling Bernese-doodle, often fell asleep when Trixie shared something important like what to eat for an afternoon snack. She'd be happy just listening to all these women chatter. It had become far too quiet in their big house. Maybe she could enjoy a few safe conversations with her small group.

She glanced at her nametag as Laura invited them to bow their heads for a blessing before the meal. Group number seven. That had to be a good sign. It was Trygg's favorite number.

CHAPTER 4

Dixie glanced at the clock as she entered the gym and did a double take. Early? That never happened! Bells should be ringing and confetti flying to celebrate. She went toward the side wall where the rolled yoga mats stood, selected a bright yellow one, and chose a spot in the front row. Actually, she was rarely late for yoga or pottery classes, but she always seemed a step behind in the rest of life.

"Good morning! Welcome."

Straightening from her stretch position, she found a woman beaming at her. "Good morning."

"I'm Sage." Curly gray hair piled in a messy bun on top of her head, her tie-dye bodysuit was certainly eye-catching. "I've been leading the yoga classes here for three years and in my own studio for thirty. I'm glad your travels yesterday didn't wear you out too much."

"Yoga is my sanity break, so even if I had to crawl, I'd have made it. I'm Do—Dixie." She held back an eyeroll. Now Sage would call her DoDixie going forward. "Dixie Jackson," she clarified.

"A pleasure to meet you. We'll get started in a few minutes. Thanks for coming." The older woman floated away before Dixie could reply.

She returned to her stretch with a smile. Sage was like a colorful butterfly flitting through the room, alighting gently on each attendee. A sweet welcome to not only the retreat but this moment of peace she desperately needed.

The morning yoga offering was one of the major reasons she'd come. She could always retreat here if things got too hankie-ish out there. At least she wasn't the youngest attendee, from what she saw last night. She shifted to a side stretch, the wall of mirrors in front allowing her to watch women arriving behind her. Most seemed middle age and healthy, not frail women in their eighties. *Thank you, God.*

As the room filled, Sage floated to the front and held out her arms as if to hug them all at once. "Welcome, welcome. How lovely to see all of you this morning. My, the room is getting very full. We'll have to squish together a bit more. Move on up, ladies. This front row can join me so we can add a row in the back. Yes, welcome! Come in! We'll make room."

Having expected to be one of a handful this morning, Dixie looked at the women on either side. Perhaps there was hope for this group after all, since so many appeared to be yoga enthusiasts like her. Letting her gaze run over the reflection of the crowded room, she wasn't surprised that her van-mate wasn't here. That woman would need a *lot* of yoga classes to get loosened up.

"Again, welcome everyone. It looks like I might need to add an afternoon class to accommodate everyone! How wonderful. Let's get started, shall we? You may have found that simply breathing these last months or years has been difficult on your grief journey. Taking this time for yourself to focus on all aspects of your health is going to make an enormous difference in how you feel throughout the day.

"Now, place your feet firmly on the mat a shoulder's width apart. Give your arms a shake, roll your shoulders back. Draw a deep breath and lift your arms wide. Be careful of your neighbor, since we're squished together. Touch your fingertips high above your head. That's it. Exhale and lower your arms. Wonderful! Again."

Dixie closed her eyes and focused inward, relaxing into the familiar pattern and rhythm of stretching. Silencing all other sounds, she listened to Sage's breathy voice and flowed from one position to the next. Heaven on a yoga mat.

Ninety minutes later, she hurried into the dining room to see all heads bowed as Laura said a blessing over the breakfast meal and the first keynote speaker. She'd had to ask directions to this room, finding it around the corner from last night's meeting room.

"Can I help you find your table?" someone whispered beside her.

Dixie nodded. "I'm at, let's see, Table #7." Lucky number seven, Bobby would say.

"Right over here on the left."

Instead of rows like last night, this room held ten tables with four seats. As they reached her table—right in front, of course—the blessing ended. Laura's head lifted and she smiled at Dixie. "Ahh, here's our Vegas lady. Now we're ready to start."

Dixie waggled her fingers and sank into the open chair. "Sorry," she said to her group.

"Not a problem," the blonde to her left said.

"At least you made it before the meal was over," another said.

Dixie looked to her right and met the raised eyebrows of her van-mate. Of course Trixie Tongue-tied would be in her group. And pass judgment on her tardiness. "Well, I certainly enjoyed my morning yoga time, so if I'd have missed the meal, it would have been worth it."

"I probably *should* miss a meal once in a while," the woman across the table said, patting her round tummy. The others smiled awkwardly.

Plates of quiche, hashbrowns, a muffin, and a fruit cup were delivered to their table of four. Dixie nearly salivated at the aroma. Although there was muted conversation throughout the room, this small group remained silently focused on their food.

"Don't forget to use the trifold in the center of your table if you need a few ice breakers," Laura said from the podium.

When no one reached for it, Dixie plucked it from the middle. "Okay, Lucky Table #7 ladies, here's your first question. Where were you born and where did you travel from?" If the questions stayed this bland, she wouldn't have to share anything remotely deep. When they remained silent, she added, "I guess I'll start. I'm Dixie Jackson. I was born in warm, beautiful Hawaii, and I came here from icy, snowy Wisconsin."

"Hawaii!" several exclaimed, their expressions dreamy.

"I lived there until I was one week old. I surprised my parents and arrived seven weeks early."

"Another grand entrance," Trixie said.

"That might explain why I'm always late. Your turn."

"I'm Trixie Tungsfeldt. I was born in the U.P. of Michigan and came here from Holland." When the women's eyes widened, she added quickly, "Michigan. Holland, Michigan."

"You're a Yooper!" Dixie exclaimed. "So was my dad."

"A Yooper?" another woman asked.

"People living in the Upper Peninsula of Michigan are called Yoopers."

"Why?"

Trixie shrugged, and Dixie jumped in. "Because they're a strange bunch, so Yooper fit." She looked at Trixie with a wide grin. "You went from a simple Gander to a Yooper. A double whammy!"

Eyebrows lowered, Trixie opened her mouth, but the woman across from Dixie said, "I'm Chantal. I was born outside Des Moines, Iowa, and I came here from the Ames area. And no, I didn't grow up on a farm."

Dixie hooted. "I thought everyone lived on a farm in Iowa."

Does she really have to comment on everything everyone says? Sorry, Lord. Not very charitable, am I?

"I didn't grow up on one," Chantal said, "but I didn't say I don't live on one now."

"You *do* live on a farm?" Trixie asked.

"No."

The women looked at each other.

"Okay, wait," Dixie said. "You do or do not live on a farm?"

"I don't. I was just messing with you."

"Oh, you are my kind of girl," Dixie said with a laugh. "Always keep people guessing."

"Ladies." Laura had returned to the podium. "I'm happy to hear all this chatter, but it's time to finish up so we can hear from our first keynote speaker. Five more minutes."

The fourth woman at Table #7 leaned in. "I'm Nicole, and I was born in Washington state. I came here from Washington, D.C., but I don't live there."

"This is the most confusing group of women," Trixie said, shaking her head. "Where *do* you live?"

"Nashville, Tennessee."

"Ooh, I love Nashville," Dixie said. "Great people, great food, and the best music."

"I've lived there most of my adult life. I love it, but I'm thinking it's time to move closer to where my kids are in Indiana. It's way too quiet in our big ol' house now."

The others nodded, smiles fading. Dixie loved their house filled with a lifetime of memories, but the financial mess would no doubt require she sell. She blinked the thought away.

"All right, ladies," Laura said. "I'd like to introduce our keynote speaker. She's a writer and speaker, a marriage and family therapist, an artist, an avid golfer, and a widow of five years. She has a very popular podcast for women and has recently published her sixth book. Let's welcome Anita Martin!"

"Hello, ladies! Thank you for that warm welcome." Anita smiled at them from the podium. "I'm delighted to be here with you. Let's start off this session with prayer. Father in heaven, thank you for this opportunity to gather here, to listen and share, to learn, and to feel the love and support from others who know our heartache and who have similar questions about what you have in store for us. Open our hearts and minds, speak through me, and touch the hearts of your daughters here. We need you, and we love you. In Jesus' precious name, amen.

"All right. It's good to know God is right here in this room, isn't it? Even now, five years after my husband's death, I cling to His promise that He will never leave us. He'll never forsake us, which means He won't turn His back on us and let us suffer and struggle and question alone. Anybody here ever have doubts and questions?" She raised her hand, and the rest of the room did as well. "Anyone wonder where God was during the suffering, the sleepless nights, the moments of not knowing what to do next? I sure did."

Trixie and Chantal exchanged a nodding glance.

"We aren't the only ones. The Psalms are full of questions, doubts, anger, and great sadness. But they're also full of joy, praise, singing, and the assurance that even in the midst of trouble and sorrow, God is good and present, strong, protective, and loving. Amen?"

"Amen," Trixie said softly. Her faith had been the only thing that kept her from going under after Trygg's death. Even so, she'd often wondered why God had allowed that wretched disease to break their family apart.

Anita briefly shared the journey she'd been on with her husband and the impact his death had had on her emotional and physical well-being. "At your tables, I'd like you to share your husband's name and when he died. No more information than that. I'll give you five minutes. The tallest woman at your table will start. Go."

At Table #7 they looked at each other, then pushed to their feet to see who was taller. The room filled with noise as other groups did the same.

"Yippee," Dixie said, plopping back into her chair. "I win. Again. My husband was Robert, although everyone called him Bobby. He died about two years ago." She looked at Trixie. "Next."

"Trygg. He died eighteen months ago."

"My husband was Steven," Chantal said. "He died two years ago. Feels like twenty years and twenty minutes at the same time."

Trixie pressed a hand over her ever-aching heart. "I know that feeling."

"I was married to Alan, who died three years ago," Nicole said.

Anita urged them to finish sharing, then continued. "Most of you are probably familiar with the stages of grief, but I'll review them briefly. Remember, these stages aren't set in stone. We will experience them in different orders, spend longer in one stage while breezing through another. There is no right or wrong way to grieve."

She turned to look at the slide on the screen. "Stage one, according to Katherine Kubler-Ross, who studied the topic for years, is denial. We don't want to believe it, can't and won't accept it. We can't make sense of what happened because it doesn't seem real. The next stage is anger. This one surprised me because I didn't know how deeply angry I was at Nate. I was angry at him for leaving me, for not going to the doctor sooner, even for going to heaven and leaving me to deal with our children's grief. That stage also lasted the longest for me. Counseling was a huge help to get through it.

"Then we may move into bargaining. We're grasping at something, anything, that will help us stay afloat. We may tell our story to anyone who will listen—friend or stranger. I remember telling the gas station attendant about Nate. Poor kid," she said with a laugh. "I'm sure he was thinking, 'Lady, just pay for the gas already.'"

Dixie leaned toward Trixie. "I did that to the cashier at the bank. Had a line six people deep behind me. I'm surprised they didn't call the cops."

Trixie nodded, rolling her eyes. "Me at the post office."

Anita continued. "We've been stunned, and then angry, and now confused by the change in our life. It's not really a surprise when depression hits. We want to hide from life. We don't want to face this new reality. We may have panic attacks for the first time in our life. Staying in bed sounds better and better. Life is too hard.

"Friends, it's absolutely imperative that you reach out to someone during this time, even though you're afraid you're bothering them. We may barely have the energy to keep breathing, but for our sake and those around us, we absolutely must ask for help. Tell a friend or make an appointment to see your doctor. It's not a sign of weakness; it's a sign of strength and determination.

"The final stage is acceptance. That doesn't mean we're glad it happened, or that we're ready to zoom back into a full life. It means we are at a point where we can understand what happened, recognize how our life, our very being, has changed, and that we're becoming whole in a new way. Even if we remarry, the loss of our spouse never truly goes away. We are simply at a point where we're ready to start moving forward."

The women at Table #7 exchanged thoughtful nods. Trixie blinked against the burn in her eyes that matched the one in her heart. Moving on meant leaving Trygg behind, and that was as unfathomable as sprouting wings and flying.

"It's not at all unusual to move back and forth among stages, and that's okay. Truly. We need to give ourselves grace to cry sometimes and laugh other times. We can look for the beauty in each day, accept help when we need it, and do the same for those around us.

"The cocoon of grief has been our safe place, where we could hide from the world and stay in the familiar sadness. But God is there in that cocoon as well, and change is going on even during the darkest days. Our loving Father is not content to let us wallow too long in our grief. He takes that pain, the silence, and sadness and loneliness, and creates a transformation within our soul. When enough change has occurred, He urges us out of that safe space to discover who He has changed us into."

She held up a clear glass butterfly, painted in pastels. "Did you know that, when butterflies emerge from the cocoon, they are at their most fragile? The struggle from coming out of the cocoon is essential for their new being to fully develop. If they're forced out, or even just helped too much, they won't finish the necessary process and will die. Once they're fully out, they need time for their wings to dry and strengthen before they can fly."

In the silence of the room, she looked out at them. "Ladies, you are here because it was time to leave the cocoon. Yes, even those of you who felt coerced to be here. *You* were the final decision-maker. Something deep inside called you to take these first steps out of your familiar cocoon of grief, to join other emerging butterflies. You aren't launched yet, but you've come out of the darkness and are now sitting in the light, gaining the strength and courage to fly.

"Many, if not most, of you are thinking you can't do it, or don't want to do it without your spouse. If you're like me, my hubby was the only guy I dated, the only one I wanted to spend my life with. I had never experienced adult life without him. And I didn't want to."

Trixie dabbed at her eyes. Trygg had been her whole life.

"But when he was called Home, I was left with a choice," Anita said. "Not one I wanted but one I was faced with, nonetheless. I could remain living in pain, in the safety of my grief, so I didn't have to face a scary world without him. *Or* I could grieve for a time and then decide that, since I was still alive, there must be more for me to do. It took a while," she assured them, "but eventually I realized my soul was reaching out to God, toward light and life. The steps I took were teeny baby steps, but it was forward motion. I know, without a doubt, that this can and will happen for you when you ask God to guide you."

Sniffling echoed around the room. Trixie saw Dixie pull a tissue from the gigantic purse on her lap and felt a strange sense of comfort. If this woman, so self-assured and full of life, was struggling, then they at least had that in common.

"That's all the time we have for this morning. We'll continue this conversation this evening. For now, you have a thirty-minute break to get up and stretch, take care of the necessities, and find your first breakout session. As you leave, please choose a butterfly from the vases at the back of the room to remind you of the changes God is making in you. We are all becoming new creatures every day."

The room emptied in relative silence as the women filed past the vases to choose from an array of beautiful glass butterflies on wooden dowels. Trixie selected a pale blue, Trygg's favorite color. Behind her, Dixie chose a multi-colored butterfly, which not only didn't surprise her but for some reason made her smile.

Chapter 5

Clutching the stem of her butterfly, Dixie wandered out to the expansive courtyard and pulled in a deep breath of the warm, flower-scented air. Stuck in knee-deep snow for months every winter, it was easy to forget there were places like this enjoying warm sunshine and blooming plants. This wouldn't be her last trip south during the long Wisconsin winters.

She settled on a bench and set her purse and folder aside, then paused to admire the beautiful landscaping. She didn't recognize many of the plants but did know a few of the flowers. Her favorite, hibiscus, in stunning reds and orange, filled ceramic planters. Palm trees waved fan-like arms along a winding, paved walkway. Wooden benches at discreet distances welcomed visitors to relax and soak in the peace and tranquility of this fragrant, hidden world.

Pulling in another breath of sage and eucalyptus, she turned her attention to the butterfly. Its bright colors sparkled in the sunlight as she studied it from all sides. She'd loved butterflies as a child, determined that someday she would fly as gracefully as they did.

Anita's words floated to mind. "You're here because it's time to leave the cocoon. Something deep inside called you to take these first steps out of your cocoon of grief, to join other emerging butterflies. You've come out of the darkness and are sitting in the light, gaining the strength and courage to fly."

Strength and courage. The figurine blurred and she lifted her gaze to the clear sky. So many dark days and nights. Was she ready for the light?

What if she couldn't do it on her own? The tangled mess of her finances had paralyzed her. The loneliness ate at her, but the thought of getting the house ready to sell made her nauseous.

She knew pottery and yoga, shopping, and decorating. Hardly the skillset to take her successfully into the future. She'd completed a few classes at the junior college—decades ago. She wasn't a particularly good cook, her spelling was atrocious, her typing skills passable for texting. Releasing a heavy sigh laced with tears, she closed her eyes and prayed softly.

"Lord, what good am I in the world now? I'd like to be a butterfly, but I don't have anything to offer. If you can create something out of this old, bumpy caterpillar, I'm all for it but you've got an awful lot of work to do. Help me be open to whatever you have planned. And maybe make me a little braver? I'm scared to death."

A bell tinkled in the distance, coming closer. Laura opened the door to the courtyard and reminded those scattered on various benches that they had five minutes to get to their first breakout session.

Dixie pulled in a sharp breath and rolled up her wilted spine. With no clue what God had in store for her, she might as well gather as much wisdom as she could from this group before going back to her cold, silent world.

Seated in the back row of the small meeting room, waiting for the first breakout session to start, Trixie mulled over the amazing things Anita had said. It had certainly felt like she'd been cocooned in her grief these past months, but Anita was right—something deep inside had beckoned her here, pulled her from the safety of home to see if there really might be something more for her. And here she sat, a butterfly resting on the ledge of new life, waiting for the strength to fly. Could she? Fly where? How?

She folded her arms over the flutter in her chest. God had called her to this retreat to discover . . . something. Herself, perhaps. The next step. How to live life without her handsome best friend.

As the presenter moved to the front of the room, a door in the back swooshed open and someone dashed in, dropping into the chair next to Trixie. She didn't have to look to know who it was—the perfume was a dead give-away.

"Sorry," Dixie whispered.

Trixie turned her head and met the wild child's sheepish gaze. Maybe she needed a watch. She glanced down at the leather band on Dixie's wrist. Okay, perhaps a watch that worked. Shaking her head, she rolled her eyes, and a heartbeat later they broke into silent giggles.

"Hi everyone. I'm Margie Wilcox. Welcome to Tennis 101," the blonde at the front said, then waved a hand in dismissal. "Just kidding, although I'll be using lots of tennis analogies as we talk about being 'Singles on the Doubles Court.' Like it or not, we've been ejected from the game of doubles and are now figuring out how to swing at the ball of life without our partner."

"I hate tennis," Dixie said in an aside.

"I was pretty good in high school. Haven't played since."

"I suppose you play pickleball?"

Trixie glanced sideways and shrugged. It was one of the few things she could still do now that she'd passed sixty.

"Who here plays or has played tennis?" Margie, the presenter, asked.

Dixie grabbed Trixie's wrist and raised it. Trixie stared at her, stunned.

"Oh, do you two play doubles together?"

With a quick shake of her head, Trixie yanked her arm down while Dixie said, "Actually I hate tennis, but Trixie here is a pro."

"What?! I played in high school," she explained quickly before elbowing the crazy woman next to her. "Now it's more on par with pickleball."

Margie laughed and turned her attention to the other women who had raised their hands—without help.

"I'm never telling you anything ever again," Trixie muttered.

An unladylike snort from her seatmate was followed by, "You probably wouldn't have raised your hand."

"So?" Trixie demanded in a whisper.

"So it's okay to toot your own horn once in a while. But I bet you don't even have one."

Ouch. Was she that obvious? Yes, she was sitting in the back row again, wearing beige—again. But the Bible was clear about not boasting, and also about putting others before self. Why toot a decades-old horn? "And you probably have ten."

Dixie glanced at her, lips pursed. "I wish I did."

Their attention turned back to the presenter, and Trixie frowned. What a strange comment from someone who wasn't afraid to make an entrance or dress so flamboyantly.

"One of the first things we need to learn," Margie was saying, "is how to play singles, especially if we've never been on our own before. While the overall scoring is the same for both singles and doubles, the rules are tweaked a bit to fit each setup. There's a lot more court to cover on our own, a lot more responsibility to hit the ball, so to speak. How many of you have had to climb ladders to change lightbulbs or take your car in for repairs? Okay, how many of you with your hands raised did that before losing your spouse? Good for you two. The rest of us were probably content to leave maintenance things to our husband.

"It may sound silly but that was a huge rule change for me after Rick died. Of course I knew *how* to change a lightbulb, but suddenly it seemed like they needed replacement every week! Simple things needed doing, and I didn't know how. That was demoralizing, and it made me even more mad at Rick for leaving."

Heads were nodding around the room, and when she invited people to share some of the issues they'd encountered, hands shot up in every row. Trixie listened in astonishment as one woman after another described her life over the past few years. Stupid little things had left her in tears, feeling angry and abandoned. But they also shared the tiny spark of pride when they figured something out on their own or at least knew whom to call.

She and Dixie looked at each other, eyebrows raised. Everyone had these problems?

"Thanks for sharing, ladies. Doesn't it feel good to know you aren't alone, you're not crazy, nor are you totally inept? Since I've always been a bit techy, computers weren't an issue for me, but I didn't even know how to start the lawn mower! A great way to deal with this is to find someone who needs your kind of help, and you can swap skills. Ask around at church or at work."

To her pages of notes, Trixie added a reminder to check at church to find other widows who needed help. She could handle a computer fairly well, and she did still love to cook but never bothered for herself. That was a place to start. Funny how that simple idea felt empowering.

The rest of the presentation flew by, making her handwriting nearly illegible as she struggled to keep up. When the session ended, she shook the cramp from her hand. The woman had discussed emotions, steps to make the transition easier, strategies for facing events that felt extra awkward alone, resources to dig into, and how to face playing the singles game with dignity and determination. Thank goodness for the handout to help her fill in the gaps.

"Well, that was a firehose of information," Dixie said. "Good stuff but a lot to take in."

Strolling toward the dining room for lunch, they shared the nuggets that had struck them as the most surprising, ideas that they might try to implement. And how much of what she and the others had said that was exactly what they'd been experiencing.

Over a salad lunch, they shared their findings with Nicole and Chantal, eager to hear what they'd learned in their breakout sessions. They agreed that, after only one keynote and one breakout session, they already felt less isolated, less like they were "handling" their grief wrong. Knowing there were so many others experiencing similar things helped ease the sense that no one else could relate to their journey of grief.

Trixie hid a smile. Tansy would be thrilled to know she'd been right. Trixie was glad she'd come.

CHAPTER 6

Dixie settled into the front row of the "Discovering New Interests/Rediscovering Old Hobbies" breakout session with a smug smile. Too bad Trixie wasn't there to see her actually early. It helped that she hadn't been waylaid by taking photos of the flowers in the courtyard and hadn't needed the restroom. Trixie didn't need to know how easily distracted she was.

Oh, to be able to focus on something without a thousand other things clamoring for attention. She hadn't been this flighty before Bobby's illness. Or had she? Caring for the cantankerous ogre through his cancer journey had sucked every speck of creativity from her.

She shook her head and sighed. The last year of his life, the Bobby she'd known had disappeared. Aside from the weight loss, his normally cheerful personality had taken an ugly turn, arguing over everything, complaining about her caretaking abilities and attitude. Only the last few weeks, when he'd accepted that he was dying, had they been able to talk. Before that, she'd gotten to where she hadn't even liked him.

She glanced at the women who were filling the rows. What would they think of her for such thoughts? They'd probably been able to hold it together and kept a smile on their face for their husband, while she'd gritted her teeth so hard for so long that she'd needed dental work to repair the damage.

"Well, look at you." Trixie sat down beside her, eyebrows raised. "Not only early but in the front row."

"Sitting in the back is a lot more distracting. Being up front helps me concentrate."

She nodded. "I hear you on that. As Trygg's disease worsened, so did my ability to focus. Sometimes I couldn't carry on a normal conversation with my grandkids."

"Can I ask what he died from?"

"A strange form of dementia called FTD."

"Isn't that a flower delivery company?"

Trixie laughed. "That was my first thought. It stands for frontotemporal degeneration. It affects the frontal and temporal lobes, which is where executive function is—decision-making, critical thinking, emotions, that sort of behavior."

"I'm sorry. That sounds awful."

"It was. Watching the person you've known most of your life turn into someone unrecognizable is terrible."

Bobby hadn't had dementia, but he'd certainly become someone else.

"I didn't even like him when he died," Trixie said quietly, lips quivering. "That man wasn't Trygg. I'd lost Trygg years earlier. It was an awful feeling—both grief and relief. One of my boys called it grelief."

Dixie turned to look at her, eyes wide.

Trixie's face flushed. "Sorry. I probably shouldn't admit that out loud."

"No! It's exactly how I felt about Bobby! He died of cancer, but he wasn't the same man either when he died. I thought there was something wrong with me for feeling such relief."

As Trixie's blue eyes filled, Dixie put a hand on her arm. "I think our grief is very different from someone dealing with the shock of a sudden death, but that doesn't make us terrible people. We're warriors."

"Welcome, everyone," a woman said from the small podium. "This is the workshop where you'll be encouraged to start thinking about what you used to do for fun and what you might like to try going forward."

Trixie put her hand on Dixie's and squeezed, nodding. "Thank you," she whispered.

No, thank you for helping me realize I'm not the awful person I thought I was.

Trixie struggled to focus on the speaker. Dixie's words were a revelation. She'd heard enough people in the online support groups share similar sentiments, but she hadn't thought of herself as a warrior. The tears receded as she turned the idea over in her mind. A warrior. That described the last few years—fighting not only Trygg but what that horrid disease had tried to do to her and their kids.

I'm a warrior. The silent declaration lifted her chin.

"What we used to be and do and find enjoyment in," the speaker, Carla, said, "can now seem foreign to us. Whether you lost your spouse suddenly or over the long term, our thought patterns have changed. There is scientific proof of the difference in the brain pre-event and then post-event. Shock and grief rewire our brain as we deal with the crisis while it's happening and afterward; thus, something you thoroughly enjoyed may now seem like a waste of time. If it was something you did with your spouse, it may simply be too painful to attempt on your own. We need to find a way to be okay with that, holding onto the memories while we create new ones. What are things you enjoyed doing before the loss of your husband?"

"I taught pottery classes," Dixie said.

"Great! Teaching and pottery. Do either of those interest you now?"

"Possibly. I haven't had the energy to even do my own let alone think about teaching again, but I'm starting to get the itch to create, so it might be coming back."

The woman nodded. "If you find the interest is returning, it's worth a try. What else have you ladies enjoyed doing that fell by the wayside during your grief journey?"

As ideas were tossed out, Trixie leaned sideways and whispered, "I've always wanted to try doing pottery."

"I'd be happy to teach you, although we'd have to do it long-distance, I suppose."

"I'd love that!"

The rest of the session passed quickly as women shared ideas along with pieces of their story. By the time the hour ended, there'd been some tears and plenty of laughter.

On their way to the next session, Dixie said, "You didn't share what you enjoyed doing."

"I did a lot of things at the church. As the pastor's wife, I was expected to be part of pretty much everything."

"Trygg was a pastor?"

"For thirty years. The last few years before his diagnosis he was working in the corporate world helping a friend start a company."

"So, you didn't do anything for yourself? Only for the church?"

Dixie's incredulous tone stung. "I loved working with Trygg doing ministry."

"I'm sure you did, and I'll bet you were good at it. But what about what *you* like?"

Exactly the issue she'd been wrestling with before coming to Arizona. "I've always loved to sing. Being in the choir was my favorite thing."

"Are you still doing it?"

She shrugged. "No. I couldn't even get to church when his dementia got bad, so singing faded away. Trygg had a wonderful voice. We met in the high school choir." Memories of their much-younger selves paraded through her mind. "Now it's . . . too hard."

"Would you like to try again?"

"Maybe. I'm finding myself singing around the house now, which I hadn't done since he died. Actually, long before he died."

Dixie stopped beside an open door. "Let's talk more at dinner. I've always wanted to sing, so maybe you can teach me while I teach you pottery."

The idea brought a smile to Trixie's heart. She could do that. "Sounds good. Is this your next session?"

"Finances 101." She sighed. "Bobby handled the money and assured me he had everything under control. Once he got sick, I found out that wasn't exactly true. He *was* good with money—spending it but not tracking it. That was me, as well. I'm in a bit of a mess," she admitted.

"I'm sorry." Thank goodness Trygg had been meticulous with their finances. She wasn't rich, but he'd made sure she would be comfortable for the rest of her life. Impulsively she gave Dixie a side hug. "You go learn about finances, and I'll go learn about Cooking for One, and then we'll share our notes at dinner tonight."

"Deal. Thanks, Trix."

She continued down the carpeted hall, her heart aching for Dixie. She needed prayer and lots of it. "Lord, speak your calm and wisdom into Dixie," she whispered.

Their journeys were so alike and yet completely different. The dementia saying came to mind: "If you've met one person with dementia, you've met one person with dementia." No two cases were the same.

That adage obviously held true for widows. While they'd all lost their spouses, many in similar ways, their journeys were as unique as they were. Turning into the aromatic cooking classroom, she shook her head. The unexpected things she was learning.

CHAPTER 7

Dixie rushed along the hallway, determined to reach the dining room before the doors closed. Breakfast smelled heavenly, and she was starving. And late. *Yes!* The door was still open. She and another woman slipped in as Janice started to close it, and she slowed to walk nonchalantly toward Table #7. She stopped, frowning. Where was Table #7? Where were her peeps?

"Psst. Dixie, over here."

She looked to the right and found their table in the middle row on the right instead of front and left. Plopping into the chair, she frowned at Chantal. "Were you guys trying to ditch me?"

Her friend giggled. "They're rotating each day to allow everyone a chance to be in the front. You'll be less noticeable now when you're late—at least for today."

Trixie snorted at the comment. Nicole pursed her lips and turned her attention to the front, where Laura was giving the Friday announcements. Dropping back in the chair, Dixie folded her arms. She deserved the ribbing, since she'd been late—barely—to every meal so far, but it was still embarrassing.

Once the meal had been served, and they'd finished oohing and aahing over eggs Benedict, Chantal leaned in. "I don't know if you guys feel this way, but I'd like to know more about each of you. You don't have to share details, but I'd love to know who has kids, grandkids, pets. Stuff like that."

Dixie nodded, her mouth full. "Mm-hmm."

"That's a great idea," Trixie said. "You start."

"Okay. Well, we were married for thirty-two years. I met Steven at college. He was pre-med and I absolutely wasn't." She grinned and added, "He's the brains, I'm the beauty. Anyway, he decided he wanted to work in a smaller town where the need for doctors is great, so off we went to live in a town of 5,000 in the middle of nowhere. I'll tell you, this city girl fell in love with the slower pace of small-town America. Knowing your neighbors was a foreign concept for me coming from the big city of Des Moines."

"Is it true that everyone knows everyone's business?" Nicole asked.

"Pretty much! But honestly, I much prefer that to the anonymity of city life. It's not for everyone, but it was a wonderful move for us. Such a great place to raise kids, of which we have three—Bryan, Courtney, and Summer. They're now all married, and I have seven grandkids."

"Can I ask how he died?" Trixie said.

"Of course. He was injured in a farming accident two years ago, helping one of his best buddies. Being the only doctor for fifty miles, there was no one close enough to help. He . . ." She paused and drew a wobbly breath, eyes filled. "He bled to death before they got him to the hospital."

Dixie put her hand on Chantal's arm. "Hon, that is absolutely heartbreaking."

She nodded, lips pressed together as she dabbed her eyes. "Thanks," she said. "He really was an amazing man. Okay, someone else's turn."

Trixie shared a glance with Nicole. "Okay, I'll go. I met my husband, Trygg, in high school, and yes, that's his real full name. In choir, actually." She smiled fondly. "I can still see the cute blonde boy walking in and hear all the girl's sigh. I think both our faith and our love of singing made us a perfect couple. He pastored for thirty years and then went into the business world when a friend asked him to help launch a company. We have four kids." She pulled in a dramatic deep breath. "Tristan, Trent, Tansy, and Trudy."

For a moment, the other three stared at her, wide eyed.

"How in the world do you keep them straight?" Nicole asked.

"Did you do that on purpose?"

Dixie held up her hand. "Wait just a minute." She shifted to face Trixie. "You're Trixie and you married Trygg." She peered at her friend's nametag. While their first names were large, their last names were smaller, and Trixie's was one she couldn't remember. "And your last name is . . ."

"Tungsfeldt," Trixie said calmly.

Trying to hold in the laugh that threatened, Dixie said, "So the Tungsfeldt family includes Trygg, Trixie, Tucker, Tommy, Tortoise, and Topsy?" The laugh burst out in a hoot. "That is . . . that is . . . hysterical," she gasped.

The other women laughed as well, while Trixie maintained her calm smile, obviously used to such a reaction. When the laughter subsided, she said, "Yes, although I must correct you on the last child's name. It's not Topsy, it's Turvy."

Dixie hooted with laughter again as Nicole asked, "I'm a little afraid to ask this, but what are the grandkids' names?"

"You *should* be afraid," Trixie said. "Ready? They are . . ."

Dixie held her breath.

"Olivia, Paul, Liam, and Unknown, who is due a month from now. Not a T to be found in the group."

"Oh, my gosh," Dixie said, waving her hands to cool her warm cheeks. "You're killing me. Was that an actual plan?"

"Not at first. I'd always loved the name Tristan, not knowing I'd marry Trygg Tungsfeldt, of course. It snowballed from there."

"Well, I love it," Chantal declared. "Remind me when you lost Trygg?"

"Eighteen months ago. He had a rare form of dementia." Her gaze turned to Nicole. "Enough of me. Your turn."

"I sure can't top that," she said. "I was married to Alan for twenty years. Second marriage for both of us. We have a 'yours, mine, and ours' family. I had two daughters, he had a son right in between my girls' ages, and then we had twins together."

"Did they get along?" Nicole asked.

"They did, really well, actually. They've never referred to themselves as stepsiblings. Alan was a trial lawyer, and one day he went to work and didn't come home. He had a heart attack right at the end of his closing statement. That was three years ago."

Chantal reached for her hand. "That's awful. I'm so sorry."

"Nothing like adding some pizazz to the closing argument," Dixie thought. When three pairs of eyes swung toward her, she slapped a hand to her mouth. "Oh, heavens. I'm sorry! I didn't mean to say that out loud."

Nicole's face took on a pink hue that turned darker as she leaned back in her chair, hand over her mouth.

"Nicole, I'm so—"

"That is the funniest thing I've heard," Nicole said, laughter making her face red. "I'll bet people thought it—*I* even thought it—but no one has ever said it aloud. That poor jury!"

Dixie couldn't stop the laugh that joined Nicole's. "And the judge!"

"Stop it, you two," Trixie scolded, unable to hide her giggle. "That's disrespectful."

"Oh, psh." Dixie waved her hand. "Life is cruel and hard and tragic, but sometimes it's so absurd it's funny. We have to find ways to laugh, or we'll become bitter and angry."

Nicole nodded. "I agree. Alan's heart simply stopped. He didn't suffer or writhe around in pain. He just . . . went. I hope I do the same, although not with an audience."

"Ladies, we'll be starting the keynote address in about five minutes," Laura announced.

Trixie motioned at Dixie. "Quick, tell us your story."

She'd been hoping they'd run out of time before she had to share. At least she only had five minutes. "I met Bobby during the summer before our senior year of high school. We got married the following summer and had two kids."

"Names?" Chantal prompted.

"A daughter, Willow, and a son, River."

Trixie's round eyes matched her mouth, then surprisingly she nodded. "Makes sense."

"Everyone loved Bobby. He was fun and funny, could make conversation with anyone or anything, had a big heart and the most beautiful smile. He retired early and went into consulting. Then he got cancer and died two years later, which is two years ago. There's my life in a nutshell. Now, I need to run to the ladies' room so I can make a grand entrance when the speaker starts." She threw a grin at Trixie. "Just kidding. But I do need the ladies' room. Be right back."

Once safely in the bathroom stall, she leaned against the door and released a long breath. She'd adored Bobby just as the other women had adored theirs. But his affair right before the diagnosis had changed everything, including her belief in their marriage. No way was she going to share that with her new friends. Ever. Not even the kids needed to know. She splashed water on her face and returned to the table with over a minute to spare.

"All right, ladies! Welcome to the Ladies' Olympics here in Scottsdale, Arizona! Only the most elite athletes have been invited to participate, and that is *you*."

The women laughed and applauded where they'd gathered in the courtyard after a picnic-style dinner.

"I'm glad to see you are dressed and ready to participate." Laura turned a grin toward Dixie. "And our Vegas lady, Dixie Jackson, is wearing an especially lovely ensemble that may trip her up in some of our competitions."

Dixie laughed and curtseyed. Trixie rolled her eyes. Who wore a skirt to an athletic event?

"Each small group table is a team, so you'll be competing with your meal-mates. Over here you'll see the list of competitions." Laura gestured to her left. "Since only one person from each team will participate in the first three activities, make sure your top competitor is signed up for their area of expertise. Activities four and five will require the full team's participation."

Rope skipping was up first. Dixie accepted a jump rope and took her place with the other contestants. Right before the whistle blew, she held up a hand. Setting the rope aside, she dropped her flowing skirt to reveal paisley yoga pants. Amidst laughter and whistles, she tossed the skirt away, took up her rope, and nodded at the judge.

Within five minutes, three contestants had gotten tangled in their rope and were eliminated. Another five minutes and two more dropped out, panting and laughing. Dixie seemed oblivious to the last two competitors and skipped in a rhythmic pattern forward, then backward. Another contestant down, and Dixie faced her last competitor with a relaxed smile. Those watching cheered and clapped until Dixie won.

Table #7 gathered around her, offering hugs and congratulations, then the next competition was announced. Trixie stepped into her hoop, wondering what she'd gotten herself into. She'd loved doing the hula hoop—when she was ten. She looked at her tablemates, eyebrows tented, then laughed when Dixie gave her a double thumbs-up. Just a silly activity, although she did love to win . . .

The whistle blew and the hoops went flying. Trixie focused on a flowering shrub nearby and kept her hips moving. Trygg would no doubt be laughing and clapping along with the women. Tansy would be doubled over with laughter. The others would be staring at her, mouths open in stunned silence. The thought made her smile. Surprise, kids! Your mousey mother is actually pretty good at the hula hoop!

The clatter of a hoop hitting the pavers pulled her attention to the competition. There were only two of them left? She really *was* good at this!

"Go, Trix! You've got this," Dixie called.

Chantal and Nicole stood nearby hooting and cheering. In response, Trixie threw her hands up in the air and swung her hips more forcefully, giggling at herself. If she had to make a fool of herself, she might as well have fun doing it. And this was fun!

Finally, the other woman's hoop wobbled and fell. *I won? I never win anything!* That might have something to do with never doing anything, but— The girls danced around her, celebrating. "I won!" she exclaimed. "I won!"

The next contest was announced, and she pushed Chantal toward the starting line. "Go get 'em, girl! Let's sweep this competition!"

Cheering Chantal on, Trixie giggled at her own raucous behavior. Had she ever laughed this hard and been so uninhibited? Doubtful. Maybe because she didn't really know these women? Or because she was far from home and it didn't matter in her real life.

She paused at the thought. Her *real* life? What difference would it make if she were back home acting like this? Her heart sank. Unless at home it was all about appearance. She'd been the model pastor's wife, carefully raising their children to be model children—because the congregation was watching. Always watching.

"Trixie? You okay?"

Dixie stood beside her, frowning.

"Hmm? Oh, yes. I'm fine. Just got distracted. How did Chantal do?"

"A very respectable third place."

Trixie blinked the earlier revelation away. "What's up next?"

Dixie studied her for a long moment, then hooked an arm through hers and pointed. "We're heading to the egg toss. All hands on deck. Or at least in line."

Determined to enjoy the rest of the evening, Trixie rubbed her hands together. "Got it. My hands are ready to catch some eggs." She looked at Dixie, an eyebrow raised. "Is that how it works?"

Her friend whooped with laughter. "You really need to get out more, Trix.

CHAPTER 8

The last full day here. Dixie studied her reflection, looking for clues. She certainly felt different on the inside, but from her wavy, untamable dark hair to her sandaled feet, she looked the same outside. The Ladies' Olympics last night had been more fun than she could remember having in years. Those hours of laughter and sheer silliness had brightened her soul.

A knock at the door pulled her from the mirror. Trixie waited in the hallway holding two Styrofoam cups. "Coffee service. I believe you prefer a medium roast with enough cream to make it no longer legitimately coffee. That would be this one."

"Ooh, yes." She accepted the cup and inhaled. "Mmm, the aroma of cream with a hint of coffee. Perfect."

"Ready for a pre-breakfast stroll? I can't believe you squeezed in yoga and are dressed for the day. If you're ready now, why do you end up being late to breakfast?"

Dixie let the door shut behind them and fell into step with her shorter friend. "That is the million-dollar question. I'm so easily distracted. I probably was a bit flighty before Bobby got sick, but it's a hundred times worse now."

Trixie nodded. "Same. I'm getting better, but for the first year or so, I couldn't finish a chapter of a book. My concentration has been shot."

They went out into the early morning sun and drew a deep, delighted breath. "Ahh. I will miss this lovely aroma." She glanced at Trixie. "Do you think this distractedness is our new normal? I'm tired of getting lost in conversations and forgetting what I was going to do."

"I hope not. At least, I think if we start getting out into the world, our brains will reconnect. It was several long years of silence for me. Trygg didn't speak for the last year or so."

"That's sad. Especially if he was a singer."

"I miss his voice most of all. I'm so thankful for home videos."

They followed the packed pebble path around the building, sipping their coffee and exclaiming over the unusual plants and stunning desert flowers.

"I envy the relationship you had with Trygg," Dixie said eventually as they settled on a bench in the shade of a palm tree.

"It was wonderful. But it sounds like you and Bobby had something similar."

"Yes. And no."

Trixie glanced at her but didn't probe. Dixie drew a deep breath and blurted, "Bobby had an affair."

"No! What a rotten thing to do to you and the family."

Trixie's swift response touched her heart. She'd carried this burden alone these last years, determined to never mention it. But now that she had, the tightness in her chest eased like a knot being loosened. A knot of grief and anger and betrayal.

"I found out a few days before our anniversary party. I was trying to figure out if I could stay with him when he got his diagnosis. Part of me wanted to walk out and let his 'girlfriend' take care of him. But I just . . . couldn't."

"I'm sorry, Dixie."

Throat tight, Dixie pursed her lips to keep hold of her emotions. "We had to get married, you know, right after high school. Pretty unheard of back then. I was never sure, especially in those early years, if he would have married me without the baby. He always insisted he'd planned to marry me before I got pregnant and joked that the baby, River, asked me first."

Trixie reached for her hand and gave it a squeeze. "But you stayed married all those years."

"Somehow," Dixie said, nodding. "Women loved Bobby. And Bobby loved the attention. I tried not to be jealous, but I was, most of the time. About five years in, after Willow turned one, he had an affair. I was devastated, so I took the kids and went to my sister's. It took nearly six months of counseling before I went back. But during the counseling sessions, with the pastor of my sister's church, we both found Jesus. That changed us and our marriage. It changed everything, really."

She released a long breath. "When I found out about the second one, it totally threw me. Had he been cheating all along? Was he unhappy in the marriage? He swore he was happy but that it just 'happened,'" she said with air quotes. "The kids were grown and married at that point, so I had no reason to stay. I was angry and hurt, and I didn't trust him even though he insisted it had been just a one-time thing at a work party."

Trixie's grip tightened, and she rested her head against Dixie's shoulder. Her silent support nearly unleashed the torrent.

"Then the diagnosis came, and we were basically stuck. I'm pretty sure our vows didn't include staying married through multiple affairs, but I *had* promised to stay in sickness and in health." She closed her eyes under the weight of their last few years together. "So, I stayed."

"And God got you through?"

"He did. I couldn't have done it without Him. I wouldn't have," she admitted. "That's why I reacted like that when you said you didn't like

Trygg by the time he died. I thought I was the only one relieved at the death of their spouse."

"I'll bet a whole lot of the women here would say something similar. Even Chantal and Nicole. They said the abrupt death was especially hard because they'd been having difficulties, as we all do, but they never got to fix it or even say goodbye."

"That stinks." She sat quietly for a moment. "I guess one good thing about him having cancer was that near the end we had some deep talks. We were able to forgive each other for decades of missteps. He admitted that he would die knowing I'd forgiven him but not sure he'd have forgiven himself. I told him Jesus had, so he had to, too. That seemed to help at the end."

As they sat in the quiet of the morning, Dixie felt the warmth of Trixie's acceptance and friendship. She'd never known that from another woman, always too busy looking for ulterior motives or comparing herself to the younger, prettier women Bobby encountered.

Trixie's stomach gurgled, and they giggled.

"And on that note," Dixie said, "it must be time for breakfast."

They stood and faced each other, reaching for a hug at the same time.

"Thank you for sharing all that with me," Trixie said. "It means a lot."

"Thanks for listening." Warmth filled her face. She was making her first real friend. "I don't really have anyone to share that kind of stuff with."

"You do now," Trixie declared. "Now let's go eat!"

"Wow! You look amazing." Trygg had stood in their bedroom doorway, his eyes lit with an appreciation that made her blush. "You might out-shine the bride."

"Thank you, but that's silly. Our daughter is the most beautiful bride ever."

"Thank goodness Trudy got her looks from you." He'd wrapped her in a hug and whispered, "I'm the luckiest man in the world."

The memory blurred, leaving an aching void. Trixie dropped onto the edge of the bed, unable to draw a breath over the stab of pain in her heart. She hadn't worn this dress since Trudy's August wedding. They never went anywhere fancy enough for a shimmering gown of royal blue, but she could never bring herself to donate it. When the retreat information had requested formal attire for the last evening, she'd been excited to carefully add it to the suitcase.

They'd never needed fancy restaurants, or expensive cars, or a big house. They'd had each other and kids they loved spending time with. She'd never wanted more than that. She'd been fortunate to be adored by such a wonderful man.

A knock at the door made her wipe her face. She couldn't do it. Dixie would have to go enjoy the meal with Nicole and Chantal. She opened the door and encountered her friend's tearful, wavering smile.

"We can do this," Dixie said firmly.

"I don't think I can."

"Hey, I don't get this dressed up for just anyone." She adjusted the top with a grunt. "And it's barely comfortable, so we'd better hurry up before I bust out of it."

Trixie put her fingers to her lips, unable to hold in a snorting laugh. "If that might happen, I'm definitely not going."

"Oh, yes, you are. We aren't the dead ones, so let's go figure out how to live."

Trixie put her hands on her hips, prepared to send her friend on her way alone, then her words sank in. No, she wasn't dead and probably wouldn't be for a long time. She could stay alone in her room, mourning the loss of a wonderful man, or she could honor him by stepping back into life, starting right now. "You're right."

"I am?"

"We're not dead, but we've been living like it. Let's go enjoy a nice meal with our new friends and take pictures to remind ourselves of this lovely weekend."

"Well, okay!" Dixie held the door open, her expressive eyebrows lifted as if she still expected an argument. "Look out, world. Here comes Dixie Trix."

"What?"

"Ever hear of the Dixie Chicks? A country group? We'll be Dixie Trix. A little play on words. Get it?"

Trixie rolled her eyes. "Yes, I get it. It's weird but very . . . you."

"I will take that as a compliment."

"You do that."

Moments later they stood wide eyed in the meeting room doorway. The space had been transformed by twinkling lights, candles on the tables, and the sweet aroma of flowers. Music playing in the background mingled with laughter and conversation.

"Welcome to A Night to Remember: Roots and Wings," Janice said. "We're glad you're here. You ladies are simply stunning."

Trixie took a full look at Dixie and smiled. The flowing gown of ivory and peach, with its bell sleeves and empire waist, was the right look for her. The garland of flowers added the perfect touch. She'd look ridiculous in it, but Dixie looked regal. "Dixie's gown is stunning, isn't it?"

"Between your sparkles and my chiffon, we're quite the pair," her friend replied.

Janice pointed them toward the beverage table, where they found Chantal and Nicole holding crystal glasses of pink lemonade. For a few moments before being shooed toward their table, they shared compliments on each lovely dress and how they'd nearly not come.

Over a meal of salmon, roast beef, potatoes, and salad, the foursome exchanged information they'd gleaned from the various breakout sessions and about how much they'd learned about themselves by simply being at the retreat. The lively conversation, punctuated with laughter and teasing, made Trixie's eyes well more than once. To be part of such an amazing group of women—no, *warriors*—was the most unexpected blessing of all.

"Ladies, we have the privilege of hearing from Anita Martin one more time to close out the retreat. As the tables are cleared, you have ten minutes for photos and the restroom before we start."

"We have to have a photo in all our finery," Nicole insisted. "There's a photo booth right over there. Come on!"

Ten minutes later they were settled back at Table #7 as the room filled with applause. Anita smiled warmly at them before starting with prayer. Then she stated, "Might I say that you all look beautiful this evening. But I suspect it wasn't easy. The first time I dressed up for an occasion without Nate was a bit surreal and felt terribly wrong. We'd done everything together, especially any big events that required dressing up."

Trixie swiped a finger under her eye.

"And then he was gone, and I had to learn to live on my own, which included going to events like this. It was hard. Impossible at first. But with the help of a counselor and dear friends, I started coming back to life. I'd stayed in my cocoon long enough. I'd been invited to my niece's lavish wedding, so I picked out a beautiful dress and put it on and then couldn't leave the hotel room. I suspect a few of you had that same experience tonight.

"It felt wrong to be out enjoying life when my favorite person was dead. But you know what I realized? My sweetheart wasn't going to come back if I stayed home. He wasn't going to come back no matter how much I wished for it, or how hard I prayed. He was in heaven and, as hard as it was to accept, I had more life to live. On my own."

Trixie shared a knowing nod with Dixie.

"So, I asked God for the courage to move forward, left the hotel room in my beautiful gown, and had a wonderful time. Yes, I got teary a few times thinking how much he'd have enjoyed it, but I also smiled at the thought of him on the dance floor. He couldn't dance," she added in a loud whisper. "At all."

Laughter rolled through the room.

"My cocoon had served its purpose, and I was working my way out. It wasn't easy, but each step made me stronger and a tiny bit more excited to see what was coming. Ladies, you are working your way out of your cocoon simply by dressing up and coming to the party. I've watched you go from timid and closed off to hugging each other and sharing tissues. That's amazing growth in these few days. God is at work in this room, in each of you. He's not done with you yet.

"You can embrace the future while still appreciating the past. It's not either/or, it's both/and. The past has brought you to where you are now. You survived a great loss, and while your butterfly wings may still be wet, they're absolutely beautiful. Look around the room and appreciate the beauty, the growth, and the spark of life I see on every face."

Trixie let the tears flow as Anita's words seeped into her heart. Trygg was with Jesus, where he'd longed to be. Where she longed to be. But apparently it wasn't her time yet; there was more for her to do and experience. Kids to support and grandchildren to spoil. And girlfriends to get to know.

"My friends," Anita said, her tone warm and encouraging. "Tonight is a celebration of a life well lived and a life still to be lived. Look forward to what will be. God is already there, His hand outstretched, to walk into the future at your side. Take His hand, ladies, and know that He will lead you into new adventures, even more growth, and an ever-closer relationship with Him. Will you stand so I can say a blessing over you?"

Table #7 stood and joined hands, sharing tear-tinged smiles as they bowed their heads together.

Chapter 9

The final breakfast of the retreat was a noisy affair, the room ringing with laughter, conversation, and silverware clinking against plates. Dixie watched Laura make several attempts to quiet the group, then finally lean on the podium, chin in her hand, smiling. Excusing herself from the table, Dixie went to the front of the room, put her fingers to her mouth, and released a shrill whistle. The room was instantly silent, all eyes toward the front.

She turned to Laura and winked. "They're all yours," she said before returning to the table. Bobby had taught her that.

Laura laughed. "Thank you, Dixie. Can you teach me how to do that before you leave?"

Dixie offered a thumbs-up as she settled into her chair. Trixie was grinning at her, shaking her head. Chantal and Nicole nodded appreciatively. Apparently, no one knew how to whistle.

"I am tickled to see and hear the change in this room," Laura said. "The quiet, nervous group that sat here Wednesday evening has morphed into a lively, happy collection of beautiful women ready to take life on. Amen?"

"Amen!"

"Anyone need any more ice breaker questions?" she asked, laughing at the emphatic "no" that rang out. "Didn't think so. As we bring this retreat to a close, I'm wondering if a few of you would like to share your impressions of our time together. Anyone have ideas or plans to put in place when you get home? You don't have to come up here. Janice will bring a mic to your table."

A woman raised her hand and Janice hurried across the room to hand her the cordless microphone. She stood and faced the group. "I'm Kate from Table 8." The women at her table giggled. "I absolutely did not want to come to this retreat, but my kids coerced me. Actually, they bribed me by saying if I came for the whole four days, I could have the grandkids for a sleepover when I get back. Y'all are my witnesses that I stayed until the end."

Her remark was met with loud cheers and applause.

She turned toward Laura. "I am so very grateful for all you, the staff, and the speakers have provided to help us step out of our cocoons and into God's light. I have learned so much and shared far more than I anticipated. And I've gotten far more in return—lovely new friends that I can call once I'm home, renewed faith, and especially hope for my future. Thank you all."

Another woman stood as applause faded. After sharing similar remarks, Janice retrieved the microphone and looked around the room. Dixie pulled in a deep breath and stood, pulling Trixie up with her.

"Dixie, what are you . . ." Trixie hissed.

Dixie took the microphone, still clutching Trixie's wrist, and faced the room. "Like all of you, I came here very reluctantly. The last thing I wanted to do was spend four days with old ladies crying into their hankies."

Laughter rang through the room.

"Instead, I met women of all ages and stages of life and grief, and not a hanky in sight. I absolutely did not want to be labeled a widow. It sounded old, sad, and lonely, but now I see it as a badge of honor. It gives me a chance to talk about Bobby, and it symbolizes our commitment to each other until death parted us. In today's world, that's quite an accomplishment, and I'm not going to hide from that label anymore."

She continued through the applause and appreciative nods. "I came here with zero expectations, certainly not expecting to make real friends. But look"—she grinned at Trixie—"could you imagine two more mismatched women becoming best friends from a widow's retreat? I sure couldn't have! And now we're a fabulous foursome," she added with a sweep of her hand toward Chantal and Nicole.

She handed the mic to Trixie, whispering, "Hold this," and pulled off her feathery headband, then placed it on Trixie's head. Trixie gave the mic back before buttoning the top buttons on Dixie's blouse, her wide grin tinged with affection.

"So," Dixie said, "I just thank God for pulling me out of a snowbank and putting me on a plane to this warm wonderland. Like Kate said, I'm going home with a hopeful heart and a plan to start using my butterfly wings."

Trixie reached for the microphone, a move Dixie hadn't expected. "I echo what Dixie said. I have been blessed by each and every one of you, by the kindness and understanding and encouragement you've offered. I sure never expected the feathered, flowing, sparkling Dixie to become my soul sister, but she has, and that is thanks to God. Mostly, I want to thank all of you for giving me courage and a safe place to laugh and cry and make a fool of myself. Unlike when I came here, I'm no longer afraid of the future. Thank you."

As Janice took the microphone, they sat down, grasping the outstretched hands of their tablemates. Tearful smiles were shared, along with promises that they were now a force to be reckoned with and would have each other's backs going forward.

"We are the fabulous foursome," Dixie declared, ignoring the tear that slipped down her cheek. In the most unexpected place, God had provided true friends who had been on similar paths, and who accepted her exactly as she was. What a blessing.

The ride to the airport that afternoon was almost as quiet as the ride in, but this time Trixie held Dixie's hand firmly. What had happened in four short days that changed her inside and out, from coming here under protest to now wishing they could stay another week? Changing her heart from the cold ache of isolation and loneliness to the surprising warmth of excitement?

Trixie caught her reflection in the window and smiled at the feathery headband resting on her head like a crown. She still didn't know who she was, but fear of the unknown had been replaced by excitement to discover the answer.

On the sunny sidewalk, they said goodbye to Hannah and the other women, then faced each other with fresh tears.

"What in the world happened to us?" Dixie demanded with a strangled laugh as she wiped her face.

"Maybe it was the desert air?"

They giggled together, then Dixie reached for her hands. "We'll start planning next year's trip as soon as we get home. And let's stay longer than four days, okay?"

"A couple of weeks, at least."

"We'll have to throw out some dates to see when Nicole and Chantal are available."

"I've never seen the Grand Canyon," Trixie mused.

"What?!" Dixie exclaimed.

Trixie shrugged. "We didn't have a lot of money or time when Trygg was pastoring. And then he moved to the corporate job, and we had more money but even less time."

"I traveled a lot with Bobby, but most of the time it wasn't a vacation, so I guess there's a lot I'd like to see again to experience it."

"We'll have to plan a lot of trips."

Dixie squeezed her hands. "Definitely. Now, could I have my headband back? It's one of my favorites."

Trixie removed it with a laugh. "It's too big for me anyway."

"I beg your pardon!" Dixie said, settling it into her dark waves. "And to think I'd planned to remember you every time I put it on. Forget that!"

"Oh, you'll remember me," Trixie assured her with a giggle. Her smile faded. "I'll have to get myself some feathers."

"That reminds me." Dixie reached into what Trixie called her Mary Poppins bag and pulled out her brightly colored butterfly. "Let's swap butterflies. That will remind us of each other and this retreat whenever we look at them."

Trixie pursed her lips, an eyebrow cocked. "Do you promise not to paint mine as soon as you get home? I picked blue because it was Trygg's favorite color."

"I didn't know that. Yes, I promise," Dixie said solemnly then added, "as long as you promise not to stick mine in a dark closet somewhere."

"I promise." Trixie pulled hers from her carry-on and they swapped. "You know," she mused, studying the sparkle in the bright colors, "I think it will mean more to have yours with me."

Dixie was silent a moment. "I think so," she said in a strangled whisper.

"Oh, now, don't start. If you cry, then I'll cry, and we'll get on our planes with red, blotchy faces."

"Good point." Dixie pulled in a sharp breath. "So, when do we start my singing lessons?"

"The same time we set up my pottery lessons. It's going to be a lot easier for me to teach you to sing online than it will be for you to teach me pottery."

"Then you'll have to come to Holland for some one-on-one lessons."

"Oh, I'd love that! It's a deal."

"In the meantime, I'm expecting you to rejoin the choir when you get home." She frowned. "Don't make me have to call the choir director."

The threat made Trixie smile. "I'm kind of excited to go back," she admitted. "And I expect you to start getting the house ready to sell. One room at a time. No more putting it off."

Dixie sighed. "Motivation is a problem for me."

"Then we'll do a video call, and I'll chat while you sort. I'm happy to tell you what to toss and what to keep."

"That would help a ton."

They were silent a moment, carefully putting their butterflies away. Then Trixie set her shoulders and forced a smile. "All right, my friend. Let's not put this off any longer or we'll miss our planes."

"You're right. How terrible to have to stay in this warm, sunny, wonderful place for an extra day or four."

Trixie put her hands up in protest. "Cut that out. It's too tempting!"

They hugged once more and then laughed when Trixie said she'd be texting as soon as she got to the gate. "This is just 'see ya' for now."

"Right. Take care. Safe travels."

"Back at you, my friend."

They rolled their luggage into the terminal together, then parted for their different airlines. Trixie checked her bag and nodded when the ticket agent asked if she enjoyed her time in Arizona.

"More than I ever dreamed possible," she said, walking away with a smile in her heart and on her lips. *God is so good.*

A Note From the Author

Dear Reader,

Thanks for reading our *Skipping Winter* anthology, and my story, "The Butterfly Sisters." Widowhood isn't exactly a light topic (I'm a widow, myself) but there is so much more to life than the labels we are given. I hope you saw that through Trixie and Dixie's separate yet similar stories. I had fun writing these two characters—some of each of them based on real people, some not so much. But all of it was written to show God at work in our lives no matter what journey we're on.

Until next time,

Stacy

ABOUT THE AUTHOR

Stacy Monson is the author of the award-winning Chain of Lakes series and is a founding member of The Mosaic Collection. She lives outside the Twin Cities metro area with many chickens, an old dog, and lots of wildlife (which includes seven grandchildren).

Learn more at https://stacymonson.com/

Titles by
Stacy Monson

Stories that reveal an extraordinary God at work in ordinary life.

THE MOSAIC COLLECTION: NOVELS

My Father's House Series:

When Mountains Sing (Book 1)
When Valleys Mourn (Book 2 – releasing 2026)

THE MOSAIC COLLECTION: ANTHOLOGY STORIES

"Mountaintop Christmas" in *Hope is Born*
"A Summer of Reckoning" in *Before Summer's End*
"The Sweetest Sound" in *Song of Grace*
"Whispered Miracle" in *A Whisper of Peace*
"Piper's Sweet Dream" in *Sounds Like a Plan*
"The Christmas Kiss" in *A Weary World Rejoices*
"Misguided deVotion" in BirdSong

The Chain of Lakes Series

Shattered Image

Dance of Grace

The Color of Truth

Standalone

Open Circle

LET'S CONNECT!

I'd love to hear from you. Let's Connect!

Facebook	https://www.facebook.com/stacymmonson/
Instagram	https://www.instagram.com/stacy_monson
Pinterest	https://www.pinterest.com/stacymonson/
Goodreads	https://wwwgoodreadscomstacy_monson
Email	stacy@stacymonson.com

THANK YOU FOR READING

We hope you enjoyed *Skipping Winter*, Mosaic's 2025 Christmas anthology. If you did, please consider leaving a short review on Amazon, Goodreads, or BookBub. Positive reviews and word-of-mouth recommendations are so valuable and appreciated, as they honor an author and help other readers to find quality Christian fiction to read.

Thank you so much!